THE ODIN INHERITANCE

◦VICTORIA L. SCOTT◦

Grey Wolfe Publishing, LLC
PO Box 1088
Birmingham, Michigan 48009
www.GreyWolfePublishing.com

© 2015 Victoria L. Scott
Cover Design by TheCoverCounts.com
Published by Grey Wolfe Publishing, LLC
www.GreyWolfePublishing.com
All Rights Reserved

First Edition ISBN: 978-1628280951
Second Edition ISBN: 978-1628281521

Library of Congress Control Number: 2015944808

The Odin Inheritance

Book One of The Pessarine Chronicles

Victoria L. Scott

Dedication

For my parents:
Timothy and Jerelene Scott;
Nancy and John Bazzetta;
and
Dale and Joyce Rondeau.

"....*forsan et haec olim meminisse iuvabit...*"
~Vergil's *Aeneid,* Book One, Line 203

Acknowledgements

The author would like to thank:

Riley Pohlman, Rohan Kheterpal, Daria Chamness, Deborah and Ron Hodges, for being friends and willing readers.

The Janda family, for being great friends and offering me a soft place to land in hard times.

Dr. Niketa Dani, my best friend.

Debbie Lamson and Mike Wilson, my Steampunk partners in crime, along with my fellow Emerson School teachers and staff members.

All of my 8th grade and Latin students who have been supportive and excited about this novel since the beginning. I honed my own skills as a writer while I instructed them in writing and thinking about language.

Diana Kathryn Plopa, my enthusiastic editor. The Rondeaus of Spruce MI and Portage IN; and the Thomsons of Ossineke, MI. Y'all will be family always.

And last but not least: Red 'the Wonder Husky', my favorite traveling and writing companion.

Chapter One

"Roll up, roll up! Come try your luck against the best hand at darts south of Hadrian's Wall!" Max Lester, Captain of the *Bosch*, shouted to the pub customers in his deep baritone voice. Even though I was accustomed to Max's method of garnering attention, I winced inwardly.

Big, broad and loud, everyone in the pub heard his pronouncement whether they wanted to or not. Heads turned to look us over, their glasses frozen mid-quaff for a moment as the patrons puzzled over which of the five of us was the darts player. Now, many in the pub stared at the large muscular man in the leather aeronaut jacket as if he'd grown purple feathers in awkward places.

I sighed. We'd only been at The Crown Pub near the Penzance docks for an hour or so. We'd barely had enough time to have a drink and get a feel for the place. It was warm, smoky and crowded due to the press of bodies and the output of the fireplaces, but it had a well-used elm dartboard, which was just what we needed. Most pubs had them, but the pubs farther from home were more lucrative for money-making purposes, as we'd discovered the hard way.

Max had figured a good place to try this time was somewhere about three hours' flight away from Cambridge, as the airship soared. Max had pointed out Penzance was within that radius, so the rest of us agreed to go along for the adventure. I'd drawn up the navigation charts, and once Max approved them, I'd set the appropriate steering logarithms and away we went, with Needle at the helm. Even if we didn't succeed in generating more ready cash, any excuse for a trip in the *Bosch* was good enough for us. Named after the Dutch painter Hieronymus Bosch in a moment of ale-assisted mad inspiration, ramshackle as it was, our ship was a second home. It even sported a rendering of Bosch's *Ship in Flames* on the envelope of the airship's cigar-shaped balloon as a tribute to the imaginative artist.

Despite a headwind, the *Bosch* had made fine time on the journey southwest, arriving just before dark. We'd secured her in a makeshift airship berth at a local farm, and travelled into Penzance proper in Griff's Technacart, hopping and clanging the whole way. We'd arrived at the pub with a cloud of steam and a terrific bang.

Most airship captains enjoyed being the center of attention, and Max was no exception. Completely unruffled, Max reveled in the stares, smiling like a madman and hooking his thumbs in his suspenders like a proud father.

"Come now, gents," Max declared, "have we no takers? No one interested in a wager?"

Needle Greene, the *Bosch's* tall and lanky pilot; Griff Baldwin, our mechanics expert; and Lizzie Fournier, our First Mate all took nonchalant protective stances about me, making it clear that they'd be able to handle themselves should necessity require it. I stood in the midst of them, wishing the earth would swallow me whole. I nervously smoothed my simple dark skirt and tucked a wayward red curl behind my ear.

"Do you really need to bellow quite so much, Max?" I asked, speaking low and from the side of my mouth. I hoped I looked inconsequential; my smaller form hidden behind my giant of a friend and the rest of my companions. "Not everyone here plays darts, and saying I'm the best 'below the Wall'? Your hyperbole will have them calling the constable."

"Ari, my dear," Max said, his smile brilliant and his hazel eyes twinkling as he looked over his shoulder and down at me, "you are the best below the Wall, as you've proven time and time again and it's worked out very well. You want money to start your business. We need money to keep the *Bosch* in the air. I've shown I know how to get it, and we'll come by it honestly. I don't care if they call the constable..." He said with a wink, "...so long as we're well away by the time he arrives."

"Which we will be," Griff whispered confidently. He grinned under his dark brown handlebar mustache, his bib overalls peppered with grease stains. "I've been tinkering with the Rover. She's the fastest Technacart these chaps, constabulary or otherwise, could possibly imagine. We're safe as houses."

"Oi!" came a shout from the innards of the pub, close to the fireplace. It was an older gentleman, hair shot with grey and skin tanned to leather by sun and ocean spray. His clothes were well made, but well-worn and mended in spots. "Who's this that's the best at darts, you say?"

Max winked at me and turned toward the shout. "Why, sir, I'm glad you ask!" he bellowed. He reached around, grabbed me under the arms, and picked me up, turning to place me directly in front of him. I instantly became the focus of every set of eyes in the pub. I tugged my plain dark jacket down a bit, checked the collar and cuffs of my white shirt, and did my level best to act as if I didn't mind the attention.

"That little ginger thing?" someone called and the pub erupted in laughter. "Can she *see* the dartboard, then?"

"Since when do they let children down to the pub?" another male voice exclaimed. "She can't be more than ten if she's a day!" The pub rebounded with more chuckles and guffaws.

I'm not really that small, I grumbled mentally. In fact, I stood a solid and perfectly respectable five feet three inches tall. Unfortunately, Max stood six feet five inches tall, so compared to him I looked positively tiny. I looked at the beamed ceiling, making my best attempt at an unperturbed demeanor.

Max held up his hands in a gesture that begged for jocular but polite attention. "Now, gents," he began, "my fine friend here's willing to take on all comers at a friendly game of darts. She's as good as I say. All it'll cost you to see for yourself is a shilling a game."

The older sailor from the fireplace stood up and made his way toward us. I stiffened, and Max placed a gentle hand on my shoulder to hide my nervousness from the crowd.

"A shilling a game?" the sailor asked, coming closer. His dark grey stubbled face showed his disbelief at my skill. His brown eyes looked me over speculatively. "She's got to be Enhanced if she's *that* good, chap."

The pub grew quiet. Enhanced people – those who had been altered with mechanical parts – were relatively new to England, though they'd been in Europe for over fifty years. Most of the Continental Enhanced possessed subtle, very life-like mechanical limbs, making them hard to differentiate from the non-Enhanced. The poor chaps who had the misfortune to acquire artificial limbs in the Empire got far cruder and less aesthetically pleasing limbs, particularly if they couldn't afford a trip to France or Germany for a better prosthetic. Whether or not the artificial limb was easily identified, most in the Empire viewed someone who allowed a mechanical addition to his or her body with suspicion and even hatred. Ten years ago an accusation that one was Enhanced often resulted in fisticuffs or worse. Times were changing, true enough, but slowly. Nevertheless, the sailor's suggestion that my skill was due to mechanical alterations was nearly as bad as being called a whore.

I swallowed, focused on keeping my annoyance in check and playing my role as instructed. After all, my being Enhanced was a frequent explanation for my skill at darts among those who didn't know me, but it was tiresome to deal with the accusation every time I showed up in a pub. The other *Bosch* officers shifted behind me, their attitude one of cautious vigilance. Lizzie slid one hand down the outside leg of her trousers, ready to retrieve the knife she kept in her right boot should it be needed. She loved trousers, and they made access to the weapon she preferred easier. Griff tucked his hands inside the bib of his denim overalls, blew out his breath and tensed. He'd grown up protecting himself with his fists, and would use them to protect me, should it be required. Needle, who was taller than everyone in the pub except for Max, scanned the crowd to provide a warning in case someone tried to get too close.

"Barkeep, I trust you have a Gauge handy?" Max asked, unruffled. Such a device existed in every pub in the Empire since many establishments refused to serve the Enhanced.

"I do," the bearded man behind the counter responded. He put down the rag he'd been using to wipe the bar, reached underneath it, and pulled out a black box the size of a loaf of bread. He pointed the open end at Max and flipped open a top panel to reveal a Gauge, its current reading at zero.

Max turned back to the sailor who'd questioned my humanity. "Ari can prove she lacks Enhancements. Will that clarify that she's without mechanical assistance?"

The sailor looked at the barman. "That Gauge true, Charlie?"

The barman nodded gravely. "Tis, Cap'n. I swear it."

The Cap'n looked me over again and nodded. "You let yonder box take a reading, and if it shows you be all girl, I'll try my hand against you, lass."

I looked up at Max, and he smiled reassuringly. "Go on, Ari," he encouraged.

I turned and walked around Max while he and my other friends stepped aside so the bar patrons could see me take the test. I approached the counter, took a seat on the stool nearest the Gauge, and placed my right hand inside the box. The first time I'd endured a Gauge scan I'd vomited before the test finished. I clamped my mouth shut and waited for the discomfort I knew so well. A wave of nausea passed over me as the instrument searched my body for any sign of Enhancement, mechanical or otherwise. I closed my eyes. The sensation of being so carefully examined made my teeth ache as my stomach roiled in protest.

The feeling faded as abruptly as it began. I opened my eyes and saw the barkeep's eyebrows go up in surprise. He looked at the pub patrons and shrugged. "The reading is 0%, ladies and gents," he announced. "The needle didn't even move. Anyone who takes this lass on'll be trying his luck against her skill, and nothing more. T'will be a fair contest."

The pub patrons began speaking in low tones, and the Cap'n smiled. He pulled out three shillings and held them up. "Let me see if I've got this right. We each pay a shilling a game. If I do better than the lass, I get my shilling back and her shilling to boot. That about right?"

Max nodded. "It is. Shall we have Charlie here hold the stakes?" He indicated the barman.

The Cap'n and Charlie both nodded. Max pulled out three shillings to match those of my challenger and placed them on the bar. I pretended disinterest. It was almost the last of our collective coin, having spent most of our ready money on Griff's most recent improvements to the *Bosch* and the Rover, and then our smaller coin on the drinks. We had some money set aside as a safety net, of course, but one of the reasons I continued my monthly forays into pubs for pick-up dart games was to keep our safety net as big as possible. More than once we'd come close to losing it all due to a particularly costly repair, even with all of us chipping in what we could from their wages and my allowance.

That was the thrilling thing about the life of freelance, part-time aeronauts. You tended to live on the edge of technology, safety, gainful employment and financial liquidity. You never knew what piece of equipment would break next, or if you'd have the funds to fix it.

That's how I'd come to join the crew of the *Bosch*. I had a side business making small, personal mechanicals for home use. I constructed unique mini-machines that laced corsets, buttoned dresses or even combed hair if a woman found herself without a maid to assist with her trousseau and hairstyle. I also constructed mechanical insects like dragonflies with phosphorite bulbs as heads which could hover and illuminate places that had minimal light. Both types of devices sold well. So far as I knew, no one else had thought to use the technology in that way, and I made a bit of money doing it.

Lizzie worked during the day at the ladies' boutique in Cambridge that sold my devices intended for ladies. Impressed by the fine nature of their construction and the ingenuity of the designs, Lizzie had shown my unique handiwork to Griff, who worked at a local blacksmith shop; Needle, who worked as a law clerk; and Max, who possessed a decent inheritance with a regular dividend that allowed him to live decently and be an airship captain at the same time. Max did a variety of odd jobs from hauling coal to carpentry and masonry work on top of the inheritance and was well known in Cambridge. The four *Bosch* crewmembers looked over samples of my work and agreed my devices showed I could create the navigational instruments they needed.

When they'd asked for my help, I gladly used my skills on their behalf, learning the ropes of airborne navigation and the needs of an airship guidance system as I went. The process of navigation and creating instruments to enable accurate flying fascinated me. I loved being up in the air, braving the air currents and vagaries of weather. Eventually, I'd earned a spot as the Navigator on the ship though no one in my family knew I flew through the sky on a homemade airship when not immersed in my university studies.

We weren't the only aeronauts local to Cambridge. The *Bosch* was part of a group of seven other airships, collectively called the "Icarus Squadron." It had earned the name due to the frequent mishaps, minor explosions and crashes the homemade ships suffered though thankfully, no one had been seriously hurt. The installation of my devices on the remaining ramshackle Squadron ships at Max's urging greatly improved their efficiency and accuracy on their flight paths, and thereby reduced accidents.

The Squadron had started as a hobby for a few Cambridge students and interested city residents, but now some pondered making the airships into a business. That's what we hoped to do with the *Bosch*. If we succeeded, Needle, Max, Griff and Lizzie wouldn't have to work their day jobs, and I'd be closer to my goal of starting my own aeronaut supply business.

Though I was just a mathematics student and not 'in trade', even I knew I'd need capital to get my business up and running. I'd been at a loss as to how I could manage to collect the money I needed without relying on my parents or alerting them to my intentions too soon. It was while pondering that problem and tossing wrenches and other tools into their bins and onto hooks in the *Bosch* air shed while Max watched in astonishment that a method for generating ready money became apparent.

"Why don't we have a little game, Ari?" Max had suggested.

"All right," I'd answered, a little confused.

He'd drawn a dartboard on the wall of the shed with some chalk and pulled some darts from deep in a drawer. It'd taken him a couple minutes to explain the rules, and then we'd played. I beat him ten times in a row that afternoon. Once we finished, Max beamed with enthusiasm for his newest plan and I wondered what I'd gotten myself into.

Max sat all of us down a few days later. "I have a business proposition," he began, "based on Ari's newly discovered skills."

"You mean getting involved in that aeronaut storefront plan?" Griff asked, looking thoughtful. "You come up with more little mechanicals or new navigational instruments?"

I opened my mouth to reply, but Max beat me to the punch. "Oh, no, my friends," playing it like he was on stage and about to introduce a new act, "Ari has a talent for dart throwing."

"Dart throwing?" Needle asked, "What sort of business can you start throwing darts? Don't the pubs have it pretty much in hand?" Lizzie nodded in agreement, her face showing confusion.

Max pushed himself up from the table and motioned all of us to follow him back to the dartboard drawn on the wall. "Watch this," he said and indicated I should throw the darts he handed me.

I did so, striking the center of the target one at a time, leaving a six-petaled dart flower blooming in the middle of the board.

Griff let out a low whistle. "That's pretty good," he allowed, "but she can't hit a target like that every time, surely?"

Max grinned wickedly. "Ari, close your eyes. Needle, mark six spots at random with chalk along the walls and ceiling of the shed." He walked over and tugged the darts from the wall. "Let's see if she can hit the spots, shall we?"

Griff shook his head and moved to obey.

I groaned. "Max," I complained. "I don't—"

"Hush, you," he ordered with a wink. "Convince the doubters assembled here, and then I'll explain the plan."

I grimaced and closed my eyes. Max put the darts in my hand. When he told me to open my eyes, I did so, quickly located the chalk marks and hit them square in their centers with the darts. Shocked silence rang in the shed.

Max rubbed his hands together and looked at us. "Now, ladies and gents," he said, "let's discuss the plan."

****

After that, we travelled around the country one weekend each month and challenged people to dart games for money. We shared the winnings 50/50, with the crew using their part of the take for improvements to the ship. I saved my portion, along with what I could spare from my allowance and the sales of my devices, for the start-up funds for my business.

I didn't want to consider what my parents would think of the plan. As the daughter of the Duke of Albemarle, after I completed my mathematical studies at Towson in June, it was entirely possible my parents would want me to marry. Going into trade and running a business wasn't on the menu for someone of my station, but the idea of it thrilled me. I loved air travel. If I succeeded, I'd have a chance to live my life among aeronauts and perhaps someday have my own airship. I knew my devices would improve the overall safety and efficiency of airship travel, assuming I could generate enough capital to make a real start on the endeavor.

I just had to win every single dart game I played. So far, I had.

The Cap'n placed his shillings on the bar beside our own and took a long moment to look me up and down, now that he was close to me. I met his gaze and quirked an eyebrow, forcing a chuckle from him.

"You're a bonny, green-eyed lass," he said, the beer on his breath potent and slightly sweet. "Freckled, ginger and lovely as a spring morning, you are. It's glad I am you've not been altered." He turned to the patrons. "Clear a space, lads," he bellowed. "I've three shillings to win!"

A flurry of activity ensued. The patrons moved the pub tables to create an aisle from the bar to the dartboard. Charlie placed a slate on the bar. "I'll keep score, if it's all the same to you, miss," the barman said, holding up a piece of chalk.

I nodded. Then Charlie turned his attention to the many orders for pints of ale or stronger beverages, and several minutes elapsed while the crowd paid for and received their drinks. I removed my jacket and rolled up my sleeves while I waited.

Once everyone settled down, Charlie flipped a coin to see who'd go first. The Cap'n won. Someone handed me three darts with dark blue fletchings, and I saw that the Cap'n held three darts with red fletchings. He took his place at the line to throw, and in quick succession his darts sailed to hit the target. The game was one where we counted down from 301 points with the goal of reaching zero, and the Cap'n had made a very good start, based on the roar of the crowd.

"Atta boy, Cap'n!" someone yelled, "you'll get your shillings in no time!"

"Give up now, girlie," someone else commented, "we'll not hold it against you!"

The room resounded with other similar encouragements, which I ignored. Then it was my turn.

Taking my place at the line, I looked down at my right hand holding the dart, and then up at the painted elm circle that served as the target. A calm focus descended upon me as it always did. My extreme concentration on the task at hand made my conscious mind fade into the background. I became a disinterested, somnolent spectator of my body's actions. I saw only the target, and the only part of my body I was aware of was my throwing arm. In quick succession my three darts flew, but if the crowd reacted to what I had done, I wasn't aware of it. I paid no attention to the score and didn't care who played against me.

I distantly felt Max guide me away from the line when it wasn't my turn, and then lead me back to the line when it was. Darts appeared in my hand, and with fluid motions struck the target. My mind drifted into a dream, punctuated by brief images of pint glasses, the flickering flames, laughing faces, and darts flying at the dartboard.

I don't know how long I spent throwing, but it took a hard shake and a small measure of rum from Max to clear the fog from my mind. My shirt and underclothes were damp, my right arm ached, my red hair had fallen from its pins and my throat was raw. I looked in surprise at the patrons around the pub, who somehow had doubled in number and seemed ecstatic with the evening's entertainment. The Cap'n tugged his forelock at me in salute as he left, and countless others jostled up to offer their congratulations.

The sheer mass of humanity around me was astonishing. The crowd of men and women pressed against the walls of the pub, spilled out the door and into the street in a loud, happily roiling cloud of faces and bodies. I nodded to the well-wishers in their apparent hundreds as politeness required, wondering where all the people had come from. I sought out my airship companions in the sea of unknown faces. Griff, Lizzie, and Needle stood near the door, beaming from ear to ear. Max winked at me from behind the bar as he tucked a wad of pound notes into his capacious inner jacket pocket. Charlie pumped Max's hand with energetic thanks.

Griff surfed his way through the crowd and leaned in toward me. "Finish the rum, Ari," he shouted over the voices. "We need to leave if we're to get back to Cambridge by dawn."

He was right, of course. The Towson house-mother, Mrs. Gildersleeve, thought I was away visiting relatives for the weekend, but it made no sense to press my luck much further. I downed the rum in one gulp, coughed as it blazed its way down my throat, grabbed my jacket and in a trice the crew of the *Bosch* was back in the Rover, clanging back to the ship and eventually, Cambridge and home.

The Odin Inheritance

Chapter Two

Once we got back to the *Bosch*, floating placidly at its farmhouse berth, Max, seeing my exhaustion, ordered me to the small cabin I shared with Lizzie while the others started the engine and prepared the ship for takeoff. I was too tired to argue and made my way down to the quarters. I hung my short jacket on a convenient hook and looked around.

There wasn't much to see or do in the darkened cabin. I reached up and tapped the phosphorite globe that that hung from the middle of the mish-mash of wood and metal that served as our cabin ceiling. The swinging lamp flickered to life and illuminated a small fold-away wash basin, with two bunks that folded up into the wall and a *Pirates of Penzance* poster from the Savoy Theatre on the wall opposite the basin. I dropped down the bunk that was mine so I could sit, ignoring the two trunks that served as seats when the bunks were stowed. Other airships could afford bigger spaces for the crew, but as the *Bosch* was a low budget vehicle, we spent most of our money on the bridge and motive equipment like the hydrogen ballonets, the rigid airship frame, engines and steering mechanisms, not to mention the fuel. One didn't make a rigid frame airship from scratch with the intent of spending time in the cabins. The goal was the air, the speed and above all, freedom.

The *Bosch* lurched into life, and I felt the lift of the air balloon and thrum of the propellers in my bones as the ship started our journey home.

***

I sat in the cabin for a few minutes watching the play of light and shadow across the walls and furnishings of the small room. I was very tired but didn't know what to do with myself. I pulled my trunk out so I could grab a brush and attend to my unruly hair, which perversely refused to go back up in its pins. I resorted to braiding it, tying off the end with a bit of ribbon and letting it hang down my back. I put the brush back in the trunk, slid it back into place and sighed, wondering what else I could do. I was too tired to do any studying, and my mind was too worked up to allow sleep. If I stayed in the cabin I'd only end up pacing back and forth, so I made my way down the hall to the bridge.

I took a moment at the door to watch my crewmates work. Needle, tongue out as he concentrated on holding the ship's wheel on course, piloted the *Bosch* in conjunction with my navigation equipment while Lizzie monitored the other ship systeMs. Phosphorite lamps swung above their heads, illuminating their stations without flames or sparks. Max moved around the bridge, his attention focused on the feel of the ship around him. The chadburn dial, a waist-high pillar next to Needle with a rounded top and various designations for locomotion indicated by a stout handle and black pointer, read 'half full ahead', and I knew the corresponding chadburn in the engine room mimicked the order. Griff was down there with his beloved engines, making sure everything was 'Bristol fashion' below. There was a speaking tube at Max's station so he could speak directly to Griff if he wished, but other than notifying Griff of changes in engine speed it sat largely unused. Griff spoke most eloquently through the efficiency of his engines and didn't like to make small talk while he worked.

I looked at my empty seat near the navigational and meteorological instruments which whirred and clicked as they monitored wind speed and direction, air temperature, altitude and barometric pressure, among other variables. The hydrogen in the ballonets reacted to changes in temperature and pressure, which in turn affected how well the ship handled. My instruments kept track of the changes and kept the bridge informed so the maneuvers of the helm compensated as necessary to keep the ship on course.

Max stopped his perambulations to stand near Needle, both of them peering out the front window of the bridge. The sky outside the window was dark and studded with feebly twinkling stars, the full moon's brightness outshining the more distant heavenly bodies.

"Don't let her blow too much to port," Max said, turning his attention from the window to the binnacle, where the compass sat. "We don't want to go so far west that we miss Cambridge, after all."

Needle nodded. He turned the wheel to account for the wind and straightened our course. The *Bosch* shuddered for a moment and settled into its new direction, slowly swinging back and forth like a boat on a gentle sea. Max checked the chadburn dial, thought for a moment and decided to leave the needle where it was.

"Fuel level, Lizzie?" Max asked.

"Plenty to get us home, Captain," Lizzie said, scanning the console in front of her, "but we'll need to refuel once we get back."

Max sighed. "Understood. What's the status of that strut on the port side?"

I frowned. The strut in question helped to hold the oblong aluminum frame for the hydrogen ballonets to the areas of the ship we occupied, which included the cabins and the bridge, not to mention the engines and their vital propellers. A storm on a prior journey had twisted it, and though we were relatively sure it was still sound, we'd all agreed it should be taken out and replaced. It wasn't the only strut we had holding the ship together, of course, but none of us liked the idea of leaving the twisted one in place.

"Holding her own," Lizzie reported, "but I've got Griff's word he'll be finished with the replacement so I can make the repair by Wednesday." She looked over and saw me. "Looks like the navigator's on deck," Lizzie said, indicating my location in the doorway with a lift of her chin. The others looked and beckoned me in to join them.

"I knew she wouldn't be in her cabin for long," Needle said sagely.

I stepped onto the bridge. A beaming Max moved to intercept me and then enveloped me in a bear hug that lifted me bodily from the floor. He was a naturally demonstrative fellow, coming from a big, very loving family. In my family, we were much more reserved. Mother disapproved of that kind of physical contact, particularly in public, and, as a result, it had taken me some time to get used to Max's ebullient greetings.

"How goes it?" I asked, ducking my head into Max's shoulder so it missed a low-hanging aluminum strut. "Is she handling well?"

Lizzie scoffed from her place at Needle's right hand, keeping an eye on the engine gauges. "Course she is. It's only a bit of a wind, after all. You know better than that. The *Bosch* is right as a trivet."

Max laughed and put me down. "You did well tonight, Ari," he said.

"I'll say she did," Lizzie agreed. "I've never seen anything like it."

"You met every challenge. Some of the throws you made..." Max shook his head. "I've no idea how you do it. From across the pub, even blindfolded... you hit the mark every time. It was head and shoulders above what you've done before."

I cleared my throat, a bit unnerved that I didn't remember being blindfolded. *How had I hit the target without seeing it?*

"Good to know," I said, covering my discomfiture. I rubbed my sore right arm. "Did they call the constable?"

Max laughed. "The constable was the one who paid to see you throw three darts blindfolded."

"He lost a half crown with a smile on his face," Needle added. "Never thought to see a Peeler happy to lose money."

"In fact," Max said, "I think he was the one who brought all those others into the pub. Charlie and the Crown made a pretty penny tonight, and no mistake. Nearly the entire population of Penzance saw you hit the mark every time."

I nodded and rubbed my right arm. *That explained the soreness*, I thought. "How'd we do, then?"

"Including the money Charlie gave us in thanks for the increase in his custom? Ooooh, about twenty pounds, give or take."

I gaped, my aching arm momentarily forgotten. "Twenty pounds?!"

His smile widened, and he pulled the wad of pound notes out of his pocket, dropping them on his desk. "That would be *each*, my dear. Twenty pounds for the *Bosch* and twenty pounds for you.

Not a bad evening's work."

I nearly fainted in surprise. Forty pounds was unbelievable. If we made that much every time we went to a pub between now and June, with that amount added to what I'd already saved, I could start my aeronaut supply shop free and clear, far sooner than I'd hoped. I'd be able to give up the allowance I received from my parents and truly live on my own. The notion took my breath away.

Max pointed to my usual station. "Have a seat. I don't think there's much for you to do, and goodness knows you must be bone weary. But worry not, we'll have you back at Towson before sunrise. All right?"

I nodded and moved to sit. Once I did, Max knelt down beside me. "You've never told stories before. I have to know. Where'd you learn them?"

"Stories?" I asked, confused.

"Oh, Ari," Needle said, waving a finger at me with one hand while he turned a knob with the other, "You've been holding out on us."

I blinked. "I have?"

Max nodded. "Charlie said he'd not heard those old stories since he was a boy... and the way you told them... none of us've heard the like in our lives."

"They were amazing!" Lizzie cut in. "Poetic, magical... as the words flowed through the room, the story unfolded in our minds like a magic lantern show!"

"Folks stayed in the pub and drank just to hear your tales," Needle added. "You told... what... five or six?"

"Oh," I said, stupid with astonishment. I wracked my brain to review the evening's activities, but I didn't remember telling any stories. My throat felt like I'd talked a great deal, however. I didn't understand what they meant. As a mathematics student, I didn't *know* any stories – not like a History or Literature student did. I'd tended to react badly to stories growing up, which was why my parents had encouraged my scholarship in other areas. *What had happened?*

"Erm... what story did you like the best?" I asked. Perhaps if I knew what they'd heard, I'd remember what I'd said.

"I liked the one about Thor dressing up as a bride to get his hammer back," Lizzie offered. Needle and Max laughed, clearly remembering the tale.

I nodded as if I knew what she meant, but I didn't. *Who was Thor?* I had no idea. I certainly appreciated the efficacy of a hammer, but for the life of me I couldn't see why a gentleman would be inclined to dress as a bride to get his hammer back. *Surely it'd be simpler just to purchase a new one?*

"It was like we sat as guests at the wedding ceremony with the wedding feast laid out before us," Griff said. "As you spun the tale we saw the big fellow in the dress – looked right ridiculous he did, beard and all – eating the groom out of house and home, and that before the ceremony, no less!"

"I'm glad you enjoyed it," I managed, my mind straining to remember the details that didn't seem to exist in my brain. *What had I done? And how?*

"Then there was the bit with Aeneas and the fall of Troy," Max said. "Squire Howland made me read that blasted poem in school. 'Vergil was a great poet' he'd croak, and then assign fifty lines to translate for the next day. I hated the damned thing." He stood up. "But when you told the tale of Aeneas going back into the burning city to find his lost wife, I couldn't believe how real it was. We smelled the smoke of the burning buildings, the fear, and the blood... heard the cries of the dying and the screams of the women..." He met my eyes and I saw his tears welling up.

"I swear I saw the ghost of his wife hovering in the middle of the room, and all of us were as stupefied as Aeneas was. And then... when he tried to embrace her ghost – "

"Twern't a dry eye in the place," Needle said. He shook his head. "That poor, poor man."

I looked up at Max, feeling fear start to scurry up from somewhere in my ribcage. I forced it back down.

He wiped his eyes and smiled. "If only Squire Howland had brought you into the classroom... if he had, we poor long-suffering lads would have loved Vergil, the poor bugger."

I swallowed, buying time so my brain could digest the new information. "So you knew the story, then? Of Aeneas?" I asked. I didn't, but I couldn't very well tell my friends that.

"Oh, aye," he agreed and moved over to sit at his post in the command chair. "I knew it, but it wasn't the familiarity of the story that appealed, Ari," he said. He sat, then leaned back and thought for a moment. "It was... it was like you put all of us – the entire pub – within the story. We saw what the characters saw, felt what they felt... like we were *them*, in some way."

"That's not a magic lantern show..." I said, a little dizzy and more than a little worried. The desperation began its slow climb again.

"You're right," Lizzie agreed. "It was just plain magic."

The word *magic* set the fear I'd forced down afire. It reached my brain in a whoosh, releasing a panic into my already whirling thoughts. I didn't recall anything I'd said. I didn't know the stories they said I'd told. I didn't know how to do magic. Magic didn't exist.

"If I didn't think it would be too distracting, I'd have you tell more stories while we're flying about in this bucket of bolts," Max said, smiling gently.

Oh, God, I thought, feeling a little lightheaded at the prospect. I couldn't do that. I just… I just couldn't. I didn't know how I'd done it in the first place, and Max wanted me to do it again. *Oh God*. My stomach lurched in distress, but I had no wish for the *Bosch's* crew to see how I really felt. They thought of the evening as a triumph. I saw it as an increasingly unpleasant nightmare. I swallowed hard to keep both the rum and my worry down.

"But so far as the storytelling goes, I wish you'd done that earlier," Max continued, thankfully oblivious to my distress. "We made as much from the tales as we did from the darts." He laughed. "I dare say, you enchanted everyone in Penzance like one of the bards in the myths of old. They couldn't give us their coins fast enough!"

Panic flared white hot within me, which I hid with difficulty. The others turned back to their stations and instruments, their pleasure in the night's success palpable. I turned to face my wall of instruments, with its gears and pointers spinning. It was a device of my own creation, but I barely saw it as my mind rolled in alarmed confusion.

What had happened?

The disconnect that occurred when I had a challenge requiring projectiles made archery, target shooting, in fact, anything that involved hitting a target easy. I'd grown so used to it I'd not wondered about my evident prowess or how I came by it. No one else had seen a change in my demeanor or seemed to notice what happened in my mind, so no one knew it wasn't *quite* me doing the throwing. They had just thought I had excellent, if somewhat unusual, aim.

My parents, once they realized how good I was, had steered me away from such pursuits. Mother explained it was unseemly for a woman to be an expert marksman unless she worked in a Wild West Show. Unfortunately, my request to apply for such a position was summarily rejected. Father pointed out that where we lived in London was neither 'wild' nor 'west', and therefore, since both civilization and geography stood against me, I should try something else. I quickly turned to mathematics and mechanicals. I loved mathematics because it was logical and precise, and mechanicals because I enjoyed creating new machines almost as much as dismantling old ones. Getting gears and cogs to line up and move on their own was a wonderful puzzle to solve. I'd only picked up the darts again as part of a bet with Max about eighteen months ago.

Letting my consciousness float while something else – whatever it was—took control had seemed natural. I'd never been frightened by it before.

Now that seemingly benevolent... *thing*, for lack of a better word—had started to take liberties with my body and mind. How could I tell such fantastic stories? How was I neither aware of it while it happened nor remember what I'd said afterward? What if this... *thing*... decided to try other activities, like tightrope walking or burglary? *If I didn't know I did it, how could I stop myself from doing it?* I wondered.

I gripped the edges of my chair. I had no idea why this was happening to me. My life-long trust in my unusual ability now seemed foolish and potentially dangerous. *Was I going mad? Was I already mad?*

Suddenly the bridge felt too small. I stood up, startling the other members of the *Bosch* crew. Max looked up from his charts.

"Do you mind if I take a turn around the deck?" I asked in a tone that was a bit too loud.

Max nodded though his brow furrowed a bit in concern.

I took a deep breath and tried again, modulating my tone to the proper level. "I need a bit of air."

"Are you all right?" Lizzie asked.

"Just tired," I lied.

Max looked skeptical but decided to let it pass. "With the wind and cloudless sky it'll be cold as blazes out there, so grab your coat. Tether yourself to the rail for safety's sake," he said and turned back to his charts, but he kept one eye on me.

I fled the room, made my way back to my cabin, and dragged a thick brown wool coat from my trunk under the bunk bed. I pulled the coat on, grabbed the matching mittens and knitted wool hat out of the trunk, and made my way up to the deck as fast as I could go.

I needed out. I needed time to think.

I climbed the stairs from the cabin and burst onto the deck that ran above the airship's cockpit and crew cabins. The wood decking was solid under my feet and the rigid aluminum struts of the balloon covered in pegamoid silk curved above me. The bow of the gondola stretched out to my left, with the full moon in front of it illuminating everything with a grey light. I gasped for air as panic overtook me. My heart raced and I felt my palms start to sweat. I closed my eyes and focused on slowing my breathing, and managed to bring my racing heart to heel.

As Max predicted, it was frigidly cold, due to it being early spring and the altitude we'd reached. I tucked the hat and mittens under one arm, reaching for the safety harness on the wall by the door. My hands shook as I buckled it around my waist over the coat, but I managed to cinch the belt tight. I grabbed the railing with my right hand, holding tight as I moved to the front of the deck. Once I got there, I clipped the harness to the front rail, thereby ensuring I'd not go far if I fell.

Wind whipped around me, pulling at the bottom of my heavy coat and causing my braid to loosen and strands of hair to flap wildly about my face. I tugged the wool cap onto my head and over my ears, tying it in place under my chin, then pulled the mittens on my hands. I looked out over the countryside below me, illuminated by the full moon. I could see the lights of cities in the distance ahead of us, illuminating the sky above them with a yellow hazy glow. The sky above held a few dim stars and an occasional wisp of cloud. The rigid balloon sloped up over my head and out about seventy feet in front of the gondola. Its grey-brown silk moved with the wind and ripples flowed up and down the sloped surface above me like wheat waving in a field. The contours of the landscape below wavered between shades of grey, brown and black, with the occasional dim light from a lantern in a farmhouse visible. I could make out forests with skeletal trees, fields beginning to frost over and muddy roads stretching in all directions. The air smelled crisp, and I only caught whiffs of smoke from fireplaces somewhere below us. The propellers beat the air behind me as we moved forward, and over the rush of the wind I could hear dogs barking in the distance. As my mind cleared with help from the solitude and brisk wind, I thought about what had happened to me as calmly as I could.

How bad is my situation, on balance? I wondered. *I've not done anything illegal, and I've not actually been hurt. Disconcerting as it is to hear reports of things I've done that I don't remember, I suppose it's not all that different from what inebriates suffer after a night of overindulgence. It's an unsavory comparison, but a valid one, based on what I've seen others experience.*

I hadn't hurt anyone, thankfully. No darts had struck anything other than the target, and my stories hadn't caused a brawl. I knew Max and the others would have stepped in if something had gone wrong, which, clearly, it hadn't. If anything, the stories had increased the happiness and camaraderie of the Crown's patrons. And, despite the press of the crowd and sheer volume of humanity I'd seen when I'd 'come to,' for lack of a better term, I was myself uninjured.

We'd made a great deal of money as a result of both my dart throwing and the storytelling, which we needed. *Is my concern enough to put a halt to our collective plan? If it is, what possible reason can I give?* I certainly couldn't tell my friends what happened to me when I threw darts. They'd think I was insane, particularly when they discovered I didn't remember telling the amazing stories they'd heard.

I gripped the railing tighter. *What happens if I start to do more than throw darts and tell stories when I'm in the semi-conscious, highly focused state? What will I do then?* It was troubling and frightening to know I'd done things I didn't remember, but... *is it so frightening that I want to stop?* My heart sank as considered my options. *Can I afford to stop?* I wondered. I wasn't sure.

I sighed and looked up at the impassive and ancient moon, idly wondering if it could answer my questions. As a child, I used to believe it could, and I smiled grimly at my own childish fancy.

At five or six years old, I'd thought the Man in the Moon was my personal protector. I believed he followed and watched over me, making sure I was safe. On the rare occasions my parents took me out for a function at night, I refused to leave the house if I couldn't see the moon. In fact, I'd learned to read *Mason's Almanac* so I'd know its monthly phases, and left my bedroom curtains open during the full moon so the Man in the Moon could visit me.   I even remembered having some sort of tea party with the fellow one late summer evening, waking to find the cookies eaten, the weak tea drunk, and myself tucked in bed with my rag doll, Bow-Bow. It had probably been Papa or Nanny who had eaten everything and put me in bed, obviously, as if my phantom protector had been Father Christmas.

Standing on the deck of the *Bosch* at nearly eighteen years old, I knew there was no Man in the Moon, just as I knew there was no Father Christmas. The moon didn't pay special attention to me, and it certainly couldn't protect me. I crossed my arms over my chest, the heavy coat making the move awkward. *How much better I'll feel if he, or anyone, watches out for me as I thought the moon did all those years ago,* I thought wistfully.

"I don't understand what's happening," I said, staring up at the lunar body hanging in the sky. "I need help, or an explanation or… I don't know… something."

I shook my head. It was a foolish statement made from the heart, more suited to my childhood self than who I was now. It was neither logical nor reasonable, and I prided myself on being both. *Better to use my head,* I mused, turning from the rail, unhooking the harness from it and heading back along the deck to return to my cabin. I'd try to sleep, and leave finding the answers to my dilemma for later.

Chapter Three

The Monday night following my excursion to Penzance found my nose back in my mathematics books, working on my most recent assignments from my tutor. I'd been so absorbed in my derivations and equations I'd missed dinner, mostly because I didn't want to think about the revelations of the previous evening in Penzance. Immersing myself in my studies kept my worries and unanswered questions at bay.

As the clock in the hall struck midnight my stomach, usually sanguine about food, complained bitterly about its empty state. I tried to ignore it, but the noises it made and the ache of hunger pains forced me into action. Sighing, I rose from my desk and books, picked up and lit my candlestick so I could see in the hallway and turned off my phosphorite desk lamp. I tip-toed down to the kitchen. I wasn't sure what I'd find that was edible and accessible, but it was worth a look.

I snuck into the dimly lit kitchen, my candle a tiny beacon in the darkness. I scanned the counters and shelves for a quick snack. I wanted to get in and out as quickly and unobtrusively as possible with enough of something edible to stop the hunger pangs but not so much it'd be noticed. Mrs. Gildersleeve frowned on residents of Towson House helping themselves to the larder at ungodly hours, and the stories of her pouncing on hungry late-night scholars were legendary. I definitely didn't want to be her next victim.

I thought I saw a wheel of cheese on a far shelf and made a move to investigate when I heard a snuffle in the darkness. I froze. The noise had been human in origin, but the expected verbal assault from Mrs. Gildersleeve for being out of bed and in the kitchen 'trolling for vittles' didn't materialize. The snuffle came again.

"Who's there?" I hissed into the darkness, turning my candle toward the sound.

"Sophie," was the soft Gallic response. "Good evening, Mademoiselle Trevelyan."

I moved toward the voice and my light revealed a figure seated in a corner, dressed in a black dress with long sleeves. A prim white cap sat pinned on a head of dark curls. She held her right arm cradled close to her body as if she had an extremely bad bellyache, the hand flexed as if cramped. Her reticule, also black, sat in her lap.

I relaxed somewhat. Sophie Gaspard was a French girl on staff at Towson House. Well-liked and constantly busy, my fellow students appreciated how she assisted the poor unfortunates struggling with the finer points of the French language. More than once I'd heard her helping someone conjugate French verbs while she dusted, the words flowing off her tongue in melodious alto tones in stark contrast to the halting, uncertain utterances of the girl she helped. Sophie's command of English was very good though she did speak with a bit of an accent. Since I wasn't a language student, I didn't know her very well.

No one knew what part of France Sophie came from, or how it was that she ended up working at our residence. I'd guess she was perhaps in her twenties, but I had no way of knowing for sure. She was very private, even living in her own rooms away from Towson House rather than in the servants' quarters the residence hall allowed. It was unusual for her to be here so late.

I moved over to Sophie, bringing the candle down so my body obscured its light from the hallway. No point both of us getting ambushed. "Why are you still here?" I asked. "Gildersleeve put you on guard duty?"

Sophie shook her head. "No. She knows I would not inform on anyone no matter what they took." She paused, obviously considering her next words carefully. "I had nowhere else to go. I am... unwell, I am afraid."

My stomach gurgled. "A stomach complaint?" I suggested, looking down at the noisy region of my own body. "Must be the season for it," I added ruefully.

"No," Sophie said, lifting her right arm and hand briefly. "It is my hand, you see. It is damaged and does not work. I have had to make my way for the past few days working with only one hand. Madame Gildersleeve has ordered me to the doctor to have it checked. She says she has no use for a girl on staff who has but one arm."

I took that in. She was frightened, which seemed misplaced to me. "But you've not gone to the doctor, I take it?"

"No."

"Is it a financial concern?" I asked. "You know there's money set aside—"

"You are very kind, but, no, it is not the money."

That stymied me. "Are you in pain?"

"No, there is no pain. The arm does not function, and I am afraid a doctor cannot assist me."

That was a puzzler. I tried to think what would make a doctor unable to help. It wasn't a language barrier. Dr. Sanburne spoke French, for a start. He was a gentle man who Towson House residents saw when they had medical issues. I'd heard nothing but good reports of his medical knowledge and ministrations.

The unusual words she'd used to describe the problem resonated in my mind. 'Damaged,' not 'hurt.' 'Does not function' rather than 'broken' or 'injured.' Then it hit me. "You're Enhanced, aren't you Sophie?" I asked in a whisper, astonished by my own realization.

Fear bloomed in her brown eyes, and I held up my free hand in a soothing gesture. "I'll not tell anyone, I swear," I said. "But that's why you can't go to the doctor, isn't it?"

"You will not tell Madame Gildersleeve?" she whispered, a tremor in her voice. "I cannot afford to lose this position, and there are those who would not welcome someone like me working in this house."

I shook my head. "No, Sophie. If Gildersleeve doesn't know, I see no reason to tell her or anyone else. Your secret is safe with me." I sat down on the floor next to her and placed the candle carefully on the floor beside me. "What I'd like to do is help you if I can."

"It is hopeless," Sophie said, slumping her shoulders in defeat.

"How so?" I asked. "Surely, even in England there are doctors who treat the Enhanced."

Sophie shrank from me. "No," she said with certainty. "The doctors in this country who repair us are evil people. They change one... make them even less human. I will not go near one of those butchers."

That was a surprise. It hadn't occurred to me there'd be difficulties finding an appropriately trained Enhanced physician in England though I wasn't sure if she was being accurate with her 'butcher' comment.

"How do you know this?" I asked.

Sophie looked at me. "I have friends who are..." she paused a moment, "...who are like me. A few of them went to one of those who claim to treat us when we break. When my friends returned, they were not themselves. They cared nothing for their friends or family. Before their repairs, their Enhancements had been hidden, as mine is, but after they returned they had metal in new, visible places. Their eyes..." she shuddered, "...turned to metal spheres, and their souls were broken. Despite this, they reveled in their new bodies, which were stronger and faster than they had been. I found the cost of their improvements to be too high." She looked down at her non-functional arm. "Being more powerful, or faster or stronger is not better. I am less human than you, but I will not lose what humanity I still possess."

I opened my mouth to say something and then shut it, at a loss as to what to say. *Why did they increase the speed and strength of their patients while reducing their human nature?* I wondered. *Why did they turn the eyes of their patients into metal spheres? What sorts of people were these so-called doctors? Why were they allowed to practice if they gravely damaged their patients?*

I thought about how people treated me in the pubs we'd visited before my non-Enhanced status was proven. Even if Sophie had the desire to report the horrific nature of medical treatment

---

her friends received, who would listen? What would be done? *Probably nothing*, I told myself. *Damn and blast.*

"That's awful," I finally said, concern for Sophie growing. "Why do you think this happened to your friends? Can anything be done to reverse the damage?"

She turned her head to regard me. "I do not know, but I will not let it happen to me. I have sat here most of the night because I am afraid to return home. I worry the ones with the silver eyes will force me to go to their evil doctor. Then I will be like them." She took a deep breath and let it out slowly. "I would rather be dead than be like them."

I agreed with that sentiment. What she'd told me of the unpleasant alterations done to her friends chilled my soul. "Where would you have to go to get treated properly?" I asked.

"France," she said, her accent particularly strong as she said the name of her home.

"Ah," I said, understanding the problem clearly now. The French were the best at Enhanced technology. Their innovations in the discipline far outstripped anything done in England, mostly because of the negative attitude toward the Enhanced here. "It would take too long for you to return home and come back here, then? Not to mention expensive?"

"And it would reveal my... anomaly," she agreed. "Entering this country for the Enhanced is difficult. I am here legally, but papers and further approvals are necessary for re-admittance."

"I know a professor who might be able—"

"No," she said, cutting me off. "It is bad enough you know my secret. I will not risk further exposure."

"Then I'll have to help you myself," I said and pushed myself to a standing position.

"But—" she protested.

"I know a thing or two about complicated mechanical devices, Sophie. You know that." I leaned over and picked up the candle, bringing the warm circle of light it shed back up around my face. "It may be that I can't do anything, or that the mechanism that's giving you trouble is too complicated for me to fathom."

"I do not want you to get in trouble," she said.

"With whom?" I asked. "I dare say, no one would care either way."

"If it is known you helped me —" she stopped, thought for a moment. "The ones I fear… if they know you work on the Enhanced, it might be bad for you."

"I don't plan to advertise," I said, shrugging, "and you have no reason to tell anyone what I do here tonight, do you?" She shook her head.

I motioned for her to stand up. "If I can figure out how to help you, then you don't risk further exposure or possible harm at the hands of those who would alter you further. You don't have to make the trip to France, and you can keep your job here at Towson House."

She stared up at me for a long moment. "You are truly willing to help me?" she asked.

I shrugged. "I'm willing to make the attempt. I'm not well versed in Enhanced technology, but I can at least offer what help I can."

Sophie stood, gripping her reticule in her left hand while she continued to press her right forearm into her belly. "You speak sense. I will go with you and we can see if you fix me, yes?"

I nodded, and my stomach growled loudly. I gave Sophie a sheepish look. "Do you suppose we could grab something to eat before we start? I'm famished."

Sophie giggled. "Yes," she said, motioning toward the other end of the room. "Bring your light. I will make you something and Gildersleeve will never know. Come."

Chapter Four

My hunger sated, Sophie and I went to my room. I shut and locked the door so we would have some privacy. At nearly one o'clock in the morning, I doubted anyone would interrupt us, but it seemed foolish not to take the precaution. I thanked my lucky stars I had no roommate.

I took my seat at the desk, turning on my desk light. I put my candle on the desk's surface and indicated Sophie should take a seat on the bed beside me. She did so, looking nervous. Her left hand gripped her reticule tightly. I closed my mathematics books and set them aside with my homework, then reached into my left-hand drawer to pull out my box of tools and spare parts, setting the boxes on the desk in front of me. I moved the desk lamp closer to Sophie so I'd have the best light possible.

"Can you tell me the nature of the problem?" I asked.

Sophie nodded. "There is a small box inside my arm. I must have it replaced every four years. I do not know what the box does, nor why it must be replaced. Once I realized my arm began to malfunction in the way I recognized from before, I wrote to my parents and they sent to me a new box. They thought, as did I, it would be a simple matter to find a technician to make the repair." She held up her reticule. "I have the box here."

"You've had it replaced before, then?" If what needed to be done was a part of regular maintenance, logic dictated that it would be something easily accessed.

"Oui," Sophie said. She set her reticule down on the bed and used her left hand to move her right arm away from her body, laying the unmoving right hand palm up on her right leg. I noticed that the hand looked remarkably human. The color was normal, the fingers fleshy and well made. The nails even had pink nail beds, but something about the sheen of the skin wasn't quite right. Nevertheless, it was close enough to the real thing that I found I suddenly understood at least one aspect of the English discomfiture with and dislike of the Enhanced. The notion that man could create something so like a human limb brought into question the nature of humanity itself. It was a difficult notion to grapple with, particularly when one considered the logical conclusion of the technology... whole mechanical bodies, perhaps?

Sophie pointed at the area just below the elbow, covered with the black sleeve. Her motion and redirection pulled me out of my philosophic reverie.

"It goes in here," she said. "The little box."

I reached over and took her right hand in mine, surprised that it was warm like actual flesh, though the feel of it was slightly waxy, like she'd used too much lotion or hand cream. I swallowed hard. I hadn't expected that. It put me a bit out of sorts.

"Sophie," I said, hoping she couldn't see I was uncomfortable and doing what I could to squash the feeling, "What's under the sleeve?"

"It is a thin covering that looks like flesh but is not. It is also warm, like the flesh of the hand, but where the covering meets there is a..." she thought for a moment, "...*le joint*... a seam, I think you call it in English. My uniform usually covers it."

I looked down at the hand again, contorted and frozen. "This workmanship is incredible. I've seen nothing like it before."

"Oui," she said. "It is only here in England the Enhanced must suffer with ugly, obvious alterations. The doctor who made my new arm took great care that it would look just like the uninjured one, to the best of his ability."

I let go of her hand. I brought my own left hand to my head and rested the elbow on the top of the desk, pondering the skill and technology required to do what Sophie obviously considered to be normal. *How much does such a limb cost? How do the fingers move? Can she sense pressure and temperature with her artificial fingers?* I supposed she must, chewing my lip as I thought about it. *How does the limb know what her mind tells it to do?* Sitting there and looking at Sophie's artificial arm, I marveled. It was far more advanced and complicated than I'd initially thought. Maybe helping Sophie was beyond my skills.

"Ah... can I see the box your parents sent?" I asked.

She reached over and opened her reticule with her good hand. She dug within it until she withdrew a glass container. Inside it sat a small silver box that was the size of a thimble. It had three thin wires protruding from it, colored red, black and white. She handed the glass container to me and I examined it very carefully through the glass. It looked like a switch of some kind. I'd never seen anything like it and it was more proof of the superiority of French Enhanced engineering. I wondered what other applications the little silver box could be used for.

"Does your arm have an independent power source?" I asked, setting the small device in its glass case on the desk. *That's what I would do,* I thought, *considering the size and complexity of the mechanism her arm requires.*

"Yes." She pointed at her right armpit. "It resides here."

"When you had this device replaced last time, did you see what the doctor did?"

"He opened the covering along the seam here," she pointed at the point below the right elbow again, "making an incision about two inches long. He parted the two flaps, pulled out the box that needed to be replaced, and disconnected the wires that attached it to the mechanism. Then he attached the wires from the new box, slid it back into the arm, and sewed the incision shut."

I blinked, imagining what it would be like to witness such an operation on my arm, whether or not it was a mechanical appendage or my own flesh and blood. The notion made my skin crawl. "Didn't that hurt?" I asked.

Sophie shook her head. "No. When I deactivate the arm, it does not feel pain. The skin on the arm is merely a thick membrane to hide the mechanisMs. It is not like the flesh of the rest of my body." She tilted her head to the side slightly. "If you do not wish to try, I will understand. It is perhaps more complicated than you thought?"

"I won't know that until I see what's under the membrane," I said. *In for a penny, in for a pound,* I thought. "Could you expose and deactivate the arm?"

"Oui," she said, and in a minute she had her bodice unbuttoned and the arm exposed, resigned to the necessity but understandably shy. I doubted she'd let anyone other than a family member see her Enhancement in such a way.

I let out the breath I hadn't realized I'd been holding. "Oh, Sophie," I said, "It's beautiful."

A thin ring of silver metal around the middle of her upper arm served as the join between the artificial limb and the living flesh. Pink scarring striped the flesh of her arm above the ring of metal, but otherwise the transition from living flesh to mechanical appendage was a smooth one. The seam of the membrane ran along the inside of the arm, visible but not obvious. There was a similar seam around her wrist. At a distance, the arm would have looked normal. Up close, if someone clasped the hand as I had done, they could tell the arm was artificial, but it mimicked the real thing with impressive accuracy.

"I deactivate it with a key," she said, producing it from her reticule. It looked like a small key meant for winding clocks. She lifted her arm at the shoulder, put the key in a small keyhole on the arm's underside close to the metal ring and turned it. The hand and arm went limp.

"Right. Let's see what can be done, shall we?" I said with more confidence than I felt. I opened my toolboxes and picked out the instruments I thought most likely to be of use, including a spool of fine white silk thread and a sewing needle. Gertrude, our resident biology student and bloody-minded in the extreme, had given me a scalpel handle and blades to put in it though I'd doubted I'd ever need to use them. Gertrude had insisted I take them, no doubt thinking I'd make some sort of diabolical surgical device with the lot. I pulled them out as well and attached a blade to the handle. I turned back to Sophie.

I positioned the arm so the area of the seam I needed to open was easily accessible and used the scalpel to pop the tiny stitches that held the membrane together in the small space Sophie had indicated. Sophie sat perfectly still as I worked, watching with interest.

I gently parted the membrane to expose the inner workings. Thin wires filled the space in the midst of long metal rods of different sizes and types that mimicked the bones and muscles, I supposed. My mind filled to bursting with questions about what I saw. It was hard to resist the urge to cut away more of the outer membrane to get a better look at the rest of the arm's innards, but I would not use Sophie as a source of curious exploration. She was a person, not one of my mechanical devices, and I had a very specific job to do.

I put down the scalpel and pulled out a thin wooden probe, gently parting the wires to see if I could find the component I needed to replace.

"How are you doing, Sophie?" I asked, looking up at her from my prodding.

"I am well," she said. She indicated the candle on the desk. "Shall I hold the candle so you may see into the arm better?"

I nodded. In a moment, the area was much more illuminated. I picked up a pair of very fine narrow tweezers, and with a few more pokes and gentle moves with my probe and tweezers, I saw the box attached to a thicker wire than the others. With both hands and a very gentle touch, I used the tools in tandem to tug gently on the larger wire. I smiled as I felt it move easily toward me. I pulled it out into the open air.

"Halfway home," I said to Sophie.

"Oui," she agreed, relief suffusing her face. "You have very steady hands."

I set down the probe and picked up a pair of long pliers. I carefully moved the box and the wire so I could see how they attached to each other. The three thin wires wound around three contacts on a metal plate through which the wire travelled. I could see now why Sophie couldn't do the repair herself. Replacing the box took two hands, since the wires were so delicate and the space they occupied was so small. Once I got my bearings it was the work of a moment to unwind the wires and remove the old box, then put the new box in place and wind the new wires where the prior ones had been. Then, putting down the pliers and using the tweezers and the probe once again, I gently pushed the box and its attached wire back into the arm cavity, aiming for the space it had occupied before.

I put down my tools, took the candle from Sophie to place it back on the desk, and heaved a sigh.

"Let's see if it works," I said, leaning back on the chair.

Sophie inserted the key in its slot and turned it to the right. The mechanism emitted a brief mechanical whirr, and the arm came back to life. Sophie looked down at her hand and ran the fingers through a few quick motions while she bent the elbow back and forth. Other than the whirr at the beginning, the arm made no other mechanical noises. Sophie beamed.

"You have done it," she said and leaned over to embrace me in a spontaneous hug with both arMs. The French were clearly a very demonstrative people. "I cannot thank you enough!"

I hugged her back, laughing a little. "Yes," I agreed, relieved I'd been successful and glad that Sophie had two working arms again. "I have to sew up your arm yet," I pointed out.

She let go of me. "Yes. Do you sew as well as you work with mechanicals?"

"If you want fancy embroidery and needlework, then no… but simple stitches such as these are within my ability." I reached over to take up the silk thread and needle. "Unless you'd like to do it?"

"No," she said. "I do not feel pain in the arm as you do, but the idea of sewing up my own—"

"Understood," I said, realizing I'd rather not sew myself up either. "A few more minutes and you'll be back to normal."

Sophie watched as I sewed up the incision I'd made with stitches as small as those I'd cut had been. It took longer than I thought. When I finished I put the needle on the desktop with my other tools, put the box I'd removed from Sophie's arm in the glass container, and then leaned back and rubbed my face for a moment. I was weary to the marrow of my bones.

"I do not know how to thank you," she said as she dressed herself, sliding her artificial arm back into its black sleeve. "Will you take money? I can pay you—"

I shook my head. "No," I said and held up a hand to cut off her protests. "I was glad to help. Keep your money." I pulled the glass box off the desk and held it out to her. "Here's your... erm... spare part?" I said.

"Do you have these things in England?" she asked, taking the glass container from me and sliding it into her reticule.

"Perhaps," I said, "but I've never seen them. I'm not really sure what that little box does, if I'm honest." I stretched, and joints popped as the muscles pulled them. "Surely it's too late for you to head back to your lodgings," I said. "May I suggest you sleep here?" I indicated the rug. "I can grab the cot from the hall closet, and I have an extra blanket you could use."

Sophie looked uncertain. "I do not think that would be appropriate," she began.

"Much of what happened this past hour or so has been less than appropriate. I'd feel better if you spent the night here." Her description of what had happened to her Enhanced friends made me concerned for her safety. Perhaps once they saw she was back to normal she'd no longer need to fear them, but then again, perhaps not.

Sophie considered for a moment and nodded. "I will help you get the cot. In the morning, we will think of what to tell Madame Gildersleeve, yes?"

I smiled and shrugged. "Should be easy enough."

The Odin Inheritance

Chapter Five

The rest of the week passed in a blur. Sophie went back to work, prepared with the tale that she'd been helping me with translating a French mathematics text. Gildersleeve was so glad to have her best employee back to work with two hands she didn't bother asking why Sophie had spent the night in my room, which was fine with us.

I spent the majority of my waking moments after that continuing my preparation for my final examinations in the Mathematics Tripos and thereby the completion of my studies at Towson. As a woman, I couldn't earn an actual degree, much to my great consternation, but I still wanted to place at the wrangler level.   To be sure I'd score high enough I worked with my tutor, attended classes, and did a great deal of math homework. When I needed a break, I dreamed up new mini-mechanical devices, often creating them at my desk in my room at Towson from materials found or purchased in Cambridge or elsewhere.   I also worked on my aeronaut navigation devices, and when I could, I met with a General Sciences professor for private tutorials on the newest theories and studies of physics, meteorology, and astronomy.

Sophie came to see me briefly each day, and a true friendship began to develop between us. She asked about my mechanical devices, so I showed her my various inventions and talked about how I constructed them. I asked about what France was like, and she told me about the village in the Loire Valley she'd grown up in. It sounded quaint and friendly and she spoke warmly of her parents and siblings. I wondered what had prompted Sophie to move from such a loving place to England, where her Enhancement was a source of mistrust and derision.

I tried to convince her to move into the servant's housing at Towson House, since I worried her steel-eyed former friends would do her harm. She shrugged off my concerns.

"They only get very insistent when one is injured, you see," Sophie explained. "I am no longer broken, so they do not concern themselves with me anymore. They have not even been around where I live for the past few days. It has been very quiet."

"That's as may be," I said, "but won't they try to drag you to this awful doctor for him to examine you or something?" I clasped my hands in my lap tightly, trying to contain my agitation on her behalf. "Since your arm is of French manufacture, isn't it possible they'll want to..." I swallowed, "...take it apart and see how it works?"

She shook her head decisively. "No. My Enhancement is minor, for the most part. Its basic construction and wiring diagrams are well known, even if the technicians here refuse to consult them. I am of no value from a mechanical point of view." She put a hand on my clasped hands in reassurance. "I appreciate your concern, but I am fine where I am."

That ended my attempts to get her to move into Towson House, but not my concerns for her safety.

My various activities, therefore, left little time for actual aeronautics, so I didn't see my fellow crewmates from the *Bosch*, and spent no time that week at the Icarus Club, the 'home away from home' for the members of Cambridge's Icarus Squadron. The fear and worry I'd experienced from the unexpected events in Penzance had faded somewhat, but I was still uncertain what to do about the whole affair. Not seeing the *Bosch* crew made the issue moot, at least for a bit, and dropping wholeheartedly into my mathematics studies pushed it out of my mind most of the time.

Saturday arrived. As was my usual habit, I ate breakfast and made my way to the Faraday Library to spend the day working on the assignments for the upcoming week. My long-time tutor Dr. Maitland, a venerable member of the mathematics and sciences faculty, pulled no punches on the workload he assigned me despite my being a member of the fairer sex. Therefore, when I wasn't floating across England in the *Bosch* on a weekend, the Faraday's long wooden tables and dark reference shelves became my home.

Mr. Avery, the Faraday librarian, knew me and my habits well. That morning he welcomed me into his book-filled sanctum with a smile and the small box of books he held for me behind his desk, since students were not allowed to take books from the library. Other students—exclusively male—trickled in around me in various states of awareness depending on how they'd spent the previous night. Those who had overindulged moved slowly as if the air touching their skin was excruciating. Those who hadn't, moved with the somnambulant air of the not-quite awake.

I took up my usual spot on the left-hand side of the middle table of the room, pushing my box of books to the right of my seat. I pulled a phosphorite lamp close to illuminate my work area and touched its glass globe to turn it on. Its circle of warm light enveloped me as I sat down, pulled my things from my bookbag, set out my papers and began to work.

As often happened when I was absorbed with my calculations, the library around me faded from my attention. The sounds of my fellow students as they snuffled and shifted seeped from my notice. The numbers dancing in my equations occupied my whole mind. While they did so, the world I inhabited was ordered and... while not predictable *per se*, at least it operated according to set rules I knew well. In recent days, my life had been decidedly peculiar. It was a relief to immerse myself in my usual routine.

I relaxed into the work and tackled my assignments in a state of satisfied industry. Hours flew by unheeded.

I'd come to the second to last problem in my last mathematics assignment when something, or rather some*one*, interrupted my work. "Excuse me, *fraulein*," came a male, German-accented voice behind me.

I turned around in my chair and peered up at a man I didn't know. Handsome in an exotic way, the man was tall, thin, dark-haired, and grey-eyed, with a small patch of dark hair in a diamond shape in the cleft of his chin. Everything about him was very, very German. In fact, I was surprised to see he wore full-length trousers with his grey suit coat and stiff collared shirt, since the lilt of his voice made me think of Matterhorns and lederhosen.

"Yes?" I asked, curious despite myself.

"I wonder," he asked in a stage whisper, "do you know where I could find a librarian? There are none at the reference desk."

I looked around. The reference desk of the library did indeed seem to be empty. In fact, the German and I were the only ones in the reading room. *How odd. Where had everyone gone?* I wondered.

"I'm sorry," I said. I indicated the books in front of me on the table. "I was very absorbed in my studies and didn't see where he went."

"Oh," the German said, an embarrassed look coming over his angular features. "I did not mean to interrupt your work." He peered at the pages I'd filled with equations and his eyebrows went up in surprise. "How interesting. You study mathematics?"

"I do."

"Don't most college ladies in England study at university to become governesses? Do you require that level of calculus to instruct children in the nursery?"

I bristled but did my best to hide my irritation. "I am not training to become a governess," I explained. "I enjoy the sciences and have an aptitude for mathematics. Therefore, I study them."

"But you cannot pursue those professions as a woman," he said, confusion crossing his face. "Why study them in depth?"

"Why not?" I responded. What he said was true – in England, at least. I'd have a better chance at an academic career in France if I wanted one, which I didn't. "You don't think there is value in careful study for its own sake?"

"Of course there is value in such study, but the value increases if use can be made of the knowledge gained," he said with a shrug, "and unless doing high level mathematics is required of Englishwomen as wives, such study on your part seems frivolous."

I gave up my efforts at remaining polite in the content of my speech but maintained an even tone as I responded to him. "You know nothing of me or my life, sir. I dare say if I were a male student you'd not feel the need to be so rude, nor would you be so audacious as to suggest my course of study was a waste of time," I said, my gentle tone in direct contrast with the meaning of my words. "Tell me – is boorish behavior the hallmark of all German nationals, or unique to you alone? Were you transferred here because your colleagues back home grew tired of your rude comments or is Cambridge especially cursed, somehow?"

"Ah," he said, genuine surprise crossing his features at what I'd said. He looked at the floor for a moment before meeting my eyes apologetically. "I am very sorry. I did not mean to offend. Sometimes what I say in English doesn't come out exactly as I intend. I did not know that Englishwomen could be ardent scholars of such... masculine material. It seemed unusual."

I narrowed my eyes speculatively at the man, not sure whether to believe him or not. "I do not believe gender determines intellect, or that certain subjects are masculine or feminine," I said, "though there are others who do. Is that the philosophy of German scholars?"

"There are differences of opinions on the matter in Germany, as there are here," he said. "But," he looked around, "...is this not the Physics library? I know Dr. Oberlin, the head of the department, disapproves of women at this university. I am surprised he allows you to study here."

The German fellow seemed to be remarkably well informed, I noticed. He'd met the one professor in the sciences department who did believe gender determined intellect. In fact, Dr. Silas Oberlin thought that women were less intelligent than men simply because they were women, despite mounting evidence to the contrary. Sadly, the mounting evidence only served to make Oberlin even more intractable in his views.

I took in a deep breath and let it out before I spoke. "Dr. Oberlin does not command all aspects of university life and facilities," I said with some asperity, "though he certainly acts like he does."

"I agree," the young man said. "You stand as the proof that he does not."

I cleared my throat. The sooner I passed this fellow off to Mr. Avery, the happier I'd be. "You were looking for the librarian?" I inquired. "His name is Mr. Avery."

The man nodded. "*Ja.* I'm trying to start on my own research, which I can't do without this Mr. Avery. I'm new to Cambridge, you see. I am Dr. Oberlin's newest student."

That explains it, I thought; *this fellow is a misogynist in training.* I put down my pen and stood up, pushing my chair back from the table. "Let's see if we can find Mr. Avery so you can get to work."

The young man looked alarmed. "*Bitte* no, Fraulein," he said, holding up his hands, "I have troubled you enough. I don't want you to—"

I waved off his concern. "It's no trouble. I needed a bit of a break anyway." I pushed my chair back under the table and then motioned for him to follow me. "Come on. Mr. Avery doesn't go far."

He followed. "*Danke.* I'm Augustus Laufeson – I just transferred from the University of Halle-Wittenberg."

"This way, Mr. Laufeson," I said. We walked to the end of the reading room where the reference desk sat, unoccupied. I looked to the left and right and noticed the office door on the left hand wall was ajar. I pulled out the small pocket watch from my vest pocket. It read four o'clock. Thankfully, I spent enough time in the library that I knew Mr. Avery's habits well.

"Mr. Laufeson," I said, indicating the open door on the left, "it would seem that Mr. Avery is on a tea break. Give him a few minutes and he should be back at the reference desk."

"Tea break?"

I nodded. "It's tea time. You'll note that you and I are the only students here at the moment," I said, indicating the empty reading room around us. Books sat open and unattended at various tables around the room. "The other students have gone off to procure their own tea." I turned and headed back to my spot in the reading room.

"Why haven't you done as they did?" Laufeson asked, following me at a distance. "Do you not drink tea?"

"I lost track of time," I called back. Since we were alone in the reading room, I didn't have to whisper. "Happens a lot when I'm studying," I explained. *I could do with a cup of tea and a scone,* I thought with a pang. My stomach rumbled at the thought of food. *Too bad I have too much work to do.*

Mr. Laufeson took several quick steps so he walked even with me, then pursed his thin lips together for a moment, thinking. "Do you know the library well enough to help me find books? You did say you needed a break."

Arriving at my study table I turned to the German man and shook my head. "Women are only allowed in the reading room," I said.

The German indicated the books on the table where I'd been working. "Then where did these come from?"

"Mr. Avery retrieves the books I request. He keeps them in a special bin behind the desk, along with the other books used by female students. When I come to the library, he assigns me to a desk and I work there until I'm finished or the library closes."

Mr. Laufeson looked unpleasantly surprised by my explanation. "They allow you to attend classes, but not to retrieve your own books?"

"If you know about Dr. Oberlin's feelings on the matter, you can hardly find that a revelation," I said. "There are too many dark corners where ladies might find themselves 'with a gentleman and unchaperoned' is what we're told," I said. I didn't believe that was the reason, but I didn't say that. I thought it was just another odd rule Oberlin and Cambridge used to remind women they didn't quite belong at the fabled university, just like the one that refused women an actual Cambridge degree after four years of study. It was annoying, but Mr. Avery really was a dear in his efforts to get the books we ladies asked for. Therefore, I kept my feelings on the issue to myself and appreciated Mr. Avery's assistance.

"But you and I are alone and unchaperoned in this reading room," he countered, "and there is no taboo about that?"

I turned from the table and stared at him for a moment. "Ah," I said, discomfited by his observation. "Yes. Well, presumably the reading room is public enough that my unchaperoned status will not lead to any... erm... difficult situations. Mr. Avery has also left the door to the staff room open. Were you to make an advance of some kind, he's only a shout away."

Mr. Laufeson took a small step toward me. "I see," he said, nodding thoughtfully. "What sort of advance would make you inclined to shout, I wonder," he whispered, a hint of mischief in his voice.

"Best not to find out, I think, Mr. Laufeson," I responded, my voice frosty. *Who does this fellow think he is?* "I'm a scholar first and foremost. Surely you don't want your library privileges revoked." I knew I intended to keep mine, no matter what.

He took another small step forward. The combined scents of rosemary and clove drifted toward me as he brought his face close to mine. It was an oddly familiar scent that made me uneasy, but I didn't know why.

"You are an attractive woman, Miss Trevelyan," he said, his voice smooth and seductive. "I'd like to get to know you better. Surely you and I could go somewhere and chat?"

There was a warmth to his tone that took a little of the edge off my uneasiness, but something deep in my mind screamed a warning about the man. *Had I told him my name, or not?* I wondered, but couldn't remember, which bothered me. The dark grey of his eyes was cold and calculating, in direct contrast with the warmth of his words. The look on his face reminded me of a cat anticipating a quick but deadly game with the mouse he'd just caught.

"I don't think so, Mr. Laufeson," I said, taking a step back and turning so I could sit down, hoping the odd fellow would leave me alone. Had his request for assistance just been an excuse to insult and then flirt with me? It certainly seemed that way. *Best to cut him off here and now.*

"I have no desire to get to know you better." I cleared my throat. "I'm sure Mr. Avery will assist you with what you need. Good afternoon, Mr. Laufeson," I said over my shoulder. I pulled my chair out from the table and moved to resume my studying, a clear dismissal of the man and his rudeness. I hoped the fellow would just go away.

Mr. Laufeson spoke a few words in a language I didn't recognize. Distrust and unease drained from my mind like water down a drain. I stopped, stalled by his words. I felt so... strange. *What's happening?*

I felt a hand on my left sleeve near my wrist, attempting to draw me away from the table. "Oh," Mr. Laufeson said softly, "I think you should make the time, don't you? You want to make the time. You'd like to come with me."

I struggled to speak as his words snaked into my mind and settled like fog into my thoughts. Laufeson moved his fingers so they touched my skin and spoke more words I didn't understand. Disorientation bloomed and the room spun around me. Strands of black desire tugged at the edges of my thoughts. His hand on my wrist became the center of my attention. The incomprehensible words he'd spoken echoed back and forth between us seductively. I wanted to go with him and damn the consequences... but something in the primitive, animal part of my mind maintained a drumbeat of alarm. My heartbeat pulsed in my ears in panicked distress. I opened my mouth to speak – to say *yes* despite everything—

Suddenly, Mother's words blazed in my mind, cutting through the fog. *No man touches you without your permission, Ariana, and one who does is a blaggart of the highest order. Feel free to resort to violence if necessary against such an impertinent fellow. Your honor is at stake.*

I managed to shake my head, indignation at the man's hand on my wrist boiling up from Mother's reminder and fueling the movement. The desire to go with him tugged at me still, but I fought it down.

"No," I gasped, fighting to form words. "I... don't. Leave me alone."

He pulled me away from the table and wrapped his arm around my waist so far that his hand snaked around to touch my stomach. His body was warm against mine, and the scents of rosemary and clove enveloped me.

"You're mine," he hissed. "The spell holds even after all this time. I've come to collect you. You belong to me."

Spell? What spell? He casts spells? How is that possible? I wondered, worried and confused. The idea that I had to get away from him somehow burned like a coal in the back of my mind, hot and bright.

Laufeson said more unknown words and the strange lethargic feeling grew. The black strands at the edges of my mind became roots, pushing other thoughts aside and urging me to comply with my captor's wishes. My left wrist started to ache and something moved inside it, like a snake waking up from a long sleep. Even though Laufeson's hold on me was not restrictive, I couldn't pull together any impetus to move away from him. *It would be so much easier just to give in and go—*

"Here, now," came Mr. Avery's outraged voice from the reference desk. "You there – take your hands off Lady Trevelyan."

And with that, whatever hold Laufeson had over my mind broke. I took in a shuddering breath and thanked my lucky stars that Mr. Avery was a rapid tea drinker and not a typical librarian. A large man and former policeman, Avery had salt and pepper hair and a booming voice. He'd been known to throw students out on their faces if they broke rules or caused a disturbance. He had no patience for 'nonsense in his library,' as he put it. He was particularly protective of the women of Cambridge, as he called students like me.

The pressure of Mr. Laufeson's hold on my body lifted. The lethargy left my thoughts as the panic and fear within me bloomed in full force. I spun and slapped the German across the face. The palm of my hand stung from the blow, the pain clearing my head completely as I quickly stepped away from him. I glared at the man who'd tried to claim me as 'his.' *How could I have ever thought to go with him?*

"Get the Hell away from me," I spat, fury in my tone. "I am not yours to touch."

Laufeson's eyes narrowed in calculation, a glint of venom in them. "The raven has talons, I see," he muttered. "How intriguing." He moved quickly to close the distance between us, malice and fury on his face. I backed up to avoid him and hit the table with the back of my legs.

In response to my slap and Laufeson's continued pursuit of me, Mr. Avery launched himself from behind the reference desk and ran toward us, the soles of his shoes slapping on the tile floor of the reading room. He brought a silver whistle to his lips and blew two short blasts on it to call other library staff or students to his aid.

"Oi!" he shouted, shaking a meaty fist over his head as he barreled toward us.

Laufeson reached out to grab me again and I moved quickly to avoid his grasp, then put up my hands in what I hoped passed for a boxing stance, prepared to defend myself again.

"We'll have none of that in this here establishment," Avery said, reaching us and grabbing the back of Mr. Laufeson's jacket collar. Laufeson stumbled as Avery yanked him out of arms' reach of me. I kept my fists up, watching the odd man carefully, not sure what he intended to do next.

Two male students I didn't recognize bounded into the reading room and slid to a halt, taking in the scene.

"Steady on," the shorter one of them said, watching in amazement as Avery hauled Laufeson toward the door. "Bloody Hell, Alfred! We've got an interloper!"

Avery continued to drag Laufeson back, the man going along without a struggle though his anger-filled eyes never left me. I held my ground despite his glare though my knees felt wobbly. I'd be damned if I'd let the ruffian see he'd frightened me.

Avery turned his attention to the two students his whistle had called. "You there – Ted, is it? Fetch Mrs. Sneed to assist Lady Trevelyan. Alfred," he said to the taller of the two, "help me show this fellow the door."

Ted nodded and ran for Ms. Sneed, the housekeeper of the residence next to the library. Alfred reached out and grabbed Laufeson roughly by the right arm. Together they escorted him out the reading room door.

Chapter Six

I sat down in my library chair with a thump. I started to shake, due in part to a need for food, but primarily because I had the distinct feeling I'd barely escaped with my life. I had no idea why Laufeson had decided I was 'his', or what he'd said in that guttural language to dull my fear of him... but his attempt to abduct me shook me down to my soul. As I sat there shaking and gritting my teeth against waves of panic, wispy memories of pain and blood flitted back and forth in my mind like ghastly butterflies.

The world sort of greyed out in a mixture of shock and fear for a few minutes after that, the solid chair under me my only connection to the here and now until Mrs. Sneed arrived with Ted, Mr. Avery, and Alfred.

Mrs. Sneed, she of white hair and stained apron, went into full caretaker mode. She hauled me up from the chair in a swift motion and clutched me to her ample body as if I were a child. I smelled shepherd's pie on the apron and nearly wept in relief at the familiar, safe odor.

"Stop your shaking, m'Lady. I don't know who the fellow was," she cooed gently, "but he's gone now. We'll not let him near you again. Now, let's get you settled." She turned her attention to the gentlemen around us. "Boys – off with you. James, I'll need your help."

"Right-o," said Ted, and the two young men departed, reliving their part of the excitement of the encounter with Laufeson in hushed tones as they left. Mr. Avery remained, looking angry and worried.

Mrs. Sneed released me from her embrace and looked me up and down. "For the love of Mike, she's pale as a sheet!" she exclaimed. "It's good you had the boy fetch me, James," she said as she took me by the left arm and we made our way into Avery's office, "she's all flustered, and no wonder!"

Mr. Avery took up a position on my other side, clutching my right arm as our pace to his office increased. "Let's get her in a chair," he responded, guiding us into his inner sanctum. "Once she gets a bit of Nelson's blood in her, she'll be able to tell us who that chap was and what he wanted with her."

"Nelson's blood?" Mrs. Sneed asked. She steered me to a chair next to a side table and sat me down. I saw the tea things spread out on his desk: crumbs on a plate, a little butter and jam, a brown betty teapot and delicate teacup resting on the blotter.

"Brandy," Avery clarified, going to a cupboard behind his desk and pulling out a bottle with three small glasses. "They brought Nelson back from Trafalgar in a barrel of brandy. Sailors being what they are, when the *Victory* returned to England, the barrel was empty of everything but Nelson's body."

Brandy sloshed into glasses, its non-sanguineous aroma filling the air. I'd never had brandy before, but it certainly smelled potent.

Mrs. Sneed took a glass from Avery. "That's positively barbaric," she said, then pressed the glass into my hand. "Have a sip, Lady Trevelyan," she urged. "It might have served to pickle Lord Nelson, God help us, but I dare say it'll calm your nerves."

I lifted the glass to my lips, nearly choked on the pungent aroma and lowered the glass. Mr. Avery motioned with his hand that I really should partake. Reluctantly I took a small sip. The taste reminded me very much of the fuel we used in the *Bosch's* engines as the brandy slid down my throat with all the subtlety of a bonfire on November fifth. I squeezed my eyes shut and waited in dread for the fire to reach my stomach.

I'd always wondered why brandy was the drink people offered those who'd endured a shock. I now understood that the taste of the infernal stuff was enough to obliterate the memory of whatever prior shock had been endured. The brandy exploded in my belly like a shattered oil lamp. My eyes widened and started to water. I exhaled slowly in hopes that it would dampen the fire in my abdomen. I also hoped I could get away with consuming as little of the noxious stuff as possible without offending Mr. Avery.

"That's better," Mrs. Sneed said, noting the change in my expression.

Better? I thought and coughed, surprised that flames didn't jet out of my mouth. *Good God.*

Mrs. Sneed took the glass Avery offered and had a sip herself as she sat in a chair to my right. She looked at the librarian. "Is there a chance the fellow you chucked will be coming back here?" she asked.

Avery shook his head and drew up a chair to sit in front of me. "I didn't ask for particulars as I showed the gent the door, but I made it clear he weren't welcome. Foreign chap he was. Did you know him, Lady Trevelyan?"

I forced my mind to work. "No," I managed, my first words coming out in a croak. "He approached me while I studied in my usual spot."

Mr. Avery narrowed his eyes. "While I was conveniently absent," he noted. "Right odd no one else was here. You aren't the only one who works right through teatime. What happened next?"

The explanation of what had happened tumbled out of me. "He said his name was Augustus Laufeson and he was a transfer from the University of Halle-Wittenberg. He needed help finding books. I told him I wasn't allowed in the stacks. Then he noticed we were alone in the reading room and he asked me to join him in private."

"Thank my sainted aunt I was nearly done taking my tea," Mr. Avery said. "I shudder to think what might have happened if I'd not been close by."

"So he tried to take you away with him, then, my dear?" Mrs. Sneed asked, placing a reassuring hand on my knee. "Is that what happened?"

I nodded. "I told him I didn't want to join him. I went to sit down and get back to my studies, but he said or did something to me that made me stop. He spoke of a spell and how I was 'his'. He said he'd come to 'collect me'. I didn't want to go with him," I said, struggling to put what I'd experienced into words, "but he made me want to do whatever he asked." I mistakenly took another sip of brandy, its noxious taste and fumes obliterating any other tastes, smells or coherent thoughts. I waited for it to burn its way down my throat, coughed and continued: "Then you showed up, Mr. Avery. I suppose you know the rest."

Avery let out a low whistle. "I thought you looked a bit odd, but I never thought I'd see the day. Someone using mesmerism to have his way with a lass? It's disgraceful."

"Mesmerism? That spiritualist nonsense? You mean to tell me that bunkum actually works?" Mrs. Sneed exclaimed. "I can hardly believe it."

Avery took a sip of his brandy and motioned at me. "Drink up, my girl," he ordered. Holding my breath, I brought the glass to my lips and allowed the liquid to touch, but not pass them, holding my breath to avoid the fumes. I lowered the glass and acted like I'd swallowed some of the stuff in the interest of politeness and discretely wiped my lip to remove the small amount of brandy left there.

"I don't know how it works, or why, Mrs. Sneed," Avery said, "but I've seen those chaps on stage mesmerize folk, and Mrs. Avery dragged me to one of those séance thing-gummies about a year ago. It's a rum business, but as that fellow Hamlet says: 'There's more in Heaven and Earth than our philosophies dream of.'" He rubbed his chin. "What she's describing is classic mesmeric influencing. I'll have to add it to my report on the incident for the dons."

"He tried to put the 'fluence on you, my girl," Mrs. Sneed said, patting my knee soothingly. "It wasn't your fault."

Avery snorted. "She got a good slap in before we grabbed him and then she put her fists up, ready to take him on... all 'Marquis of Queensbury rules' and spit and vinegar. I dare say he'd have had a run for his money trying to get her out of the reading room on his own, 'fluence or no 'fluence. She's stubborn as a bull." He winked at me, obviously proud. "That's my girl, m'Lady."

I put the glass of brandy down. I felt oddly warm and slightly dizzy. I could feel sweat blooming under my corset and chemise. "Yes," I said, "thank you, Mr. Avery. I appreciate your help, and yours too, Mrs. Sneed. But," I continued, "I'm afraid I've not had much to eat since breakfast." I resisted the urge to grab the chair I sat on for dear life as a wave of dizziness went through me. "Though I am most grateful you came to my aid, I think perhaps it's best I head back to Towson House. I can get something to eat and rest there." I also didn't want to return to the residence smelling of brandy, of all things. If I had to keep pretending to drink the nasty stuff much longer, I'd be redolent of a distillery by the time I got home.

Mrs. Sneed shook her head. "Oh no, my dear, you're not walking back to Towson House alone. James, you and I will make sure she arrives safe and sound, yes?"

Avery nodded. "I'll pack up your things in the reading room and close the library early. After we get you home, we'll drop by the central office and make a report."

I nodded, grateful for their offer of an escort. I didn't want to be left alone if Laufeson decided to try grabbing me again.

"Right then," Mrs. Sneed said, setting down her own brandy and standing up. "Come along. Help me tidy these things while Mr. Avery takes care of your books."

Chapter Seven

The walk home from the Faraday Library was uneventful. Mrs. Sneed walked with me arm in arm carrying on conversation meant more to soothe than anything else, while Mr. Avery walked on my other side and carried my bookbag. I felt protected between them, but I scanned the route ahead and around us just in case Laufeson made a reappearance, though I didn't know what I'd do if he did show up again. Thankfully we arrived at my residence without incident. My companions left me and my bookbag on the Towson House steps and made their way back to make Avery's report.

I grabbed my bookbag, slung it over my shoulder wearily and climbed the stairs to the door of the residence, then let myself in. My housemates were scattered across the main rooms, their papers, books and conversations in the dining room, sitting rooms and living room bringing life and cheerfulness to the residence.

Towson, while not nearly as big as Girton, was home to young women with a passion for learning and a certain *joie de vivre*. Lady Ahisa Sato, the foundress and financial backer of the residence, personally chose all the girls who lived at Towson House, and she looked for women who were 'unusual, practical and benevolently devious', according to her somewhat mysterious standards. A small, intense Japanese woman, she interviewed all the girls and decided who to admit to our merry band, distributing scholarships as needed. She came to visit the house occasionally, usually unannounced, and frequently found the residents of Towson covered in grime while engaged in un-lady-like activities, such as playing rugby in the back garden or building a trebuchet behind the kitchen. Luckily, Lady Sato didn't mind our 'messing about', as she called it. Mrs. Guildersleeve, the house manager, did mind, of course, but with Lady Sato's tacit approval on our side, there was little she could do.

Therefore, my housemates were all outstanding scholars but pursued unusual hobbies or worked with philanthropic associations to effect societal change in addition to their studies. Even a small cross-section of Towson women who lived on the third floor of the residence revealed a great diversity of interests. I had my airship extra-curricular activities; Cora, a Classics major, was adept at practical jokes, cooking and battle tactics; Gertrude, a Biology major, studied poisons and tried her hand at taxidermy when she could, and Melisande, the resident expert on Icelandic sagas, painted watercolor landscapes and was a proud suffragette. Despite our being individually eclectic and even slightly eccentric, we Towson girls hung together despite our diversity and genuinely enjoyed living in our quirky little house.

The snippets of conversation that I caught here and there exemplified the usual mix of intentions for the later part of a typical Saturday afternoon and evening. Some girls planned an evening out while others made study arrangements with fellow classmates. Mrs. Guildersleeve shooed students out of the dining room, speaking to the staff about setting the table for the final meal of the day as she did so. I saw Sophie in the dining room, her arms full of tablecloth and napkins ready to be put on the dining room table.

Amid the chatter and engulfed by the warmth that was Towson House, the tension from what happened in the library, which I'd not realized I'd been holding, released. I relaxed. I was home, where random German fellows couldn't grab me. Friends surrounded me, and they'd help keep me safe. I no longer had to be vigilant. Relief coursed through my body, bringing exhaustion in its wake.

Someone approached me from the dining room area. "My God, Ari," my good friend Cora Allerton said, seeing me standing in the doorway and moving to join me there. She shut the front door behind me and handed me a small package wrapped in wax paper that she'd concealed in the skirts of her burgundy day dress. Somehow she always knew when I needed to eat.

Cora blew a wayward strand of brown hair out of her face. "You look absolutely done in. I knew you'd forgotten lunch. You were gone far too long and you always forget about food at the damned library." She indicated the package I held. "It's a sandwich I snuck out of the kitchen – with Sophie's help, of course."

I looked at the sandwich, safe in its paper wrapping. "Ah," I said. "Thanks. I could do with some vittles."

Cora narrowed her eyes at me a moment, then seemed to come to some decision. She reached over and took my bookbag, and then bustled me over to the stairs. I went mostly willingly, too tired and numb to resist all that much.

"By Hercules, something unpleasant happened to you today, Ariana Trevelyan," Cora hissed in my ear so no one else overheard. "You smell of brandy and you look like you've seen something awful."

I frowned. Apparently I hadn't stopped with the brandy in time.

"I'll be damned if you don't spill all the details to me toot-sweet, up in that gear and spring-filled workroom you call your bedchamber."

I nodded dully and we made our way up the stairs to my bedroom. Cora dumped my bookbag on my desk, then pointed at my bed. "Sit. Eat," she commanded as she made her way over to shut my door. Then she took her place in my desk chair.

I sat. I opened the wax paper and took out half of the sandwich, my mouth watering. It was beef, cheese and mustard on some hearty white bread and it tasted heavenly. I consumed the first half quickly, feeling vitality return to my body and mind as I ate. I went slower with the other half of the sandwich. Once I swallowed the last bit, Cora handed me a ginger beer, already uncapped.

"How did you—" I asked, taking the bottle. I looked her up and down. I hadn't seen her carrying the bottle, nor had I seen her open it. "Where did you—"

"Later," she admonished. "Drink now, then talk."

I nodded and took a long sip, then sighed. My extreme hunger made it seem like the best ginger beer I'd ever tasted.

"Now," Cora commanded, "tell me what happened from the beginning and don't leave anything out."

I took another swig from the bottle and handed it to Cora, who put it on my desk. Then I started the story of Laufeson and our unpleasant encounter in the library. Cora listened attentively and didn't interrupt as I described the mesmeric influencing the fellow had attempted and how Mr. Avery came to my aid. Once I finished the story, Cora emitted a low whistle.

"Good grief," she said, "Germans trying to mesmerize female students? How rude. It's bad enough their operas and philosophers put one to sleep. We'll have to put out a campus wide alert so all college females know to avoid the fellow."

I nodded, hugging myself. Now that I wasn't starved and had time to go over the events with a clearer head, I started to feel truly frightened. *Who was Laufeson?* I wondered. *Why had he chosen to go after me, of all people? What would have happened if Mr. Avery hadn't—*

"Mrs. Sneed gave you brandy?" Cora asked, interrupting my train of thought like a herd of cows on the railway tracks.

"Sorry—what?" I asked.

"Brandy?" she prompted. "What did you think of it? Did it help calm you down?"

"It... certainly made me think of something other than the man who grabbed me," I said, grimacing. I could still taste the stuff though I wasn't sure if that was the residue on my lips or a resurgence of the unpleasant memory of my imbibing. "I am sure the beverage has many uses, but I fear most of them are industrial in origin."

Cora smiled in delight at my quip. "That's what I've always thought, too. No idea why it's touted as such a remedy. I dare say it'd do fine service as a floor cleaner, so long as the ventilation was excellent." She tilted her head, thinking. "So Sneed and Avery brought you home. What happens now?"

"Mr. Avery is making a report to the dons and the constable. He swore Laufeson would be kept well away from me. I suppose Mr. Avery will be the one who suggests the 'campus-wide alert,' as you call it. It also wouldn't surprise me if he moved my study spot at the Faraday to one more near his reference desk just to be safe. I think I'll be studying here at Towson for a few days for my own piece of mind, anyway."

Cora picked up the ginger beer from my desk and handed it back to me. I took another sip as she leaned forward and looked me in the eyes.

"He rattled you all the way through, didn't he?" she asked softly. "You don't want to admit it, but that's the truth."

I looked away and nodded.

"I have a suggestion and a request," she said gently. "First, the suggestion. You make sure you go nowhere alone. I will speak to the other third floor girls and we'll coordinate schedules so someone will always be available to walk you to class, go with you to the infernal *Bosch* hangar or study with you at the library for a while – just until you're less frightened or the ruffian is well and truly off university grounds. Is that all right?"

I looked at Cora gratefully. "That would be a great comfort. Thank you. What's the request?"

"Tell your Aunt Miranda about this Laufeson blaggart in the next letter you write to her. She's the most level-headed woman I know, and she'll have some useful advice for you. She sees around corners, if you know what I mean. She'll have a solution, or plan, or something that will help. She might even know how to combat mesmerism."

I put up a hand to stop her. "I don't—"

"Better her than your mother," Cora countered. "If the formidable Duchess of Albemarle hears about this, she'll drag you home faster than boiled asparagus and not let you come back. You've only a few months before the Tripos and once you finish the exam, you get your certificate. You don't want to be languishing at home taking tea with widows and matrons instead of studying that awful mathematics you seem so fond of, do you? You tell your Aunt Miranda first, and she can run interference if your mother does find out."

I smiled a little. "Yes," I agreed. "You're right. I'll start the letter later tonight while the details are fresh in my mind." Since the incident happened on school grounds and not as the result of something I'd done with the *Bosch*, I realized, I could fill my aunt in and not worry about revealing my aeronaut activities.

"Excellent." Cora rubbed her hands together eagerly. "Now —leave the logistics to me. I'll need a copy of your schedule along with where your usual classes and haunts are. Do you want me to ask your escorts to have weapons?"

"Weapons?" I stammered, "since when do Towson girls have weapons?"

Cora smiled conspiratorially. "Gertrude has a new neurotoxin she's dying to try out on a living person, as a start," she said.

"Neurotoxin?" I squeaked, alarmed, "she can't – "

"—and Towson females are nothing if not responsible. In fact," she pulled a small throwing knife from each of her boots and handed them to me hilt first, "best you have a couple of these."

I gaped, looking first at the knives in my hand and then up at Cora. "Knives? You carry knives?"

Cora shrugged. "Only on weekends. Weekdays I usually get by with my parasol, fan or reticule, the staples of a lady's wardrobe."

"Good Lord." I put the knives on the bed beside me. Lizzie carried knives with some regularity; particularly when we went on a dart-throwing outing on the *Bosch*, but she'd had never had a reason to use them, so far as I knew. When I threw anything, I never missed. Therefore, I threw darts at targets, not knives at people.

I regarded Cora with skepticism. "You've turned your accessories into weapons?"

"No," Cora said, "I just use them like weapons." She mimicked swishing an umbrella about. "For instance, this is mostly a lot of pretending the 'brolly is a sword, but it works in a pinch. Hidden weapons, no matter how pedestrian, offer distinct advantages. Pen nibs, hairpins, certain brooches... all have offensive possibilities if you use them properly."

"I can't believe I'm having this conversation with you," I said. "You've been reading too much Lao Tsu and Caesar, surely. Pen nibs and hatpins as protective devices? It's daft!"

"A modern woman needs to defend herself," Cora said decisively, "and if you can't see those sorts of items as weapons, that vouches quite eloquently for their advantages in a pinch. That being said, I agree the neurotoxin is a bit much. If Gertrude hits herself with the stuff instead of an attacker, well... I'm actually not sure if she's made an antidote for it yet."

"I see your point, but I hardly think such enthusiastic precautions are called for," I said, trying not to imagine Gertrude with a neurotoxin.

Cora's expression grew serious. "Men are frequently bigger and stronger than women," she pointed out, "and unless you start thinking strategically about how to deal with ruffians, you may well become the victim of one as you almost did today. You're the daughter of a duke who's a powerful member of Parliament. You don't think someone would attempt an abduction to get your father to vote a certain way? Or to secure a ransom?"

I stilled. That hadn't even occurred to me. "It seems a long way to go to get—"

"Precisely," Cora said, pointing at me. "This Laufeson fellow didn't go 'a long way,' as you put it, and persons with agendas have only their goals in mind. You don't even know why the dratted German wanted you in the first place. His first, and hopefully only, attack failed. Vigilance will be required to make any other attempts equally unsuccessful." She pointed at the knives. "Take those, at least, if only to make me feel better. I have several I keep in my room, and Papa will send me more, if I ask."

I marveled that Cora's father would give her more knives, but kept my thoughts on that to myself. I could see the logic of her argument, but the possibility of my use of knives against anyone made me distinctly uncomfortable. "I will, but I doubt I'll actually use them." I took another sip of ginger beer and asked: "From what did Gertrude make this neurotoxin, by the way?"

Cora shrugged. "Something slimy that lives under rocks, or something terrifying and multi-legged she liberated from the Biology department, I should imagine. She's also carefully maintaining a colony of spiders in her room, and plans on relocating them to one of the yew hedges in the garden once the weather allows, so I suppose they could have been the source. Guildersleeve will have kittens if she finds out, of course. We've a bet going on how long it'll take the woman to catch on. Want to throw in a shilling or two?"

I laughed. Cora delighted in tormenting our house manager. "No," I said.

Cora stood up and motioned to my desk. "Write up your engagements and itinerary for the week, and I'll start making arrangements for escorts."

"I'll do it right now," I said, standing, "and thank you."

Cora waved off my thanks as she moved to my door. "You helped me through my math course last year," she said, "so it's the least I can do." She pointed at my desk. "Get writing. I'll be back in a bit to get your schedule, and you need to get the letter to your aunt squared away.   You can post it Monday."

Cora left and I sat down, pulling writing paper from the top drawer of the desk.   It took a few minutes to write out my schedule for the week.   I set it aside and started my letter to Aunt Miranda.

Chapter Eight

I stayed in my room rather than go down to dinner. Cora came by after the meal to check on me and pick up my schedule, then left, knowing I wanted to be alone. I spent the rest of the evening crafting the letter to my Aunt Miranda. It came out at a whopping four pages long, which was unusually verbose for me. I put it in an envelope and planned on dropping it in the post on Monday morning. Then I did some more studying, tinkered with a few Ladies' Devices and lay down to try to sleep at some wee hour of the morning. Sleep didn't come easily, and when it did, I dreamt of ravens, wolves, snakes and arctic cold. I woke only slightly rested and distinctly unnerved Sunday morning.

As I prepared for church that sense of unease increased, crawling up my spine and sitting hard in the back of my mind. *What will I do if I meet Laufeson on the way to church? Can he use his mesmerism on me from a distance?* I worried. I thought about giving church a miss, but knew that would generate questions and unnecessary concern in my friends. So, I squashed what worry I could and finished dressing, hoping no one would notice how jumpy I was.

I moved into the Towson foyer, tugging on my gloves to hide my apprehension. Other girls stood in corners in groups, making the final adjustments to their clothing as they spoke quietly to each other. I turned my attention back to my gloves when I found myself flanked by three Towson females bearing parasols. Gertrude, Melisande, and Cora, dressed in their Sunday best, held the rain repelling devices at what could only be called 'parade rest' and exuded an air of heightened vigilance.

"Is it supposed to rain?" I asked, dismayed. "Shall I get my parasol?"

Cora shook her head. "Not until you've been properly trained in its use," she said gravely.

"Oh, good heavens," I muttered. "You can't be serious."

"We're your guards," Melisande told me with a wink. Her blond hair, striking features, and nearly turquoise blue eyes emulated the Nordic heritage she studied in her Viking saga curriculum with Professor Einarsson. "Don't worry. Cora's briefed us on what needs doing. We'll be escorting you to classes and that horrid air shed and disreputable clubhouse until further notice. She even spoke to Millie to send a message to Max and your other *Bosch* friends so they know to be vigilant."

I rubbed my forehead with the heel of my hand, now worried Laufeson would try to hurt my friends. "I appreciate your concern, but doesn't this seem... I don't know... a bit more martial than is really necessary?"

Cora snorted. "For some it isn't nearly 'martial' enough." She indicated Gertrude.

"Cora won't let me bring my neurotoxin to church," Gertrude muttered dejectedly, giving her parasol a shake. Her light brown hair hung in ringlets that framed her face and neck, making her seem more like a china doll than an avid dissector of dead animals of all kinds.

Cora rolled her eyes. "Poisoning the parishioners is hardly Christian, no matter how enthusiastic you are about the stuff," she responded. She looked Gertrude up and down. "You aren't packing any spiders, I hope?"

"No," Gertrude answered lightly. "According to the reverend, insects have no souls, so they're quite beyond salvation and Heaven, the poor things."

Melisande shuddered. "Spiders. I can do without those wee beasties at church, thank you very much."

Cora pointed at the door as our fellow housemates moved toward it, ready to head out. "Let's go. We don't want to be late."

The Odin Inheritance

Chapter Nine

On the way to St. Bene't's Church, my protectors surrounded me on three sides and kept a careful watch on everyone we passed. Melisande, who guarded my right side, maintained a running monologue at me as we went, mostly about house and town gossip. I listened politely and didn't interrupt. Then she grew thoughtful.

"The name of the fellow who attacked you – what was it again?"

"Augustus Laufeson," I told her. "Spoke with a German accent, said he was a transfer from Wittenburg."

"Laufeson… Laufeson…" she mused. "An interesting name. Do you know what it means?"

I snorted. "I'm as good with languages as you are with calculus, Mellie," I told her. Melisande was notoriously bad with suMs. "So I've no idea what the name meant, and it didn't occur to me to ask." *I'd been too busy fighting whatever mesmeric influence he'd tried on me,* I remembered with a shudder.

"Laufeson means 'Son of Loki,'" she said, then looked at me as if I should know what the significance of that was.

I shrugged. "Trevelyan means 'Village of Elian,' though I've no idea if such a place even exists."

"You don't know who Loki is?" Mellie looked hurt. "How can you not know that?"

"My area of study is the sciences and mathematics. I've never been one for myths and stories—" I paused, remembering the stories Max had described my telling in the pub in Penzance. Part of me—a part I didn't control—knew stories... though I didn't. A chill went down my spine, but I continued; "—just ask Cora. She's appalled I've not read the *Iliad* or *Odyssey* or some such nonsense though I have read Aristotle... in English, at least."

"Loki is the trickster god of the Norse pantheon," Mellie explained. "Sometimes he helps the Norse gods, and sometimes he hurts them. He engineered the death of Baldur, and Odin punished him by binding him under the dripping fangs of a venomous snake for eternity. He's a shapeshifter, illusionist, a sorcerer, of sorts... and a liar."

"In the stories you've studied, did this Loki have the ability to mesmerize someone?" I asked.

Melisande nodded. "Without question. Under certain circumstances, he can put thoughts in someone's head or make them believe things that are not true."

That made me pause. "You speak of this Loki fellow as if he's more than a myth."

Melisande grimaced. "There are those—my professor among them—who think Loki exists as a force in the modern world."

"I can't believe I'm even entertaining this idea," I said, "but let me make sure I understand this.   You think Laufeson's name is no coincidence, and you're suggesting this 'Son of Loki' might possess some of his mythological father's traits or abilities?"

"I know it sounds very odd," she said, "but in some places in this world such a notion would be perfectly reasonable."

"I've been experiencing some odd moments recently," I admitted, "though I can't figure why Loki—or a son of his, metaphorical or otherwise—would want me.   I've no connection to Norse myths."

Mellie shrugged.   "Nor can I, but mark my words… something about your attacker is linked to Loki… whether or not you believe the god exists."

Another chill ran down my spine at her words and a sense of foreboding filled me.   "Lovely," I murmured.   "Bloody lovely."

Gertrude, my protector opposite Mellie, hit my left forearm in gentle admonishment.   "Language, Ari!" she hissed.   "You can't speak like that on a Sunday!   What will the reverend say?"

"Sorry," I said, trying and failing to shake off the dread I felt but couldn't explain.   "I will endeavor to keep my speech pure for the Sabbath."

****

The church service was uneventful, if long.   I said the prayers and made the responses as I always did though usually I paid closer attention to the sermon.   Instead, my mind kept replaying what happened in the library as Melisande's words echoed through the memories.   The reverend's words faded to a drone.

Laufeson had spoken of how 'the spell still held' and that he'd come to 'collect me'. It was a choice of words more indicative of a magic user than a random mesmerist. *Can Mellie be right? I wondered. Is Loki real? If so, what would such a being want with me? How could such a being exist?*

Gertrude, ever the proper churchgoer, nudged me to bring my wayward thoughts back to the service. I straightened and did a better job of at least looking like I paid attention, though I didn't, really. The irony of pondering the existence of a pagan god while I sat in a house of worship for the Christian deity wasn't lost on me. I prayed the whole thing was an incredibly bizarre coincidence and asked the Lord for protection from future attacks and abductions while those around me murmured about forgiving trespasses and avoiding temptation.

Then the service was over, and flanked by my parasol-wielding companions, we made our way back to Towson House. The journey was, thankfully, without excitement. Laufeson made no appearance, and my protectors felt they'd done an excellent job keeping me safe. I thanked them for their efforts on my behalf, declined a vial of Gertrude's neurotoxin, much to her dismay, and retired to my room.

I was bone weary. The worried thoughts that had occupied me during the reverend's droning sermon had drained me, and that, combined with the poor night's rest, left me wrung out like a dishrag. I plopped down on my bed with a thump. Melisande's revelations about Loki, Laufeson's attempted mesmeric abduction, what I'd done without knowing it in the pub in Penzance and repairing Sophie's Enhanced arm all swirled about in my exhausted brain as I tugged on the fingers of my gloves to remove them. I dropped the gloves on the floor beside my bed and lay down, too tired to even bother undressing. Sleep grabbed me and I lost consciousness, grateful for oblivion.

****

"There you are," someone called. "This is no time for slumber—wake up, girl!"

I opened my eyes and looked around in astonishment. It was night, and a full moon—oddly bright—illuminated a huge field of wild grasses and flowers that extended as far as the eye could see in all directions. Despite the light of the moon, the stars of the Milky Way galaxy twinkled as brilliant shining spots of light. Directly in front of me was the largest tree I'd ever seen, its leaves a dark forest green and in full foliage, vibrating with life.

"She's beautiful, isn't she? It's a shame so few people ever see her anymore," came the voice.

I sought the source of the voice but seemed to be the only one in the meadow. A breeze wafted past, chilling me.

"Who are you, and where am I?" I called into the moonlit expanse of field and tree, clutching myself in an attempt to keep warm.

"The tree is Yggdrasill," responded the voice, "and this is some northern region of your world, though I admit I pay very little attention to what you humans call your small bits of earth."

I looked down at myself and saw that I stood in my nightdress, barefooted... in some northern region of the world. I seemed to recall lying down in my church clothes, but they were nowhere to be seen. Such was the random nature of dreaMs. "And you are...?" I asked the air around me.

A tall, breathtakingly beautiful blonde woman appeared before me, her deep blue eyes sparking with intelligence and wry humor. She wore a light blue gown of fabric that shimmered in the moonlight, with a simple silver necklace curved around her neck. Next to her stood the largest boar I'd ever seen in my life. It was grey and white with huge tusks, and it matched a pony for size. Intelligence sparkled in his eyes. I couldn't help but get the feeling my presence in my night clothes in the midst of a meadow at night amused him. I gaped.

"I am Freya, she of the Vanir and now of the Aesir. This," she indicated the boar, "is Hildisvini, my boar."

I dropped a deep curtsey, feeling a bit of a fool doing so in my nightdress, but the woman who stood before me was obviously royalty of some sort. "A pleasure to meet you, my lady," I said, "and... erm... you... Mr. Hildisvini?"

The boar inclined his head graciously in acceptance of my greeting. Freya smiled. "You have no notion what's going on, do you?"

I opened my mouth to respond, thought better of it and shut it. I shook my head. My feet were starting to go numb and the air around us cooled down even further as the night deepened.

She looked at Hildisvini. "You were right," she said. "The Pessarines were thorough. That Seneschal of theirs is almost as crafty as Odin himself. How delightfully unexpected." The boar snorted in agreement.

Freya turned her attention to me. "You are Ariana Grace Trevelyan, are you not?" she asked, "daughter of Aiden and Elaine?"

Something oddly powerful about the use of my full name shimmered through my nerves. "Yes, my lady," I said, hiding my unease.

"You and I are..." She paused, thinking, "...cousins, of a sort. It's not an exact explanation of our shared heritage, but it will do for now. This tree," she indicated it behind her, "is the conduit between the world you're from and the world I inhabit. This is a place of great power."

I looked up at the tree spreading its branches above us. It was beautiful in an other-worldly sense, and I felt that the part of the tree I saw was only one aspect of its presence in the universe. "What kind of a tree is it?"

"An ash tree. Yggdrasill is also known in mythology as the World Tree. Do you recognize it? This place?"

I blinked. "No. I've never seen this tree before, and I've never been here in my life," I said. "Why have you brought me here?"

"Well, cousin," she said as she absent-mindedly rubbed the top of her pet boar's head, "I've been watching you from my home in Asgard and I wanted to meet you. The only way I could do that was by invading your dream. My power in the waking world is extremely limited."

"Where is Asgard?" I asked.

Freya pointed upward. "It sits at the top of Yggdrasill. This," she indicated the field around us, "is Midgard, where you live." She pointed at her feet. "Below us are the lower realms."

I rubbed my shoulders in an attempt to stay warm.

"How are we related?" I asked. "My parents have no siblings, and I don't recall them mentioning your name. You also said 'you humans' earlier. If you aren't human, what are you?"

Freya shrugged. "You look for your 'one answer' in this, as if figuring out where I fit in is a mathematics problem. Life is rarely that simple. I am essentially an ancient god whom few worship anymore since your Christian Jehovah holds sway among those who used to revere me. I still have some power, though I'm considerably limited in scope and influence. As to our kinship, we're related in a sense that is more... symbolic than biological. We do not share a bloodline. We share something else."

I tried to make sense of her words but felt another shiver start in my body due to the cold. I tried to keep my teeth from visibly chattering. If this being was a goddess, perhaps she had information I would find useful.

"Do you know Loki?" I asked tentatively.

"The Liar? The Tricker of Gods?" Freya responded, and then spat on the ground in disgust. "Yes, the Bound One is known to me. He suffers a just, eternal punishment." Her brow furrowed. "How do you know of him?"

My shivering increased. "A friend told me about him."

The boar snorted and indicated me with an inclination of his head. Freya looked down at him, then at me.

"You're cold," Freya said. "My apologies. Allow me to remedy that difficulty."

Before I could say anything Freya waved her hand and replaced my nightdress with a high-necked, long-sleeved gown of soft, finely woven dark-blue wool. A golden belt cinched my waist, fur boots covered my feet, and my unruly red hair now dropped in a neat braid down my back. I brought my hand to my head and felt a simple circlet there, the metal curving gracefully across my forehead.

"That attire is much more fitting to a daughter of the All-Father," she said, looking me over. "You should no longer feel the cold. When you meet with my kind in your dreams in future, this will be your attire, if it pleases you."

I'll be meeting with more beings like her? I marveled but remembered my manners. "It's beautiful," I said. "Thank you."

"It's the least I could do, having brought you here unprepared for the climate," Freya said simply.

"Begging your pardon, my lady," I ventured, "but how did I become related to an ancient god? Who is the All-Father? Of what are you a deity? What, if anything, does Loki have to do with me?"

"That isn't important." Freya beckoned me forward. "Come and place your hand on the trunk of Yggdrasil," she said.

"It isn't?" I moved forward as ordered, intrigued. "I beg your pardon, but it seems rather important to me."

"I have little time. You must touch Yggdrasil."

"Why?"

"The World Tree knows you," she said, indicating the tree. "Come greet her, cousin." Freya took my hand. Hers was cool to the touch and oddly calloused. In my mind's eye, I saw her in armor, surrounded by armored men fighting a massive battle.

"Come," Freya beckoned, tugging my hand. In two strides, we were at the base of the huge ash tree, covering the distance in the blink of an eye, the boar now beside me, warm and intent. Freya smiled gently and drew my hand to the tree trunk. "Do not be afraid," she said and placed the palm of my hand on the tree. The bark was rough under my fingers.

"You know the blood of this woman, Yggdrasill," Freya said, looking up into the tree's branches. "Make yourself known to her."

Images and sensations crashed into my mind. I tasted blood, coppery on my tongue. I saw the dark silhouette of a young girl, black against a huge full moon that was far too close to Earth to be astronomically possible. The girl, moving slowly within her bonds, hung from the branches of the great tree that surrounded me. I felt blood drip from my limbs to splatter on the roots of the tree. I felt the bone-weary exhaustion of the girl tinged with fear and a determination to be brave. Alarm spiked within me. Very little kept the girl from sliding away into death.

"Ari?" came a call from far away. I turned my head at the sound of my name. The dream-world I stood in shook like a massive earthquake around me, rattling my teeth in my head.

"Ari?! Wake up!" I opened my eyes to find Cora leaning over me. "Freya?" I asked, confused.

"Not hardly," Cora snorted.

"I was having the oddest dream…" I muttered. "Big boar… big tree… blood…"

"A fine time for dozing," she chided. "According to the schedule you gave me yesterday, we're supposed to trek out to that infernal air shed in half an hour."

"Oh!" I exclaimed, pushing myself to a sitting position. The details of the dream slipped away. "Quite right! Give me a few minutes to change into my work clothes, and I'll be right down."

Cora took a step back, shaking her head. "I'll get Sophie up here to help you, and get the bicycles ready, shall I?"

"If you would. Thanks."

Chapter Ten

Twenty minutes later I stood in the foyer of Towson House listening to the daily noises of my fellow students studying, chatting and drinking tea in the dining room as I prepared to leave. It was a pleasant, familiar sound and part of me regretted missing teatime, again. It seemed like I regularly missed tea for one reason or another. Pulling on my riding gloves, I read the new, hand lettered flyer tacked to the back of the front door. "Save Towson House" it declared. "Prevent the stodgers from driving women out of Cambridge! Strategizing meeting seven o'clock Friday evening, Drawing Room!"

I shook my head. *This nonsense again?* I mused. It wasn't like women studying at Cambridge was a new innovation – females had attended classes at the venerable institution nigh on twenty years. Other universities with less ancient and regal reputations even allowed women to take classes and earn degrees, though Cambridge didn't. Usually, it was some misogynistic faction of male students who mooned about, lamenting the presence of women as students at 'their college'. Now, some of the older, tenured professors of our male-dominated institution, led by some particularly unpleasant gentlemen in the Physics department, lobbied to have the women of Towson and Girton—the other women's college at Cambridge—denied access to Cambridge classes. I had no doubt the detestable Dr. Oberlin was involved in the campaign. If the flyer was to be believed, they'd gotten a surprising amount of support from professors in other departments, using the rallying cry "Deny the women and Enhanced, Keep our college far-advanced!" as if admitting women and the Enhanced would somehow regress the college as a whole.

I'd no idea why they wanted women out, other than the fact that we weren't men, of course, but I knew it wasn't because our scholarship was deficient. Towson and Girton women were rare birds who took their academics seriously and we could hold our own with the men any day. I also knew it wasn't because we'd been behaving in an 'unladylike manner'. Our houses were at least two miles from the men's colleges, making unladylike behavior inconvenient at the very least. We also knew our behavior would have repercussions for the women who followed us, so we took great care to make no waves. It wasn't the first time men had attempted to drive women from Cambridge, I knew, but this effort seemed oddly forceful. Tying the idea of women as students with the British dislike of the Enhanced was a new wrinkle on an old debate. Personally, I saw no reason why Enhanced folk couldn't attend university, but I knew I was in the minority. So far as I knew, no Enhanced person was a student at Cambridge.

Cora joined me, dressed in her green bicycling clothes and carrying her matching gloves. "Bicycles are on the side of the house, ready to go, and I detected no signs of sabotage," she told me.

I furrowed my brow. "Who would sabotage a bicycle, and how would Laufeson know which one was mine?"

"Doesn't matter. I feel better knowing nothing was done to them." Cora indicated the flyer. "You don't want to get Mellie started on this 'women out of Cambridge' business," she warned me. "She's got the suffragette contingent armed and ready to confront the blighters and she'll pin a 'Keep Women at Cambridge' button to your lapel as sure as look at you."

I motioned at the flyer. "You going to the meeting?"

"Of course," she huffed. "Bloody men. Why do we have to fight for every single thing?"

I made a mental note as to the time and day of the strategizing meeting. "I'll go as well," I sighed.

"Did you really dream about a big boar?" Cora asked.

I struggled to recall. "Yes, but most of the details seem to have slipped away. It had a name."

"The dream?"

"The boar," I corrected. "Shall we head to the air shed?"

Cora bowed slightly. "Your grace," she intoned.

I rolled my eyes and opened the door to head out, my mind filling with what I planned to do that afternoon. I wanted to re-calibrate the barometer of the *Bosch* for a start and then try attaching a new gauge to the navigation console.

I took a step onto the front stoop and found my path blocked. Looking up, I saw a familiar face.

"Aunt Miranda! What—I mean, this is a surprise!" I stammered, "My goodness. I nearly knocked you over!"

"Indeed, niece," my Great Aunt intoned, non-plussed by my flustered greeting. "Clearly you are on your way to something important. Have I come at a bad time?"

I'd been looking forward to spending time crawling about the airship, making myself useful and getting my hands dirty. Clearly that idea had to be abandoned. Politeness dictated I give up my plans to work on the airship and serve as a gracious host or, as was more likely, be a companion to my aunt for the duration of her visit. One never knew what to expect with her.

"Of... course not," I said quickly, still stammering a bit.

"Hmpf," she responded eloquently.

It wasn't that I was unhappy to see her. I loved Great Aunt Miranda a great deal. Since I'd been five, we'd exchanged letters every two weeks, keeping each other up to date on our respective lives. Her letters were far more interesting than mine were, particularly since I'd taken great care to keep my airship activities out of my half of our correspondence. Aunt Miranda traveled widely and seemed to make friends wherever she went. Other travelers wandered about with their noses stuck in their Baedecker or Thomas Cook guides, refused to speak anything but English and saw only the 'approved' sights. My Great Aunt Miranda always had experiences beyond those of regular travelers. She dined with mystics in Istanbul, rubbed elbows with adventurers in Africa and took tea with rajahs in India. She managed these miracles easily, and her tales made for fascinating reading.

In many respects, Great Aunt Miranda was more of a grandparent to me than a distant aunt, particularly since my grandparents had all passed away when I was very young. She sent me fabulous birthday presents, slipped me pocket money for sweets—though I'd usually spent the money on mechanical bits and pieces—and always had peppermints in her reticule. I saw her maybe four or five times a year and her visits were always pleasant... but she'd never shown up out of the blue before.

I took a deep breath and tried again. "I apologize for my awkwardness, Aunt Miranda. It's just such a surprise to see you here."

My Great Aunt Miranda's right eyebrow went up. "Of course it's a surprise, child," she said, her mild Scottish brogue tinged with asperity. "If I'd wanted you to know to expect me, I'd have informed you I was coming. I meant to ambush you." She turned her attention to my companion. "Good afternoon, young woman," she said. "I trust you are possessed of better manners than my grand niece?"

Cora dropped a quick curtsey. "Your ladyship," she said, her delight obvious. "I am very happy to see you."

Aunt Miranda looked from Cora to me, and back to Cora. "Miss Allerton, I believe?" she said, raising an eyebrow. "I am pleased to see you as well though I find your joy at my arrival here somewhat unexpected."

Cora curtseyed again. "Begging your pardon, your ladyship," Cora said smoothly, "but I know how Ari enjoys spending time with you. If you don't mind, I'll excuse myself to put away our conveyances and head back to my studies so the two of you can have a proper visit."

Aunt Miranda inclined her head. "As you wish, child," she said and watched as Cora skipped back into the house, shutting the door behind her.

"These modern females," she tutted, "always in such a hurry."

"Yes," I said. "Quite."

Aunt Miranda looked me up and down. I had on my brown bicycling outfit that doubled as my work togs, the high-necked and long-sleeved jacket being perfectly respectable for someone of my age and standing, even if it was a trifle last season. I'd repaired my ripped stockings so the stitching remained hidden in my boots, not wanting to spend money on anything new if I could avoid it. The bloomers, which allowed my calves and boot-clad feet to show, were perhaps not as appropriate. I'd pinned my hair tightly to my head with only one stray curl bouncing on the back of my neck. I never seemed to catch them all when I did my hair myself. I even had a hat—a small brown fascinator with a feather. I wore my riding gloves as well.

"Ariana, what in the blue blazes are you wearing?" she asked. It was her turn to be surprised. She looked down. "Good Lord – are those your legs?"

"I was about to take a bicycle ride with Cora," I said defensively. "I tried that once in full skirts with unpleasant results." I frowned, remembering. My petticoats stopped the bike's chain mechanism unexpectedly and I'd flown over the handlebars, tearing the damned skirt. I'd landed face-first in a hedge and it had taken a week for the scrapes on my face to heal.

"As a result," I continued, "I wear bloomers and boots so I don't end up in a heap in a bush."

Aunt Miranda, silver-haired and regal, took that information in, her blue eyes sparkling. "Hmmm... yes," she admitted, "I can see how Newton's laws and petticoats are somewhat at odds on a bicycle."

She indicated her own ensemble, a navy blue silk affair with an impeccably tailored bodice and French bustle skirt, topped off with a matching fascinator, reticule and kid gloves dyed to match. "I dare say this outfit will never do for riding one of those two-wheeled contraptions. Perhaps if I had informed you of my arrival, I could've dressed for that sort of riding. Ah, well."

It was my turn to raise an eyebrow, imagining my nearly eighty-year-old Great Aunt riding a bicycle. "I do know how to ride one of those things, you know," she said. "Don't you give me that look." I dropped the eyebrow.

"We will, therefore," she declared, "have to take a hansom cab."

"Hansom cab?" I asked. "Where? Why?"

"Indeed. You do know what they are and how we can find one?" she asked pragmatically.

"Well, yes, but—"

"Capital," she said and took me by the elbow in a surprisingly strong grip, leading me down the front stairs of my Cambridge women's residence. "It's tea time. Let's go someplace pleasant for tea and you can fill me in on all your college activities."

"Oh?" I asked, suspicious. "You came all the way down from Aberdeenshire just to have tea?"

She stopped our forward progress at the bottom of the stairs. "I came all the way from Aberdeenshire to see you and do a few other things – but that part isn't important right now. Tea is merely the civilized liquid we shall consume as you explain why you've been lying to your parents, Mrs. Guildersleeve and me."

Chapter Eleven

I felt my cheeks warm with a blush. It had been a necessary, and I believed successful, deception. Apparently I'd been wrong. *How had she found out?* I wondered. I knew I hadn't written her anything in my letters that would reveal what I'd been up to.

"Ah," I said, trying to sound unconcerned, hoping it would put my aunt off the scent. "That."

Aunt Miranda propelled me forward again. "Yes, child, THAT." She looked up and down the street. "Which direction is the cab station?"

"Didn't you come here in a cab?" I asked.

"Of course not," she said. "I walked. More stealthy and healthy that way. Can't stand fat old ladies. Cab station?"

I pointed to the left. She steered me in that direction. "Please tell me how is it I hosted you at Brentwood Close twice and in London three times in the past fifteen months, yet I have no memory of these happy encounters?"

"Erm…" I bleated, "I… um…"

"You'll need to do better than that, my dear," she said sharply. "Always have some sort of reasonable answer prepared when you're engaged in covert activities. How do you think I've managed all these years?"

"Covert activities?" I asked. "What covert activities?"

She saw a cab at a distance and waved, managing to get the driver's attention. He nodded to indicate he understood and urged the horse into a walk toward us.

"If you needed an alibi, you should have asked me for one," she continued, slowing our brisk walk to a more leisurely stroll.

I blinked in surprise. "If I needed a… what?"

"Keep up, child," she chided. "An alibi. I am quite capable of creating convincing ones, and I've reached such an advanced age that no one dares to contradict or question me." She sniffed. "It's one of the few advantages to being an ancient personage. I do like to be useful."

The hansom cab reached us. It was well-kept and clean, drawn by a bay horse that was equally well cared for. The driver, a young man with an impressive mustache, tipped his hat at us politely. "Afternoon, yer ladyship," he said genially. "Where can I take you two young ladies this fine afternoon?"

Aunt Miranda smiled pleasantly at him. "Where is the best place in Cambridge for tea, my good man?" she asked.

"My Mary does the afternoon tea at the Old Vicar, m'lady. I find it's the best to be had for fifty miles or more."

"Then the Old Vicar it is," she responded jovially, "and you are?"

"They call me Aylmer, m'lady," he said, then indicated the horse. "This here's Pip, like in Mr. Dicken's story, at yer service."

"I am Lady Miranda Brentwood," she said. "What's the fee to hire you and Pip as my personal conveyance for the next few days?"

It was Aylmer's turn to be surprised. "I don't rightly know, yer ladyship," he said, "seein' as you're the first one who's asked. I'm new to the cabbie business. Just bought it off me uncle."

"Would a pound a day to be at my beck and call serve as appropriate remuneration?"

That surprised both Aylmer and me. A pound was a remarkable sum for a cabbie's services, and she was offering him the chance to earn a few in as many days.

Aylmer, earnest and honest but not a fool, climbed down from the driver's seat to speak to us on the pavement. "It's far too much, if I'm honest," he said, sticking his hands in his pockets. "Half that amount would do for each day, yer ladyship, and no mistake."

Aunt Miranda looked at me. "He thinks I'm senile for offering him so much," she whispered. Then she turned her attention back to Aylmer.

"I can assure you, Aylmer, I'm not off my head and I'm quite able to afford the fee I've offered." She reached into her reticule and pulled out a gold sovereign. "You seem an upstanding fellow with important knowledge of this municipality, and I didn't bring my own coach for the visit. Therefore, you shall have a pound a day to be at my disposal, and I'll not pay you a penny less." She leaned over a bit. "Are those terms acceptable to you?"

He smiled. "If you insist, m'lady. It'd be rude for me to refuse."

"A wise man," Aunt Miranda said. "I trust you'll use some of your windfall to buy something nice for Mary? A new hat, perhaps?"

Aylmer beamed. "Oh yes, yer ladyship. My Mary sure does like hats."

She stepped closer to the cab and Aylmer smoothly opened the door of the cab for us. We climbed in and sat down. The cab's interior was a little worn, but clean and well-maintained.

"Now, Aylmer," Aunt Miranda said, handing him the money, "that's for today. I'll give you another one tomorrow. Take us to the Old Vicar. I'm famished."

Aylmer tucked his fee in an interior jacket pocket. "Right away, yer ladyship," he said, shutting the door. He hopped aboard himself and within four seconds the cab was in motion.

"You paid him all that money in advance," I said, settling into my seat and removing my gloves. "He could drop us off at the Old Vicar and not come back."

"True, but considering the excellent condition of this cab, Aylmer is a man who's proud of what he does and very good at it, for all that he's new to the business. Such a fellow will fulfill his end of the bargain today and come back tomorrow, and the next day and so on until the job is done."

"How can you be so sure?"

Great Aunt Miranda smiled. "I have a good eye for honest men. Trust me – he'll not let us down if only because Mary likes hats." She put her hands primly in her lap. "Now," she said, focusing her considerable attention on me, "for what nefarious activities do you require an alibi, precisely? It doesn't involve some fellow your parents would disapprove of, does it? Going out without a chaperone, perhaps? I do like a good 'clandestine paramour' story."

Shock at the suggestion struck me like a physical blow. "Of course not," I said, wide-eyed with astonishment. "Why ever would you think something like that?"

"I wouldn't," she said with a shrug, "but I thought I'd better ask, just in case. Obviously I've been reading too many lurid novels recently. Bother." She smiled. "So, if it isn't an inappropriate gentleman friend, what is it?"

I chewed a fingernail, uncertain about whether to tell Aunt Miranda the whole truth.

She smacked my hand from my mouth, and then pulled it toward her so she could get a closer look at my fingers. "Your mother would be the first to point out that ladies do not chew their fingernails, and they certainly don't have dirt and oil underneath them."

"I am a mathematics and sciences student," I pointed out. "I do… experiments. I just neglected to clean my nails as well as I usually do."

My aunt looked decidedly unconvinced as she allowed me to take back possession of my hand. "Mmmm hmmmm…?"

I stared at my lap. "I've been working on some new mechanicals," I said carefully, feeling my way along. I really wasn't sure what Aunt Miranda would say if she knew the truth.

"Like your little dragonflies and Ladies' Helpers?" she asked. "I hardly think you need to lie about those – even your mother has one of your dragonflies."

I was amazed. "She does?"

"Of course she does. I gave her one. She doesn't know you made it, of course. Too much like being in trade – she'd never approve."

"And you do approve?" I asked, curling my fingers in to hide my dirty nails.

"I appreciate fine workmanship and devastating cleverness," she said sharply. "Now, stop hedging. What are these new mechanicals of which you speak?"

"Navigational instruments."

Aunt Miranda furrowed her brow. "Navigation? But Cambridge is essentially land-locked. Are you telling me punts on the Cam need compasses and such like? How odd. Seems to me river navigation is rather straightforward." She leaned forward and pointed a finger. "You follow the river... or at least that's what I did on the Yangtze."

I shrugged.

"I see," she muttered, eyes narrowed as she considered my silence, pulling back her finger and leaning back on the seat. She settled her elegant hands in her lap. "So... your instruments must be for something else. Is it some sort of new device for bicyclists? You are dressed for it."

I remained silent.

"Come now," my aunt chided. "It's my intent to be a help, not a hindrance."

In for a penny, I thought. "The navigational instruments are for an airship," I said.

A pause. "Ah. Is this a functional airship? It flies? In Cambridge?"

I nodded. "It does."

"So when you take off in this airship, you claim to be staying with me? Why?" Aunt Miranda asked.

I looked at my hands for a moment. "It isn't exactly an appropriate activity for the daughter of a duke," I admitted.

Aunt Miranda leaned back. "Ah. Yes, I can see how your mother would disapprove. 'Life at risk' and all that."

"Actually, no. It isn't terribly dangerous. After all, these sorts of technological advancements are for the good of the Empire, even if the people involved are—"

She held up a hand to stop me. "You protest too much, child. I take it your airship companions are not of the peerage, then?" Aunt Miranda asked.

I bristled. "They're good men and women—"

"I never said they were bad people," she said, "I just asked if they had titles, which clearly they do not. It isn't like that matters to me. If they're friends of yours, I'm sure they're fine. I've never known you to befriend people who were… how shall we say… unworthy of your regard."

"But Mother— "

"—is less understanding of such things. I know. As some people get older, they become more set in their thinking, and that's certainly the case with your mother. She pays far too much attention to rank, though being a duchess, I suppose that's understandable." Aunt Miranda looked out the window as the cab drew to a stop. "My thinking has always been infinitely malleable, so I, thankfully, don't suffer from that particular affliction of the aged. If only that were true of rheumatism." She sighed.

"Let's go in, get our tea, and you can tell me all about this airship business." She patted my knee. "All right?"

Chapter Twelve

The Old Vicar Tea Room, situated in an old vicarage on the Cam, was indeed one of the best tea shops in Cambridge by reputation though I'd not been there before. Mary seated us in a windowed alcove with lace curtains and a view of the garden. After complimenting Mary on her fine choice of husband, Aunt Miranda ordered afternoon tea. We made small talk until the waitress brought the tray with the teapot, teacups and tiered tray with the cucumber sandwiches and scones, complete with butter, clotted cream, and jam.

I poured the tea, and once we had everything distributed and settled, Aunt Miranda continued her interrogation.

"So," she began, her blue eyes dark with interest, "with whom are you engaged in this airship adventuring?"

I told her about Max, Needle, Griff and Lizzie, my fellow crewmen of the *Bosch*, how I'd come to know them and eventually join them on the ship. She listened with great interest, not interrupting me even though I talked for a long time. When I finished, she poured herself another cup of tea, clearly thinking about what I'd said.

"*Bosch*, eh? Sounds a bit like 'bosh' to me. So you fly about in this ship with these people. Where do you go?"

"Oh, it depends," I hedged. "Max chooses the destinations."

My aunt took a sip of her tea. "What criteria does he use to make his choices? The weather? Access to a landing field?"

Do I tell her we go to places with pubs where I throw darts to earn extra money? I wondered, thoughts whirling. She might be open to my being friends with common folk—even with floating about in an airship—but gambling in pubs? *What would I do if she told Mother?*

"Are you sure your life isn't in some sort of danger?" she asked, seeing the turmoil of my thoughts echoed on my face.

"No, Aunt Miranda," I said, "I'm just afraid you won't approve, and then you'll tell Mother."

She rolled her eyes. "When have you ever known me to do that?"

"Never, but—"

"Young lady, unless you're hurting yourself or others, or you're knowingly putting yourself in some sort of danger, I see no reason to tell your mother what you've been up to. Besides, if you're using me to hide your activities from your parents, I deserve the truth."

"Erm…"

Aunt Miranda frowned.

Best to just plunge right in, I thought. "We fly to different cities and go to pubs," I said, imagining Mother's response if she were to find out.

Miranda's eyebrows went up in surprise. "Oh? I didn't take you for an ale drinker. How interesting. Seems a bit much for a trip down the pub, but—"

"I throw darts at the pubs we visit, and we," I swallowed, my throat suddenly dry, "…we encourage the other patrons to make bets on how well I throw."

There was a flash in her eyes then: something venerable and crafty with the hint of menace in it, and then it was gone. She set down her cup and looked out at the garden for a full minute before she spoke. I spent that minute convinced she'd tell Mother despite her assurances to the contrary. My heart sank.

"How do you do," she asked, "throwing the darts in pubs?"

"Very well," I said carefully. "We use the money to help with the upkeep of the airship." I shrugged. "I never miss."

She nodded as if my accuracy was not a surprise to her. "It takes a lot of money to maintain an airship, then?" she asked absently. "I should imagine so. If your clothes are any indication, you're spending your dress allowance to help fund the endeavor. Your mother will have a fit if she finds out."

I nodded though that wasn't entirely true. I saved some of the money I made throwing darts so I could start my own airship-related business.

"I wish you'd told me sooner. I could have increased your allowance with funds of my own, but you will insist on doing everything the hard way. I can at least keep you well supplied with proper underclothes. There's no reason you need to be sewing up tears in your stockings, for Heaven's sake."

"How did you know—?"

She waved off my question. "Please," she said airily, "I've seen your embroidery. The beginning end of one of your repair attempts is just peeking out of the top of your left boot."

I looked down. She was right.

"You may be a deft hand with tiny mechanicals, but you sewed that stocking like a drunk, myopic dock worker." Aunt Miranda came to a decision then. "I'd like to see this *Bosch* airship of yours," she told me.

"Sorry?" I asked, not sure I'd heard her properly.

"I want you to take me to see this airship. I'd like a tour and, if such a thing is possible, I'd like to take a ride in it. Perhaps we could go to a pub somewhere."

I sat, open-mouthed in astonishment.

"Ariana, shut your mouth. You look like a fish."

I shut my mouth. "You want a tour?" I asked, the 'at your age' in my thoughts, though I was smart enough not to say that out loud.

Aunt Miranda looked mildly offended. "I'm not going to break, child," she admonished. "I am nearly eighty years old, true enough, but that doesn't mean I can't go places and do things. I've travelled the world – climbed the Pyramids, sailed down the Mississippi River, walked the Great Wall – and I did all of those things before these airships existed. I'm a tough bird."

She'd written about those experiences in our correspondence. "I know, but—"

"Despite my age," she barreled on, "I've an interest in technological advancement. I also think riding in an airship would be an interesting and enjoyable experience. If the issue is money, then I'll pay for my passage. Will that suit you?"

"I... ah..."

"How long would it take you to set this up?"

"I'd been about to head to the shed where we keep the *Bosch* when I met you on the steps," I said. "I usually ride my bicycle out there. Max and the others had scheduled a work day today."

"I see," she said and took what was almost a gulp of the tea.

I continued to stare.

Aunt Miranda waved her hand at me impatiently. "Finish up child," she chided. "We've a hansom at our beck and call, and I'd like to see this flying contraption before the sun sets. You can tell me more about your fellow crewmates and your collective adventures on the way."

The Odin Inheritance Victoria L. Scott

Chapter Thirteen

Aylmer followed my directions and we arrived at the *Bosch's* airfield and hangar about half an hour later. The doors of the hangar were open and the tan, curved envelope of the airship's rigid balloon frame was visible, moored to the buoy. A rendering of Bosch's *Ship of Fools in Flames* graced the middle of the cigar-shaped balloon, the mast of the odd boat rising out of the head of a robed figure while other humans sat in the curved hull warming their hands on the burning craft. It was an odd, nonsensical image that matched the roaming, illogical nature of our expensive and time-consuming hobby. The big difference was that while Bosch's flying boat seemed to burn with a lazy sort of flame, if our airship caught fire, the hydrogen in the ballonets inside the rigid frame would explode with enough force to send all parts of the ship and its unlucky crew spewing away across the countryside in tiny bloody bits.

That was a piece of information I had no intention of sharing with my Great Aunt. I hoped my crewmates were wise enough to keep that fact to themselves. Due to our rigid safety protocols, the chances of an explosion were slim, which was only reassuring so long as the ship didn't explode. *Anyone who operates an airship like ours and rejects the chances of an extremely violent mishap is a fool,* I thought. Problem was that while another lighter than air gas was known and slowly becoming available for use—namely helium—it was prohibitively expensive and not buoyant enough for our particular needs. Hydrogen was easily obtained, inexpensive and very much lighter than air. At the moment, there was enough hydrogen in the ballonets to keep the *Bosch* upright, but not much more. I hoped Aunt Miranda wouldn't inquire much into the gas we used for buoyancy.

We exited the cab, and while Aunt Miranda instructed Aylmer to wait for us, I made my way into the hangar.

I couldn't see anyone inside on ground level. I called out, and Max came down the gangplank of the ship, wiping his hands on a rag. He saw me and smiled broadly.

"Ari! I wondered what kept you. Is everything all right?"

"Hello, Max. Sorry I'm late. Can... we give someone a tour of the *Bosch* this afternoon?" I asked, looking back and seeing Aunt Miranda approaching, looking up at the balloon of the airship in wonder.

Max noticed. "Who is this lovely lady?" he asked, moving past me to greet my aunt, smiling his most charming smile.

Miranda turned at his approach and took in his appearance. He'd rolled his work shirt-sleeves up past his elbows, and standing there with the rag in his hands, in grease-stained shirt, suspenders, pants, and boots, he was the epitome of an airship captain. He held out a greasy hand, realized it was greasy and dropped it, wiping it self-consciously on the rag.

"Hello, madam," he said, making a small bow and tucking the rag in a pants pocket. "My name is Max, and I'm the captain of this bucket of bolts we call the *Bosch*. Ari said you'd like a tour?"

Miranda beamed. "My, my," she said, eyes twinkling, "aren't you a pirate. Ari didn't mention that about you."

Max looked at me and then back at my aunt, his smile intact. "You have me at a disadvantage, madam," he said, "and we've not ventured into piracy just yet." He moved his shoulder like it hurt. "Waving cutlasses aggravates my rheumatism."

Aunt Miranda shook her head sadly. "I always preferred a pistol," she said. "Saves wear and tear on the joints."

Max turned to me. "Who is this esteemed personage, Ari?" he asked.

I opened my mouth to introduce her, but she beat me to the punch. "I'm sorry," Aunt Miranda said, stepping forward. "I'm Lady Miranda Brentwood, Ari's great aunt. I asked for the tour."

"Oh!" Max said, understanding dawning. "Lady Brentwood, we'd be honored. Let me get the rest of the crew out here." He shot me a slightly amused look as he turned to head back up the gangplank and disappeared into the ship.

"I see why you like this," Aunt Miranda said, walking over to join me. "He's very pleasant. Are you sure you aren't—"

"No, Aunt Miranda," I said. "He's just a friend."

Aunt Miranda sniffed. "Shame."

"It's a great deal of work keeping the ship in top shape," I said, changing the subject quickly. "I don't think we can take you out in the *Bosch* today—but tomorrow should work, assuming the weather holds."

Max emerged from the ship with Griff and Needle behind him, all of them stained to varying degrees with oil and grease. Griff's handlebar mustache drooped slightly, giving him a tired appearance. Needle was taciturn and angular as always. Lizzie, I knew, was at home helping her mother, and wouldn't be joining us until later.

Max made the introductions, and Aunt Miranda greeted my friends warmly. I didn't say much, mostly because I knew my Aunt wished to evaluate my friends and our 'hobby' on their own merits. If I hogged the conversation, it'd seem like I was trying to hide something from her. She wanted the truth in its unvarnished, simple form from my crewmates.

Max, Griff, and Needle seemed flattered by my aunt's interest and soon they chatted like friends.

"Ari always speaks of you with great affection," Griff said with a warm smile. "It's a pleasure to meet you."

"You asked for a tour," Needle said. "That'll involve a lot of climbing over struts in the balloon and the engine room is dirty. Are you sure you want to risk your clothing on our foolishness?"

Aunt Miranda looked up at the envelope. "You can go inside the balloon? Ye gods."

Max laughed. "There are smaller rubberized ballonets inside the rigid frame. We need to be able to walk around inside the frame to maintain and repair the ballonets and the frame. Come on," he said, motioning her forward, "I'll show you."

Together we made our way up the passenger gangplank into the lowest level of the ship. The part of the *Bosch* that wasn't the aluminum-framed envelope for the hydrogen ballonets was an actual boat the others had repurposed. They'd replaced the wooden framing of the boat with steel, and reapplied the planks to the new frame. They'd also removed the keel and flattened the bottom so it sat flat on the ground for repairs. The oak was weathered but strong, and a thin line of tar between each board kept out the wind.

To the left was the large gangplank we used for Griff's Technacart. The large gangplank was drawn up, but the space where the Technacart sat was empty. Griff had it elsewhere in the hangar, probably in pieces as he worked to improve his design. He took a few minutes to explain what the Technacart was to Aunt Miranda, who nodded in understanding and looked elsewhere in the room.

Coiled ropes and other random bits of tackle hung from the walls opposite where we stowed the Technacart while containers of fuel for it sat strapped into bins below them. Narrow stairs to the next level spiraled upward at the prow of the ship. The room smelled of petrol, tar, wood, oil, and rubber.

"How in the world did you have the time, energy and funds to create this?" she asked, obviously impressed. "I thought the exterior was wonderful... but this—"

Max beamed. "That's a long story I only tell over a pint of Guinness, your ladyship," he said. "But, since you're Ari's favorite aunt, I'm willing to give you the short version. My friends and I pooled our resources. I inherited a lot of aluminum struts, along with this land and enough money to build the hangar and commence airship construction from an old friend of my family. Bit of a magnate he was, with no sons to whom he could pass on his legacy, so he left me enough to get the airship enterprise started and still eat while I did it. Griff knew a chap who knew a chap who had a boat we could buy cheap. Needle and Lizzie drew up the plans for how to modify the boat and attach it to our balloon. All four of us worked to make the necessary modifications, cobbling together engines and propellers and whatnot in our spare time."

Aunt Miranda nodded. "I see. What contribution did my niece make to this grand endeavor?"

Griff sidled up to stand next to my aunt. "Your niece is a mathematical and navigational genius," he said. "Lizzie sells Ari's little Ladies' Helpers in the shop where she works. You know about those, I hope?"

"I do. Ingenious devices. Have a few with me whenever I travel, particularly since I never take a lady's maid with me."

"Indeed," Max agreed. "Were I a lady, I dare say I'd have them myself."

"Well," Griff continued, eyeing Max oddly, "Lizzie asked Ari if she'd try her hand at devices we could use. Y'see, your ladyship, we built the *Bosch* and actually got her to fly... but steering was a bit dicey. We had no reliable way to compensate for the wind or keep track of our position relative to the ground. Figuring when and how much gas to put in or take out of the ballonets was a right puzzle." Griff pointed at me. "She came out, looked the old girl over, rode with us a couple times and got to work. She figured out how to navigate the *Bosch*. She made the instruments to determine pitch, roll and yaw, created devices that track wind speed and our position in the sky, and developed the system by which we know how much gas to put in the ballonets. If we move up, down, left, right or sideways... well, it's because Ari figured out how to do it."

"We don't crash anymore," Needle added, ever the pragmatist. "That's lowered the repair bill considerably."

Aunt Miranda looked at me. "Crashes? There were crashes? Good Lord."

I started to respond, but Max beat me to it. "No one has been seriously injured," he put in quickly, "but before Ari applied her considerable intelligence to the problem, all the amateur airships and their crews in Cambridge had the same probleMs. Pioneers frequently encounter these sorts of difficulties, as I am sure you are aware. Ariana solved them."

Aunt Miranda looked at me speculatively. "Did she, indeed?"

"She showed the other amateur Cambridge aeronauts what she taught us," Max said.

"There's more than one of these airships in Cambridge?" Miranda asked. "I'd no idea."

"We've a club," Griff said proudly, "and a clubhouse. We call ourselves the Icarus Squadron. Thanks to Ari's help, our club name is more an inside joke than an allusion to our airship mishaps. We're the best amateur aeronauts in England, says I."

"Or at least the most persistent," Needle added.

"Icarus Squadron, eh? Hmmm," my aunt murmured, thinking. "Ari, if your mother ever finds out about this airship matter, I suggest you refrain from telling her the name of your club. Well then," she sniffed, "you'd better show me the rest."

Max indicated the stairs in the prow. "After you," he said. "Next level up is the engine room and cargo hold."

"Is that the only way up to the next level? Those narrow spiral stairs?"

"No, m'Lady," Max said moving toward the stairs and encouraging us to follow him. "There's another set folded up into a closet directly opposite the way we came in, but we mostly use these stairs. There are also three other ways off the ship in case of emergencies."

We followed Max up the stairs in a line, with Aunt Miranda directly behind Max, while Griff, Needle and I brought up the rear.

The four gasoline engines: two on the port side and two on the starboard side, sat silent and oily in the metal and wooden frames that held them screwed to the deck. Steel straps held the oblong petrol tanks between the engines on both sides of the ship. Pipes with pressure and fuel level gauges jutted out from the tops of the tanks and attached to the engines. Two small mechanical beetles with phosphorite bodies sat clamped to the ceiling above the engines with tiny claws, waiting to be powered up in case light was needed in a hard-to-reach place, while larger phosphorite globes in sconces dotted the walls. Drive shafts extended out from the engines through the walls of the ship to the four propellers that moved the *Bosch* through the air. The chadburn, its white dial and bronze handle gleaming, stood in the center of the room, its pointer indicating 'Stop'.

Aunt Miranda looked over the set up in silence, taking in the scene with obvious interest. "So these engines move the ship through the air," she mused, "but what are you using to give the *Bosch* buoyancy?"

I bit my tongue and waited for disaster.

"Hydrogen gas, my lady," Needle said, cutting to the chase as usual. He was calm and obviously proud of our hydrogen gas system. "We've tanks that keep it under pressure on the next level up, and we control how much gas goes into or out of the ballonets with valves controlled at the helm. The chadburn here," he pointed at it, "tells the engineer when to speed up or slow down the engines. Combined with the navigational devices, we're able to maneuver the old girl pretty as you please."

Aunt Miranda nodded and the temperature of the room seemed to drop as she considered Needle's explanation. "I'm not a chemistry student, but I seem to recall hydrogen explodes rather violently when it comes into contact with a spark or an open flame. How is it in your previous..." she paused and looked at me, "...crashes, you've not been blown to Kingdom Come?"

I winced. I was in for it now.

Max noticed my discomfort and cleared his throat before he spoke. "Well, there's some that say we're too stubborn to blow up," he began, but quickly decided on a different approach when he saw Aunt Miranda's withering glare, "...but, mostly, we're careful not to make sparks, and the rigid aluminum frame helps keep the ballonets from being punctured."

"Are you the only airship in Cambridge that uses hydrogen?"

"No, ma'am," Max responded, "and we've a healthy respect for the stuff. Every safety precaution possible has been taken." He indicated the room around us. "We only use phosphorite bulbs for lighting. The engines are as far from the ballonets as possible. No smoking of any kind is allowed on the ship. We've several ways to escape if there's an emergency, and each exit has several parachutes to facilitate a safe landing should we have to... um... abandon ship."

"I see," Aunt Miranda said coldly. "How many people have been injured in your airship escapades?"

"Old Toby broke his arm," Griff said, "but to be honest, he was drunk and he'd sort of... hijacked the *Folly,* one of the other ships in the Icarus Squadron. He floated into a tree, panicked and jumped out of the cockpit."

"We don't fly drunk," Needle said gravely.

"Other than that," Griff continued, "there have been some scrapes and bruises, and a bit of blood, I'll admit... but there've been no life threatening injuries. With Ari's navigational instruments, we've had a run of several months without a mishap for the whole Squadron."

I held my breath, waiting for Aunt Miranda to respond.

"Max," Aunt Miranda intoned, "are there other safety precautions that can be taken?"

"We could use a few more fire extinguishers," he said cautiously, "and a couple more parachutes."

"Ariana, do you know where those items can be purchased?"

A glimmer of hope shimmered through me. "Yes, Aunt Miranda," I said.

"Very well. I will purchase what you require, Captain," she told Max, "and in future, should you require other such equipment, you will let me know. Is that understood?"

Max clicked together his heels and saluted my aunt smartly. "Yes, your ladyship," he said with a grin.

I released the breath I'd been holding, grateful that my aunt was such an understanding person. I saw my crewmates also relax.

"Well, don't just stand there saluting, young man," Aunt Miranda ordered, waving her hand at Max dismissively, "show me the rest of the ship."

Chapter Fourteen

We climbed and crawled all over the *Bosch* after that, our delight at Aunt Miranda's interest fueling a more thorough tour than we might otherwise have provided. We showed my aunt the hydrogen gas tanks, the bridge, the crew quarters and the ballonets safely secured inside the *Bosch's* cigar-shaped, pegamoid silk-covered aluminum frame, each of us taking turns to explain where we were and what she looked at. Max spoke of how he wanted to try and make the *Bosch* a commercial vessel, hauling cargo or even passengers, pointing out how Americans used such ships to cut travel time from one place to another down from weeks to days. By the time the tour ended, Aunt Miranda's carefully coifed hair was askew, her hands and dress were covered with grime, and her mood was jovial. The rest of us were equally dirty and happy.

"I thank you, gentlemen, for showing me around and for keeping an eye on my niece," she said, shaking his greasy hand with her own. "I'll see you get those fire extinguishers and parachutes right away. Now—can we discuss the possibility of my taking a trip in the *Bosch* sometime tomorrow?"

"Thank you, Lady Brentwood. I'll consult with my crew," he indicated Needle and Griff, who both grinned and nodded excitedly, "and determine when we'll be ready to launch. But don't you worry. We'll continue to watch out for Ariana, particularly after what happened in the library yesterday," Max said, beaming.

I looked at the ground as Aunt Miranda frowned and dropped his hand. I'd not had a chance to send the letter I'd written, and her appearance had been so unexpected, I'd forgotten to bring the incident up. Clearly Cora's promise to make sure my airship friends knew of the attack had been fulfilled. Now, whether or not I wanted to tell Aunt Miranda about Laufeson, it seemed I had no choice.

"Library?" Aunt Miranda asked.

Max faltered. "I thought that's why you'd come," he said. "I guess Ari hasn't told you about it?"

"No," Aunt Miranda said, and I could feel her eyes boring into me. "She didn't mention it."

"Ah," Max said. "Sorry about that, Ari."

"I'd love to get my hands on the lout," Griff declared.

"A disgrace, really," Needle said, "that German fellow grabbing her like that."

"Grabby Germans?" Aunt Miranda echoed. "Really. Well, I'm sure Ariana will tell me all about it as we head back into town. Won't you, my dear?"

I looked up and nodded. "You surprised me and—"

"It's all right. Save it for the carriage ride," she ordered gently but firmly. "Thank you again," she said to my friends. "In light of this news, you will understand if I ask that my trip in the

Bosch be postponed to a later time.   Ariana and I have a lot of catching up to do.   I'm sure I'll see you again soon."

Max struggled to hide his disappointment and worry that he'd gotten me in trouble.   "Yes, ma'am.   We look forward to our next meeting."

Aunt Miranda turned to me.   "Let's go," she said, striding past me.   I sketched a quick wave at Max, who mouthed an apology as I turned and walked with her back to the carriage.

Alymer stood beside the door and smoothly ushered us into the cool interior of his cab.   He made no mention of our dirty and disheveled appearance as he shut the carriage door and took his own seat.   He turned to open the trap door that allowed him to speak to us from the box.

"Where to next, m'lady?" he asked through the rectangular opening.

"Cambridge Arms Hotel if you please, Aylmer.   We'll need to clean up before dinner."

"Yes ma'am," he said, then shut the little door.   The carriage began to move and Aunt Miranda skewered me with her gaze.

"What, precisely, happened to you yesterday?" she asked in a tone that brooked no refusal.

****

Aunt Miranda listened with intense focus as I described Laufeson's attempt to kidnap me from the Faraday Library.   She frowned intently when I reached the point where the ruffian grabbed me and talked about spells and how I was 'his'.   She relaxed a little when I described how Mr. Avery had leapt to my defense, and seemed grateful that Cora and my other friends were intent to keep me from harm.

"Had you seen this fellow before?" she asked.

I shook my head. "Never in my life, and I hope never to see him again."

"Understandable," she agreed, "but are you sure there was nothing familiar to you at all about the man?"

I thought carefully, going over every detail of the encounter in my mind. "He smelled of rosemary and cloves," I said, "which made me feel... I don't know... uneasy? Wary?"

"I see." She looked out the window of the carriage for a long moment and then regarded me with a grim smile. "You've not told your parents, I assume," she said.

"No ma'am. Cora suggested I tell you in case they found out. I wrote a letter telling you all about it, but you beat me to the post... as it were."

"Yes," she murmured, seemingly lost in thought, "yes... so it would seem." She shook herself out of her reverie and the ancient and crafty look I'd seen in her eyes appeared again, and then drifted away. "It is best that we keep this bit of news to ourselves. In that I am in agreement with your friend Miss Allerton. Your mother would insist you come home, and that isn't the place for you right now. In future, please make sure you are not left alone as you were in the Faraday."

"I will," I responded.

Aunt Miranda tilted her head in thought, looking me up and down. "Have there been any other... how shall we say... unusual happenings? Other than unpleasant gentlemen attempting to abduct you?"

"What qualifies as unusual?" I asked.

She leaned forward. "Have you done unexpected things? Had strange dreams or..." she waved a hand as she sat back, "a sense of foreboding for no good reason?"

"I started telling stories."

"Oh?"

"The last time we went to a pub and I threw darts, I followed up the games with stories."

Aunt Miranda became still for a moment, as if what I had said confirmed something unfortunate. "You've not had much exposure to literature," she replied with care. "In fact, as I recall your mother forbid you to read myths and stories after the unfortunate incident in the garden with her best silver."

I felt my cheeks redden. "The story never really explained how the sword got into the stone in the first place. How was I to know silver wasn't as strong as steel?"

My aunt laughed. "You've always been an experimenter and seeker of knowledge, my dear; though it did give your mother fits to see the knives bent in half."

I clasped my hands in my lap and tried to seem unmoved by her laughter. "They bent them back good as new, you know."

That made her laugh harder. I looked at the ceiling of the cab.

When she'd managed to stop laughing, she grew serious again. "Telling stories, you say. Are these stories of your own unique exploits, or were they something else? And, when did it start?"

I described what Max and the others had told me about our trip to Penzance. Her face grew grave as I did so. The storytelling in the pub and my not remembering actually telling the tales had unnerved me, but Aunt Miranda seemed even more troubled than I had been. That gave me pause. I was used to Aunt Miranda knowing more than me on a regular basis, but this seemed different.

"So you brought home a great deal of money that night, I take it?" she asked. "That must have been a good result, surely."

"It was... but I don't remember telling the stories. I'd never heard the one about Thor and his hammer. How could I tell stories I don't know?"

"Anything else?" my aunt asked, ducking the question.

I rubbed my forehead as I thought, trying to remember that afternoon's dream. "I dreamt about a huge tree. There was a blonde woman, blood, and a very large pig named Hildy," I told her.

My aunt's eyebrows went up in surprise and her eyes sparkled with amusement. "Hildy? Hildy the pig?"

I threw up my hands in frustration. "There was more to it than that, but I'll be dashed if I can recall the pertinent details. Telling you about it makes it sound completely absurd, but at the time..." I trailed off, at a loss and feeling foolish. "Something about it felt like a warning... or a memory... or both. I don't know, but the woman in the dream said we were related."

"Yes," my aunt muttered, "I bet she did."

"What was that?" I asked.

Aunt Miranda patted my knee to comfort me. "It could be nothing more than your mind's attempt to work through what's happened to you the past few days."

I gaped. "A huge boar, a mysterious woman, an ash tree larger than anything I've ever seen in my life, and you think it's a reaction to the attempted abduction?"

"You said you slept poorly the night before, and you went to church surrounded by friends armed with parasols while one talked about some pagan Norse god wandering around the planet... who knows what your unconscious mind would make of that, as that Freud fellow says." She shrugged. "I can see the value of some of his theories, but some... I don't know. The man seems very set in his opinions, and that's never good when trying to understand the mind."

"Something is happening to me, Aunt Miranda," I said. "I don't know what, or why... but it feels like I'm at the center of something I simply don't understand."

"I think you need to stay with me at the hotel. I've a story or two to tell you over dinner. I'll notify Mrs. Guildersleeve so she knows you're with me, and we'll dine in my room tonight. All right?"

"But my class in the morning—"

"I'll contact Dr. Maitland to inform him I intend to impose 'Great Aunt privileges' for the next twenty-four hours."

"But—"

"I'll ask him to send over something so you don't feel like you're falling behind in your studies. Mark my words, my girl, you need to spend this time with me, and I'll not take no for an answer."

Chapter Fifteen

We arrived at the Cambridge Arms Hotel, an imposing Georgian edifice of butter-colored stone that filled most of a city block. Aylmer helped both of us out of the cab and promised he'd be waiting for us the following day when we needed him. We thanked him and made our way through the baroque cavernous lobby to the hotel's front desk, a malachite and mahogany monstrosity that would have looked more at home in a cathedral. Despite its large and somewhat gaudy presence, it served well as the administrative center of the place.

Aunt Miranda breezed up to the counter, disheveled, grimy and completely oblivious to the stares her déshabillé engendered. She caught the eye of an older gentleman behind the counter. Impeccably dressed in a grey suit and meticulously groomed, he glided over and bowed slightly in greeting, his bearing genial but business-like.

"Lady Brentwood," he intoned, "you are looking well as always. How nice of you to join us. It has been some time since your last visit."

Aunt Miranda rolled her eyes. "Come now, Sanderson," she said, "I look as I always look when I come here—grimy, completely disarranged and in need of a wash. You're just too polite to mention it."

"Yes ma'am," he said.

She turned to provide me with an explanation. "I've been staying here on and off for nigh on..."

"Thirty years," Sanderson helpfully supplied.

"...and this fellow has been at the front desk as the concierge since that time. We are both old and wise in our respective ways, are we not, Sanderson?"

He bowed again slightly. "Indeed, madam."

Aunt Miranda winked at me and turned back to the concierge. "So, what news?"

"I took the liberty of having the package from London delivered to your room, and the staff are ready to draw your bath immediately, if you wish. I took the liberty," Sanderson cleared his throat, "of assuming you would require one."

"Messages?"

Sanderson picked up a short stack of envelopes. "The usual number, madam. Shall I send a boy up later to retrieve your responses?"

My aunt took the proffered stack from Sanderson and glanced through them briefly. "I will need you to telephone Towson House and inform the house mother that my niece Miss Trevelyan," she indicated me, "will be spending the next night and following day with me." She flipped through the envelopes with her thumb thoughtfully. "These responses can wait to go out until the morning, if you please. I wish to take dinner in my room with my niece tonight. I trust that can be arranged?"

Sanderson inclined his head to me in greeting. "Welcome to the Cambridge Arms, Miss Trevelyan. I can see the family resemblance to your aunt." He turned his attention back to my aunt. "I will see to dinner, madam. Will your niece require a room? I have one available that adjoins your suite."

Aunt Miranda turned to me. "Would you like your own room, my dear?"

I indicated my own disheveled appearance. "I should wash up though I don't have a change of clothes."

Aunt Miranda smiled. "Oh, I think you'll find that's not a problem." She nodded at Sanderson. "Put her next to me, send Elissa and June up to start our baths, and whatever the chef prefers to send up for dinner in an hour will be fine, I have no doubt."

Sanderson turned, pulled two keys from adjoining cubbie holes and handed them to my aunt. "I shall make your wishes known, madam. Do you have any other needs?"

Aunt Miranda took the keys, handed me one and considered his question. "Do you have any rum?"

I had to steel my face to hide my surprise. *Rum?*

"Of course, madam," Sanderson said, non-plussed. "Do you require the usual variety, or would you prefer a different kind?"

"The usual will do, thank you."

"Shall I have it sent up after dinner?"

Aunt Miranda smiled. "Yes, that would be best. Thank you, Sanderson." She turned to head to the lift on the far left side of the lobby and caught my eye, indicating with a motion of her head to follow me.

I took a few quick steps to walk beside her. "Rum?" I hissed.

"I find it to be a far superior beverage to brandy, don't you?"

I couldn't really disagree with that. "But—"

"Some conversations are best with tea. Others with coffee, others with rum... and the most unpleasant conversations usually require brandy or grappa." She pointed a long finger at me. "This one will require rum, unless you would prefer brandy?

I shook my head quickly. "No thank you," I said with a grimace.

"Mind you," she continued, "how much rum we'll need will depend on two factors."

"Such as?" I asked.

"The number of glasses and the quality of the rum," she said, brow furrowed. "Have you learned nothing practical at this university? There is more to life than sums, child."

The elevator dinged and a bellboy pushed aside the door and grate to the small lift and indicated we could step inside. We did so. "Third floor please, young man," my aunt intoned.

The bellboy, a lanky, angular boy who couldn't have been much more than fifteen years old, knuckled the brim of his cap in response, pulled the grate and door shut, and started the lift. We stood quietly as the small room ascended to the third floor, then departed it after the bellboy opened the conveyance and let us out. The hallway was long and wide with maroon paisley wallpaper and dark green carpet. The doors of the rooms were a dark brown, their room numbers in bronze in the middle of the doors. Phosphorite globes dotted the walls on either side.

Aunt Miranda indicated we should head to the right. "There have been many improvements to this hotel over the past thirty years," she said as we walked toward our rooms, which were 333 and 335 respectively. She indicated the walls of the hallway. "I can't say this wallpaper is one of the better improvements but thank goodness they don't use the ghastly stuff in the rooms."

"It does seem…" I searched for the proper term, "…exuberant."

"That sounds like something your mother would say," my aunt remarked with a smirk. "Diplomacy is all well and good, child, but in matters of wallpaper and horses, one must speak plainly and to the point. Ugly wallpaper speaks directly to the character of the person who chose it, and the ownership of an inferior horse shows others you are either foolish or stupid or both. None of these are attractive qualities."

"No, Aunt Miranda," I intoned obediently.

We reached the door of room 333, and noises could be heard coming from within. Aunt Miranda nodded. "That would be the bath preparations," she murmured and turned the key in the lock.

We entered a spacious room done in gentle greens and golds with no unpleasant wallpaper in sight. The furnishings were elegant in dark wood. Two bedside tables flanked the bed, one of which sported a black candlestick telephone. Light globes sat in sconces above the head of the bed. There were two armchairs, a dresser and a dressing table with mirror, along with an armoire. Aunt Miranda's trunk sat open and empty in the middle of the room, and a large brown paper package sat beside it. The door to the bathroom was open, and light, steam, and voices poured out the door. A maid's head peeked out from the bathroom. Seeing us she stepped into the room, dropped a quick curtsey, and indicated the bathroom.

"The bath is started, Lady Brentwood," she said. She looked into the bathroom and motioned for whoever was in there to come out. A second maid, taller and older than the first, came out to stand beside the first and also dropped a quick curtsey. They were both pretty women though the stark black of their dresses gave them an air of austere efficiency. Their aprons and caps were brilliantly starched white accents to their black garb. I thought of penguins for a moment, remembering a picture Gertrude had shown me.

"These ladies would be Elissa," my aunt indicated the taller woman, "and June." She indicated me. "This is my niece, Miss Trevelyan. June, would you take her to her room, help her undress, have a bath and then put on one of the new outfits that just arrived?

"I would be happy to do so, Lady Brentwood," June said, moving toward the door.

"New outfits?" I asked, looking from my aunt to June and back. "What new outfits?"

"That's what's in the package. I thought you'd like a few new dresses and some other things, so I bought them in London and had them sent up." She sighed. "I had hoped you'd wear them at an assignation with a clandestined gentleman friend—" she teased.

"I don't—"

"—but since you don't have one," she continued smoothly, "you'll just have to wear them for me tonight and tomorrow."

Aunt Miranda shooed me off in the direction of the door, where June waited patiently. "Off with you, child. June knows what to do. I'll see you in an hour."

Chapter Sixteen

June was a model of efficiency. As Aunt Miranda had requested, I was undressed, bathed, and re-dressed with new undergarments and stockings which June then covered with a new peach-colored cotton dress in the height of fashion. June buttoned the dress up the back and then pulled my unruly hair up in a soft Gibson-style bun, leaving some red curls to frame my face. Looking at myself in the mirror after her efforts, I could see why my crafty aunt had hoped I'd wear the dress to some sort of assignation. It was beautiful and suited me perfectly though it was not an outfit I'd ever have chosen for myself. I thanked June and made my way to Aunt Miranda's room and the dinner she'd ordered.

In her room, a table for two was set in the middle of the chamber while two waiters quickly and quietly set out the food covered with silver domes that came from a wheeled cart beside the table. My aunt sat at the dressing table with her back to the door. She was responding to some of the correspondence she'd received earlier, seeming very relaxed. She wore a simple white cotton dress that was high-necked. She'd covered that with a blue silk kimono that had a pattern of gold medallions woven into the fabric. Her hair was up in a chignon, per usual, and she turned as I entered the room. Taking in my appearance, she was obviously pleased.

"I knew that dress would be lovely on you," she said, nodding. Putting down the pen and turning over the paper so what she'd written couldn't be seen, she waved a hand at the waiters. "I told Sanderson I wanted us to eat family style, without staff. I hope that's all right with you?"

"We eat that way at Towson House," I said. "So that's fine with me."

"Excellent." Aunt Miranda got up and looked over the progress of the dispersion of food. "What do we have on offer, gentlemen?"

What followed was a list of French dishes I didn't really recognize. As the waiters lifted the silver domes I could see baked herbed potatoes; asparagus grilled with cheese; some sort of baked chicken that smelled heavenly; a plate of cheeses and fruits, and finally a fruit trifle in a stemmed bowl. There was a carafe of white wine and two glasses on the cart yet to be placed on the table. The sight of the food made my stomach rumble.

"Please tell the chef he has outdone himself," my aunt said. "This is perfect. You may leave the cart and I'll call down when we're done."

"As you wish, madam," one of them intoned, and the two of them left us to the meal without further comment.

We sat at the table and Aunt Miranda took it upon herself to serve me, loading my plate with portions that were hearty without being un-ladylike, and then doing the same with her own plate. She picked the glasses up off the cart, set them on the table and poured each of us some of the wine, setting the carafe back on the cart.

"Please, child," she said, picking up her fork with one hand and a napkin with the other. "Eat. I can hear your innards growl. We can speak of trivialities over the meal, and get to the heart of the matter with the rum."

The meal was outstanding. Everything was flavorful and well prepared, and the white wine suited the food admirably. As we ate, I spoke about my current assignments, the upcoming Tripos exam and the recent campaign to get women kicked out of Cambridge. Aunt Miranda regaled me with a tale of a London society dinner party where the hostess's dachshund had somehow made it onto the table in the dining room and sampled morsels from all the first course plates, which had been pre-set, covered in food. Then there was a catastrophic chase through the house after the beast, who yipped and yapped his way through the crowd and barreled through the legs of several of the ladies present, tearing petticoats and causing mayhem in his wake.

"I stood along the wall of the hallway and tried to stay as flat as possible," she said, smiling as I chuckled, "while the host—a pleasant but horribly rotund man who shouldn't ever run anywhere —bobbed and weaved his way down the hall, chest heaving from the exertion. I believe he was a bit too familiar with some of the ladies he encountered as he bounced from one wall to the other though I doubt he intentionally wished to cause offence."

"And the dog?" I asked, setting down the wine glass.

"Caught by a footman. The poor thing was overwrought by all the excitement and expelled digested food in various forms from both ends. That effectively ended the evening. I took a cab back to my house and had Cook make me a cheese sandwich." Aunt Miranda looked at my plate. "Done, my dear?" she asked.

"Yes, thanks," I said, wiping my mouth with a napkin. "That was a wonderful dinner."

"I'll call down and have them come take the food and the plates. Will you put our dishes on the cart for me?"

I did so, and shortly after the call, the waiters arrived and took the dinner remnants away, leaving a bottle of golden brown Jamaican rum on the table with two small glasses. Aunt Miranda opened the bottle and poured half an inch of the rum in each glass, then sat down opposite me at the table.

"We don't need much, and you've already had half that glass of wine," she explained. "No need to overindulge." I agreed.

"You're worried you're at the center of something you don't understand," she began. "The storytelling, the attack by that Laufeson fellow, the dreams... yes?"

"Yes."

"I can provide some insight, I think," she said, drawing her glass of rum closer to her, "but you may find my explanation to be too..." she pursed her lips in thought, "...pedestrian, perhaps?"

"I think I'd prefer pedestrian," I said.

Her eyes sparked at that. "Wouldn't we all?" She took a sip of rum, swallowed it and set the glass back on the table. "Are you aware that your mother lost three babies before she finally gave birth to you?"

I blinked in surprise. "No," I said, and I couldn't keep the shock from my voice. "We don't discuss such things, and it never occurred to me to ask." I ached for my parents, imagining how sad they must have been. "That's horrible. What happened?"

"There are those whom God gifts with the ability to have children easily. Your mother, bless her, was not so fortunate. There were three boys lost to miscarriage in the first years of your parents' marriage despite your mother's and the doctors' best efforts." Aunt Miranda looked down at her right hand and traced circles on the tablecloth with a finger. "I felt so sorry for your parents then, the poor dears. The loss of those boys affected them greatly, and when your mother found she was pregnant with you, whatever joy they might have felt was tainted with the sorrow of prior losses and the knowledge you might be lost as well."

I nodded, understanding and sorrow in my heart.

"Then, about six months in, your mother started to bleed. The doctors warned that she was losing you and that this time, she might die as well."

I brought a hand to my chest. No one had mentioned any of this to me, ever. *Why had nothing been said?*

"Your father, desperate, called on me for help," my aunt continued. "I have, as you know, travelled widely, and, therefore, have friends with medical and other skills that differ from those of English doctors. He and your mother were willing to try anything to keep you alive so your mother could carry you to term. My good friend, a healer named Jeremiah, came and managed to save both of you though he told your parents there would be no children after your birth." She smiled gently and looked at me. "Thus you came into the world."

I reached over and picked up my glass of rum, taking a small sip and feeling the warm liquid flow down my throat. "So far," I said, setting the glass down, "this hasn't seemed a very pedestrian conversation." The revelations about my parents were saddening and somewhat alarming, to be sure, but I didn't see what any of that had to do with recent events in my life.

Aunt Miranda tilted her head and conceded the point, then sat back in her chair, regarding me thoughtfully. "You're odd creatures," she mused. "Every one of you. Odd, and delightful, and maddening and worrisome."

"Creatures?"

"Children," she clarified. "I never had any myself, of course, but I've cared for several in my time. I never cease to be amazed by the resiliency of childhood even as parents find themselves stunned by what the product of their love has wrought on their lives. They think they know what the child will be like—they know themselves and assume a result of their union will share their traits and personalities. Sometimes that's exactly what happens. Often, it isn't, and the resulting loveable creature," she pointed at me, "is a complete mystery to those who brought her about."

That was hardly news to me. I knew I'd confounded my mother daily growing up though Father had been more understanding even as my childhood exploits astonished him. They loved me greatly—and now I had a clearer picture of why that love was, at times, fierce in its intensity—though I knew they didn't quite understand me.

"You, my dear," my aunt continued, "walked at ten months and ran at eleven. You refused to wear shoes and disrobed at the most inconvenient times. The nurse had to put your clothes on backwards so you couldn't wriggle out of them."

"Yes," I said, a little embarrased.

"You started speaking in full sentences by the time you were eighteen months old, and your father taught you to read at three so he could have a moment's peace while he worked at his desk. You then proceeded through all of the children's classic stories and your parents hired a governess to help guide your avid mind into more... how shall we say... appropriate avenues of scholarship. Then you had an accident."

That brought me up short. "Accident? What accident?"

Aunt Miranda held up a hand. "No, you wouldn't remember. You were four at the time. You were very gravely injured—the particulars of how you came to be injured would take too long to explain tonight. Suffice it to say the medical skills of my friend Jeremiah and others had to be employed to save your life. After that, at my request, you lived at Brentwood Close with me in Aberdeenshire for a year while you continued your recovery."

I swallowed. "I don't remember living with you for a year," I said, not sure what to make of what I'd been told.

"Hardly a surprise. It was a difficult time for you. You didn't sleep regularly for months. You refused to go anywhere without Bow-Bow, your long-suffering stuffed muslin rabbit, and more than once we had the groomsmen and locals out in the countryside looking for you after you'd made yet another escape from my house. You were very good at escaping."

I nodded. I'd been good at escaping all my life, as Mother's stories of my very early days showed.

"I stayed up with you when you couldn't sleep, and we made a fair dent in my library at the Close. We read the myths of various cultures together, along with the Roman and Greek classics. Had you stayed longer, we probably would have started on Shakespeare next. When you were not with me, our noses pressed into some tome, you trundled about the house and garden, 'helping' the staff. You weeded the rose garden by pulling up all the roses, wanting to find rose bushes that had no thorns. You took apart the library mantle clock with surgical precision one afternoon, and it took the local clockmaker three weeks to reassemble the damnable thing. You half unraveled a tapestry in the dining room—but you get the idea."

"I'm sorry," I said, amazed at and troubled by the activities of my younger self.

Aunt Miranda waved off the apology. "You did none of these things with malicious intent, Ariana. The accident presented your mind with experiences you didn't understand, and everything you did while you stayed with me was a childish effort to figure out what had happened to you. After that year, you returned to London and your parents, and while some of your unique exploits continued—"

"Like trying to insert the knives in the boulders in the garden," I interjected.

"—you'd grown out of many of the others," she finished. "Once we realized it was the stories that encouraged you to act out, your parents encouraged you toward mathematics and the sciences. With time, your year with me and everything you did at the Close faded from your memory... until now."

I leaned forward. "You're saying that the stories I told at the pub—the ones I don't remember telling—came from the reading the two of us did together when I stayed with you?"

Aunt Miranda nodded. "I think so, and I think the odd dream with the pig and the huge tree is part of that as well. We read the *Aeneid* and the Norse myths all those years ago. This time, instead of acting out the stories, you created vivid versions of them to tell for the entertainment of others or, at least so far as the dream goes, for yourself."

"But I don't know how to tell a story—not like that," I maintained.

"Nonsense," she replied. "You tell a fine story – they just tend to be factual or science-based."

"Lizzie said my stories were magical, but magic doesn't exist in the real world."

"Spoken like a scientist." Aunt Miranda thought for a moment. "Shall I tell you a story?" she asked.

Chapter Seventeen

Aunt Miranda cleared her throat. "Here's a tale I know you've never heard," she began. "One of the items you'll inherit when I pass on is a small island in the Orkneys. It's so small as to be nearly worthless, but my father and I spent a very eventful few weeks there when I was about twenty years old. Father was a bit of an amateur archaeologist though that's not what we called it then. There was a Viking tomb on the island. We went there and dug it up."

I furrowed my brow, doing the math on when this excavation had happened. If Great Aunt Miranda was nearly eighty now, that meant when she and her father excavated the tomb it had been –

"You and your father opened up the tomb in 1845?" I asked. "That's... what... thirty years before Schliemann started at Troy?"

"It is." Aunt Miranda smiled. "Father was far more careful and fastidious than Schliemann was, but he had that sort of mind. Everything documented, everything in its proper place was his way of doing things. Schliemann was a thief and scoundrel."

"So I've heard," I agreed, my interest in the story growing. "So... what was the island like?"

"It was terribly windy there, since the island had no trees or large rocks to block the gales."

Aunt Miranda continued to speak, describing what the island looked like in detail. I could see it then, framed by a windswept sea. The air smelled of salt with a hint of dead fish, and the pebbles at my feet clicked against each other as I walked. There was no soil to be seen, and a few unfortunate plants fought for life here and there, stunted and twisted by the wind and lack of earth. Waves hit the rocky shore in rhythmic slaps, and small whitecaps appeared and disappeared on the water's surface in reaction to the winds.

It was midday. The sun warmed me despite the constant wind that pulled my hair from its pins. Through the winding tendrils of my loosening hair I could see one end of the island in front of me, pointed west. I turned to see the other end, which rose to a hillock that also held the mound of the tomb and the billowing white tents beside it. I marvelled. The whole island was only a trifle bigger than Towson House and its garden, and it would take perhaps ten minutes to walk the perimeter of it. The islands around the tiny island I stood on looked equally rocky, but they were bigger and had more grass and soil on them.

Aunt Miranda's words came to me on the wind. "Our tents blew down every other day, and there were some nights we couldn't keep a fire lit due to the winds, but we soldiered on. After a few days of digging, we found two skeletons in the tomb: a man and a woman. Father was overjoyed to find the tomb hadn't been looted, and we spent the next two weeks cataloguing the artifacts the tomb contained."

I walked toward the tomb. It was the size of a London omnibus, and it stuck five feet above the hillock. Large grey-black granite slabs, carefully fitted together and spotted with moss and lichen, made up the walls and roof of the tomb. Smaller stones and gravel sat in patches on the roof and in piles along the walls. One rectangular slab that had been the entrance to the tomb lay on its side, revealing the dark interior of the structure. It was clear from the piles of earth around the entrance that opening the tomb had taken time and effort. Two shovels stuck out of one of the piles.

"What did you find?" I asked, staring at the tomb.

"The inside of the tomb was damp and smelled of mold and decay," Aunt Miranda told me. "The structure itself was very carefully constructed, but the constant moisture destroyed many of the more fragile items."

I walked toward the tomb and ducked my head to enter the dark space, partially lit by the sunlight streaming through the entrance. Under the cover of the tomb, the wind stopped whipping my hair around. It took a moment for my eyes to adjust to the dimness inside, and the smell of damp earth and long decayed wood and animal skins overwhelmed me briefly. When I could see, I found myself standing between two stone beds made of granite slabs just like those that made up the walls and roof of the tomb. Each one contained a skeleton in the repose of death. No flesh remained on the bones, and scraps of fur and coarse-woven wool were the only indications of clothing, now rotted away. The skeleton on the left had a helmet and shield placed near him, indicating his masculine gender. An ornate gold armband that resembled a wolf in full run drooped on his right armbone, and in the midst of the jumble of his finger bones at the end of the right arm was a simple gold ring.

I looked at the skeleton on the right. Wisps of long red hair clung to the skull, and I had the distinct impression I saw the remains of a woman. I wondered if she was the wife or daughter of the warrior on the left. She had a delicate gold ring mixed within the white bones of her left hand, and a necklace of gold chain framed her neck.   From the chain a gold pendant, shaped like some sort of bird, rested on her exposed breastbone.   Around the edges of the tomb other grave goods sat: metal and ceramic pots, weapons, and the metal fastenings for wooden items, the wood long ago rotted away.   I could see how it would take a fortnight to document all of the artifacts.

"I sketched both the tomb and its artifacts as we found them in it, and then the artifacts separately, filling three or four books with drawings and notes." Aunt Miranda chuckled.   "Father sat beside me, eyes wide with excitement, speculating on the origins, uses, and reasons for each artifact."

It became dusk.   I saw the two of them in one of the tents, seated on stools with a flickering lantern illuminating their work.   I saw a much younger version of Aunt Miranda, her hair a beautiful chestnut brown, her body young and healthy.   She wore dirty, old-fashioned clothing I'd only seen in old prints.   She sat next to a bearded older man who held one of the pots from the tomb.   His eyes flashed in the lamplight and he spoke with great animation.

"Most of the artifacts Father sent to the British Museum.   A few of them he kept for himself, and some of them he gave to me."

With a jolt, I found myself back in my chair in the hotel room.   Aunt Miranda took another small sip of rum and indicated I should do the same.   I did so and set the glass back down, amazed by what I'd just experienced.

"That's what Max and the others described," I said, amazed. "I was on the island—I saw the tomb."

"I've always found it fascinating how a tale, well told, can transport people to a different place and time," Aunt Miranda said simply.   "It isn't magic, Ariana, it's the power of language and imagination.   You seem to be developing the skills to tell stories like I've just done."

"Yes, but—"

"Didn't you tell me once that when you aim at something your mind alters somehow?"

"I did," I said, thinking about that.

"Perhaps the telling of stories is merely a new aspect of that... I don't know... alteration? It seems a more reasonable explanation than magic, doesn't it?"

"I suppose it could be," I said uncertainly. "That's a more logical one, at least."

"Quite," my aunt responded.

A question occurred to me. "You said your father sent some of the artifacts from the tomb to the British Museum, that he kept some, and some he gave to you. What did he give to you?"

Aunt Miranda held up her two hands, palms facing me. One delicate gold ring sat on the ring finger of her right hand while the other – bigger and obviously meant for a man's finger – sat on the middle finger of her left hand. I'd seen them countless times before, of course, but I'd not made the connection to the tomb excavation until now.

"He gave you the gold rings from the skeletons?"

"As well as the necklace and the armband. I have all of the artifacts on my person at all times."

I grimaced. "That seems a bit morbid," I remarked.

"There are those who would love to get their barmy hands on these bits of gold," she told me. "That tomb held a priest and priestess of one of the Norse gods, and there are some who believe these items," she waggled her fingers at me, "have great power.

Father knew that and gave the gold to me, since a woman wearing gold rings is less remarked upon than a man doing so."

"Mellie said that about Loki on our way to church today," I said. "She says there are those who believe the Norse gods still hold sway here on Earth. Do the artifacts you wear possess some sort of power?" I asked, then frowned at myself. *That was a foolish question*, I mused. Gold artifacts from an ancient tomb holding some sort of mystical power? There was no basis in logic and science for such an idea. I felt my face flush with embarrassment.

"I'm sorry... I..."

"That's a tale for another time, my dear," my aunt said, winking mischieviously and standing up. "I'm afraid I'll have to play the part of Scheherazade and put you off until another time. It's late, and I'd like some sleep. I dare say you could use some as well."

I stood up. "I'll see you in the morning, then?"

"You will," she agreed, then came around the table to embrace me. Her hug was comforting and soothing, not brimming over with crushing enthusiasm as Max's tended to be. "I hope what I've told you helps you feel less confused," she said as she let me go.

"It's given me a lot to think about," I admitted. Her story helped explain the happenings in Penzance, but not Laufeson's abduction attempt. My aunt's excavation of the priest and priestess's tomb seemed to indicate there was some sort of familial Norse connection though I didn't know what to make of that just yet. Laufeson making the connection between me and my aunt's antique Norse jewelry seemed far too unlikely to be possible.

I made my way to the door. "Goodnight," I said, and headed to my hotel room.

Chapter Eighteen

I found an assignment from Dr. Maitland waiting for me on the bed in my hotel room when I returned. After catching a few hours of thankfully dreamless sleep, I woke up in the very early morning to work on what he'd sent. I had much of it done by the time June arrived at eight in the morning, bringing breakfast and a message from my aunt. She had a full day of errands ahead, the brief note said, and I should be ready by nine to accompany her on said errands.

I reported, as ordered, to Aunt Miranda at nine o'clock dressed in a new tan day dress. Aunt Miranda had chosen to forego her usual blue dresses and wore a green ensemble, complete with fascinator and reticule.

"Excellent," she said, stepping out into the hallway to join me. "Aylmer is waiting for us downstairs. Let us away, and toot sweet!"

We spent much of the morning after that visiting various shops. I looked around while Aunt Miranda conducted her business, which ran the gamut from purchasing new gowns for her maids to inquiring about having phosphorite lamps installed at Brentwood Close.

"I do prefer candle and lamp light," she confided, "but I'm not getting any younger. Phosphorite is less likely to set the house ablaze if I stumble in my eventual feebleness and drop a lamp. Candles are not so forgiving, and I'd hate to lose the old place."

We stopped for lunch at a pub, and Aunt Miranda insisted Aylmer join us—which, after a certain amount of disagreement, he did. Our postprandial activities included picking out no fewer than three hats for Mary, since my aunt declared Aylmer's taste in hats to be appalling.

"No woman wants to wear a chapeau that looks like it came from a barnyard or was constructed of obscure cooking utensils," she'd said, astonished by one of Aylmer's first hat choices. It had been a green thing with no fewer than three artificial birds attached at odd angles, with something that looked like a mini-cheese grater gracing the middle of the monstrosity. The sales clerk had called it 'avant garde.'

"Ye Gods. More like 'be on your guard'," my aunt had responded with some asperity, and we'd left the shop.

Luckily, Aylmer appreciated my aunt's assistance, and he beamed as he carried the three awkward hat boxes, knowing Mary would like the hats very much.

Then Aunt Miranda ordered Aylmer to take us to the Dean of Mathematics and Sciences at Cambridge, providing him with the address of the dean's private residence. The cab lurched into motion. She looked at me.

"His name is Dr. Fieldstone, is it not?"

I blanched. "It is, but—"

"I thought so. I'd like to have a word with the fellow, and now's as good a time as any."

"A word?"

"Indeed. Odd German persons attacking my niece in a library? Not on my watch, or I dare say, on his. No, sir."

"But—"

"If he's already aware of Saturday's altercation, all the better. If not, it will be my great pleasure to inform him of the matter."

I swallowed, thinking quickly. I wasn't sure if my aunt's intent to have a word with the head of the department in which I pursued a degree would help or hurt my reputation. Dr. Oberlin's dislike of me was well-known, but I didn't know Dr. Fieldstone very well. I didn't know what he'd make of my formidable aunt.

"It's the middle of the day on a Monday," I offered. "He may not be home." I sort of hoped he wasn't.

"Nonsense," my aunt said, her tone business-like. "He'll be there, and he'll see me without an appointment."

I slumped in the seat as much as my corset would allow and looked out the window at the street and buildings rolling by, feeling nervous and a little doomed.

I felt a hand on my knee. "Trust me, my dear," Aunt Miranda soothed. "I'll do nothing to jeopardize your standing and hard work here, and I'll do nothing to encourage the man to dislike you, though I don't know why on earth he'd not like you."

I nodded, the feeling of doom increasing.

"I want to speak to him for my own piece of mind and to be sure he's aware how little I appreciate my grand niece being accosted." She leaned back. "This is what ancient great aunts do, you know, and far better it come from me than from your mother, I think."

I shuddered a little. That was true enough.

"Everything will be fine. You may wait in the carriage with Aylmer while I speak to the man if you'd like."

"If I may, I think I'd prefer that."

She put up a hand indicating I could please myself. "As you wish."

Aunt Miranda's meeting with Dr. Fieldstone was mercifully brief. When she returned to the carriage, she ordered Aylmer to take us back to the hotel, then turned her considerable attention on me. The cab began to move and sway as Pip headed out under Aylmer's gentle hand.

"You will be assured to know that the good dean has been made aware of what the lout did to you, and he was in complete agreement with me that a punishment was required. In large part due to your Mr. Avery's description of the event and Dr. Maitland speaking very eloquently on your behalf, he barred Augustus Laufeson from all Cambridge libraries for a month."

I couldn't believe it. "A month? Good heavens. There's no way he'll be able to do any work assigned by Dr. Oberlin if he's barred for a month." Such a punishment, while justified, would do nothing to improve my standing with Dr. Oberlin, unfortunately, but there was nothing I could do about that. I resolved to thank Mr. Avery and Dr. Maitland at my first opportunity.

"In addition, the dean ordered the man to give you, all other female students and Towson House a wide berth lest he be kicked out permanently." Aunt Miranda sniffed. "It is hoped this month-long hiatus will encourage the man to betake himself back to Germany permanently."

"I think that would be outstanding," I agreed.

"Now," my aunt said, removing her gloves, "we shall return to our rooms, have dinner in the dining room, and I'll have Aylmer take you back to Towson House so you may sleep in your own bed tonight. I'll have Sanderson deliver the rest of your new clothes to the residence tomorrow. How does that sound?"

"That sounds lovely, Aunt Miranda," I said, "and thank you."

Chapter Nineteen

I made my way to the Icarus Club Tuesday evening, after a two-hour afternoon session with Dr. Maitland.   It had been a long day.   Towson sat a couple miles from Cambridge, so after I'd spent the morning studying, Cora and I'd ridden our bicycles to my usual math class, which I followed with my meeting with Maitland in the same building.   Then, meeting Mellie, I rode with her another two miles out of Cambridge in the direction opposite Towson to get to the Icarus Club.   Mellie kept up her usual banter as we rode.

The smell of spring blossoms hung in the air, and I smiled at the heartening sight of budding trees and new flowers pushing up through the soil.   We passed the familiar fen lands, farms, and recent roadwork set up beside an old cemetery.   We curved around the abandoned wheelbarrows side-by-side, full of cobbles, mislaid shovels, and piles of dirt, with me noting how much progress the workers made on the road since I'd last passed by the site.   By the time we arrived at the Club entrance, it was nearly dusk.

Upstream of Cambridge, the Squadron had lovingly re-purposed an old flour-mill on the Cam to serve as their club.   The exterior walls of the three-story building consisted of rectangular grey stones, which remained exposed on the inside of the building. The Mill's grinding wheel, with the bar counter on top of it, sat in the corner opposite the door, along with much of its hardware as the bar's backdrop. The waterwheel still spun merrily on the side of the mill as the Cam River flowed by though the wheel's power fulfilled a different purpose other than turning wheat into flour. Now, it kept the Club warm in winter and cool in summer.

Everyone in the Squadron contributed time, materials, or money to the endeavor, since we all used the building as a gathering place. Max had headed up the renovation scheme due to his experience as a mason and a carpenter while apprenticed to his father. He and a handful of volunteers had removed the intervening floors between the basement and ceiling, putting in balconies that jutted out from the stone walls at different levels. He'd constructed them to look like carriages, old-fashioned air balloon gondolas, and the decks of ships of various kinds, leaving the blue wide-planked floor free for dancing on Thursdays and daily acquisition of beverages at the grindstone bar.

A sculpture of the Squadron's emblem - *Icarus bewinged with a sun d'Or sinister in a field azure* – hung from the center of the tall ceiling, capturing Icarus in the midst of his delight at flight, before he went too high and plunged to his death. It spun slowly, allowing Icarus's upturned eyes to scan the entire ceiling of the Club by way of gyroscopes and a gear system of my devising, hidden in the beams and unseen below.

Many small globe lamps provided light in the ample, airy space, and Squadron members and their guests lounged in the balconies at their leisure, stood by the grindstone bar ordering drinks, or took a tour around the room. Comfortably and elegantly ramshackle, it reflected the rough and tumble life many airship crewmembers lived. I loved it.

Once I arrived, I thanked Mellie for the escort. She turned to head back to Towson while I climbed the short staircase of the usual nook the *Bosch* crew inhabited, which was done up like a pirate ship complete with Jolly Roger. A worn wooden table with seven chairs sat in the middle of the space, covered by plans, drawings, and nearly empty glasses of various sizes. I dropped my bookbag in the corner with a satisfying thump and inhaled deeply, taking in the smell of pipe and cigarette smoke, leather, metal, iron and grease, feeling the tension in my shoulders and neck abate. I took a moment to check that my red wavy hair remained coiled firmly to my head. I dusted off my dark green bicycle trousers, linen shirt and jacket. Satisfied that I was presentable, I sat down with my crewmembers, who welcomed me warmly.

It took no time at all to catch up on what my friends had been up to over the course of the previous few days. Griff told me all about more improvements to the Rover, which seemed to include padded seats from a demolished theatre though he'd need a couple more days with it to get it fully operational. He'd left it at the shed. Lizzie regaled me with her adventures replacing the twisted strut on the *Bosch*. Needle, a taciturn fellow whose fingers were always ink-stained, grunted and nodded at the appropriate moments in the stories, while Max laughed. Max then related how he had regaled everyone in the Icarus Squadron with tales of my phenomenal success in Penzance. I tried to avoid saying much on that issue and mostly succeeded by nodding and shrugging. I, in turn, told them about my exploits with my aunt and confirmed that the safety equipment she'd promised to contribute was on its way.

While the others argued about where we should take the *Bosch* next, an attractive blond-haired man sidled up beside me. He stood over six feet tall. Muscular and well built, but not overly so, he wore a grey suit with a white shirt and black tie though he didn't look very comfortable in them. His blue eyes sparkled with intelligence and mischief within a tanned, handsome face.

"Hello," he said to me, his smile bright and warm as he sat down to my right. "I hear tell you're the red-haired young lady who throws darts so well."

I blinked in surprise to find the stranger's accent indicating an American origin. I opened my mouth to answer, but Max intervened in his usual boisterous style.

"Andrew!" he bellowed and reached over to clasp the man's hand in a firm handshake. "I'm so glad you've come."

"As am I," murmured Lizzie, taking in the handsome fellow in a long, interested look. She was a classic English beauty with blonde hair, blue eyes, and cream-colored skin who never lacked interested suitors. Even clad in her work dress, a navy blue garment that was well cut but otherwise unremarkable, she was a vision. I wasn't sure if she had a beau at the moment, but I knew she only teased the newcomer. I stifled a smile and she rolled her eyes at me, mimicking a swoon.

"I'm sorry I'm late," the American said, not noticing Lizzie's theatrics. He inclined his head at me slightly in apology. "It took longer to walk here than I'd thought."

"Ladies and gents," Max said, making an expansive gesture that included all of us, "allow me to introduce Mr. Andrew Michaelson, late of Southern Texas by way of Cambridge, Massachusetts. He comes to us with high marks from the Harvard Aeronauts, and seeks enlightenment from our merry band in addition to a graduate degree in something meaningful," Max faltered, "though for the life of me I can't remember what subject he specializes in."

Andrew laughed... a warm, pleasant sound. "Physics," he said. "If Cambridge allows Americans to study such things." Max introduced us and Andrew shook hands with each person in turn.

"I must say, I've found everyone in the Icarus Squadron to be friendly and helpful in the few days I've been here," the American said. "My American colleagues warned me that you British chaps were standoffish and painfully polite."

"I'd be more than happy to extend an even warmer welcome to you, Mr. Michaelson," Lizzie cooed, a sparkle of mischief in her eyes.

Mr. Michaelson barked a laugh. "Please, y'all, call me Andrew." His smile was brilliant and mischievous as he bowed politely to Lizzie. "I thank you for the offer, ma'am, but I'm afraid I'll have to decline."

"Oh, pooh," Lizzie said, laughing. Clearly, she hadn't taken offense at his refusal.

To my surprise, Andrew turned to me. "Max says you're a Math major who dabbles in other sciences. I hoped you'd be able to give me some insight into the Physics professors before I meet with them tomorrow."

"Those Physics chaps don't know a gem when they see it," Griff growled. "Most of them wouldn't give our Ari here the time of day."

"Don't like smart women," Needle confirmed, nodding agreement with Griff.

Andrew's jaw dropped. "Really?"

"Surely this comes as no great surprise, coming as you do from Harvard," I said, my voice tight. "Women are not admitted to that university, or even allowed to attend classes there."

Andrew dipped his chin, looking at the table's surface, thinking. Then he looked up and met my eyes. "You speak the truth," he admitted, "Harvard doesn't admit women. It's not a policy I agree with. I had hoped, since I know Towson women take Cambridge classes, that attitudes here would be more," he paused, "egalitarian. I'm sorry to find that is not the case."

"As am I," I said. "Though the Physics department may be short-sighted when it comes to women's abilities and education, they are well versed in their subject area. Dr. Oberlin, the head of the department, is an expert in his field, and has many books in his personal library you will find useful."

I knew I would have found them useful, had I been allowed near them. There was a reason why people called Dr. Oberlin 'Obstinate Oberlin' and worse. I believed all of the nasty nicknames people used for the unpleasant fellow were richly deserved. I'd come up with a few of the more colorful ones myself.

"So long as you ignore the books with titles like *Why are Women Redundant?*" Griff added. "I've been to his worship's office for a job or two and seen his books. Hard to like the man, knowing how much he's against gals like our Ari."

Andrew smiled. "You have true friends here, Miss Trevelyan," he said, indicating Griff, who still looked affronted on my behalf. "I will take your counsel, and theirs, to heart." He looked at the glasses on the table.

"It seems to me the table is dry," he said. "May I buy the next round? I'm eager to hear what improvements you've made to your airships. Perhaps my knowledge of the Harvard Aeronauts will come in handy, if you're so inclined."

We were, and Mr. Michaelson headed to the bar to place our order, leaving us to ourselves for a moment.

"Seems a nice fellow," Needle drawled, "for an American."

"Good man with a wrench, the Harvard chaps say," Max added, "and on horseback and with a gun though I suppose that's because he's from Texas. Savage place, I'm told." He clasped his hands on the table. "Showed up at the airfield yesterday with letters of introduction, and I spent several hours chatting the fellow up. Seemed a decent chap, so I invited him here tonight. What do you think? We'll need another hand for the *Bosch*, and he's pleasant enough. Knows his way around an airship, and no mistake."

I put my chin in my hands and pondered Andrew as he stood at the bar talking to Gibson, our barkeep. We planned to add more cabin space to the *Bosch* so it could carry cargo and perhaps a passenger or two, but that meant a proportional increase in balloon, engine and fuel tank size to accommodate the extra weight. We'd all helped with drawing up the plans and determining our needs for this next step, and it was true another crewmember was part of the expansion.

"How certain is it that Cambridge'll have him?" Lizzie asked. "If he's not admitted, I doubt he'll stay here just to be part of the crew. As it is, most of us need jobs outside the *Bosch* to make ends meet."

"True enough. What do you think, Griff? Will Devil Oberlin take the American on?" Max asked.

Griff snorted. "He's not a lass, so he's got a fair chance so long as he keeps his mouth shut about uppity females."

"Don't know that he'll like *that* old bastard," Needle opined, "but he seems fair interested in our Ari here."

"What?" I said, surprised. "You're barmy. He's only just met me, for Heaven's sake."

"Ah, but he already perceives the value of your many charms," Max said with a devious smile. "Mostly because I detailed them to him at length."

It was my turn to roll my eyes. "Oh, Max—you didn't. Please tell me you didn't."

He looked singularly pleased with himself. "I did, and why not? He ate the stuff up! Besides, he seems a nice fellow from a rich American family. I bet your parents would think him a fine catch."

"I have no interest in catching anything until after the Tripos is over," I told him, annoyed. "And after that, I'll be more interested in catching a storefront and some aeronaut hobbyists or professionals than some chap my parents like."

My crewmates laughed at me. "Oh, we know that," Lizzie said, shaking her head as she chuckled, "but it's such fun to watch."

Andrew arrived at that point, a tray full of drinks in his hands. "Here we go," he said, setting the tray on the table. As he passed out the glasses to us, he eyed the plans on the table with obvious interest.

"These the expansion plans you mentioned yesterday, Max?" he asked, sitting down beside me again. Lizzie hid a smirk by taking a drink of her small ale.

"They are," said Griff. "I'd be curious to hear your thoughts on them," he said, waving a hand over the papers.

What followed was a long discussion of airship design, punctuated by the scribbling of bits of machinery and equations on the corners of the plans, general opinions as to the best shape for air balloons and propellers, and a great deal of friendly arguing and laughing. Max was right: Andrew did know airship design, and he impressed all of us with his breadth and depth of knowledge on the subject. Before we knew it, two hours had passed.

"I have to go," I said, standing up. "It's a long bike ride home, and I've some studying to do before I sleep. Must get in before Gildersleeve checks beds for curfew."

Andrew looked up at me, alarmed. "You're going to ride your bicycle home through Cambridge alone and at night?"

I stiffened. Who did this American think he was? "Well, usually Griff gives me and my bike a lift but the Rover's back at the airfield. So, yes, it seems I will be riding my bike home through Cambridge alone and at night."

"But it's dark," Andrew insisted.

"Ari," Max warned, "what about that Laufeson chap? You're not supposed to go anywhere alone, according to that Miss Allerton and my Millie."

"I know, but what are the chances the fellow would have followed me here? It's been days and he's been ordered to leave me alone."

"Millie said Miss Allerton would string us up if we let you go home alone," Needle stated bluntly, "and I dare say she looks the type to do it."

I moved over to where I'd dropped my bookbag and picked it up, slinging it over my shoulder. "It's not even nine o'clock. I'll be faster on the bike than if I were to walk, and I know what streets to avoid. I should be fine."

"I insist on coming with you," Andrew said, standing up and walking over to me. "I refuse to let you make your way home alone."

Griff, Max, Needle and Lizzie exchanged a meaningful look.

I looked up at the American and struggled to remain polite. One of the reasons I avoided romantic entanglements was because the gentlemen involved became proprietary, thinking they had the right to tell me what to do. "I do not need a protector," I told him, gently but firmly.

"I don't mean to be one," he countered, "since you seem to think you'll make it home without incident. I need to head back to my hotel, and I'd like to ask you some more questions about the Physics department." He shrugged and put his hands in his coat pockets. "As a rebel colonial, it may be that I'll need *your* protection." He smiled. "What do you say?"

Part of me found the idea of a long walk alone with Andrew to be a very good idea indeed, but the more practical part squashed the notion, helped by my annoyance with his unnecessary masculine protective instincts. "It would be inappropriate for me to walk home with a gentleman alone," I said, "even if you need a bodyguard."

"Quite right, my good man," Max interjected. "A lady of her standing has her reputation to think of. She's pushing her luck hanging out with us as it is, barbarians that we are."

Andrew turned to look at Max, clearly not understanding what he meant. "What's her standing, then? Mathematics student?"

Griff rolled his eyes. "She's the daughter of Lord Aiden Trevelyan, Duke of Albemarle, you prawn," he said. He looked at Needle. "Colonists," he said disparagingly, and Needle nodded sage agreement.

"That means she has a title?" Andrew asked, frowning. "Since we don't have such things back home, I don't even know what the proper form of address for a duke's daughter would be. I'm sorry – I hope I haven't caused offense."

"If we were being formal, and if Ari allowed it, you would call her 'Lady Ariana'," Max told him. "Since she does not allow such a thing among her aeronaut friends, you'll just have to make due with calling her 'Miss Trevelyan' or 'Ari.'"

"Only our barman Gibson calls her 'Lady Ariana' here. Drives Ari up a tree, but he'll not stop," Griff added.

"I see," Andrew said, thinking. "So, your social standing will not allow you to walk home with a man, but riding alone across Cambridge unattended is acceptable?"

"No," Max said, a grin spreading across his face, "but she's stubborn. Half the time one of us follows her home in the Rover, but we don't tell her."

I opened my mouth in shock. "You do not!" I insisted. "Follow me home in the Rover? Not bloody likely!"

Max tisked. "Language, your ladyship," he teased, then looked at Lizzie. "Do you think...?" he began.

Lizzie hopped up and smoothed her skirt as she came to stand beside me. She hooked her arm in mine. "I'll go along to protect your honor, Ari," she said with a wicked grin, "So long as the colonial agrees, that is."

I shot Lizzie a dark look, but she shrugged and nudged me with her shoulder.

"Two protectors, then?" Andrew said with a smile. "How could I possibly refuse?"

"As you wish," I responded, and tugged the strap of my bookbag further up on my shoulder, doing my best to salvage a little dignity from the situation. "I'll walk with you so I can keep you both from harm."

"Might as well leave your bicycle here," Max suggested. "If you're walking back to Towson, no need to drag it along. Griff can bring it by and put it in the shed tomorrow morning."

That seemed reasonable.   "All right," I said.

"Excellent," Andrew said.   "Once we get to your residence, I can hire a cab to take me to my hotel." He indicated the door. "Shall we?"

Chapter Twenty

There was about a mile of countryside between the Icarus Club and the outskirts of Cambridge. Andrew took my bookbag despite my protests, and we began our trek back into town, Lizzie on one side, Andrew in the middle and I on the other. It was a cloudless and, therefore, chilly evening, but the light of the stars and a waning moon provided some illumination on the road. Lizzie, as always, was a dazzling conversationalist, and she kept up a lively dialogue with Andrew as we walked, asking about his home in Texas and America in general. I found I didn't really want to talk much and was content to listen as Andrew answered Lizzie's questions.

"My parents own a great deal of land in Texas," he told her, "and earned much of the family fortune raising livestock initially, and now, drilling for crude oil. I wanted more than that kind of life. My parents agreed to pay for my education at Harvard, and now at Cambridge... if they'll have me, anyway. My younger brother is keen to follow in my parents' footsteps. He'll take the farm, the drills, and the land, and I'll find my way somewhere else, I hope."

"Really? Your parents don't expect you to take over the business?" Lizzie asked, surprised.

"No, ma'am. I suppose you think it odd, but I'm not cut out for that kind of life, and my parents know it. So long as I'm happy and can make my own way, they don't mind. Jeffrey is far better at managing the place than I am." He chuckled. "My mind is always on flying, or the moon, or airship design. Never liked cattle much, and I'm only interested in crude oil if it can be used to power an airship."

"Sounds like me and the shop," Lizzie remarked. "Pays me enough so I can live, but my heart isn't in it. It'll be grand when the *Bosch* can go independent and I can fly to earn a living."

"I know how you feel," Andrew said. "I feel closer to home, somehow when I'm on an airship." He turned his attention to me. "Is that what it's like for you, Miss Trevelyan?" he asked.

I shrugged. "In many ways, yes," I said, marveling at Andrew's loquaciousness. I didn't like to talk about my family very much. He seemed quite willing – and even eager – to share what he could about himself with us.

Not wishing to say anything else, I turned my attention to the road ahead of us and saw the road construction site I'd passed on my way to the club. The tools, wheelbarrows, and cobbles sat where they'd been earlier, coated in shadow. I peered into the darkness, squinting my eyes in a poor attempt to see better. The group of men resolved into four tall male students I didn't know led by a short, stocky man I knew only too well. He walked like a toad, swaying back and forth and using his arms to help him keep his balance. The students, oddly, wore tinted glasses even though it was dark.

"It's Dr. Oberlin," I said, hardly believing my eyes. "What in the world is he doing out here at this time of night?"

"Lizards usually hide under rocks at night, don't they?" Lizzie muttered. "Maybe he's tired of eating ants and other loathsome creatures and decided to take a bit of air?"

"He's got a wild look to him," Andrew remarked. "Look how his clothes are rumpled and he's got a fevered glaze in his eyes. It's like he's been 'ridden hard and put away wet', as we say back home."

Andrew was right. As they got closer, I could see Dr. Oberlin's shirttails hung limply outside his trousers and only one suspender did the job of keeping his pants up. He usually wore his hair in a horrid comb over in a failed attempt to hide his wide bald pate, but the long hairs usually covering the vast expanse now hung long and loose on the left hand side of his head, making the man look oddly lopsided. His bespectacled companions looked equally disarrayed.

"They all look a bit off the mark," Lizzie noted. "Are they drunk?"

"They're certainly unsteady on their feet," I pointed out. "Oberlin is known for taking a glass of ale with a few students every once and a while... but not to this extent. I can't fathom what's going on."

"There she is," came Dr. Oberlin's squeaky tenor voice, slightly slurred with drink, "that's the Towson girl!" He pointed at me with a stubby arm that ended in sausage digits. "She led Augustus on with those green eyes and a promise of a good time, and then turned nasty when Avery showed up. Augustus got barred from the Faraday because of her!"

I ground my teeth in annoyance. So that was the story Laufeson had been telling, was it? The whole thing was my fault? Of course Oberlin would believe the blasted German.

"That's a bloody lie!" Lizzie yelled before I could stop her. "He attacked her!"

"So much for a quiet walk back to town," Andrew muttered.

"I say we teach the trollop a lesson," one of the male students cried. I didn't recognize him or any of the others, but it hardly mattered. Clearly they knew me.

The other students grunted their agreement with the plan as Oberlin shook his fist in the air. "We'll show you what the proper place for a woman is!"

I looked at Andrew and Lizzie. "Run for help," I told them. I now regretted my decision to leave my bicycle at the Icarus Squadron headquarters. It would have helped me make a quick getaway, assuming Oberlin and his students only wanted to cudgel me and would, therefore, leave my companions alone. "I'll try to draw them off the road. Maybe if I hide in the cemetery, I can lose them."

"Not bloody likely," Lizzie remarked. "What if you can't outrun the blighters? No dearie - I'm staying with you."

"As am I," Andrew agreed. He took a quick look around and pointed at the road construction near the cemetery. "Let's head over there-we can use the cobbles and shovels to keep them at bay. Maybe we can convince them they have better ways to spend their time than roughing folks up on the road."

We ran back down the way we'd come fifty feet to the wheelbarrows full of cobbles. Three shovels lay on the ground next to them. Oberlin and the students ran after us, somewhat unsteady in their gait, but drew up short when they saw us pick up the shovels.

"That's no fair," Oberlin said and pointed an accusing finger at me. "She deserves a good drumming for what she did to Augustus. Step aside and let us administer a proper penalty."

"Is this really the proper behavior for a professor of your standing, Dr. Oberlin?" Andrew shouted back. He groped within his shirt and pulled out something on a chain. Then he held the shovel in one hand while he clutched at the pendant on the chain around his neck. "Surely you don't want to tarnish your reputation with an accusation of assault on a woman?"

"Shut up, you!" He replied in a growl as he pushed up his sleeves and started to stalk toward us, the students in a line behind him mimicking his actions.

Andrew looked up at the moon and whispered something I couldn't quite catch. To my amazement, the moonlight seemed to coalesce around him in a dim grey-white aura that disappeared almost as quickly as I noticed it.

What the Hell? I thought but didn't have time to wonder about it much more than that as Oberlin and the others continued their approach. Andrew dropped the pendant and gripped the shovel in both hands. Lizzie and I did the same.

"Give it up Oberlin," Andrew said, swinging the shovel in a wide arc across the front of his body. "Someone else is controlling your thoughts and actions. Fight that influence! We don't want to hurt you!" Oberlin growled like an animal and continued to walk toward us, fists clenching and unclenching in fury.

I was less certain about not wanting to hurt Oberlin, if only because the old fiend had done everything in his power to get in the way of my studies. It was hard to resist the urge to get a bit of my own back. Wisdom prevailed, however, since he was very clearly not himself. As much as I disliked him, it wasn't right to hurt him if he was a victim. *Who*, I wondered, *controlls Oberlin and the others, and how do Andrew know that is the case?* The answer came to me in an instant.

"Laufeson mesmerized them," I said, my voice low.

"So it would seem," Andrew ground out.

I shook my head in wonder. "Damn and blast! Who is the damnable fiend and what does he want from me?"

Andrew swung the shovel across his body again. "Laufeson is a powerful manipulator. He wants you in his control very badly if he's resorted to this. I just hope we can get out of this mess without having to hurt anyone."

"Or get hurt ourselves," Lizzie remarked grimly. "Mesmerized or not, these blokes are serious."

The three of us turned our backs inward to stand in a triangle, shovels at the ready. The wild eyed group ran at us, ready to fight, faces grim with violent intent. They leapt on us and our struggles began in earnest. There was a confusion of fists, shovels, and limbs. Grunts of pain and the blows of fists and shovel blades hitting flesh sounded around us. Spectacles went flying, the eyes behind them wild with fury and sporting what I could only describe as a weird silver sheen to them, like someone had painted the exposed eyes with a thin layer of silver paint. I'd never seen anything like it.

I used my shovel to block the hits I could see coming at my head or at Andrew and Lizzie, but I felt fists strike my body in various places, knocking the wind out of me. I struggled against the onslaught, but eventually resorted to swinging at whatever fist came in range. I heard grunts of pain and thuds of impact as my companions did their best to keep from being injured.

A fist connected with my head and I fell to the ground, dazed. I dropped the shovel as I fell to my hands and knees, my head spinning. Someone tall grabbed the back of my shirt and jacket and hauled me to my feet only to wrap an arm around my throat and choke off any cry I might have made. I struggled to free myself. The ruffian strengthened his grip on my throat so I saw stars and couldn't draw a breath.

Andrew shouted words I didn't recognize and suddenly another mind—ancient, masculine and grimly resolved—gently eased my mind aside and I became a passenger within my own body very much like when I threw darts. It wasn't frightening, oddly. Somehow whatever was within me was a familiar and comforting presence, though I didn't have a lot of time to think on the matter too much... the world around me browned out as the arm continued to squeeze my throat.

My right elbow drew forward and back with great force, striking my assailant in the abdomen hard enough to knock the wind out of him. He yelped and let go of my neck as he doubled over in pain. My body then stepped forward, turned, and as my hands grabbed the student's hair, my knee came up to strike the fellow hard in the face. I heard the crunch of bone as his nose broke. He collapsed, the fight knocked out of him.

My body turned to look over the rest of the combatants. Lizzie still had her shovel, but it was clear she was tiring quickly as she kept two of the students at bay. Andrew fought the other two men, one of them the odious Oberlin. My body moved quickly to one of the wheelbarrows. My hands thrust down into the cobbles and I felt my mouth and throat working as I spoke though I couldn't hear what I said. My hands came out of the cobbles and spread wide. To my great surprise stones rose to float in mid-air between my hands as blue symbols I didn't know traced across the stones' surface.

Another few words growled from deep in my throat and the blue symbol-covered cobbles flew toward the remaining assailants with great speed, knocking them unconscious with such precision it was as if the cobbles had minds of their own. It was the most extraordinary thing I'd ever seen. Once the stones struck, I felt all of the energy drain from my body, as if the blue symbols had used my vitality to fuel their attack. I sagged and nearly dropped to my knees as the presence that had summoned the power drifted away, leaving me in control of my own body once again. Unfortunately, though I commanded the movement of my limbs, I didn't seem able to do much more than pant for air and stay upright.

Struck by the cobbles, Oberlin and the three students dropped to the ground like sacks of grain as Lizzie and Andrew looked at me in astonishment. Andrew got an alarmed look on his face as he pointed behind me.

"Look out!" He cried as he tried to step over Oberlin to get to me.

A hand grabbed my right shoulder and spun me around so I faced the student whose nose I'd broken. My consciousness swam with exhaustion as I stared at him, blood streaming down the lower half of his face and onto his shirt, his eyes silvered and narrowed. He held a cobblestone in his right hand and brought it down on my forehead despite my attempt to stop the blow. There was an explosion of pain and I felt something crack inside. The ground flew up to meet my limp form as darkness and pain consumed me.

Chapter Twenty-One

    I awoke, gasping for breath and shivering. My brain throbbed painfully, and it felt like my skull was too small to contain it. I'd never had such an awful headache in my life.

    It took a panicked and confused moment lying in the dark for me to realize I was in my own bed in my room at Towson. The smell of white cotton sheets and a wool blanket surrounded me, and the sheets felt familiar and smooth on my skin. I had no memory of making it home, or undressing to go to bed, yet I was in my cotton nightgown and my hair was braided down the back of my neck. I brought a hand up to my head and felt gauze and padding wrapped across my forehead and around my skull.

    I didn't remember having any wounds dressed. In fact, at that moment I didn't remember receiving any wounds. I gripped my bedsheets, stared at the dark grey ceiling and forced my racing heart to slow. My mind tore back and forth over my recollections of what happened on my way home from the Icarus Club with Lizzie and Andrew.

The memories washed over me in a horrid rush. We'd encountered Oberlin and other men on the road home. Then we'd been... attacked?!?

I sat up, desperate to find out what had happened to Lizzie and Andrew. I tore the sheet and blanket off my body, then swung my feet over the side of the bed in a rush. The room whirled at a fantastic speed around me, and I fell back onto my pillow, nauseated and dizzy. My skin bloomed with sweat.

"Easy there, Ari," a soft voice soothed from the desk chair to the right of my bed. "You're all right."

I swallowed, tasting bile, and closed my eyes, hoping that would make the room stop spinning. "Lizzie?" I croaked. "Is that you?"

"Yes," Lizzie confirmed, and I felt her put my legs back up on the bed and then sit down beside me.

I opened my eyes and tried to get up again, and again flopped back on the bed, dizzy. Why did the room refuse to stop spinning?

I forced myself to speak. "Are you all right?" I asked. My eyes couldn't focus on her, but I had a basic idea of where she was. She still wore the blue dress she'd had on at the Club, which meant I'd not been unconscious for all that long. "What time is it? How is Andrew? Those men—"

Lizzie shushed me and placed a hand on my arm. "We're fine, Ari. It's about five in the morning. The only one hurt was you. Andrew has your books, and I'm sure he'll bring them by later today or tomorrow. You'll not be fit to go anywhere for a bit, I'm afraid."

"They attacked us—"

Lizzie sucked in her breath, then made a low whistle. "You did get your brains addled. What attackers are you talking about?"

I looked at her, able to focus better now. Her face was in shadow and hard to see in the darkness of the bedroom. "The students and Oberlin on the road. We went to the wheelbarrows, grabbed the shovels—"

"Those men were workmen heading home from a night at the pub. They didn't attack us."

I brought my hands up to clutch my aching head. I distinctly remembered a group of men. Andrew and Lizzie had reacted as if we'd been under attack. I also remembered a group of drunken workmen singing songs in inebriated camraderie as they swayed past us, but that memory seemed to be overlapping the previous one.

That wasn't right, I thought. *The men weren't drunk. They weren't workmen. What in blazes is going on?* The memory of drunkards floated in to cover the thought. I viciously shoved it aside and forged ahead with what I knew was the truth, *blast it.* My head started to throb faster, but I grit my teeth. *Ill be damned if I let pain get in the way of knowing what really happened,* I thought stubbornly.

I closed my eyes and concentrated. I remembered hearing and saying snatches of a language I didn't understand. Images of cobblestones covered with glowing symbols flying out of a wheelbarrow swam through my thoughts.

Suddenly, my head felt as if it split in two. My stomach lurched, and I swallowed heavily and decisively. Vomiting would not help my throbbing head or my apparently weakened constitution.

"Well then," I croaked, deciding discretion was the better part of not throwing up, "why don't you tell me what you think happened, if I don't have the right of it."

"You need to rest," Lizzie protested. "I can tell you—"

"Now," I interrupted. "Tell me what happened *now*."

Lizzie sighed. "Stubborn as always," she muttered. "You're right that we did encounter a group of men, and as a precaution we went over to where the wheelbarrows were. The men passed us, and we went to go around the wheelbarrows, but in the darkness you missed your footing. You fell against a wheelbarrow and hit your head so hard it knocked you out."

I felt the bandage again. "I hit my... head?" I had only a dim recollection of that, but, just like everything else I recalled, it didn't match my memory. I seemed to recall... yes... someone had hit me with a cobblestone. "That's not what I—"

Lizzie nodded and adjusted her placement on the bed, patting my shoulder to calm me down. "Scared us, you did, and no mistake. There was blood everywhere, and we couldn't revive you. Andrew stayed with you to do what he could to stop the bleeding. I hiked up my skirts and ran like the Devil himself was after me into Cambridge until I found a cabbie with a free carriage. I directed the cabbie back to where you and Andrew were, and we brought you back here. Mrs. Gildersleeve sent Andrew on his way despite his protests, and I ran for Dr. Sanburne. He examined you, bandaged you up, called it a severe concussion and posted me on watch until dawn, when Millie takes over."

Millie was the upstairs maid, Max's girlfriend, and also a friend of mine. She started her duties at sunrise. I wondered idly where Sophie was.

"Mrs. Gildersleeve gave Andrew quite a tongue lashing, you know," Lizzie said.

I grimaced. Mrs. Gildersleeve had a low opinion of my extra-curricular activities though she wasn't certain what they were. She knew I helped aeronauts with navigational devices, and perhaps suspected I traveled in an airship occasionally, but she had no firm evidence. I took great care that she never found any, since I didn't want her telling my parents. Luckily, my parents were not the sort who required constant updates of my activities while at school. Regardless, bashing my head on my way home would only confirm Guildersleeve's belief that the Icarus Club was no place for 'proper young ladies'.

"What happened to Oberlin?" I asked.

Lizzie stilled for a moment. "Oberlin? That horrible professor?" she asked. "I've no idea. Should something have happened to him?"

I felt my heartbeat in my temples but forged ahead. "He was one of the men who came at us."

"I..." she began, "I... don't recall that," she said, but she didn't sound very certain.

"But—"

"Ari, the men we saw on the road were drunk. They didn't mean us any harm. They went on their merry way and you fell and hit your head. It's as simple as that."

Lizzie's version was a reasonable if somewhat embarrassing story of how I'd ended up with a throbbing brain pan, a protesting stomach, and a spinning bedroom. I could see the events unfolding in my mind as Lizzie described them, at least until I blacked out... but I knew without question no matter how reasonable her tale seemed, it was not the truth. We'd used shovels to defend ourselves. I knew I'd spoken odd foreign words and watched blue symbols flow across the cobbles –

My skull exploded in pain again, and this time I couldn't prevent the loss of my stomach contents. Lizzie was ready for it and held the basin while I retched up bile. She took a cloth from my nightstand to wipe my mouth when I finished and handed me a glass of water. She even held my head to help me take a sip.

"You need to rest, but not for long stretches," Lizzie told me as she laid my head back on my pillow. "I'm supposed to let you sleep for a couple hours, and then wake you up. If you don't wake up, we're supposed to call the doctor back. The nausea and pain are all part of the concussion."

"Wonderful," I whispered. "How long did Dr. Sanburne say I'll feel like this?"

"You're on bedrest for two days at least, and no doing mathematics or anything mentally strenuous until the doctor determines you're better."

"Not bloody likely," I said. "I have the Tripos coming up. I can't spend time lolligagging."

"You need to rest," she said. "Recovery from this sort of wound isn't lolligagging, and I dare say you'll be too tired and confused to make any sense of your mathematics until you're better. Now be still and let your body heal."

A wave of dizziness rolled over me. "Did someone tell my parents I'm—"

"Yes—Mrs. Gildersleeve telephoned them after the doctor left. Now hush," Lizzie ordered.

I slipped into sleep. I dreamt of an ancient, one-eyed wanderer making his way through a frost covered field with the worried waning Moon following behind him.

Chapter Twenty-Two

I quickly discovered that Dr. Sanburne's prediction as to my overall mental capabilities was sadly accurate. I spent a day sleeping in short spurts, monitored by various members of the Towson house staff or one of my housemates to be sure I didn't sleep too much or too deeply. My housemates, in particular, tried to ply me with everything from mango chutney to beef tea, but I couldn't bring myself to take anything but water. My stomach rejected everything else.

I did have some visitors other than my housemates, of a sort. My mother telephoned the house the afternoon following the encounter in the street to find out how I was and whether I should be shipped home for my recovery. Mrs. Gildersleeve wrapped me in a blanket like a Christmas parcel for my trip downstairs to take the call. After I lied about why I'd been out on a road instead of safely studying in my room, I assured my mother I didn't need or want to come home. I did this with one eye open and one shut to limit the spinning of the sitting room to a slow barrel-roll. Mother reluctantly agreed to let me stay but expressed her intention to come get me unless I was right as rain in a few days. It was a notion that filled me with dread. I loved my mother, but she hadn't understood my desire to get a college education in the first place. I worried if she packed me off home, she'd not let me come back.

Father called a little later, urging me to be more careful and to heal quickly. He sent Aunt Miranda's love, since she was in France somewhere, he said. He knew how much I loved my studies and, therefore, didn't suggest I leave Towson, but he did order me to take it easy until I felt better. He told me he loved me and rang off. Mrs. Gildersleeve trundled me back up to my bedroom, and I resumed my purgatorial bedroom existence.

Andrew brought my books by the house the morning after the incident on the road but wasn't allowed to see me, though he'd asked if he could. Mrs. Gildersleeve told me, with her usual bluntness, she 'didn't like the cut of the young man's jib' and urged me to avoid 'colonial entanglements' with an exaggerated roll of her eyes. Thankfully, her other comments about 'damnable aeronauts' and 'infernal bicycles from Hell' faded from my consciousness as sleep gobbled up my mind once again.

I spent much of the time I was awake and unable to concentrate staring at the four walls of my room which was sparsely, yet comfortably furnished. I eyed my bookcase to the right of my bed, desk and desk chair with longing, wanting something – anything – to take my waking mind off the tedium. At one point, I managed to get myself across the room to my bookcase. I grabbed a copy of Aristotle's *Complete Works* in English translation during a brief moment when I wasn't being watched though the effort made my head swim. I discovered that the words on the page might as well have been in Ancient Greek for all the sense I made of them. It was as if the letters slid off the page into my lap, danced a tarantella, and leapt back on the page in random order. Frustrated, I dropped the tome to the floor with a thump.

My friend the bright-eyed Cora Allington, who, like me, had Tripos exams coming up, dashed into my room at the sound of the thump. She was relieved to find it was Aristotle and not me sprawled on the floor.

Cora picked up the book and tutted at the title. "Aristotle is hardly appropriate for someone in your current frame of mind," she chastized, then sniffed. "He's better in Ancient Greek, anyway."

"I'll have to take your word for it," I said, crossing my arms over my chest. "Never was any good at languages, and the only 'frame of mind' I seem to possess is a broken one."

Cora shook her head and deposited Aristotle on my desk. "Since the professors know you're not able to meet them for lessons, you shouldn't try reading anything until you're better. It isn't like they're assigning you homework while you're ill."

"At this rate, it'll be a month before I can get back to my usual level of comprehension," I moaned.

"My goodness... aren't you the glum one. Would you like to go outside?" Cora asked. She walked to the window on the other side of the bookcase, moved aside the curtain, and peered out. "If we bundle you up and you promise not to wander off, you'd have a chance to enjoy the sun for a bit. We'll sit in the garden. I could look over my Cicero and keep you company."

"Gildersleeve would never allow it," I muttered glumly, twirling the end of my braid in my fingers. "You'd have to spirit me up the chimney or out a window."

"Hmmmm," Cora said, thinking fiercely. "Getting you out the window would require construction of a winch or something else tiresomely mechanical. Do you think if I got a message to your aeronaut friends, they'd be able to fly you out of here?"

I stared at her in amazement. "I know I'm the one with the concussion, but did you really just suggest spiriting me away by way of the *Bosch* right under the nose of Guard-Dog Guilders?"

Cora smiled brightly.   "I know you travel in that infernal flying machine at least once a month, and it's been easy enough to keep Guard Dog in the dark about it all this time. What she doesn't know won't hurt her. Let me see who's around. I bet we of Towson House could keep Gilders busy while we sneak you out the back. We'll keep the *Bosch* idea as the back-up plan."

My mood lifted. If there was anyone who could get me into the garden, it was Cora. She'd employed her tactical mind to keep me guarded against Laufeson following his attack, after all, and I was grateful for her help then and now.

"Cora," I said, "I'd love to get out of this room, and if you could do that—"

"Say no more," she said, moving back to the bed and patting me on the arm. "I'll find some co-conspirators. Sit tight. We'll have you sitting in the sun in no time."

****

The next thing I knew, I'd been placed in a wheeled laundry bin, covered with sheets and towels, bumped down a staircase and propelled into the garden. Cora retrieved me from the laundry and helped me into one of two wrought iron chairs beside a small matching table in a sunny corner.   It was a location conveniently hidden from Towson House windows and Mrs. Gildersleeve, surrounded by three elder trees and a weeping willow, all of them only starting to leaf out, their foliage peeping forth with tender, yellow-green shoots. Birds chirped in the trees. Daffodils, tulips, and hyacinths turned their blooms up at us from their beds under the trees, and the scent of the hyacinths filled the air. The grass at my feet was bright new-green, and everything about the spot Cora had chosen was pleasant and tranquil. She tutted at my still being in my nightgown and, therefore, made sure she wrapped me up in my wool blanket appropriately so none of the nightgown showed. She patted me on the head as if I were a cocker spaniel, took the seat beside me and promptly immersed herself in her Cicero text.

I took in the fresh air, revelled in the sunlight, and rejoiced to be out of bed in a muddled, fuzzy-brained way. Even though I had been carried to the place I now occupied, I was still immensely tired, mostly because I still couldn't keep anything but water down. I watched a raven circle overhead, enjoing the smooth, effortless loops the dark bird made.   It must have seen me watching it because it flew down and took up a perch on one of the branches of the willow tree. It turned its head to look at me, and the two of us took the measure of each other in companionable silence. The raven's black feathers had a blue sheen in the sunlight, and he had a speculative, intelligent look in his eyes. I wondered, idly, what he thought of me, bandaged, brain-addled, weak as a baby and wrapped in a blanket as I was.

The raven must have found me acceptable company. He made a low grumble in his throat and turned his attention to preening himself, the picture of relaxed contentment.

I closed my eyes and tried to sleep, but oddly, sleep wouldn't come. My mind felt clearer in the sun-lit garden than it had since the night I'd been hurt. It must have been the fresh air. With no book to read and nothing particular to do, I again started to ponder what I remembered of the events on the road into Cambridge. I'd been trying to puzzle it out, but I kept losing bits and pieces of my recollections as time passed. That worried me. If I couldn't keep something as simple as a walk home straight in my mind, what hope was there I'd heal well enough to pass the Tripos in June?

My head twinged in pain, and I felt my stomach rumble in warning. I started with logical conclusions, as I'd been doing in fits and spurts since I'd been confined to bed. *Right,* I said to myself, *obviously, some of what Lizzie told me of the events was true, since I certainly feel the pain of the wound and have the symptoms of a concussion.*

I'd also seen the gash on my head. It was an angry red cut about half an inch long above my left eye, stitched with black thread, purpled with bruises around the edges that expanded out to the size of a crysanthemum blossom. The eye below the gash was impressively blackened and bruised though that was fading slowly to a sickly greenish-yellow as time passed. Right now, my eye was purple-blue in the middle and green-ish yellow at the edges.

I refused to believe that my memories differed from Lizzie's due to the delusions of an injured brain. More had happened that night than my being clumsy. As if in response to my thoughts my headache increased, but I ignored it.

I reviewed what I remembered that differed from Lizzie's account. I had seen Oberlin, who'd threatened me, I was sure. Lizzie didn't seem to recall him at all. And, progessing further through the events of that night, I tried to recall what else had happened. What were the strange foreign words Andrew had spoken? I had to know and I was sure they were important.

"Ari, you're looking paler. Is everything all right?"

"Here you are!" exclaimed a male voice behind us. The accent was American, and I recognized Andrew's distinctive baritone. "That Gildersleeve woman is looking for you ladies," he said, walking carefully through two elder trees to join us. He was more casually dressed than when I had last seen him, wearing dark blue trousers, boots, a brown shirt with a matching paisley vest, and a long leather overcoat. "I managed to put her off the scent, at least for a bit."

"Oh? How did you do that?" Cora asked, clearly intrigued. She shot me a worried look Andrew didn't see. Apparently she thought I was not at all well. Since the world continued its slow barrel roll so far as my senses were concerned, perhaps she was right.

"I let her think she chased me off from visiting a certain concussed Mathematics student," Andrew continued.

He's come to visit me? I marvelled. Having something else to occupy my thoughts made my discomfort fade, which was a relief. I was tired to my soul with feeling sick to my stomach.

Then I realized with a shock I still wore only my nightgown and my blue wool blanket, and I felt my cheeks warm as I blushed. I didn't even have my robe on, my hair was down, and my feet were bare. How could I excuse myself from the garden to the house without his seeing my lack of proper clothing? I wasn't even sure I could walk a straight line.

I attempted to divine possible routes out of the embarrassing situation, but my mind just wasn't up to the task. I determined there was nothing I could do and winced. If my mother knew I was out of doors talking with a male who wasn't a relative while in my night clothes, she'd have my head on a stick, or worse. I curled up in a ball and pulled the blanket in closer about me, even covering up my head. Maybe if I made myself as small and as hidden as possible?

Andrew bowed slightly to us. "A pleasure to see you again, Miss Trevelyan," he said with a dashing smile. He turned his attention back to Cora. "I'm afraid I've not made your acquaintance, Miss—"

Cora shut her book, stood up and shook Andrew's hand. "Cora Allerton, at your service," she said, matching his smile with her own. "You must be Ari's American savior, famous for helping to get her home? Very dashing, I must say. Thank you for taking care of her," she looked at me, cowering in my blanket and rolled her eyes, "since we at Towson House would hate to do without her... even with her somewhat... odd habits when we have guests."

Andrew bowed again over their clasped hands before he released the handshake. "Don't discount Lizzie's efforts, Miss Allerton," he said. "She found the cabbie and was instrumental in the success of the rescue."

Cora waved that off.   "Yes, we know, and we thanked Lizzie too, of course. I just don't know your name, sir."

"Oh! I'm sorry. Andrew Michaelson, native of Texas at your service, ma'am," he said. "Very pleased to make your acquaintance." He indicated my crumpled, embarrassed form. "How goes it?" he asked. "Max has made a number of early morning visits to see Millie but hasn't been able to get a satisfying amount information on the patient. Her other *Bosch* friends wanted to come by, but since they work during the day, they asked me to come as their representative. What can you report about Miss Trevelyan I can pass on to the others, Miss Allerton?"

"She is a bit befuddled, somewhat bruised, and not able to hold her breakfast," came Cora's matter-of-fact response.

I couldn't believe what she felt free to tell this fellow I barely knew.

"I am quite capable of speaking for myself, Cora," I said, flustered. I pulled the blanket from my head. "Good heavens. I hardly think the disposition of my breakfast is Mr. Michaelson's concern."

Andrew's smile grew more bright. "Ah, feeling better, I see," he laughed. "And feisty besides! I'm glad."

"Feisty indeed," Cora scoffed. "She had her hands on some Aristotle earlier, contrary to doctor's orders. For her own health, we had to get her out here."

Andrew looked around and nodded his approval of our warm spring weather refuge, taking in the trees, flowers, and the raven. "A nice spot you have here, Miss Allerton. Even yon raven approves your choice. I commend your strategy of hiding in plain sight. Very bold."

Cora made a quick curtsey of acknowledgement of the compliment. "I have sentries posted," she said. "You got through our perimeter precisely because Mrs. Gildersleeve doesn't like you much - "

"Cora—" I said, a low rumble of caution in my voice.

"—and wouldn't let you visit Ari," she continued breezily. She scanned the garden like Caesar sizing up the site of a battle. "Do you mind keeping the invalid company? She's somewhat better, but still very weak, and I don't want her left alone. I've got to do a reconaissance with my auxilliary troops. I'd feel much better if you stayed here while I do so."

I opened my mouth to protest, but Andrew beat me to it.

"I'd be happy to oblige," he said.

Cora smiled, put her book on the table, and left us to check her security measures. I had the distinct feeling she'd be gone for quite some time. *Why is everyone so keen to throw me into the company of this American?*

The Odin Inheritance Victoria L. Scott

Chapter Twenty-Three

"I am not an invalid," I clarified, once we were alone.

The expression on Andrew's face turned serious. "No, I suppose you aren't though you do look the part." He indicated the seat Cora had vacated. "May I join you, Miss Trevelyan?"

I nodded, and he sat down. "I'm sorry you continue to feel unwell," he said. He looked worried. "You're very pale."

"I haven't had an opportunity to thank you for helping me when I had my... accident," I said, finding a brief refuge from my mortification in the mechanics of polite discourse.

He chuckled. "I could hardly have left you there," he pointed out.

"Nevertheless, I am thankful you assisted me." I frowned. "It seems I needed a protector after all."

"You're welcome," he said. "Is there some way I could help you now? A particular food I could bring? Tea perhaps? You need to gain your strength back, particularly with all the blood you lost."

"I quite agree," I said with some asperity, "but my stomach remains unconvinced, and it has the final say in gustatory matters." I sighed, recalling the tedium of my bedroom. "It's only very bad when I try to recall what happened on the road, which is really all I have to occupy my mind."

Andrew sat up very straight in the chair. "What have you been able to recall? The tumble into the wheelbarrow?"

"Hardly." My head twinged. "What I remember is different from what Lizzie remembers, which confounds me. Bits are simply missing. I know what I experienced, and I know what Lizzie told me as if I experienced it, but I know her version isn't the right one. Lizzie seems firmly convinced those men were just workmen, while I remember them as being distinctly different. Those men meant us harm, and I'd known one of them. How can I have two memories of the same event? I've been wracking my brain about it, which invariably leads to nausea and... well, I suppose you can imagine the rest."

Andrew nodded gravely but sat back into the chair, rubbing his forehead. He looked overly concerned about me for someone who was only an acquaintance. "I certainly can," he said. "Two sets of memories would be very confusing indeed." He leaned forward and looked me in the eye. His gaze drew me in.

"Miss Trevelyan, this is very important. You need to let your recollections of that night go until you're feeling better," he said as if he had some sort of claim over the workings of my mind. "Head injuries are tricky."

I shook my head, annoyed that he felt he could tell me what to think, of all things. "I beg your pardon," I said, my tone affronted. "I'll think what I like."

Surprise flitted across his face, followed by a sort of resignation. "Clearly," he said dryly.

"Since I'm not allowed to read anything– " I continued.

"Not allowed to read?" he asked, shocked. "Why? With your Tripos exams coming up, you need to study. That's why I brought your books back."

"Yes. Mrs. Guildersleeve took the doctor's instructions that I do nothing 'mentally strenuous' quite to heart, and she hid my bookbag away somewhere. I've not been able to study." I pulled the edges of the blanket in and tried to get smaller within the wool cocoon. "It wouldn't matter if I did have the books. I try to read, and the letters on the page become word soup. I can't concentrate long enough to read one equation, much less study for the Tripos."

Andrew looked troubled. He reached into his shirt and clasped that pendant, or was it a crucifix? I remembered from when we'd walked back from the Club together. I had a sudden vivid memory of his speaking odd words I hadn't understood. In my mind's eye, I saw cobbles wreathed in blue symbols fly from my hands and strike—

"What was Dr. Oberlin doing with those men?" I asked, and instantly regretted it. My mind exploded with fire and pain. I brought my hands to my head and squeezed, trying to keep my brains in my skull, bringing my head to my knees and gasping.

The next thing I knew I was on the ground in a tangle of blanket and nightgown, Andrew's handsome blue-eyed face swimming before my watering eyes, the world spinning slowly around us. His gold pendant hung from his neck between us though I couldn't make out what it was, I could see it wasn't a crucifix. The neck of his shirt was open, and I saw odd gold tracery running up and around his upper chest. It looked to be a part of him. Confusion and fear gripped my heart. The gold metal curves I saw reminded me of the thin ring of Sophie's artificial arm.

On the ground beside me I also saw the raven, his black beak and head a part of the slowly whirling kaleidescope of spring landscape. Pain was the only sensation that kept me conscious, and I held on to it like a raft in a swirling storm at sea.

Andrew took my right hand in his and gripped it tightly. He closed his eyes for a moment.

"Stop," he whispered, and in an instant, the world righted itself. The pain left me as if Andrew had removed the source of discomfort by pulling it directly out of my mind. *Is that an ability that goes along with the gold tracery on Andrew's chest?* I wondered. I felt my thoughts settle, and in a rush all my memories of the encounter on the road took their proper places. I re-lived what had happened. Oberlin had been there with four very odd men. They'd threatened to hurt me. Lizzie, Andrew and I used shovels to protect ourselves until Andrew said those foreign words and that paternal presence that had overtaken me. I made cobblestones fly through the air as weapons, and then I'd been struck in the head myself. I felt bone break under the blow. Had my skull been cracked? What the bloody Hell had happened to me?

I thought my headache had been prodigious, I heard Andrew say, but his lips didn't move. He inspected me for exterior damage and gently moved a red curl off my forehead. *They warned me. I should have listened. At least the sleep she'll have after this will be the recuperative kind.*

I realized I heard the words inside my mind. My heart sped up in surprise. I felt panic grow, but I squashed it before it overtook me. I was tired of being frightened, blast it, and decided to try an experiment. Two could play at this game. Using my thoughts, I turned my attention to *his* mind. I wanted to know who Andrew was. I wanted to know what had taken me over on the road.

My mind filled with images and snippets of information. I saw the moon, a one-eyed man in grey and had the sense of great age and power. Andrew's fear tinged everything: fear for me, primarily, but also for the world. A picture of a huge tree and a bloody child hanging within its branches crossed my thoughts, fading into a small table covered with a child's tea set. My Bow-Bow sat in one of the chairs, his worn, jaunty smile peeking over the tabletop as toy teacups held in disembodied hands moved back and forth across the table.

My arms and body moved before I could form a thought and I scrabbled to get away from Andrew's touch. In response he picked up his hands and moved back in surprise, and then watched as my frantic backward crawling moved me several feet away from him, leaving the blanket behind. I waved an accusatory finger at the surprised American.

"What in the bloody Hell are you?" I demanded, tucking the bottom of the nightgown around me. "What did you do to me?"

The raven looked at Andrew and squawked in a tone that seemed to be remonstrative.

"I don't know," Andrew said to the raven, and it was clear he thought the bird understood him. He turned his attention to me and put up his hands in a pacifying gesture. "Ari? Are you all right?"

I gripped the grass in an attempt to ground my confusion and remind myself of the real world around me. "I heard your voice in my head," I said, "and you put the true memories of the road back into my mind." I looked at him angrily. "I want to know what you did to me."

"Ah." Andrew rubbed a finger under his nose. "The blow to your head cracked your skull. I... well, I healed the break and did what I could to stop your brain from swelling."

"What power or being possessed me and made me shoot the cobbles Dr. Oberlin and the others?"

Andrew winced. "One that cares for you, and one who has been part of you for many years. I asked for his help."

I narrowed my eyes. "Is Oberlin all right? What about those odd students with him?"

Andrew nodded and put out a hand as if to calm me down. "He's fine, and he doesn't remember anything that happened. As you now are able to recall, he was under the influence of another mind when he and the others attacked us. I took advantage of that and erased his memories of our hitting him with shovels. Those students, as you call them, were anything but."

I took that in, recognizing he spoke the truth, but not able to make much sense of what he said. "How do you know what the inside of my childhood bedroom looks like?" I asked.

The raven's glance at Andrew burned with anger, and it flapped its wings to bring itself closer to me. I shied away from the black bird.

Andrew dropped his hands. "Ah," he said and settled himself on the grass in a kneeling position. "That's going to require a conversation we don't have time to do properly here and now."

"*Try*," I spat at him.

He sighed and rubbed his thighs, obviously choosing what to say next very carefully. "Up to this point you have lived much of your life in a world without stories or..." he paused, "...magic. Now you've been thrust into a conflict between two supernatural forces where stories matter and magic is commonplace. Hugo," he indicated the raven, "and I are here to keep you safe and to help you understand the new reality of which you are a vital and important part."

I glowered at that pretty bit of spoken nonsense. "Pull the other one," I said, my tone even and too calm.

Andrew looked at the raven, confused. "Hugo... I don't... What did she say?"

Something unseen passed between the two, and understanding dawned on Andrew's face. "Oh," he said, "You think I'm playing some kind of joke. 'Pulling your leg,' as it were. Well, I'm not." I glared at him. "...and obviously you don't believe that," he said. "Marvelous."

"You're Enhanced," I said. "That's how you put thoughts into my head. That's how you manipulated my memories and Oberlin's and Lizzie's. Are you trying to become the first Enhanced student at Cambridge? Is there something you want from me?"

Andrew shook his head vigorously, alarmed. "No, Ari – no, I'm not Enhanced... I swear. Think! There's no way a mechanical Enhancement would allow the transmission of thought from one person to another. My abilities aren't mechanical – they're magical."

"Magic? Please. All that talk about Texas and the rest... it was a lie," I said bitterly.

"No," he said, his alarm increasing. "All that *is* true. I want to study Physics at Cambridge. I love to fly in airships. My brother *will* inherit from my parents." He smiled uncertainly. "You see, I've already received my destined inheritance," he said, pointing at the gold on his chest and the lump of gold that hung from the chain around his neck. "I'm a Facti. I'm the Heir of Khonshu, the Ancient Egyptian god of the Moon. That inheritance makes me a member of a group that fights the man who wants you in his power so badly. My connection to Khonshu allows me to speak mind-to-mind with the people I touch, and lets me heal injuries like the one you sustained on the road."

"I've never heard of Facti," I said, "and you really expect me to believe you're somehow connected to an ancient pagan moon god?"

He scratched his head. "It would make things much simpler if you did," he muttered.

I said several very unladylike words in response. Andrew blanched a little.

"Ah," he said. "I'm afraid I don't quite know how to respond to... erm... How did the daughter of a duke learn to swear like that?"

The raven turned his head and gestured at Andrew.

"Cora's on her way back. It would be awkward if she found us like this. Can you– " he picked up the blanket and indicated the chair, "return to your seat?"

I stood up, wobbled, then moved forward carefully. I took the blanket from Andrew, forcing down my anger. Cora couldn't see what had transpired between us. I wrapped the blanket around myself and returned to my wrought iron chair. Andrew turned and walked over to stand beside the table, while Hugo flew over to land on the table beside me. Suddenly I was tired and chilled, no doubt due to the excitement of the previous few minutes and the fact that I hadn't eaten in days.

Andrew looked down at me, worry on his face. He started to button up his shirt to hide the gold coiled in his skin. "I owe you an explanation, I know. But please – you're in danger. It would be best if you left Cambridge. Postpone the Tripos. Let us – let the Facti take you somewhere you can be safe."

"Absolutely not," I said.

His shirt re-buttoned, he dropped his hands. "But—"

"I don't know what you're playing at, Mr. Michaelson," I said, "but I'm not going anywhere with you."

Cora appeared from around the willow tree. "Hello? Everything all right over here?"

"Yes," Andrew said, all politeness. "Troops still in place?"

Cora stopped in front of us. "Yes," she said. "Why Ariana, you still look too pale, but better overall. Your eyes have their old spark back. Mr. Michaelson must have had a healing effect on you."

I eyed him cynically. "Oh, he's had an effect," I said, my tone ironic.

"—and I have a gift for the invalid," Andrew put in quickly and indicated the raven. "This is Hugo. You'll find he's very well-behaved and pleasant to be around."

"Mr. Michaelson," I rumbled.

He kept talking. "I'll have Hugo's things brought by Towson House later today."

Cora clapped her hands together in delight. "A raven as a pet? Guildersleeve will go mad. How marvelous!"

"But—" I protested, and shot Andrew a look. The very public way he'd presented Hugo made it impossible for me to refuse the "gift". He'd just made sure I'd have the raven with me whether I liked it or not.

"With that, ladies, I take my leave," Andrew said, his smile wide, fully aware of what he'd done. "No doubt Miss Trevelyan will wish to rest, and surely you have more studying to do?"

Cora smiled back. "Very glad to have made your acquaintance," she said. "I hope you'll come by and see us again."

With that, Andrew bowed and left.

Cora turned and looked at me and the raven. "He's quite a pleasant fellow," she said, "don't you think? Somehow, your having a raven as a pet suits you perfectly."

Damn and blast, I thought. "That Mr. Michaelson... he's *something*, all right," I said and yawned in spite of myself. "I'd like to go back in, please," I said, standing up and gathering the blanket about me. "I'd like a little broth, and I should rest."

Cora put an arm around my shoulder. "Indeed! Let's not forget about Hugo—I can hardly wait to see Guildersleeve's face!"

Chapter Twenty-Four

Once I was back in Towson House, I tried to puzzle out the odd things Andrew had said along with the strange things I'd seen and experienced. I didn't get very far in my ruminations, however. Once I'd consumed and kept down a cup of beef tea under Sophie's watchful eye, weariness overtook me in short order.

"*Mon Dieu*!" Sophie exclaimed, "you look like you could sleep here in the pantry!" She gripped me firmly by the shoulders and helped me up and out of the kitchen and into my own bed. Once there, my whole body went loose-limbed and any attempt at fighting the slumber failed miserably. I slept the sleep of the dead until an exclamation shocked me awake.

"I have had quite enough of this!" a strident female voice cried.

I awoke with a start, tried to get up and ended up on the floor of my bedroom next to my bed, cocooned in its tumbled sheets and blanket. The bandage on my head unravelled, and I had to pull it aside so I could see. I looked up to find Mrs. Gildersleeve glaring down at me, shirt-sleeves rolled up, apron soiled with something food-like but otherwise unrecognizable, and greying hair askew around her face. She was a frightening vision of Celtic vengeance on the best of days, but she was more than usually Boudicca-like at that moment.

"Sorry?" I said, pushing myself up to a seated position, extracating myself from the bedclothes. I pulled the bandage completely off and dropped it on the floor.

"You've been asleep for hours and hours," Mrs. Gildersleeve grumbled, "nearly slept the clock round, you have – and your infernal raven won't stay out of the house!"

I took that statement in, rolling it around in my thoughts. Considering how much better I felt, and—miracle of miracles—I was actually hungry, I supposed the sleep had been sorely needed. As to my raven being in the house...

"Raven?" I asked.

Just then Hugo walked out from behind Mrs. Gildersleeve's skirts and presented himself to me, nodding his head slightly in greeting. His eyes glittered with intelligence and Mrs. Gildersleeve's distress didn't bother him in the slightest.

"Ah," I said, now remembering what Andrew had done and cursing his existence to an infernal Texan Hell, "my raven."

"Yes, your raven!" Mrs. Gildersleeve thundered. "I put him out of the house, and five minutes later he's back in your bedroom. I've no idea how he does it, but I'll put you out, I will, if you don't control the blasted bird!" She waved a fist at it. "By God, if I thought he was edible he'd have been in a stewpot long before now!"

I looked at the raven, who seemed calm, non-threatening and almost gentlemanly. I certainly had to admire the bird's tenacity to stay by my side. I pondered my situation for a moment.

I still wanted answers and I simply refused to take 'magic' as the solution to attempted kidnapping and random road brawls. The damnable American claimed he wasn't Enhanced, stating it was his role to protect me from Laufeson or whoever Laufeson answered to. He'd also engaged in some sort of discourse with the bird currently under animated discussion with the fist-waving Guildersleeve. Therefore, considering all I'd been through over the past few days, it seemed wise to keep the bird nearby in case it could provide some insight into my experiences or Andrew. I felt the 'Goblin of the Perverse' take hold of me, and I determined to make sure 'my raven' got to stay in the house.

I looked back up at Mrs. Gildersleeve. "What, exactly, has the raven done to make you so angry? Did he snatch something off the table at dinner?" I asked.

"No," Mrs. Gildersleeve admitted.

"Has he poked a hole in a wall or ripped any of the furniture?"

"No," came the grudging response.

"Has he left droppings about the house?" I asked. "If he's been here for a day, surely he'd leave droppings behind somewhere." I scanned my bedroom quickly. "I don't see any in here."

At that Hugo looked insulted and fluffed his feathers in a gesture I took to mean annoyance.

Mrs. Gildersleeve stopped and thought for a moment. "No..." she said uncertainly. "I've not found any droppings."

"Has he bitten anyone? Has he bitten you? Does he sqwawk or caw too loudly or at inappropriate moments?"

"No he hasn't," she faltered, "...I mean doesn't... but that's not the point—"

I pulled myself up to sit on my bed, and the raven walked over to stand by my feet, looking up at Mrs. Gildersleeve. "Do the other girls object to his presence in the house?" I inquired.

"They don't," she rumbled. "They think he's adorable and want to adopt him as the house mascot for the love of all the saints. He isn't a puppy."

"I see. But you object."

Her Boudicca aspect returned. "I do indeed. It isn't natural to have such an animal in the house. Ravens are death birds, they are. Bad omens and all that. And they're dirty, too! In fact, I found the bloody thing in my kitchen this morning eating a mouse, of all things! Disgusting it was!"

I smiled. Mrs. Gildersleeve had just hoisted herself by her own petard. "Hmmmm. Didn't you say last week that mice had gotten into the flour cupboard and pantry and that the 'wee beasties' had foiled both the cat's and your efforts at eradication?"

Boudicca deflated a bit. She hadn't thought about that. "Well... yes.. but—"

"So you want the raven gone."

Boudicca returned. "Yes I do!" she demanded.

"Even though he is obviously an excellent mouser?" I continued doggedly.

Mrs. Gildersleeve threw up her hands. "He's a raven. You can't keep a raven in the house."

I sighed, looking down at the two-foot long black bird, tranquil and patient at my feet. "He is quiet and respectful, has bitten no one, damaged nothing, left droppings nowhere, earned the love and respect of all the house residents except for you, and has the potential to keep the entire house mouse-free... but he can't stay?" I scratched the back of my head. "Why, then, are we keeping Budgie the cat? He's got a worse record than the raven does on all those points."

"Now, don't you be smart with me, Ariana Trevelyan! Birds are dirty," Mrs. Gildersleeve stated definitively. That was the only objection I hadn't countered.

I shrugged. "So we bathe him," I said.

Mrs. Gildersleeve's face lit up in alarm. "Bathe the monster? You can't bathe a raven!"

"Why not? People frequently put birdbaths in their gardens, so I'm sure the raven is at least familiar with the idea." I reached down with my right hand. "Care to take a ride on my shoulder to the bathroom, Hugo?"

"You've given the thing a name? Good heavens!" Mrs. Gildersleeve cried.

Hugo eyed me for a moment, then stepped calmly into my outstretched palm. I lifted Hugo up off the floor gently, stood up myself, and placed him on my shoulder. I figured he weighed about three pounds, and although he had to grip my shoulder with some effort to stay on his perch, it wasn't painful to have him there. I regarded Mrs. Gildersleeve.

"If I can guarantee that Hugo will continue his excellent streak of behavior while in the house, and I make sure that he bathes regularly, will you allow him to stay? Ravens are known for being extremely intelligent," I said, though I had no real idea if that were true or not. "Seems to me he'll be a valuable asset to your mouse removal efforts." Hugo trilled in agreement.

Mrs. Gildersleeve's mouth opened and shut a few times in complete astonishment. When she'd recovered herself, she narrowed her eyes. She'd realized I'd outsmarted her, but couldn't come up with an effective counter argument.

"Fine!" she spluttered, "If you can bathe that bird and he doesn't put up a fuss, then... well... all right. But if he puts a talon out of line, he's got to go. No arguments!"

"Agreed. I dare say, once he's an approved resident of the house, you'll not have to waste time putting him outside or chasing him about. That will certainly make your life easier, will it not?"

Mrs. Gildersleeve balled her fists. "There are days when I hate this job," she muttered and stormed out of the room.

I looked at Hugo. "Did you understand all that?" Hugo nodded and fluffed himself a bit.

"Yes," I said, "She has that effect on me, too." I chewed my lower lip in thought. "Mother will be even less welcoming," I said. "We'll have to come up with a plan if this is to be a permanent arrangement." Hugo sqwawked quietly.

"Time for a bath," I said, and we headed off to commence our respective ablutions.

Chapter Twenty-Five

Bathed, dressed, and ravenous, I made my way downstairs to see what the rest of the house was up to. I still felt a bit off kilter, but I managed to negotiate the hallway without much trouble, led by the scent of breakfast. The sticking plaster over the cut on my forehead hid the stitches, but the cut itself seemed to be healing well. My left eye and forehead were still blazoned in a riot of purples, blues, greens and yellows, but there wasn't much I could do about it. I'd braided and pinned up my unruly mop of red curls successfully, for the most part. My brown skirt and linen shirt felt a little loose on my body since I'd gone a couple days without eating, but I hoped to make up for the deficit as soon as possible.

Hugo, also freshly bathed, hopped along beside me on the floor, easily avoiding the other house residents, items of furniture and even Budgie the cat, who hissed at our approach, then hid under the couch in the sitting room. Hugo and I turned from there to enter the dining room, the biggest room in the house. It was the site of all our meals and the center of studying late into the evening. It had ivory-colored walls, three different entrances, with one of those for the kitchen, and three windows on one wall that looked out into part of the garden. The massive dining room table in the room boasted seating for twenty people, with enough space in the room left over for two sideboards on the wall opposite the windows. For breakfast we served ourselves, and the sideboards brimmed with plates full of eggs, various meats, kippers, toast, tea, coffee, and juices. The smell was heavenly.

My fellow Towson students, twelve present and accounted for at breakfast, cheered my arrival in the dining room. There was a flurry of conversation about my injury, how well it was healing, the Maths Tripos, Guilders and Hugo, and the handsome American who'd come to call repeatedly. That last bit of news was imparted with fluttering eyelashes and inquiring looks, which I did my best to ignore. I loaded up my plate with everything except kippers, snagged a cup of coffee and made my way to the table. I sat down next to Cora. Melisande, having finished her breakfast and now nursing a second cup of tea, read out the important news stories of the day from the *London Times*, though she usually started with the Society page and worked her way forward from there to the front page with its national and international news. She regaled her listeners with the most recent exploits of one of the princesses of the realm in the midst of the din of plates, silverware, and various separate conversations.

I managed to answer the many queries that came my way between bites of a prodigious breakfast. I savored every morsel and closed my eyes in bliss at the bitter, lovely taste of the coffee on my tongue. Hugo stood on the floor between Cora and me, looking up hopefully for dropped food.

Cora frowned. "Here, Hugo," she cooed, taking it upon herself to see that Hugo ate by slipping him morsels of food under the table. Apparently, she had been the one who'd taken care of him while I was asleep.

"I've got a perch, a cage and a few other things for Hugo, which I'll deliver to your room later today," she said. "I must say, having only had cats and dogs as pets at home, I can see the appeal of a raven. Hugo is charming. He seems to understand everything we say, and he's got a prodigious memory. No wonder they keep them at the Tower."

Hugo nodded, then flapped his wings a little. Cora handed him a bit of toast with jam.

"Your handsome Mr. Michaelson dropped them off," she said.

"He is not my handsome anything, Cora," I said definitively. "I barely know him, remember, no matter how 'heroic' he was on the road."

The mysterious American had struck again. I sighed. The past few days had been filled with bizarre happenings. I hadn't had time to contemplate everything, but Andrew Michaelson stood in the center of the mystery.

Part of me trusted Andrew implicitly for no reason I could fathom, which frustrated me no end, while the rest of me worried over the golden tracery I'd seen embedded in his skin. He believed in the existence of ancient pagan gods. He'd helped to protect me from attackers and clamed to have saved me from serious injury, but he'd also mucked about in my head without my consent. It was disconcerting to know he could project and read thoughts mind-to-mind. I, at least, knew what he'd done to me. *What did Lizzie know about what he'd done to her?*

I realized then that Hugo had probably led Andrew right to me in the garden yesterday. An icy tremor crawled down my spine. "What did he tell you about Hugo?" I asked, hoping my unease didn't show.

Cora handed Hugo a bit of ham, which he gobbled up eagerly. "He went on about how to care for the bird, which I wrote down for you."

So, is Hugo his spy, then? I didn't know. "I appreciate that, Cora. Thank you. Andrew didn't mention an intent to come by and visit again, did he?"

Cora thought for a moment. "Not to speak of, but it wouldn't surprise me if he did. He seems quite keen to get to know you better."

"That's what I'm afraid of," I muttered to myself.

"I didn't quite catch that, Ari," Cora said. "What did you say?"

"I said, have you any idea where Guilders hid my books?"

Cora handed down another piece of ham. "Hugo found them. They're in my room, but the doctor says no reading until he examines you again."

"Oh dear," came Mellie's clear soprano voice, "it seems some Enhanced fellows have caused trouble in London." All eyes turned to her. Anything involving the Enhanced made most people uncomfortable.

"Read us the article then," Cora suggested. "Sounds serious, if a bit daft."

Mellie cleared her throat. "Yesterday, in Seven Dials, a group of thirty Enhanced men looted several stores and pubs. They broke windows, stole items from stores, destroyed furniture and injured several people, two of them fatally. The police employed Gauge guns to stop the mayhem, but even after several of the Enhanced men were disabled, they managed to continue their spree of violence. The police eventually employed deadly force after the ruffians set three buildings afire, thereby endangering the whole neighborhood. Firefighters managed to extinguish the flames before the fire spread to other buildings. Unfortunately, none of the Enhanced men involved in the incident could be identified. Any information the public could provide would be most welcomed, and persons wishing to help should make their reports at Scotland Yard."

Mellie took a bite of toast. "Sounds like it was a bit of a mess," she said around the morsel. "Since when have the Enhanced caused trouble like this?"

Cora whistled. "Gauge guns? I didn't know the police had those."

"What are Gauge guns?" I asked. Suddenly, I wasn't hungry anymore and I put down my fork. The news story in the *Times* worried me, and I tried to divine why. I knew Seven Dials was a crime-ridden, very poor area of London. Father had called it a slum, in fact. The newspaper wrote about brawls and other difficulties there frequently. What made this story different than the other stories? Certainly this was the first time I'd heard about a specific incident with Enhanced people involved, but considering the neighborhood, was it really that surprising?

"I'm told they work on the same principle as the Gauge mechanisms that test people for Enhancements," Cora said. "Only the Gauge guns use some sort of magnetic whatsit to disable the Enhanced. Depending on how, well... modified a person is, it could just make them unable to walk or use an arm... or, if the Enhancement runs deeper, it could kill them."

"But the article says they didn't work," Mellie said. "It didn't stop the blighters. So were they not very Enhanced, or not Enhanced at all?" She handed the paper over to Cora, jabbing a finger at the illustration that accompanied the article. Cora took the paper and placed it between herself and me. I looked at the picture and swallowed hard.

Staring up at us was the face of an angry man with pupil-less, metallic sphere eyes. It was what Sophie had described had happened to her Enhanced friends after the 'butcher' had worked on them. Sophie had spoken of the increased strength and odd detatchment of those who'd been altered in that way. I remembered her saying she'd rather die than become like them.

I shivered. *Are these ruffians victims of the same evil doctors as Sophie's friends had been?* Then another thought occurred to me. *Is a new, dangerous form of Enhancement being created? If so, to what end?*

"And what's this business about not being able to identify the blokes?" Margaret asked in her heavy Scottish brogue. She was the one studying mythology or anthropology or something, I remembered though I didn't know her very well. "Were the Peelers not able to catch any of them? It makes no sense."

"Whatever's going on, it's a trend that can't bode well for anyone," Cora pointed out. "If this escalates it could get very, very bad."

Mrs. Guildersleeve stormed into the dining room then, letter in hand. My fellow housemates stopped talking, and the room fell into a hushed silence. Guilders snorted, then came over to where I sat and dropped the letter beside my plate. "This came for you this morning," she told me, her tone sharp. She turned, waving her hand to indicate we should get back to our usual business, and vanished into the kitchen.

I looked down at the letter, recognizing my mother's distinctive handwriting on the envelope. My mouth went dry.

"Oh bother," I muttered. "This can't be good news." I reached for the missive, then turned away from my plate so I could open it. Suddenly Hugo was there directly beside me and deftly snatched the envelope from my hand. He jostled it a bit to get it more firmly in his beak and hopped back, making a run for the hallway. He disappeared behind the wall, obviously off to hide the letter. I looked at Cora.

"Did Mr. Michaelson mention the mail-stealing tendencies of ravens?" I asked dryly.

"No reading until the doctor examines you again. That means letters, too." Cora smiled. "I think it's sweet that Hugo cares so much about your health."

I pushed my chair away from the table. "Yes," I said, annoyed. "Sweet." *Blast,* I thought. *How am I to know what Mother wants if I can't actually have the letter, or read it?* I didn't want to telephone her, particuarly if she intended to bring me home as she'd indicated when we'd spoken a few days before.

I stood up too quickly, felt a little woozy, and grabbed the table. "Damn," I muttered and waited a moment for my equilibrium to return. "I'll head up to my room —"

There came a booming knock at the front door. Millie, the upstairs maid, exited the kitchen and moved quickly to the door, smoothing her dark hair and its cap with one hand and her apron with the other. Her black skirt and petticoats swished as she moved. I altered my course from my room to the front hall. I knew that knock.

Millie opened the door. Max filled the door frame, his beaming face a balm to my sore mind. He was Millie's beau and made a point of visiting her every morning he could. Dressed in his canvas work clothes rather than his more flashy aeronaut togs, he was as boisterous as usual.

"Millie, m' darlin'!" he exclaimed, stepping in the house and enveloping her in a bear hug. She was only a little taller than I was and was nearly lost in his huge embrace. "I'm sorry I neglected you yesterday, but I've been busy working on the *Bosch*. How lovely it is t' see ya! Are you off this Friday night? Can I take you dancing?"

"Max!" she whispered, giggling. She poked him in the ribs and he put her down, chuckling. He saw me and waved. I leaned against the wall and waved back. His comment about the *Bosch* intrigued me no end. I hoped he'd have time to stay and fill me in on what I'd missed.

"If Mrs. Guildersleeve saw you—" Millie hissed.

"She'd wish I'd take *her* dancing." He winked. "Haven't you heard? I'm quite the catch! So, what do you say?"

Millie reached up and ruffled Max's blonde hair. "Yes, Max, of course! Now keep your voice down!" She turned to me. "Is Mrs. – ?"

I laughed. "Coast is clear. Off with you before Guilders comes out here. You don't want her to make you work Friday night just to be spiteful."

Millie nodded. "Right you are, Miss. Thank you Miss!" and with that she was off back to the kitchen, skirt and petticoats swirling in her wake.

Chapter Twenty-Six

Max shut the door behind him and regarded me, hands on hips. "I got regular updates from my best girl about you, you know," he told me, indicating the retreating Millie with an inclination of his head. "You don't look like you broke your skull, thankfully. A bit pale, and the eye's a gruesome sight, all green and puke-colored, but not so much death warmed up. I'd say that's a good thing."

I moved away from the wall and indicated the seating in the front parlor. "I don't know whether to be flattered or offended by those remarks," I told him. "I'm glad you're not a doctor – with that sort of bedside manner, you'd lose all your patients."

The front parlor was the traditional place to meet male guests. Open on two sides to the rest of the house and close to the front door, it contained two large blue velvet covered couches, two or three matching chairs depending on the number of guests, and a table for tea or other libations, depending on the gentleman and his business. Blue wallpaper in a pattern twenty years out of date covered the walls, which supported the framed pictures of previous Towson classes. Because of its open plan, nothing discussed in the room was private, and Mrs. Guildersleeve made frequent passes through it to help 'maintain the virtue of the Towson ladies'. Those ladies who sought more privacy with male callers had to look elsewhere for a place to rendezvous.

Max and I, of course, had no romantic intent so it would serve us quite well as an appropriate meeting space, just as it had in the past. Max sat on one of the couches, and I put myself in the chair opposite. "Andrew said you'd be better after rest and some food. I'm glad to see he was right," Max said.

I just nodded. "How are things with the *Bosch*? Are Lizzie and the rest doing well?"

"Yes, of course, though this accident of yours worried us some."

"I'm sorry I've not been around to help with any of the improvements."

"That's part of why I came to see you today, Ari my dear," he said. "We've got us a job – permanent-like – for the *Bosch*. Hauling cargo around the world, if you can believe it. The consortium, or whatever its called, will cover all costs of updating the ship as well as fuel costs, repair costs and salaries for the crew. We've quit our day jobs, and we're going to make a real go of it. We're professional aeronauts!"

I clasped my hands together in surprise and happiness. "Max, that's wonderful! When did this happen? How soon do we start?"

"Pretty much the day after you were hurt on the way home. Soon as I found out I called a general muster of the Icarus Squadron," he said. "We've had volunteers working around the clock on the *Bosch* to speed up the re-fit. Lizzie, Needle, and Griff have been hard at work too, with help from me and Andrew, of course. Just a couple more parts coming in on today's train and we should be ready to go on our first run by the weekend."

"Congratulations!" I said, genuinely happy for them, even as I knew I'd not be going with them on their first few runs. It also meant no more trips to pubs so I could win dart games, but that was all right. I still had my exams to pass, a parentally-approved marriage to avoid, and a shop to start. If I took great care with my allowance between now and June I thought I'd be able to make a go of it. I certainly intended to try.

"Andrew's the one who found us the position, and we're meeting tomorrow to discuss the particulars and sign the contract."

That brought me up a bit short. Andrew yet again. Why was he everywhere, acting as an enigmatic savior one moment and securing jobs for the *Bosch* crew the next? What was he really up to? Was this job actually as lucrative as Max seemed to think it was? *How far could Andrew be trusted?* I wondered.

Max noticed my pause and rubbed under his nose a moment, thinking. He cleared his throat. "What's wrong, Ari?"

"How did Andrew find this consortium?" I asked, my tone wary. "He's an American, and new to Cambridge. Doesn't it seem a little odd to you that he should find this opportunity for the *Bosch* when he's supposed to be looking into a graduate program in Physics?"

Max stared at me for a long moment. "I hadn't thought of it like that," he admitted, "and those are certainly reasonable questions. Because you've been recuperating, there are a lot of bits of news you've missed."

"I'd be eager to hear all of it," I said, leaning back in the chair in an effort to relax.

"First off, Andrew managed to convince your Dr. Maitland to take him on as a graduate student, allowing for his absences due to working on the *Bosch*, once we get up and running." Max frowned and added: "He'll be working with Devil Oberlin as well, but only for a few classes once the monster returns to his duties."

That made me pause. Dr. Maitland was my main tutor, and Andrew would be working with him? Clearly he did intend to pursue a graduate degree, which only added to the mystery surrounding the man. "Oberlin's not teaching?" I asked.

"Took a leave of absence for a couple weeks," Max explained. "Claimed to be overworked."

"Hmmm..." I said, thinking quickly. *Is it overwork or something else that prompted his absence?* I mused. I wondered how the American would deal with the detestible Oberlin post attack, annoyed that gender always trumped intelligence and hard work in the thick-headed professor's mind. I felt anger rising within me, so I took a moment to compose myself before I spoke.

"I wish him joy of his new tutors, and success in his seeking the degree," I said, my voice prim and my countenance unruffled.

Max snorted, not buying my act for a second. "I bet you do," he said, a wicked smile crossing his face. "We both know Oberlin's Satan Incarnate. Andrew will have his work cut out for him."

I decided it was better not to respond to that, and forged ahead. "I take it, based upon what you've said, he's now part of the crew?"

Max nodded. "All it takes is a majority vote to add a crewmember, as I'm sure you remember. He approached the consortium about hiring us. They needed cargo and people hauled, we wanted to make the *Bosch* a commercial venture and Andrew brought the two of us together." He leaned forward. "Since he's done so much to be helpful to us and to you, it seemed natural to vote him aboard. Do you have an objection to him we need to be aware of?"

I thought for a long moment. *Did I have anything concrete I could tell Max that didn't sound completely ludicrous? What was I to say—Andrew had tampered with my mind, and Lizzie's, possibly more than once? He claimed to possess magical abilities and seemed to think I did, too?* Even though I knew that was true, it sounded completely daft, even to me.

I sighed. "There's something funny going on with him," I said. "I know you think he's a good fit for the *Bosch*, and he's been terribly helpful to all of us. I don't have an objection to his being part of the crew... or at least I don't think I do... but Max, please. You must insist on full disclosure. I'm worried..."

"You think the fellow has skeletons in his closet, then?"

"In a way," I admitted. "I think maybe you should check if he's Enhanced or not."

Max stilled. "Would it make a difference to you if he were Enhanced?"

As an educated woman, I knew that Enhancements did not fundamentally change who a person was. Sophie was a prime example that an Enhancement didn't change personality. In some instances, the Enhancements were the only way to save a person's life. Those with a more religious point of view argued that the Enhanced didn't have souls, or if they did, the Enhancements corrupted their souls in some way. If only from my experience with Sophie I knew that was rubbish.

I'd been accused of being Enhanced often enough that I'd tasted a tiny bit of what life for someone like that was like. Did it truly make a difference if Andrew were Enhanced or not? The logical, equality-minded part of me said no, but his other abilities were nothing like what one would expect from someone who was Enhanced... but what if he'd altered the minds of Max and the others? Lizzie had already been a victim...

"There's golden tracery on his chest, embedded in the skin," I said, blurting out the words. "I asked him about it. He didn't really answer me. I've no real proof, but..." I trailed off.

"I see," Max said, rubbing his chin. "Do I want to know how you got a look at his naked chest?"

I felt the blush rise in my cheeks and cursed silently as Max watched my reaction to his question. "He wasn't naked, for Heaven's sake—" I stammered. The fact that I had been in my nightgown at the time was something I thought better kept to myself.

Max held up a hand to cut me off. "Leaving the 'how' of what you saw aside, I suppose I can see your concern," Max said. "There are some folk who want nothing to do with the Enhanced, as we know, so knowing if Andrew is or isn't Enhanced is good business sense."

I nodded, at a loss. That hadn't been the reason for my awkward outburst, but it would have to do.

Max leaned toward me. "You're really troubled by something," Max observed. "If he's done some-" he stopped, not liking where that statement would take him, and tried again: "If you truly don't approve of Andrew joining the crew – "

"No," I said, cutting him off. I didn't know enough to have that sort of objection to his joining the crew. "That's not what I meant. He hasn't hurt me... like that." I took a deep breath. "I have no proof that Andrew wouldn't be good as a crew member, and he's certainly proved his worthiness to the *Bosch*. It doesn't matter if he's Enhanced or not. Whatever other issues I have... I'll talk to Andrew about them in private. They have nothing to do with the *Bosch*." *Or, at least I hope they won't,* I thought.

"Well," Max said, eyeing me and sensing my discomfort, "I'll leave that for the two of you to sort out, shall I?"

I nodded, ashamed of myself. I shouldn't have mentioned it at all. Now that I had, I couldn't take it back.

Max blew out a breath. "Soooo... um... I know you're still recovering from your injury and you've still got the Tripos to study for. Despite that, do you think you could join us at the Club tomorrow evening, around seven o'clock so you can hear all the details of our new venture? A representative of the consortium will be there to hammer out the contract and give us our first job."

I thought about it for a moment. "Yes," I said, my mind churning. Andrew would be there. If I went, I could insist on an explanation and find out, finally, what was going on. "Yes, I'll attend, though I'm sure you'll understand if I ask for a lift, if the Rover's available?"

Max beamed and stood up. "I'll make sure it is. Griff will be glad to act as driver. The old pirate has missed you, you know."

I thought about Griff and smiled as I also stood and we headed to the front door together. "Yes," I said. "I've missed him, too. I've missed all of you."

I waved goodbye to Max as he headed down the street, then shut the door. I headed for the kitchen and the telephone. Perhaps Dr. Sanburne had an opening in the afternoon and I could get approved for studying, I thought. It was at least worth a try.

The Odin Inheritance Victoria L. Scott

Chapter Twenty-Seven

A telephone call later, I had an appointment to meet Dr. Sanburne at his office for three o'clock.

Luckily, Cora didn't have any classes that afternoon, and she agreed to escort me to the appointment. Then she'd head back to the house and send Gertrude to escort me home. I didn't feel it was wise to go alone. We'd only have to walk to the cab station and go in the cab to Sanburne's office. I still had moments of dizziness, though I had no intention of mentioning that to Cora or Sanburne, but I thought I could manage the walking I'd need to do to get to and from the doctor without taking a tumble.

After I'd made the arrangements with Cora, I returned to my room to find Hugo perched on the windowsill, eyes closed, basking in the greyish spring sun. A quick look out the window confirmed an approaching rainstorm.

"Cora and I are off to Dr. Sanburne's office this afternoon. You'll be coming along, I assume?" Hugo didn't react. "I don't suppose I could convince you to hand over my letter," I ventured. He opened one eye, looked at me, and slowly shook his head. "Do you really understand what I say? Everything I say?" He closed the one eye, fluffed the feathers on the top of his head, and snuffled a bit.

Not sure if that was an affirmative snort or not, I pulled out my desk chair and sat down. I reached out a hand toward one of the books on the left edge of my desk and started to pull it toward me. It was my translation of Euclid.

Hugo growled from his perch on the windowsill.

I leaned my head on the back of my chair and stared at the ceiling for a few moments, praying for patience. *Fine,* I thought. *No reading.* I brought my head back up, pushed the book back to the edge of the desk, and opened the drawer above my knees, fumbling about for paper and a pencil. Perhaps I could write.

Hugo flew over to the desk and landed right in front of me, glaring first at me, and then at the drawer contents. I sighed and slid the drawer shut. *So much for that,* I thought, annoyed. Satisfied, Hugo hopped up, extended his wings and flew back to the windowsill.

I waited until Hugo settled. I reached down to the left hand drawer that contained my tools and parts for the non-aeronautic devices I made. I looked down at the bits and pieces and thought about what had happened to me on the road. Memories swirled in my consciousness. I saw the cobbles rising before me, commanded by some force I didn't understand. I heard Andrew speaking in that odd language, but I couldn't make out the words.

Whether it was Laufeson actively working to grab me or someone directing his actions, I'd been caught unaware by him twice. Cora's comments about using the standard kit of a lady's wardrobe as weapons for my own defense came back to me. I wondered if I could create something with my materials and my ingenuity that would keep me safe.

Hugo growled again.

"It isn't reading," I said decisively, setting my pliers, crimping tools and bits of springs and cogs on the surface of the desk. After a moment's hesitation, I retrieved the box of scalpel blades from the drawer and placed it on the desk. Razor sharp blades incorporated into what I created could be helpful, in a murderous sort of bloodthirsty way. I knew at least Gertrude would approve.

Hugo turned his head to look at me skeptically. "I can't *read*," I insisted, "or *write*, but I can tinker. Sanburne didn't forbid *that*."

The black mound of feathers emitted a chuffing noise, then subsided into silence. I turned my attention to the tools and supplies in front of me, and the rest of the world faded away as I created protective devices bristling with hidden scalpel blades.

By the time I had to leave to meet Cora and head to my appointment with Dr. Sanburne, I'd successfuly created three devices: a brooch with a glass cabochon that hid some very devious and destructive clockwork; a bracelet of gears, metal wings and spines woven together seamlessly that became a spinning blade if it was opened a certain way, and a hair clasp of springs, blades and arcing copper wire that grabbed on to more than just hair if activated appropriately. I held them in my hands proudly and hoped I'd have no reason to use them.

I applied the hair clasp to my hair, tucked the other two devices back in the drawer with my tools, and made my way downstairs with Hugo perched on my shoulder.

The Odin Inheritance Victoria L. Scott

Chapter Twenty-Eight

The weather turned wet and cold at about noon, and by the time Cora and I left Towson House a proper spring rain was in full deluge. We had umbrellas and our warmer coats, but the walk to the cab station was damp and chilly. Few people were out and about on our end of town, but I did notice a few workmen standing and chatting under umbrellas close to the cab station. Coat collars pulled up against the chill, they huddled and talked in an animated fashion as we passed.

Hugo didn't seem to be troubled by the weather and flew from tree to tree as we walked. Once we found a cab, we gratefully escaped the cold rain and Hugo followed us, flying and perching and flying again as we went. Ten minutes later we emerged outside Dr. Sanburne's office, a brown house with a substantial yard a few blocks from Great St. Mary's Church. Hugo fluttered down to a graceful landing on the roofline of the house. Cora ordered the cabbie to take her back to Towson and I entered the waiting area, the bell on the door ringing to announce my arrival. I shook out my umbrella and placed it in the stand near the door.

The room was just a touch too warm, even after being out in the wet. I quickly removed my coat and hung it on the coat rack. The other door in the room, shut as usual, was the one that opened to the hallway that led to Sanburne's examination room.   I'd been to the doctor's office a couple times before, and he tended to be prompt and on time for his appointments.   I had no problem finding somewhere to sit, since I was alone and the room was stuffed with brown furniture, most of it uncomfortable. I sat and stared at the tan walls, which the doctor had covered in paintings of country scenes with cows, rivers, shepherds and large, old trees.

At three o'clock on the dot, the door to the examination room opened and Mrs. Tirel, Sanburne's nurse, beckoned me in. A blonde woman who reminded me very much of an older, settled version of Lizzie, Mrs. Tirel usually met all the doctor's patients with a smile. When she called you back for your appointment, her brown eyes glowed with happiness or sympathy depending on how your health appeared to be. It was clear she greatly enjoyed her job. She made it a habit of talking pleasantly to everyone and had a gift for making nervous patients feel more relaxed. She was one of the reasons the women of Towson House used Dr. Sanburne when they had a medical issue.

This time was no exception. We discussed the weather for a few moments. Then we made our way down the hall. Mrs. Tirel opened the door to examination room two and indicated I should enter it, which I did. "He'll be with you in a moment," she said pleasantly and shut the door behind me once I entered the room.

I looked the room over to see if I noted anything amiss, Cora's admonition to remain vigilant ringing in my ears. The examination room had a window opposite the door, the curtains pulled aside to give a view of the rain, the wet street and the neighboring red brick building that housed a solicitor's office. Inside the room there was an examination table covered with a sheet, a cabinet on wheels that contained a metal tray with a bottle of alcohol, squares of gauze, rolls of bandage and steel instruments on it. The sight of the instruments turned my stomach. They were a nasty assemblage of sharp implements and knives, and I shuddered to think what Sanburne used them for. Between the window and the examination table was a white wooden cabinet that had a glass-windowed cupboard on top, showing jars of bandages and labeled bottles of unguents and tinctures in neat rows on the shelves. There were a series of drawers below, their contents neatly labeled with little cards in holders above the brass handles.

To the left of the window was a cupboard and tabletop that held a pitcher and basin along with towels and a bar of soap for Dr. Sanburne to wash his hands. Beside that was a wheeled stool for Dr. Sanburne to sit upon, and next to that was the door to his personal office, from which he would enter to examine me. The remaining exposed walls were white, the floor below my feet was grey linoleum, and the room smelled mildly of fels naptha soap, bleach, and vinegar.

I stood in the middle of the room, suddenly out of sorts and uncertain what to do. I rubbed my hands together, suddenly chilled. The door opened slightly and I jumped, startled. Usually, Dr. Sanburne knocked before he entered.

Then the door swung open, and Dr. Sanburne entered, flushed and nervous. He was a tall man though he was very thin and balding. His clothes, usually pressed and impeccably neat, were wrinkled and mussed up. He shut the door behind him with more force than he intended, and winced as he turned to regard me.

"Lady Ariana," he said, breathless and clearly agitated, "my apologies. Something came ... er... up, as it were." He looked back with concern at the door to his office.

Clearly, something was wrong. "Dr. Sanburne, is something amiss? You seem quite troubled and distracted. Shall I come back at another time?"

"No!" Sanburne insisted, rather loudly. I took a step back in surprise. He quickly realized his overstatement and put out a hand to reassure me. "No. You came to be examined, and I'll examine you."

"As you wish, Doctor," I said, still wary.

He moved to the basin and started to wash his hands. "Let's take a look at your head, shall we?"

I took a seat on the examination table. Sanburne finished washing and drying his hands, then stepped over to inspect my wound. My sticking plaster removed, Sanburne exclaimed at how well the wound knitted up and took a quick moment to remove the stitches with snips of small medical scissors and quick tugs to pull the threads out. The feeling of the threads coming out of my skin made me mildly sick to my stomach, and I couldn't help thinking of what I'd done to Sophie's arm.

After he removed all the threads, he felt for my pulse and looked carefully in my eyes. I had the feeling he wanted to keep me in the office, and my favorable condition was a bar to that desire.

"I dare say, Lady Ariana... ah... other than the remaining bruise, you look quite well. Have you any other complaints? Any spells of vertigo?"

"No, sir," I said. It was a lie, but I needed to get back to my studies.

"Indeed?" he looked genuinely perplexed. I saw the fear return. "I had a remedy prepared... it seems you will not require it?"

I frowned. "No, sir," I said. "All I need is permission to resume my studies. Since I have the Tripos exam coming up, I'm eager to get back to work. I've lost nearly a week."

"Ah," he said, clearly at a loss. "If you... ah... allow me to administer the remedy, I'll be... how shall we say... glad to allow you to get back to your mathematics, my dear."

"Are you sure? I'm doing quite well. Is it usual to apply a remedy when one isn't needed? I confess," I said, scratching the back of my head, "medicine isn't my profession, but anything other than allowing me to return to my studies seems unnecessary."

At that, Dr. Sanburne became very angry, much to my great surprise. "You'll have the remedy," he said sternly, "and not question my medical decisions. Now stay here while I retrieve it." With that, he turned and headed into his office, shutting the door behind him.

I had no intention of waiting around. Hopping off the table, I went to open the door to the hallway. There in the hallway, directly in front of the door, was a large man who smelled of tobacco and gin. He wore dirty tradesman's togs, including dark canvas pants, a worn linen shirt and brown canvas jacket with a wool cap, work boots, and an unpleasant smile on his bearded face. His eyes were like steel ball bearings in his eye sockets, with no pupils evident. He was Enhanced, and I stared at him for a split second, completely astonished. He looked like what I'd seen in the *Times* and how Sophie had described her former friends, but what was he doing here? Then my mind and body caught up enough to register I was in danger.

"Oh," I said, moving quickly to swing the door shut again. "Wrong door! Pardon me!"

The man stuck his boot in the doorframe, pushed the door aside and strode into the room. I backed up out of his way as fast as I could. He smiled at me, then shut the door. He stood in front of it, barring my escape.

"Oh, I don't think so, young miss," the man said, looking me up and down proprietarily. "We followed you from the cab station just so's we'd meet you proper like. No running off. You're coming with us, once the Doc does his bit."

This was the second time in a week someone had attempted to abduct me. Unfortunately, I didn't have anyone there to help me, and I wasn't certain how my new hair clasp would work against the ruffian sharing the room with me. I put my hands up, fists clenched.

"Now none of that, miss," he warned, shaking a finger at me. "No use making a fuss. The Doc agreed to make you more..." he smiled, showing brown teeth, "...compliant? We ain't allowed to bring you to our boss damaged, more's the pity."

I backed up into the examination table and found my hand resting on the steel tray with the alcohol bottle, bandages, and sharp instruments. "Who the Hell are you?" I asked, a tremor in my voice.

"Abe Drummond at your service, Miss. I work for... well... for someone who's very interested in you," he said. "You've got something he wants. So come along quiet-like, and no one gets hurt."

This was why Andrew had suggested I leave Cambridge. *Damn and blast! What am I going to do now?*

Dr. Sanburne stumbled into the examination room, held by the scruff of the neck by another large steel-eyed tradesman, the twin of the one who held me at bay. In his right hand, the doctor held a syringe full of some sort of liquid.

I felt my temper rise. *Go without a fuss? Not bloody likely.* I reached up and plucked the hair clasp from my head, and re-clasped it to the fabric of my skirt within easy reach. I'd probably lose in a scuffle, but I'd draw blood before I went down.

The ruffian released his grip on Dr. Sanburne's collar, shoving him toward me. Sanburne stumbled, righted himself, pulled down his shirt and cleared his throat, attempting to regain his professional mein. "Now... ah... if you'd roll up your sleeve...?"

I pulled myself up to my full height, gripped whatever instruments would fit in my hand from the tray and stood my ground. "I most certainly will not," I said pointedly.

Dr. Sanburne nearly melted into tears. "Oh please," he said, pleading. He indicated the two thugs. "They'll do something horrible to Mrs. Tirel unless I let them take you!"

"They have no intention of leaving Mrs. Tirel or you unharmed," I spat. "Once they've taken me, they'll kill you both."

The two men beamed. "She's a smart one, Doc," Abe said.

"Never mind, Abe, my lad," the other Enhanced fellow said, "we might as well grab the bird and leave the Doc out of it. He ain't got the stomach for this kind of work."

"Yeah," said Abe with a grin, "but we stomach it just fine, don't we, Dennis?"

Dennis reached out, grabbed Sanburne, punched him three times in the face and dropped his unconscious form on the floor. The syringe clattered to the floor, and Dennis crushed it with his boot. He motioned to his partner. "Abe," he said, shooting his cuffs, "she's all yours, mate."

Abe lumbered toward me. I pulled the instruments I'd grasped off the table with one hand while I grabbed the tray with the other. The bandages went flying, while the bottle of alcohol dropped to the floor and smashed, filling the room with its fumes. My quick moves and my waving the tray around made Abe pause in his efforts to grab me. I felt the mental suspension that came over me when I prepared to throw darts. I took that moment to hurl the handful of medical implements with as much force as I could muster at Abe's face, where many of them stuck, while the others struck his face, then clattered to the floor. Abe let out an angry howl of pain, backed away and started to pull the instuments out of his lacerated face.

Dennis stepped in and tried to grab me. I batted his hands with the tray as hard as I could. That made him draw back. Then I reached back to grasp the wheeled steel cart the tray had come from.

Abe, in the corner by the office door, wailed and continued to remove the knives from his face, hands shaking. He dropped the bloody things to the floor as he got them loose, which only increased the flow of blood from the cuts.

I added to the din, groaning as I lifted the narrow cart up with my right hand, then tucked the top end of it under my arm so I could use it as a lion-tamer did a chair. The wheels on the other end swirled about on their stems, but Dennis easily grabbed the end closest to him and pulled it from my grasp, leaving me with only the steel tray. He tossed the cart aside. It clattered against the wall and fell to the floor near Dr. Sanburne.

I transferred the tray to my right hand, then reached down with my left hand and removed the hair clasp from my skirt. It had two modes: one to distract and annoy, the other to cause harm. I toggled the switch for the second option and felt the device hum into life. He was close enough to me I didn't need to concentrate on hitting him, so I threw it at Dennis and hit him square in the chest. With a whir and a click, the device attached itself to his shirt and started crawling randomly over his torso like a mechanized spider. Blades dropped down from the center of the device and started cutting the fabric of the shirt away, the points of the blades cutting skin and the pinchers of the device's feet grabbing flesh when it couldn't grasp fabric. Dennis grunted and batted at the device, trying to knock it off, but the randomization algorhythms I'd included in the clockwork easily outmanuvered the thug's efforts. It crawled under Dennis's jacket, and he batted at the moving fabric, trying to smash the thing that chewed up his flesh. Blood bloomed in the cloth of the jacket in a random trail.

I watched, fascinated. I hadn't intended the hairclasp to do a great deal of harm. Rather, I'd thought it could be used to make an escape easier, should one be needed. It was a major distraction for Dennis, who clearly had a hard time deciding whether to get the device off before he came at me again, or to grab me and then deal with it. Unfortunately, Abe stood too close to the door for me to slip past Dennis and run.

Screaming, I brandished the tray like a club over my right shoulder with both hands. I hoped I looked menacing.

Dennis gave up on grabbing my clockwork hairpiece and let it roam over his body, wincing and growling at the cuts and pinches as his jacket and shirt continued to soak up blood. He started to move toward me, his face a rictus of pain and fury.

"You're a plucky one," he said through gritted teeth, "but even with your infernal device slicing me to bits and Abe done up with the knives, I'll still win in the end. Give up now, why don't you?" His beefy hands stretched out for my throat, and he lunged at me.

Then the window exploded inward, broken by a black pointed projectile of some kind. Dennis ducked to avoid the broken glass, only to look up into the face of a hovering, very angry raven, his talons extended. Shrieking and growling, Hugo set upon the ruffian, biting and scratching. It was Dennis' turn to scream in pain, and he called to Abe for help. Abe lumbered over blindly and I took my chance to beat a hasty retreat.

I dropped the tray and made for the door. I opened it, ran into the hallway, reached the door to the waiting room, opened it and ran in... only to find one more Enhanced ruffian there. He held a gun pointed right at me, and he wore the same sort of work clothes as the ruffians in the examining room had. I remembered the workmen I'd seen talking in a group at the cab station and cursed myself for a fool. They'd followed the cab to the office.

The man with the gun was steel-eyed and eager for violence. I started toward him, anger moving my feet forward before my brain could engage and look for other, less foolhardy options.

The thug pointed the gun at my chest. "Hands up," he said. "Do anything smart and I shoot. Got me?"

I stopped, cursing the Enhanced ruffians and my own helplessness. "I thought you fellows were supposed to bring me in unharmed," I said, trying for bravado.

The man shrugged. "We are, but if we gotta hurt you to get your cooperation, we'll do that." He motioned with the gun. "Hands on yer head and no funny-business," he said.

I put my hands on my head, feeling my heart thump in my chest at an alarming speed. Down the hall, I heard the sounds of Hugo's cries fade away and determined with great relief that he'd escaped. I hoped he was uninjured. *Hugo,* I thought, *if you're truly a spy for Andrew, I hope you get a chance to tell him what's happened, because dashed if I know what to do next.*

Dennis and Abe, bloody and furious, joined us in the waiting room. The encounter with Hugo had dislodged my device, but cuts and scrapes covered Dennis's face, torso, and hands, leaving bloody streaks on his shredded shirt, jacket and trousers. Scattered deep cuts dotted Abe's face, leaking blood in slow streams down his face and neck, dropping plops of red onto his shirt front.

The thug with the gun looked at their battered forms with some surprise. "Blimey! The little girl did *that* to you boys?" he asked, laughing.

"Watch it, Mitch," Dennis rumbled. He hiked a thumb over his shoulder. "I knocked the Doc out and tied the nurse up. We'll have to get this bird stowed, then come back to finish the job."

"I'll stow the little miss," Abe growled, leaning over and wiping his bleeding face with a handkerchief, "I'd love to pay her back for what she did to my face."

Mitch motioned toward the door. "We've got a cab waiting. Let's move. The boss wants her with him as soon as possible."

Mitch went out the door first, while Dennis and Abe flanked me on either side. We stepped into the rain, which seemed to be coming down harder and colder than it had been earlier. The grass of the doctor's yard and the pavement of the road and sidewalk glistened with the wet. Puddles twitched rapidly as the raindrops hit them.

I thought to call for help from a stranger, but the weather put a stop to that. Sensible people didn't go out in torrential downpours. The hard, cold rain soaked us almost instantly. The Enhanced men seemed disinterested in the downpour even as their clothes soaked up the rain. Shivering, I peered at the dark outline of the cab Mitch had mentioned and didn't pay attention to where I put my feet. I slipped on the wet pavement and felt a large hand grip my arm to steady me.

"Don't you fall, missy," Abe hissed. "I want my full fee for this here job."

Suddenly, a woman stood between us and the cab, covered in a brightly-colored flowing garment. Her dress, if one could call it that, gave no indication of the size of the body it enclosed, but flowed down from her shoulders like a waterfall. The vibrant colors of the fabric seemed to change as I watched. Her hair was short, black and curly, and wisps of it peeked out from under a yellow turban, decorated with one peacock feather. The woman waved a hand dismissively behind her, and a wall of rain formed between her and the cab, obscuring it from our sight completely. The watery wall expanded to encircle us, effectively cutting us off from the rest of the world. Mitch stopped. My captors stopped as well, grabbing my forearms to prevent my running away.

I didn't know what to think of the colorful woman who stood before us, but I'd never seen water behave like that before.

"Out of our way," Mitch ordered and pointed his gun at her.

"Let the girl go," the woman said simply, her accent giving her origin away. I couldn't believe it. Another American? Where had she come from?

"No chance," Mitch sneered. "Get out of our way or I'll shoot you. I'm sick to death of uppity women."

"No!" I tried to run toward the woman, but Abe held me in painful check, giving me a rough shake for good measure. Mitch took aim with the gun and fired.

Faster than my eyes could follow, the woman easily dodged the bullet. When she stopped, the American woman brought her hands together in a clap that echoed back and forth within the watery enclosure she'd created around us. With a roar, the rain increased in intensity, but only on the ruffians. Water sheeted down their faces, covering their noses and mouths so they couldn't breathe. The three men, moving with jerky, panicked strides, moved off the pavement and into the street, trying to escape the deluge and get out of the cocoon of water that surrounded them. They clawed at their faces, trying to prevent the water from shooting down their throats and up their noses, but to no avail. Seeing their struggles to breathe made my own throat close up, and it was as if time elongated in proportion to their desperate struggles for air. The horror of it transfixed me to the spot. I watched, shivering and astonished, as the three men drowned like rats.

Eventually, the Enhanced men stopped struggling. They slumped in limp poses of death, face down in the street. The wall of water fell heavily on top of the corpses. To my great surprise, the bodies melted into the rain, and as the water flowed away down the street drains, all that remained were the ruffian's empty clothes and their metallic Enhancements. The silver spheres that had been their eyes lay in the gutter along with three ugly artificial legs, tense in a rictus of mechanical mortality. The rain continued to come down in a torrent, but at least it seemed to be a natural phenomenon.

I didn't know what to do. The woman had saved my life, but why? What if she'd only killed the men so she could take me somewhere else? *How can I hope to outrun someone who controls the rainstorm itself? I don't even have an umbrella. What if she decides to melt me?*

The brightly garbed woman crossed her arms over her chest and graced me with no-nonsense sort of look. "Tell me," she said, indicating the mechanical bits of the men in the street, "do you still refuse to believe that magic is real, or shall I make another attempt to convince you otherwise?"

The Odin Inheritance   Victoria L.   Scott

Chapter Twenty-Nine

I put my hands up in surrender and shook my head to get some of the water out of my eyes. "No further demonstrations necessary," I spluttered, feeling the damp of my clothes seep into my bones. "Begging your pardon, I've no idea who you are or what you want, but… please, don't melt me."

"Melt you?" she asked, surprised by the request. "Of course I won't," said the woman as she walked toward me. "I've gone to considerable trouble to save you from those ruffians." She stuck out her hand. "Hypatia Downs, Facti and Heir to Tlaloc at your service," she offered as an introduction in a business-like tone. I noticed her eyes were as green as the jungle, and she was bone dry even though it rained all around and on me. Remembering that Andrew claimed he could read thoughts when he touched someone, I did my best to construct mental defenses against such an intrusion before I put out my hand and shook hers.

"Pleased to meet you, I'm sure," I said, withdrawing my hand, grateful my thoughts seemed to be my own. "You're a Facti?"

"As Andrew is, yes," Miss Downs said with great patience. "Take a moment to organize your mind and think things through," she said. "I often find, when presented with notions completely beyond my usual realm of experience, a good minute or two of evaluation and adjustment goes a long way toward avoiding foolish questions."

I opened my mouth to respond and she held up a hand to stop me. "Fret not, young woman. I will wait."

I nodded and pondered as ordered. Though I loathed admitting it, nothing about the behavior of the rainwater I'd just witnessed could be accounted for by any mundane force of nature I knew about. The water had formed barriers and waterfalls very clearly at the command of the woman who stood in front of me, and she had no mechanical enhancements that I could see. I didn't feel like I'd been mesmerized, and the empty clothes and Enhancements of my attackers sitting limply in the street were certainly real. The only explanation for what I'd seen her do was the use of magic, barring some other process with which I was unaware.

I didn't like that notion at all. Where did science end and magic begin? Could anyone do her sort of magic? What if someone used that sort of magic against me? Little mechanical scalpel filled devices would have no chance against something like what this woman had done. I felt very fortunate that Miss Downs seemed to be on my side at the moment.

Obviously, this woman knew Andrew, and whatever the Facti were, they meant to keep me safe. The Enhanced men worked for someone at odds with the Facti, who also cleary needed me for something. Somehow, Miss Downs had known I needed help. Had the request for assistance come from Andrew or Hugo?

"Thank you, Miss Downs," I began slowly, "for saving me from those fellows."

She smiled. "Please, call me Hypatia. You're very welcome. I trust you are not injured?"

"A little bruised, perhaps," I admitted. "Can you tell me who those men were?"

"Them?" she waved a dismissive hand at the remains in the street, "they were lost to Obscurati thrall. Best to kill the fiends when they get that way. We've yet to find a method that reverses the effects of the conversion process. The poor devils think they're choosing a path that will make them better, but it only leads to ruin."

"Obscurati?" I asked.

"The Obscurati work to bring chaos and evil into the world. Facti work to prevent their efforts at destruction as best we're able, with magic," she waggled her fingers at me, "provided by certain artifacts from certain pagan gods with whom we have a connection."

"And the Obscurati 'converted' these men? Was that conversion mechanical?"

"Partially," Hypatia said, "but the Obscurati have access to magic as we do. They worship the pagan gods they serve, which is how they get their abilities. We," she indicated herself, "do not worship the gods who work with us. Our pagan affiliations are with the... how shall we say... more positive gods of the various pantheons. The Obscurati gods are scoundrels to a deity, and they want nothing more than to cause harm at every opportunity."

"So they subvert the Enhanced as a way to do that?" I asked.

"Sadly, yes. The Enhanced are particularly vulnerable to their most recent method of 'abomination', for lack of a better term. Once the eyes of the poor buggers are full silver with no pupils, their tendency to violence increases, as does their resistance to most conventional methods of Enhanced control."

"Like the men in Seven Dials," I breathed. "Like Sophie's friends."

Hypatia inclined her head in agreement. "Indeed. The Obscurati have been very busy as of late."

I stepped closer to her hoping to avoid being rained on since I had little rivulets of water running down my back. Unfortunately, being closer to Hypatia and her brightly colored garment did not prevent the rain from finding me. I'd never been so wet in my life, and I was sure my entire body was prune-y and wrinkled. "But I'm not Enhanced. Why do these Obscurati want me so badly?"

"You're not like most people," she said simply.

"You don't even know my name," I said, hands on hips.

She sighed. "You are Lady Ariana Trevelyan, the very strong-willed Mathematics student who lives in Towson House and rides about in airships without her parents' knowledge."

My jaw dropped. "Does everyone know about the airship, then?" I demanded, annoyed. "Damn and blast!"

Hypatia laughed at me then, a rich, pleasant sound. "Your parents are still in the dark though none of the Facti are."

"Ah," I said, still annoyed but less concerned. "I suppose you do know me, then."

Hypatia smiled. "I suppose I do... if only by reputation."

I put my hands on my wet hair, interlocking my fingers so my elbows hung down on either side of my head. "How is it you see me as being not like 'most people,' as you say?"

"Aren't you?" Hypatia asked in a rhetorical tone. "Surely you've figured that out by now, university girl."

I had, but not in a way I understood. I dropped my hands from my head. "How, precisely, am I different?" I asked.

"You are consecrated and an Heir."

"Which means what?" I pressed.

"At the moment, frequent attempted abductions," she said with a tired shrug.

I clenched my fists and tried to control my frustration. "I can't control elemental forces. I can't read minds or project thoughts. I can't make people disappear. How is it, then, that I'm different?"

Hypatia crossed her arms, the sleeves of her dress folding over and blending into the body of the dress in a swirl of brilliant color. "You really don't see it, do you?" she said. "How interesting."

I ran through everything I could think of that might qualify as something that made me different, and all I came up with was: "Dart throwing? That's what sets me apart? But that's nothing like what you do—"

"—yet," Hypatia finished.

I swallowed and thought furiously. "Have you been Enhanced so you can control rainstorms and lightning?" I asked.

"What, like the men I killed? Heavens, no."

"Are you a witch or sorceress of some kind?"

"Faerie stories," Hypatia scoffed. "You should know better than that."

"Then, what are you?" I asked, frustrated, dropping my hands. "Please—you know this isn't the first time people have tried to abduct me. It isn't the first time I've seen things I couldn't explain. I don't understand what's going on, and it seems to me it'd be better if I did."

Hypatia sighed. "I am a Facti, as Andrew is. We work as a force for good."

"So you said. Tlaloc is an ancient pagan god, then?"

"Tlaloc is a rain god of the Aztecs. That gives me the ability to manipulate storms as you saw here. Surely Andrew mentioned his connection to the Moon? Khonshu is a god of healing. He employed those skills to heal your fractured skull. Surely he told you that."

"He did," I said. I crossed my arms across my chest. "I'm afraid it didn't go well."

"Ah. He suggested you should leave Cambridge, I take it?"

"Among other things," I admitted. "I refused."

"The Obscurati won't stop trying, you know," she said, then grabbed my arm and leaned in to speak quietly in my ear. "You stand at the cusp of your destiny," she said, her tone portentous. "Be careful."

I frowned. She'd said many things, but I found myself still mostly in the dark as to who or what I was, or what she was. "That was singularly unhelpful," I pointed out. "I've no idea what you mean."

Hypatia dropped my arm and scratched her left ear. "I know. It sounded better when I rehearsed it in my head, but it can't be helped."

I threw my hands up in exasperation. "So I'm just supposed to muddle through with next to no information?"

"You've done a pretty good job so far. I've found most of life is just 'muddling through', as you put it. You'll have more information than you want or need soon enough." She looked at the sky. "Storm's abating. Must be off."

"Will I see you again?"

"No idea, though I am keeping an eye on you. Whether I'll need to make as dramatic and admittedly ostentatious an appearance as this again, I don't know. Just remember what I said... and trust Andrew Michaelson. He's a good man to have on your side."

I put my hands out to stop her from leaving. "Please—"

"Good luck," she said and with that, she faded away into the rain.

"Bloody Hell," I muttered, staring at the empty space Hypatia had occupied, feeling very much like a drowned rat.

At that moment, Hugo fluttered to a stop at my feet. He shook himself vigorously, spraying me with water droplets, but since I couldn't be any wetter I didn't scold him.

"Thank you for your timely intervention," I said, bending down to rub his head. He squawked agreeably and stepped closer so I could pet more of him. His feathers were sleek and wet, but soft.

I sighed. "Let's go in, shall we? I should check on Dr. Sanburne and Mrs. Tirel, then get my coat and brolly and head back to Towson House to dry off." Hugo nodded. Together we headed into Sanburne's office.

Chapter Thirty

My time with Dr. Sanburne and Mrs. Tirel was brief. I introduced the injured doctor and Mrs. Tirel to Hugo, who received a ginger snap for his trouble and refused the offer of tea. Dr. Sanburne had been unconscious during my fight with Dennis and Abe, while Mrs. Tirel had been tied to a chair in the kitchen, so neither of them knew what had happened in the street.

They wanted to make a police report, with Dr. Sanburne, holding a cloth with ice on his damaged face, reminding me of the article in the *Times* from breakfast as the reasoning for it. He pointed out the ruffians had looked like the picture in the *Times*, and the authorities had to be informed as to this new wrinkle on the difficulties with the Enhanced in England.

Dr. Sanburne rose to make the call to the police station, and I rose to head back home over their objections. I claimed fatigue and asked that they send the police by Towson House tomorrow for me to make my report. I gathered my coat and umbrella, whistled to Hugo, and he and I left the doctor's office. As I headed down the street on the lookout for a cab, Hugo flew above me and I wondered what to do next. Much as I hated to admit it, the smartest thing would be to contact Andrew and have the Facti get me away from Cambridge, since I didn't know when the next kidnapping attempt would occur, and I wasn't certain I'd escape unharmed and free a third time. I rounded a corner, hailed the cab I saw, and chewed my lip as the driver took me back to Towson House and I pondered my future. *What would I say to my parents and tutors? Where would the Facti take me? Would I ever take the Tripos exam and start my business?*

I alighted from the cab to find another cab standing in front of the house, loaded with two large trunks. Hugo dropped himself onto my shoulder gracefully as I recognized one of the trunks as my own.

My mother, wearing a fashionable light grey silk dress, a travelling cloak, and a black feathered fascinator perched on the side of her head, met me at the door. Her right foot tapped the wood floor, a sure sign of impatience.

People said I favored Mother in my looks rather than Father. We both had green eyes, red hair and were of a somewhat petite size, so I saw their reasoning. In most other respects, we were completely different. Mother paid a great deal of attention to what was right and proper for persons in our station in life. I cared more for pursuing life in an airship. She visited and corresponded with all the right people, attended all the best social gatherings, had impeccable manners, and had very little patience for those who didn't. I rarely used my title, knew my manners were not as impeccable as my mother's and hated society gatherings. Despite her lack of height, she exuded great presence and was every inch a duchess. The only way anyone knew I was the daughter of a duke was if someone told them, since nothing about my aspect or presence indicated nobility.

She was a force to be reckoned with. I mostly just reckoned with her force.

Standing in the doorway and taking in my bedraggled, soaked form, my hair a disaster, with no gloves on and a large black bird on my shoulder, Mother's expression went from annoyance to shock.

"Good heavens, Ariana!" Mother exclaimed with uncharacteristic emotion. I must have looked very bad indeed. I braced myself for the next onslaught.

"With your face all banged up and as damp as you are, you look like you've been drowned twice with some horrible sea creature and a bathing machine!" Mother stepped forward to get a closer look. "Is that the cut from the bash to the head you took? I must say it looks prodigious. I hope it doesn't leave a scar."

I resisted the urge to roll my eyes. No doubt a scar would affect my marriage prospects, which was yet another reason why I wished to avoid marriage.

"What the devil happened," Mother continued, indicating my wet clothes, "and what in the world is that bird doing on your shoulder?" I opened my mouth to respond, but she beat me to it.

"Nevermind," she said, stepping away and waving her hand in dismissal. "You can tell me on the way. Up to your room spit spot. Make yourself presentable and stow that bird somewhere. They'll not allow it on the train loose like that."

On the *way*? *Train?* My heart froze. "Mother? With respect, why are you here? You've not come to take me home, I hope," I said earnestly. "I'm feeling much, much better. Honestly." I would have danced a hornpipe at that point to convince her not to take me home. I didn't want the Obscurati to threaten my parents, and I had no idea how to explain my current predicament to them. If I told my parents magic was real and I'd seen it used, they'd have me locked up.

Mother looked up as if asking the Almighty for patience. "I sent a letter, dear. Didn't you receive it?"

I shot Hugo a look. He had the decency to appear embarrassed and started to inspect one of his feet. "No, actually," I said, turning my attention back to Mother. "What did it say?"

"We're off to Scotland." She sighed. "Since you weren't here when I arrived, I had the upstairs maid pack your trunk though I suppose you'll want to gather a few of your mathematics texts yourself. The cab awaits. We're loaded up and will be on our way once you're ready."

I gaped at her. *Scotland? What if someone tries to abduct me on the way? How am I to tell her people have already tried to kidnap me twice? If someone like Hypatia came to my rescue, how will I explain their supernatural abilities, particularly when I don't understand them myself?*

She sighed. "Close your mouth, Arianna, my dear. It makes you look unintelligent."

I did so, mind reeling. If I told her what'd really been happening, she'd pull me out of school, assuming that too much math had unhinged my mind. *What am I going to do?*

Mother tutted. "Come now, child. We don't have a great deal of time. You need to go up to your room, change, grab a few of your silly books, and get back down here. We have to make the seven o'clock train."

"Scotland?" I ventured, stalling. "Whatever for? What about my classes and the Tripos? Surely it could wait?"

"It cannot wait. We must go now, and we'll be back in a few days," she said. "I've already informed your professsors." She shooed me toward the stairs. "Go on now. Quickly!"

"But – "

"But what, my dear?" Mother responded, her patience waning.

"What if... something bad... happens?" I finished weakly.

"Then we shall deal with it," Mother said, as if there were no other possible answer. "We're members of the peerage in an Empire that spans the world. We come from a long line of strong personalities and personal successes which have culminated in our current high social and political status. I dare say, should there be problems, those problems have far more to worry about from us than we do from them."

I blinked in surprise. "Good heavens. Do you really believe that?" I asked.

Mother pointed at the stairs. "Absolutely. Go. Now."

I made my way up to my room. The perch for Hugo sat by my desk, and he flew over to take up residence there. Millie had left out a change of clothes for me, choosing a navy blue skirt, light blue shirt, and navy blue jacket to wear. She assisted me in changing my clothes and combing and pinning up my hair. My book bag sat on the bed, a bit dirty, but otherwise none the worse for wear.

We worked quickly to get me ready for the trip. While Millie did my hair, I wrote a quick note to Max, explaining that I'd be unable to meet with them and why. Millie promised to deliver it. Then she offered to go to Cora's room to retrieve Hugo's cage, helpfully dropped off by 'that American bloke'. I shooed Millie off on her errand.

Quickly, since I wasn't certain how long I'd be alone, I opened my lower right hand desk drawer. I pulled out the two knives Cora had given me and quickly lifted my skirt, sliding one blade into each boot. I'd never thought to use my throwing skills to attack another person, but without knowing what awaited us, it seemed foolish to leave the knives behind. I wished I had more than two, but they were better than nothing.

I dropped my skirt, hiding my boots and the knives. I shut the right hand drawer and opened the left, pulling out my box of gadgetry tools and supplies. The brooch and bracelet sat on the top. The spider-like hair clasp hadn't survived the encounter with Dennis, unfortunately. I applied my remaining infernal devices to my shirt and wrist as an extra layer of defensive armament and tucked the box into my bookbag. This was what Hypatia had meant by 'muddling through', I supposed.

I was double-checking the contents of my bookbag when Millie returned with a birdcage for Hugo. He hopped into it agreeably, then leaned down and seemed to read the newspaper lining the floor of the cage.

"*Nice,*" he croaked in a graveled tenor, and both Mille and I jumped back in surprise.

"Hugo talks?" Millie said in delight. "Well, I'll be! What a clever bird!"

I narrowed my eyes at Hugo. "Yes," I agreed, re-evaluating my pet raven. "A clever bird, indeed."

I said my goodbyes, closed my bag, grabbed it and my coat, while Millie took Hugo in his cage, and we returned to Mother by the front door. She looked me up and down.

"I don't understand why you favor such dark colors," she said, "and that ensemble is a year out of date. What do you do with your allowance that you've got last year's styles on?"

I couldn't tell Mother why my outfit was that old, and I'd decided to leave the new clothes Aunt Miranda had given me behind. "I can go change – " I offered.

"No time. I suppose you'll have to do. Perhaps on our way back from Scotland we can do some shopping and get you proper fashionable dresses." She looked at Hugo in the cage. "Must we take the bird?"

"Yes, Mother," I said, bracing for an argument. "He'll be fine in the cage, surely."

"Oh, all right," she said, waving at the door for us to leave. "Come along."

I desperately wanted to know why we headed to Scotland but knew it was pointless to ask. Mother would tell me in her own time. So, as we rode in the carriage to the train station I listened patiently as Mother told me all about recent happenings in London though her account seemed to consist primarily of weddings. I made the appropriate interested noises at the right places but didn't really keep track of who had married whom.

As she spoke, though, I found myself looking at Mother in light of Aunt Miranda's revelations about the miscarriages she'd suffered. It had to have been awful for her and Father in a way that was unfathomable to me. I wondered if her focus on my future, or at least the future she believed I should have, was based, somehow, on the losses she'd suffered. Unlike my dead infant brothers, I had a future. She wanted it to be the best future she could imagine.

That realization made my eyes water a bit. My heart squeezed in understanding of my mother's motivations, even as it broke knowing that my hoped-for future was far removed from what she wanted for me. *What would she do if she knew what I've been though over the past few days,* I wondered. My life had been in danger. Had Laufeson or the Enhanced ruffians succeeded, I could have disappeared without a trace and Mother would never have known what happened to me. I found I was glad the Facti were on my side, if only so that Mother wouldn't lose me.

Mother's voice droned on, unaware of my concerns. I looked at Hugo, who returned my gaze with what seemed to be sympathy though I suppose it could have been boredom. Eventually, he took the coward's way out, settling down to sleep. I, unfortunately, couldn't follow his example. I made sure my face showed an appropriate level of polite interest and continued to nod as the carriage took us to the train station.

Chapter Thirty-One

The train station surged with activity and people coming and going. Oddly, there were many police officers standing around the station obviously watching for signs of trouble. People looked tense and nervous. Mother hailed a porter and moved to make the arrangements for our trunks while the carriage driver unloaded them. I stood near the carriage to keep an eye on the luggage, Hugo's cage on the ground at my feet. He was awake and watchful just as I was. I looked around anxiously, holding my bookbag by the strap over my right shoulder. A few news carriers stood at the far end of the station, waving papers and shouting though I couldn't make out what they said over the din of the carriages, people, and trains.

"Pastry for the train, miss?" came a timorous child's voice to my right. "Or maybe fer yer bird?"

I turned and saw a girl, perhaps nine or ten years old, holding a tray out to me with small, somewhat limp pastries on it. I saw her look with interest at the cut on my brow and the bruising around my eye, and then remember her manners, forcing her eyes to look away. Her clothes were clean if worn, and her brown hair hung in two braids on either side of her head. Her face was drawn and there was a smudge of dirt on one cheek. Her deep-set brown eyes pleaded with me to buy one of her pastries. It was obvious she was new to selling such things to travellers and had been less than successful.

"I don't need a pastry for the trip," I said and watched as her face fell, "but I will pay for some information if you'd care to oblige me."

The girl's countenance became suspicious. "I ain't gettin' anyone in trouble with the Peelers," she said, sticking out her chin. "I ain't that kind o' girl."

"You'll be getting no one in trouble," I said. I reached into my bookbag, plunged my hand into my reticule, and drew out a sixpence, showing it to her.

Her eyes widened in hopeful surprise.

"Just tell me why all the Peelers are about, and what the newsboys are saying," I said.

"It's them bad Enhanced blokes, innit," she said, garrulous. "Been makin' a mess o' trouble in London, Liverpool, Manchester and Bristol today. Burnin' stuff, attackin' folk, makin' a right mess o' things. Peelers are standin' here hopeful they can keep Cambridge from bein' next fer attack an' ruin." The girl leaned forward. "They's afrighted, and no mistake," she said confidentially. "They ain't got them Gauge guns, see. If the evil Enhanced blokes come here to wreck us outta house an' home, Peelers got nothin' t' stop 'em."

Hypatia's words about the Obscurati working to create chaos came back to me. *Was the term 'Obscurati' another name for Enhanced, or just the steel-eyed fellows I'd encountered earlier?* Clearly I needed more information. I reached back into my bag and pulled out another sixpence. "Can you run down and buy a *Times* for me? You can keep the change, and when you bring me the paper, I'll give you this sixpence besides."

The girl nodded, took one of the coins and made a quick dash to the nearest newsboy, her pastries jostling about alarmingly, which explained their somewhat battered condition. She bought a *Times*, enclosed the change in her fist and dashed back, smiling.

"Here you go, Miss," she said, holding out the paper. I took it from her.

"Thank you. What's your name?"

"I'm called Sadie Marsters, Miss," she said with a genuine smile. "Thank you kindly, Miss. Me Pa's lost his job due t' this ruckus with the Enhanced folk. Lost his leg, an' they gave him a new one, but... well, I'm tryin' t' help out, like."

I handed her the sixpence she'd been promised. Then I had an idea. "Do you know where Towson House is?"

She looked at the coin and thought for a moment. "That's where the posh college girls live, ain't it?"

"Yes. Go there, and ask for Cora Allerton.   Tell her Lady Ariana sent you, and that I said she needs to find you a job helping out at Towson House. They can always use someone to run errands, and maybe that'll help tide your family over until things improve."

She gripped the sixpence in her fist with the rest of her change, curtseyed and smiled. "Thank you, Miss. I'll do that," she said, and turning, the pastries bobbing excitedly in the tray as she walked, she disappeared into the crowd.

I saw Mother making her way back to me with a station porter in tow. I quickly tucked the newspaper into my bookbag. Mother disapproved of ladies reading the newspaper, so I'd have to wait until I was alone to read it.

"Come, Ariana," she said, waving a dismissive hand at our luggage, "these fellows will take care of our things. We need to board the train." I grabbed Hugo's cage and followed.

We made our way through the throngs of people to Platform Seven, where the train for York sat while people climbed aboard. Police officers stood there with their billy-clubs out and their eyes missing nothing. Mother blazed a trail to the first class cars. Armed with knowledge, however sparse, of the current troubles with the Enhanced and remembering with a great deal of accuracy my own very recent encounter with them, I scrutinized every person we passed, attempting to detect any trace of Enhancement or malice. I saw none, and Mother made it clear she thought my overzealous peering about to be very tiresome. In no time, we had boarded the train. Wary of attack, I followed her into our first class cabin. I placed Hugo and his cage on the seat, waited while Mother removed her coat, and hung hers with my own.

It was a standard sort of cabin, like the many others Mother and I had shared over the years. It had dark wood paneling on the walls, red velvet bench seats stuffed with horsehair, shelves above the seats for our luggage, and a wide window with a little door in the middle of it to view the world as it slid by. I put my bookbag and Mother's small valise on the shelf above my head and sat. Hugo shook himself and trilled a bit, then curled up and closed his eyes to sleep again.

Mother sat across from me, calmly looking in her reticule for our tickets. I, in contrast, was nervous as a cat. I felt the lurch of the train pulling out of the station and nearly jumped up from my seat. The steam whistle blew a strident note, nearly giving me an apoplexy, and we were off. As the train's speed increased, the cabin swayed and moved with the power of the engine and the unevenness of the tracks. I looked into the corridor beside the cabin, watching the people go by. I stiffened when the short, grey-haired conductor entered, anticipating an attack. His blue uniform with its brass buttons covered his protruding belly and wide girth like a tent, and he carried a small box with one open end that I knew all too well: a Gauge box.

"Begging your pardon, ladies," the conductor said, "but I'm afraid I'll need to check you both for Enhancements before I see your tickets."

Mother looked aghast. She knew as well as I did what regard the Enhanced held in England. Someone like a train conductor asking someone of her rank to prove she had no Enhancements was simply unthinkable. I winced, knowing what would be said next by my very rank-conscious parent.

"I am the Duchess of Albemarle," she said with asperity, "and we're seated in first class. Surely you don't suppose my daughter and I are Enhanced. Even if we were, we certainly don't behave like those London ruffians in Seven Dials." She sniffed. "I took the train here just a couple hours or so ago, and I wasn't required to submit to a Gauge test then."

The conductor knuckled his head in imitation of lifting his cap. "My apologies, Your Grace," he said, "that is as may be, but we just got word that all the passengers need to be checked for Enhancements. The Head Conductor received a telephone call a minute or two before the train pulled out that there's a fear the rascals will start targeting the railways. Been a bit of a messy day in some places, if you know what I mean. Home Office wants to keep track of Enhanced people's comings and goings."

Mother looked the conductor up and down in her best withering, high-society glance. "And what if we refuse?"

"Begging your pardon, but we'll stop the train and put you and your luggage out on the side of the track."

"Well, I never!" Mother said.

The conductor nodded. "Yes, your Grace. I have no doubt of that," he said with a droll look of his own.

"Sir," I asked, before my outraged Mother could respond, "what if we were Enhanced? Would you put us off the train then?"

"No, miss," he said. "I'd just record that you were on the train, and make a note of your destination. I'd only put you off if you started a ruckus." He rubbed the back of his neck. "Mind you, you'd be dealing with the police once you got off the train in York, just to be sure you're law-abiding citizens."

So if there are Enhanced fellows on the train, I'm still on my own. I put out my hand. "I'm ready to be tested, sir," I said.

Mother spluttered in shock across from me, but the conductor's face took on a grateful look. "Thank you, miss," he said, turning the box in my direction. "Just place your hand inside here – won't take a moment."

I did so, endured the nausea-inducing process in stoic silence, and removed my hand when the device finished. "No Enhancements," he noted, looking at the reading.

"Of course not," Mother said in a huff. "What do you take us for?"

The conductor turned the open end of the box to Mother. "If you will, your Grace," he said, "it will take just a few moments. Then I can punch your tickets and be on my way."

Mother looked at me, and I motioned that she should comply with the conductor's request. She frowned and placed her hand in the box, looking none too pleased to do so.

I watched in fascination as the Gauge read my mother. Her face paled and she closed her eyes, swallowing a few times as the nausea of the the test moved through her. I swallowed in convulsive sympathy.   The test ended, and Mother pulled her hand from the box as if she'd been burned.

"No Enhancements for you either," the conductor said. "Thank you for your cooperation." He tucked the Gauge box up near his armpit and pulled his hole-punch from its holder on his belt.   "Now, Your Grace, if I could see your tickets?"

Mother shot me a look as she handed over the tickets to the man, annoyance and disapproval of him and what she'd been forced to do coming off her in waves.   He punched the tickets, handed them back, and beat a hasty retreat, shutting the door to the cabin as he left.   I locked it, still nervous about an attack. Mother furrowed her brow in confusion.

"You seem to be very security-minded," she commented, settling into the seat and working to pull her dignity back in place. "Though I think those Enhanced chaps would find a locked door easy enough to get through if the newspaper accounts are accurate."

"You've been reading the paper?" I asked, shocked.

"Of course not," she said.   "Your father keeps me informed." She sniffed dismissively.   "Clearly the government is more worried about those awful people than I'd thought.   Imagine that conductor suggesting we're Enhanced.   The cheek!"

If only she knew the half of it, I thought grimly, and flashed back to my encounter with Dennis and Abe in Dr. Sanburne's office.

"I've heard about thefts on trains," I said in explanation of my locking the door.   "True or not, it seems foolish not to take precautions."

Mother considered this.   "I see your point," she said. "Good thinking." She reached up and removed her fascinator, setting it on the seat beside her, then began removing her gloves.

I'd forgotten to put mine on before we left. I realized I'd left them on my bed back at Towson House and Mother hadn't said a word. That was odd, I thought, and with a mental sigh added that to the growing list of oddities I'd dealt with in the past few days.

I turned my attention to the window and watched the countryside go by while I waited for Mother to reveal our specific destination, hoping the scenery would ease my mind. It didn't. I kept considering what our escape options were if someone attacked us. I noted the stop-cord along the top of the train window but knew it would probably take too much time for the train to stop to do us any good. Jumping out the little door while the train speeded along was another tricky possibility, but too likely to result in injuries. I also wasn't sure we could move our corsetted torsos enough to get out the door in the first place. Hand-to-hand combat within the cabin looked to be the only defense available, if we came under attack.

If only I knew more about why the attacks against me had taken place. What was the connection between the disturbances by the Enhanced and the attempts to abduct me? Frustrated, all I wanted to do was pace the cabin and have a good think, but I couldn't due to its small size and Mother's presence. It took every ounce of my control to sit quietly and keep my hands clasped in my lap as the daughter of a duke should.

Mother cleared her throat, dignity now fully restored. "My goodness, Ariana," she said. "You look ready to pounce or explode. Look at me, take a deep breath and open your fists before you hurt yourself." I did as instructed but felt no better. My hands tingled as the blood returned to them.

"I was unaware you were so attached to Cambridge, my dear. You're positively vibrating with agitation. I told you I spoke to your professors. They'll send work for you if we're gone for longer than I anticipated."

I leaned back in the seat, amazed. "Thank you, Mother," I said, truly grateful.

Mother rolled her eyes. "Honestly, Ariana. You're my only daughter. Do you really think I don't know how keen you are to pass the... what's it called... the Tripos exam?" She looked down and dusted something off her skirts. "It's important to get it done this June, of course, so I made sure your professors knew to send you exercises," she waved a dismissive hand, "or whatever it is they have you do."

I knew why I thought it important to be done with the Tripos in June, but I didn't understand why Mother did. "Oh?" I prompted.

"Once you finish at Towson, you'll finally settle in to your proper role in life, and leave mathematics and science behind, of course. You certainly can't do anything with your Cambridge education." She sighed. "It's not part of your future, and you've dilly-dallied long enough."

I stifled my desire to tell Mother I intended to avoid marriage and be a professional aeronaut, knowing it would do no good. "What is there in Scotland that figures so prominently in my future?" I asked, resigned. "Some duke or earl you wish me to meet?"

"No, child. We're headed to Aberdeenshire to visit your Great Aunt Miranda," Mother said.

"I thought she was in France," I said, surprised. I almost mentioned that I'd just seen her, but wisely stopped myself. I didn't want to explain to Mother why I'd seen her.

"She's on her way back. We're to meet her at Brentwood Close." My mother's face creased with a puzzled look. "She telephoned and told me in no uncertain terms I was to retrieve you from Cambridge and get you to Brentwood Close with all possible speed." She shook her head ruefully. "I couldn't get a word in to ask why, or how she was, or anything. She made me swear to get you out and was oddly forceful about it. She told your father the same thing – well, she's a force of nature, isn't she? If she wants you to do something, you do it."

"That's true enough," I agreed.

"You see your aunt occasionally on weekends, do you not? Do you know why she'd be so insistent to get you out of Cambridge?"

I immediately thought of Laufeson and our encounter in the library, which Aunt Miranda knew about. She didn't know about the attack on the road or the altercation at Dr. Sanburne's, however. I didn't want to tell Mother about any of that, or our brief trip to Brentwood Close would become a permanent trip home.

"No," I said.

"We'll be meeting a friend along the way, and she made the necessary arrangements to get us there as quickly as possible."

"So we'll be transferring to an airship when we get off this train?" I asked hopefully. It would be the fastest method, and only a few firms offered the service, as I was in a good position to know.

Mother looked horrified. "Heavens no, child. We'll travel by train, as any civilized person does. Airships may be the vogue, and I know you greatly favor them, but until Queen Alexa makes use of one, I'll stick to trains."

Queen Alexa had ascended the throne in 1870 as a young woman, inheriting from her father, Arthur II, who had died at the age of sixty-two after a forty year reign. Alexa was intelligent, the mother of two daughters, hard-working and beloved, but she, and her husband the Prince-Consort William, didn't readily embrace new technologies, following in the footsteps of the prior Tudor monarchs who had ruled England since 1485. An unfortunate, bloody incident with a flying clockwork insect during the reign of Queen Elizabeth I had put her descendants off rapid advancement of machine technology. The Empire's distrust of the Enhanced was merely one facet of that mechanophobia.

In contrast, Queen Alexa's second cousin, Victoria, actively encouraged new machines and methods, believing rivals would overtake Great Britain unless technological advancement increased ten-fold. Her husband Alfred, a German, heartily agreed and used his considerable fortune to promote new ideas and help inventors. I knew my father worried the Empire would fall behind in power and influence if he didn't work with Parliament and the Prime Minister to overcome Queen Alexa's reluctance to accept new ideas and advancements. At the moment, Great Britain 'strode the world' in colonies and territories, but through new devices and technology France, Germany and the United States were rapidly becoming influential world powers.

Therefore, Mother's opinion about travel in airships was hardly a surprise, focused as she was on rank and Queen Alexa's opinions.

"Now," Mother said, fixing her gaze on Hugo's cage, "why don't you tell me about how you came by that ridiculous raven, and why Mrs. Gildersleeve allows it in the house."

There was a knock at the door of our cabin. I tensed, then followed Mother's gaze to see who stood in the hallway through the window.

"Ah! Lady Sato!" she said and rose to let her in. I rose in welcome as was appropriate and curtseyed, amazed and happy to see the benefactress of Towson House.

Lady Sato moved into the cabin with an almost superhuman grace, wearing the most beautiful pale gold brocade dress I'd ever seen in the most up-to-date design shown in the lady's magazines Melisande favored. The fabric of the dress paid appropriate homage to its owner's Japanese heritage. Designs swirled in the weave of the fabric, reminding me of birds in flight swarming in warm sunshine. She was shorter than I was by three inches, her jet black hair pulled up on her head in the latest hairstyle, topped by a fascinator that matched her dress in elegant simplicity. Her eyes wavered between gold and brown, and she saw *everything*. There was wisdom in her gaze to depths I couldn't possibly fathom, but it was more than that. Somehow, I knew she saw what had gone before, what was happening now as a result of that past, and the future that was to come because of both with a clarity that literally took my breath away.

I'd met Lady Sato several times at Towson House and a couple times at home, since she was a friend of my mother's. I liked her very much though her seeming to understand everything with a glance made some people uncomfortable. Hugo looked up and trilled in welcome, and Lady Sato dipped her head slightly to the bird in response. I looked from Hugo to Lady Sato and back in surprise. *Hugo knows this woman? Does that mean she knows Andrew?*

Hugo fluffed his feathers and brought a foot up to scratch his neck briefly, for all the world like a normal bird. Then he turned his attention to the page from *Times* on the bottom of his cage again.

Mother hugged Lady Sato, making a demonstration of affection I rarely saw at home. Lady Sato returned the embrace with equal affection. Lady Sato then moved to me and hugged me with equal warmth. I wondered if Lady Sato knew how to fight, in case we came under attack.

That thought made me stop. *My God*, I mused, *before this week I'd had no reason to consider the combative capabilities of my companions. What sort of person am I becoming? Damn and blast! Will I be worrying about ambushes from now on, in every situation?*

Mother indicated the seat beside her when Lady Sato broke our embrace. "I'm so glad you could join us," she said, smiling. She indicated me. "Perhaps your presence will help reassure Arianna that her studies will not go neglected on this trip?"

Lady Sato beamed and took her place beside Mother. "The Tripos exam is very important, Elaine," she said, her voice melodious and devoid of any recognizable accent. "She's become a resourceful woman. Despite this interruption, I am sure she'll do well on her final examinations."

"I must say," Mother responded, eyeing me speculatively, "I did worry that letting her live in that insane asylum you call a 'women's university residence' would damage her manners and deportment."

It's good to know Mother thinks I have manners and deportment, I thought with some relief. There had been many times Mother had despaired that I'd ever gain any such social skills.

Lady Sato's eyebrows went up in surprise. "Towson ladies are never rude, Elaine. I select the young women myself, as you very well know. While it's true some aspects of life at the house are out of the ordinary—"

I thought of Gertrude with her colony of spiders in her bedroom and smiled.

"—for the most part it is as appropriate and proper a residence as Girton. Towson ladies are more resourseful and clever than their Girton counterparts, is all. Such traits sometimes lend themselves to extraordinary pursuits. Those pursuits cannot be allowed to float through the air on a random breeze. They need to be steered to a proper and appropriate mooring." Lady Sato turned a shrewd gaze on me. "Wouldn't you agree?"

My mouth dried up. Her comments and the look on her face indicated quite clearly she knew about me and the *Bosch*. *Who had told her*, I wondered? *Cora?* Several very unladylike phrases flitted across my thoughts though I at least had the presence of mind not to utter them, no doubt due to my manners and deportment.

Mother's face indicated puzzled agreement with Lady Sato, but it was very clear she didn't make any connection to airships from the extended metaphor Sato had used. That was good.

Then I remembered what Hypatia had said: the Facti knew I was on the *Bosch's* crew. Lady Sato and Hugo seemed to know each other. *Does that mean Lady Sato is a Facti? Is that even a possibility? How can I find out?* I certainly couldn't ask her about it in front of Mother. *Come to that,* I thought quickly, *how would I ask? 'Pardon me, Lady Sato, but are you connected to some ancient pagan god that gives you magic powers?'*

If I was wrong, that question would make Lady Sato think me a 'right nutter', as Griff would say. Hopeful I was right but frustrated that I had no way of knowing for sure, I cleared my throat and managed to say "Yes, ma'am," with the appropriate tone and conviction.

"Your mother and I have a great deal to catch up on," Lady Sato said, smiling warmly at me. "Can you study effectively while we chat? Or perhaps you have some other work to do? It would be a shame to waste this time we're en-route, don't you think?"

I nodded, grateful I didn't have to participate in a discussion of London society. "Yes, I think I can, Lady Sato," I said, reaching for my bookbag.

Mother beamed. "Excellent, my dear." She waved her hand at me in a shooing sort of gesture. "Get on with it, Ariana."

I felt my eyebrows rise in surprise which caused a twinge where my cut was, but tamped down the emotion along with my expression. I pulled out my books, taking care not to reveal my toolkit or the newspaper, and got to work, looking up from time to time to keep an eye on the people who walked past our cabin. It was a great relief to find the letters and numbers stayed on the page in their proper order and didn't move about like a drunken barn dance as they had a couple days before. I settled in to my work. Mother and Lady Sato spoke about society gossip and the London season in a low murmur I barely noticed, and the first leg of the train trip passed by in a blur of equations and cautious paranoia.

Chapter Thirty-Two

We stopped in York, the train pulling into the station in darkness, the platforms and train station lit by phosphorite lamps.

It was a city on edge. The police who stood in force in the station were tense and hyper-alert, scanning everyone who passed them to see if they were Enhanced. I saw three policemen holding oddly configured guns on an Enhanced man with a mechanical foot in a dark corner, his empty shoe on the pavement beside him. A fourth policeman inspected the man's travel documentation and I noticed with some relief that the man's eyes looked completely normal.

Passengers scurried back and forth, eager to make their trains or move on out into the city, but they did so without smiling or making eye contact. Over the din of the trains and the crowd, the newsboys waved papers with garish headlines, shouting about Enhanced uprisings in Manchester, Liverpool, and Bristol. I was desperate to read the newspaper I'd bought to find out more about what was happening. I clutched my bookbag in frustration in my right hand while I carried Hugo in his cage with my left. The porter loaded our belongings onto a cart and followed as Mother, Lady

Sato and I quickly made our way to a carriage that would take us and our luggage to our accommodations. Lady Sato found one, paid the porter and the carriage driver, and in just a few minutes we were on our way to our lodgings for the night.

The Royal York Hotel was less crowded than the train station had been, but the staff was clearly vigilant and security-minded. That eased my mind somewhat, but I still scanned the guests for any possible threat. Three police officers patrolled the well-appointed lobby, and one stood at the top of the wide staircase looking down at the comings and goings of the guests. I took in the tall corinthian columns and the black ironwork of the stairwell balustrade illuminated by countless lamps, impressed by the size of the place. Hugo, safely in his cage, looked around and trilled in approval. Mother ignored Hugo's commentary and asked the porter where we checked-in. He pointed us past the staircase to the left, where there was a long marble counter with red uniformed clerks behind it, helping other guests.

Lady Sato turned to us. "Allow me take care of this," she said to Mother. "I'll get the room keys and have the porter take our trunks up. Do you feel like having dinner in the dining room, or shall I ask about room service?"

Mother turned to me. "Ariana?"

"Is it all right if I just go to the room?" I asked. I wanted to give Hugo time out of the cage, and I knew that wouldn't be allowed in the common dining area. "I'm not hungry."

"I need a little something," Mother said. "Let's have them send up something simple, shall we?"

Lady Sato inclined her head. "That would be most agreeable," she said. She walked toward the counter and motioned the porter forward with the luggage cart that held our trunks.

Mother turned to me, weariness making her face drawn and pale. "This has been a very long day," she said. "It'll be pleasant to have something to eat and retire for the night."

More than you know, I thought, remembering my adventure at Dr. Sanburne's office.

"You never told me how you came by the raven," Mother said, looking down at Hugo. "He's a very well-mannered bird though I can't imagine how you convinced Mrs. Gildersleeve to allow him in the house."

"His name is Hugo," I told her. "He was a gift. As to how he became mine and what I did to convince Mrs. Gildersleeve to let me keep him in the house... well... it's a long story."

Mother looked at me for a long moment. "The last time you said that, we spent three days washing molasses off the carriage horses and staff."

I grimaced, remembering. When I was seven, I'd read about how knights defended medieval castles with my tutor Mr. Browdle. After the lesson, not having boiling oil to hand, I had climbed into the rafters of the stable and poured the entire household supply of molasses on the horses, coachman and stable boy in defense of my 'castle'. Father had laughed for days and praised my sneak attack. Mother forbade my climbing rafters and engaged Mr. Browdle in a strenuous conversation concerning my course of study. Shortly after that I'd bent the knives in my Arthurian 'sword in the stone experiments', and Mother insisted we stay away from the more 'romantic subjects' in lessons.

"No molasses this time," I told her. "Just superior debating skills."

"That's a relief," Mother said. "Less washing that way." She looked me up and down. "I hope the other dresses in your trunk are more fashionable than what you have on now. Your Great

Aunt will think your father and I neglect you if she sees you in those sorts of clothes."

Aunt Miranda had divined the true reason for my out-of-date dresses, of course, but I kept that to myself. I looked down at my plain, but perfectly serviceable garments. "Dresses fit for garden parties are not fit for riding a bicycle or participating in laboratory classes. There is no social scene in Cambridge as there is in London, and even if there were, I'm so busy with my studies I've no time to attend such soirees." *Not to mention my prefering to avoid such kinds of gatherings*, I thought.

"I suppose that's true," she said and reached out a hand to feel the fabric on my skirt, "but it makes you look so dowdy, Ariana," she complained, dropping the fabric and rubbing her fingers together as if considering something. "You're a pretty girl. I've no idea why you don't want to dress the part. No gentleman of quality will give you a second glance in that ensemble."

"Did Father base his decision to marry you on the clothes you wore at the time?" I asked, genuinely curious.

Mother pondered the question with far more care than I would have. "I don't think he based the decision on it, but my attire and bearing caught his eye and his interest from the first. After that," she sniffed, "my other qualities became known to him, and I should like to think those are what decided him in favor of marrying me."

"Ah," I said.

"That is why one's wardrobe is so important, particularly at your age and in your station in life, my dear. You neglect it at your peril."

"What time does the train leave tomorrow?" I asked, deliberately changing the subject.

Mother shrugged her shoulders, aware that I'd diverted the conversation, but not bothered by it. "I've made arrangements for a carriage to take us to the station at a quarter past nine. The train leaves at a quarter past ten for Aberdeen."

Lady Sato returned. She held up two bronze key fobs with bronze keys attached. "They'll send up some food in a bit," she explained, "and we're sharing a two room suite. It has two doors to the hallway, with two connected rooms and four beds. Your Mother and I will be in one room, and you're in the other, Ariana." She indicated the stairway. "We're on the second floor. Shall we head up?"

Chapter Thirty-Three

We climbed the grand staircase to the second floor and turned into a sedate hallway.   White wood paneling ran halfway up the walls, topped by a chair-rail.   Above the rail, light blue striped wallpaper reached to the ivory plaster ceiling, with an occasional picture or painting on the walls breaking up the spaces between the white room doors, their numbers on plaques to the right of each door.   The hotel staff had turned down the lamps in the hallway so the hall had the feel of late afternoon light rather than full-on daylight.   It was a simple matter to find my room, which was on the left and three doors down from the stairway.   Mother and Lady Sato walked past me to enter the next room over with their own key.

I entered the hotel room, locked the door behind me and relaxed somewhat.   The room had tan walls, a vanity, dresser, two armchairs and two nightstands in a light tan wood and two ponderous looking beds with white bedclothes and coverlets.   The carpet was brown, while framed lithographs hung on the walls.   My trunk sat on the luggage rack near the dresser, and the porter had lighted the lamps above the nightstands in anticipation of my arrival.   A candlestick telephone sat on the right-hand nightstand.

One wall had two windows that looked out over York, framed with heavy brocaded curtains that matched the carpet. I thought I could see the spire of York Minster out one window, grey in the moonlight. The bathroom, small and tiled, was to the right of the door. The door that led to the room Mother and Lady Sato were in was to the left, and Mother immediately opened it to inspect my accommodations.

"Not bad," she pronounced, nodding in approval, "and the hotel has no problem with our feathered friend," she said.

"I'm glad to hear it."

"The food should be up shortly. Lady Sato gave them our room number for room service. I'll let you know when it arrives, shall I?"

I put Hugo's cage on the floor and opened its door so he could hop out. He flew to one of the windows and took up a perch on the sill. Moonlight spilled through the window and illuminated Hugo so he looked more charcoal grey than raven black.

Mother watched in astonishment as Hugo settled, seeming as comfortable on the sill as he would be in a tree. I cleared my throat. "I don't really feel hungry, but I'll see what's on offer when it comes. Thank you, Mother."

"Good heavens," she exclaimed, pointing at Hugo. "Won't he make a mess if he's out of the cage?" Hugo shot her an affronted look, which even my mother understood. She bristled slightly.

"I do beg your pardon," she said to Hugo and headed back into her own room. "I'll just shut this door. You may be comfortable with such a creature milling about, but I would rather he stay out of our room."

With that, she stepped through the door that linked our two suites and shut it behind her, the latch sliding into place with a soft clicking sound.

I dropped my bookbag on the bed nearest the windows in relief, pulling out the *Times* and glancing at the headline. It read "Enhanced Troubles Continue" and a scan of the article titles below it detailed the difficulties the authorities dealt with around England.

"Well, Hugo?" I asked, looking up at him. "Do the accommodations pass muster?" He scanned the room for a moment, then nodded slightly.

I indicated the window. "Do I need to let you out to… erm… fly around a bit or anything?" Hugo opened his beak and croaked, and I had the distinct feeling he laughed at me.

"Pardon me, I must say," I responded with some asperity, mimicking Mother a little. "I've never travelled with a raven before." Hugo croaked again, shook his head and resumed his vigil looking out the window.

I sat down on the bed and read the articles fully. I felt cold horror run down my back as the details of the disturbances revealed themselves. The steel-eyed Enhanced rioters had started by attacking people at random. They'd set buildings on fire and watched as people burned alive within them. The list of the wounded and the tabulation of property damage was extensive and astonishing. The police had responded in force in all of the cities, but their Gauge guns hadn't stopped the Enhanced ruffians. The police had resorted to revolvers, but even bullets had little effect. It was clear the authorities didn't really know what to do. Bills had started in Parliament to banish all Enhanced people from the Empire. The Prime Minister had called for 'national calm' in his speech that afternoon though I wasn't sure what that meant. *How can Father leave London and go to Scotland with these disturbances taking place all over?* I wondered.

I shook my head in frustration as I folded the newspaper back up, but didn't put it in my bookbag. If I'd had a chance to speak to Hypatia longer, or have the long talk Andrew had promised, I was sure I'd have more answers, or at least know what sort of questions to ask.

My left wrist started to itch, and I scratched it absently until I realized the itch wasn't on the surface but came from within. I had a flashback to when Laufeson had made his first attempt to take me, and how that part of my wrist had twitched deep inside.

Revulsion, panic, and dread crept into me as realization dawned. Laufeson had said 'the spell still holds after all this time.' *Is that spell part of something implanted in my body*, I wondered. *If so... when and how had it happened? If something was there* – I felt it twitch again and swallowed hard.

If something is there, I began again, getting a firm grip on my fear and forcing a logical train of thought over it, *then it isn't mechanical.* If it were, the Gauges I'd used in countless pubs over the past year and a half would have picked it up. Before the past few days, I'd have scoffed at the idea of someone putting a spell on me, but now? Now I realized it was a distinct and very worrisome possibility, and I had no idea what to do about it.

Mother opened up the door that divided our rooms and I quickly tucked the folded paper under my skirt. She stuck her head around the door and looked at me.

"Room service just brought the food up, if you'd like any," she said. I nodded to indicate I understood and Mother shut the door again.

Clenching my fists, I worked to put the puzzle pieces together from the dribs and drabs of truth I'd gathered. I curled my legs up and pulled them close to my chest, grateful for once of the tight hold the corset had on my torso. Forced into measured breaths by steel-boned foundation garments, I began assembling facts in my mind with the same concentration I applied to differential equations. There were several variables to consider, and I was not dealing with a linear problem.

Andrew had said that I was part of a world where stories mattered and magic was real. Some presence had the power to take over my body and perform magic, as the blue symbols on the cobblestones indicated, but it wasn't an ability I could call up on my own, nor did I know its source. The Facti had magical abilities conferred by artifacts, Hypatia had said. Andrew's must have been the pendant and the gold tracery on his chest, I mused. I didn't see what Hypatia's artifact was, unfortunately. I'd never received any sort of artifact, so far as I knew, so I wasn't a Facti, but Hypatia implied that I would be.

The ruffians at Dr. Sanburne's office had the steel eyes that matched those who started the riots and disruptions that currently threatened England's stability. The men who'd been with Oberlin on the road had seemed to have a silver sheen to their eyes, though the disagreeable professor hadn't. *What does that mean?* I wondered.

Laufeson was a man with magical power over people's thoughts, as I knew from personal experience. He was an Obscurati, but how did he fit in with the riots? Why had he sent rioters to retrieve me? How had the Obscurati managed to affect so many people, and why only the Enhanced? What was their ultimate goal? Were they after simple chaos and death, or was there another agenda?

I frowned. I had no way of knowing what the Obscurati planned. *For what, then, did the Obscurati want me?* I wondered. Hypatia had said they wanted me because I was 'consecrated and an heir', which meant nothing to me. My repair to Sophie's arm had been minor, and certainly nothing like the sorts of things trained Enhanced physicians did in England or anywhere else. My mechanicals used no magic so far as I knew, and my accuracy with darts was handy but hardly worth the effort his kidnapping attempts had required. The attempts also seemed oddly half-hearted, which also confused me. Telling stories – my most recent odd ability—also seemed a passive skill, ill-suited to Obscurati plots. What would they have me do—tell the entire country a really good story as the foundation of a violent *coup d' etat*?

Then I reconsidered the ancient masculine presence Andrew had called to occupy my body on the road. Whatever that presence had been, it had protected us that night. I needed to know who that being was, why I was his chosen heir, and what difference my being 'consecrated' meant in the scheme of things. I knew churches were consecrated... but was it possible to consecrate people?

The thing twitched in my wrist again. I clutched my legs closer while I focused on my breathing and waded through the horror I felt. I had to think. If the Facti fought against Laufeson and the Obscurati, I needed to throw my lot in with them if I wished to stay safe and in control of my own actions and destiny. How to do that while on my way to Scotland with my mother and Lady Sato, of all people, was the next problem I had to solve. I had no idea how I'd even begin to explain any of this to them or how I'd keep them safe. If Lady Sato was a Facti—

Someone knocked on my hotel room door. I froze. Hugo looked at the door, alert and still.

Oh, God, I thought. *They'd found me.* Luckily, I'd locked the door. Would it be enough of a deterrent? Panic flared and I turned it to anger. I wouldn't go without a fight.

Not sure what else to do, I slid off the bed as quietly as I could and I reached down with my right hand to pull the knife from my right boot. Then I stood. Unbidden, I felt the calm when I threw darts suffuse me, but rather than my mind slipping into a dream, my senses sharpened. My consciousness didn't detach from my surroundings and I became hyper-aware of everything.

I stopped. That was new. *What's happening?* I wondered. The knock came again. "Who is it?" I called, listening carefully for the response.

"I've brought your dinner, miss," was the feminine response from the hallway.

That was odd. Mother had told me the food was in her room, and I doubted Lady Sato would have given my room number for room service. I listened closely. There was no sound of dishes clinking on a tray on the other side of the door, and I hadn't heard a cart approach the door. The calm grew into a presence in my mind, devoid of emotion, calculating options and possible responses like a military general. It had the mental feel of the magical being from the road, but I still didn't know who or what it was. *If it's keen to assist me in this, all the better,* I thought. I moved to stand away from the bed as my left hand pulled the other knife from my left boot.

"You're mistaken," I said, knives in both hands, ready to be thrown. "I didn't order dinner to be brought up."

"Please, miss," the voice pleaded. "I'll lose my position if the cook finds out I didn't deliver this as ordered."

"I didn't order it," I said. "Be on your way."

A key turned in the lock. The door opened wide, kicked inward by a black boot with enough force to leave the door wide open, but not so much that the door made any appreciable noise.

So much for the efficacy of the lock, I noted. *Damn and blast!*

A middle-aged woman stood in the doorway, her wide-brimmed black hat and dark glasses obscuring her face. She wore a black dress, a black scarf around her neck and long black gloves covering her hands and arms, looking for all the world like a recent widow in her weeds. She held no tray of food though that was hardly a surprise. Then she ruined the illusion of bereavement when she removed her hat and pulled off her dark glasses, throwing both to the floor.

Grim-visaged, she was Enhanced and not inclined to be friendly. Her face was leathery and wrinkled from years of work out of doors. Her brown hair hung limp around her head and shoulders, and her intent steel eyes regarded me. I noted the delicately thin silver filaments that curved from the outsides of her eyes, ran along the sides of her head, and entered her skull at her temples. That was different from what I'd seen in the news and on my prior attackers.

She took a step forward and planted her feet on the carpet of my room, looking around to see if I was alone. Unfortunately, I was. Hugo had disappeared. I hoped he'd gone for help.

"Hello, sweetie," she growled, once her gaze settled on me. "You're a hard one to find, you are. Molly's been searching all night to find you here."

How had she found me? I wondered. I held up the knife in my right hand.

"Get out," I warned.

The woman laughed, a harsh, gritty sound that came from deep in her throat. Smiling in a sickly mad way, she peeled the scarf off to reveal silver Enhanced tracery that ran in graceful curves around her neck and down into her chest.

What the Hell? The woman was more metal than flesh, I realized. *How is that possible? If the simple silver-eyed men were 'fiends', what does that make this creature?*

"I'm afraid I can't do that," she said, shaking her head. She held out her hands toward me as if pleading for me to take them. "Just let my pets get a bite of you, and you'll see it's better just to come along quietly. Molly will take good care of you."

I scanned the room looking for her 'pets', but saw nothing. Oddly, I heard the sound of ripping cloth, and as I watched silver worm-like tendrils shot from her hands through the fabric of her gloves. Metallic and segmented, they writhed in her hands like living things.

"Who are you?" I asked, fascinated and repulsed by the undulating of the 'pets' she held.

"I'm Molly Silver. I've come to take you to your new friends," the woman spat. "You're overdue for a visit, and we've got a great deal to share with you. The All-Father wants you for himself, but we'll make sure you ally with us so the old man won't claim you anymore."

All-Father? I wondered, wracking my brain. *Old man? Was that the being who currently floated at the edge of my mind?*

Taking advantage of my distraction, Molly growled and leapt with inhuman strength and speed, her arms and hands reaching for my throat. The tendrils in her hands stretched forward, their ends opening to reveal tiny metal mouths like hungry snakes, clicking against each other in their frenzy. I didn't want them anywhere near me.

I tensed, and in the space of a heartbeat the presence – the All-Father—had mapped the trajectories of my knives like an elegant math equation. Before my heart could sound another beat, the knives left my hands in a double throw at an impossible speed. One knife buried itself in the woman's neck, spurting red blood across the carpet and the bottom of my skirt in a fan of droplets, while the other knife sank to the hilt into the woman's left eye socket.

Her body hit the floor in front of me with a sickening thud, her lifeless hands and their spasming tendrils brushing the bottom of my skirt. A pool of dark red blood bloomed from underneath her head and neck while the snakes continued to snap and writhe, seeking to bite me even though their fleshly host was dead.

The presence left me and the spell I was under shattered like glass. Emotion returned, replacing cold calculation. Horrified by what I'd done, I took a step back, turned to the right, and retched what little I had in my stomach onto the brown carpet. Once my heaving stopped, I stumbled to the bed and sat down, body shaking in shock and fear, looking down in disbelief at the dead Enhanced woman at my feet.

I'd just killed a woman without hesitation... and it had been far, far easier than throwing darts. The presence that had worked with me this time had felt nothing as it calculated my responses, and I'd gone along without complaint. *What, in the name of all that is holy is going on? Is the magic I possess only good for killing people? How will that serve the Facti or do any good? Oh God. What am I going to do?*

I had to get out of the room. I got up from the bed, moved around the corpse and ran into the hallway, gritting my teeth against the scream trying to force its way out of my throat. Once out of the room I nearly collapsed, but refused to let my knees buckle. Tears pooled in my eyes and ran down my cheeks, but I didn't care. I put my hands on my knees and drew in great gasps of breath, trying to ride the wave of fear and alarm without losing consciousness.

One or two heads peeked out of doors, took in my shocked, terrified features as I stood doubled over in the corridor and ducked back into their rooms. I heard locks turning and muffled voices behind the closed doors, probably calling the front desk about the wild-eyed young lady in the corridor who'd just killed someone in her room and left the corpse on the floor in a pool of blood. No doubt the police would be on their way. *What will I tell them? Oh God—what will I tell Mother?*

A sob escaped my throat. I didn't know what to do or where to go, but—

"Miss Trevelyan?"

Before I could respond, the presence took control. It had me reach for the bracelet on my wrist and toggle the switch to transform it into the spinning blade. I turned, blade in hand and ready for another attack, my mind an island of icy calm.

Thankfully, I saw Lady Sato in the hallway with Hugo on her shoulder. She ran toward me with a fluid grace and speed despite her skirts. Hugo flapped his wings on her shoulder to maintain his balance.

The presence drained away from my mind, recognizing the Japanese woman as a friend. I stumbled to the left and put an arm out to catch myself against the wall. Another sob escaped me, this one louder and more desperate. I dropped my weapon to the floor and it popped back into a bracelet shape with a snap. Lady Sato's arms encompassed me, surprisingly strong and wiry.

"Hugo said someone attacked you," she said in a rush, "and you killed the woman with your knives. Is that true?"

I opened my mouth to respond, but bent over and retched instead, though I had nothing in me to bring up. I leaned my body against the wall and started to shake again.

"Hugo, stay with her," Sato ordered. He hopped down and ran over to lean against me, a gentle pressure on my leg. Lady Sato looked up and down the corridor to see if we were alone, then ran the few steps down the hall and into my hotel room.

She was back almost immediately. "We must leave, and now," she said, hauling me to my feet. "We'll have the trunks sent after us, and go by airship to Brentwood Close."

"But my mother—what if they go after her? "I stammered, "—and I killed that—"

"I'm with your mother right now. She's safe and will remain so."

I gaped in confusion. "You're not with her," I said, my voice high with growing hysteria, "you're here with me. If the Enhanced —"

She cut me off. "I'm with her there now and I'm here with you now."

I didn't understand what she meant. *How could she be in two places at once?* "But—"

"Let me handle this. Now—right now—you will go down to my room, number 225. The door is open—go. I will see all of us safely and discreetly away."

"But your room is next to mine," I stammered, not understanding.

"I have two rooms," she explained tersely.

"The police will want to speak to me," I babbled. "I killed—"

"In self-defense, child!" she said, "and I have no intention of allowing the police anywhere near you." She pushed me down the corridor gently but firmly. "Go!" she urged, "Now!"

I stumbled my way toward Lady Sato's other room, Hugo at my heels, fumbled at the knob for room 225, and nearly fell in as the door swung open. Hugo hopped in behind me. The room was identical to mine, but it had one bed rather than two. I shut the door and moved like a drunk to sit on the bed, my movements stilted and wobbly. Hugo hopped up on the bed to sit beside me, leaning against my arm. I wiped the tears from my cheeks.

The door opened and Lady Sato rushed in, startling me so I jumped. She wore an old-fashioned dark green gown and her hair hung in ringlets around her face. She looked younger than she had when I'd seen her in the hallway seconds before, and then she'd worn a gold dress and her hair up rather than down.

"Ariana—come with me," she said.

I stood up in shocked astonishment. "But your dress – "I yammered, "you look—"

"Not one of my best frocks, I know," she said, grabbing me by the arm. She handed me my bracelet from the hallway and I quickly put it on my left wrist. "We can discuss my haberdashery later. You need to leave this hotel."

With that, she pulled me out of her hotel room, ran me down the stairs and led me out of the lobby, then propelled me into the street in front of the hotel in a blur of silent speed, Hugo flying behind us. We moved so quickly, or perhaps everyone around us moved so slowly, they didn't notice our hasty departure. No one turned their heads as we passed them, and as we dashed through the lobby, it was as silent as a tomb despite its being full of people.

The Odin Inheritance Victoria L. Scott

Chapter Thirty-Four

Once out on the street, our speed seemed to return to normal, but the air around us rang with silence. It was still night, but I couldn't tell what time it was. I scanned the people standing around the hotel entrance, worried we'd be attacked yet again. I found to my great surprise that not only were there no threats in evidence, the people around us stood still as statues. Even the smoke from one man's pipe hung unmoving and static above the pipe's bowl. Hugo, very much mobile, flapped up behind us to land on Lady Sato's shoulder, trilling in alarm.

"Yes, Hugo," Sato acknowledged, "there has been a great deal of running about. It can't be helped."

"I don't understand any of this," I said, bewildered. "Why are we the only ones moving?"

"We're standing between two seconds," was Lady Sato's response. "I'm holding them," she indicated the people standing around us, "trapped in the moment, and allowing us," she indicated herself, me and Hugo, "to move about as we need in this infinite... pause," she finished.

I pounced on her explanation, my mind racing and grateful for the distraction from what I'd done in the hotel room. "You're saying we're existing outside the time they're living in," I said. "How is that possible? Are you making use of some new device or invention? Are these people in danger somehow?"

"Surely you recall from your study of mathematics that between two places on a line there are an infinite number of points."

I nodded slowly, taking that in. "So, you're saying that between two places in time there's an infinite amount of time?"

"It's the most basic of explanations, but essentially, yes. As to our immobile companions here in front of the Royal York," she gestured at them, "they're in no danger. To them, nothing is happening. Once I allow time to resume its usual pace, they'll not even know we were here."

"But how – "

"I have a special relationship with time," she said. "Best if we leave it there, however. Explaining how I do this," she waved a hand, "requires verb tenses that don't actually exist in English."

"You're like Hypatia," I said. I brought my hand to my face, closed my eyes and squeezed the bridge of my nose. "My God. You're another one."

"Well done, Ariana," Lady Sato said, clearly pleased. "I am the Heir of Mammetun, the Sumerian goddess of Fate and Time."

I wasn't certain who the Sumerians were or how it was possible to be an heir with power over something like time. "Oh," I said eloquently. "Where is Sumeria, exactly?"

"Focus, Ariana," she said with some impatience. "Escape now, geography later."

The Odin Inheritance   Victoria L. Scott

"Right. Ah... speaking of escaping, I think there's something in my wrist," I said, clutching it protectively. "Could it be that's how the—I choked, seeing Molly Silver die all over again in my mind, "— found me here?"

Lady Sato nodded, urging me forward and away from the hotel entrance. "We thought as much." She scanned the area. "It was the one thing we couldn't fix when we found you thirteen years ago."

"Found me?"

"The man you know as Laufeson kidnapped you from the back garden of your home in Kent when you were four. Took us three days to find you." She chewed her lower lip. "Clearly his claim on you is greater than we'd thought. I'd hoped leaving Hugo with you would throw him off the scent."

"Three days? I don't remember being missing for three days, Lady Sato," I said, "Or being found, for that matter."

She nodded. "At the time, we thought blocking your recollections was the best course of action. I'm beginning to think it was a mistake."

It took me a moment to absorb that. "Have you people been mucking about in my head for years, then?"

Lady Sato stopped, took my hand in hers and squeezed it. "We had to protect you as you grew up. Blocking your access to what happened was the best way to do that. If you ever thought to ask about it, we referred to it as an 'accident'."

"Aunt Miranda — she told me I'd had an accident and that I'd lived with her for a year after," I muttered. "Bloody Hell. She's a Facti."

Lady Sato smiled as if she'd known I'd say that. "Quite."

"Why kidnap me?" I asked, mind reeling. "What use could he make of a child?"

"Because you're related to your Aunt Miranda, and your aunt thwarted Fate to ensure you were born," she said. She dropped my hand. "Laufeson had no use for you as a child, Ariana. He had a use for an adult – you – with a connection to an ancient god, and he was willing to wait for you to grow up. Once you did, he'd take you back."

"Is this ancient god the All-Father?"

"He is." Sato looked at her feet for a moment and then met my eyes. "The All-Father is Odin, the chief god of the Norse pantheon. It's him you feel on the edge of your thoughts."

Now I had a name to attach to the presence I'd felt, but I had no idea who Odin was or what he was capable of. *Is he a good god?* "But – "

"Laufeson took you as a child because children are easy to grab, though even as a four-year-old you fought like a tiger."

I froze. *Easy to grab?* "Where is Mother?" I asked, the words coming out in a rush. I scanned the unmoving crowd to see if I could see her. "Is she in danger? And Father? He's supposed to be meeting us. How will we keep them—"

"Someone we trust is with your Father and bringing him, in safety, to Miranda's estate at Brentwood Close. In fact," she said, reaching into her sleeve, "he wanted you to have this." She pulled down and out came a long gold watch chain with a gold fob I recognized.

"Father gave you his watch chain with Old Tom?" I said, holding out my hand to accept it. It coiled up in my hand, warm and familiar. I remembered playing with the chain and fob when I was small, sitting on Father's lap. The fob, called 'Old Tom' was an old Catholic saint's medal, the face in profile nearly worn smooth. "Why?"

"He wanted you to wear it for luck. If you wrap it around your wrist, I think you'll find it'll do well as a bracelet."

I wrapped it about my right wrist as Sato suggested and attached the clasp to the fob. It reminded me so much of Father I couldn't help but smile, though it made me worry that I had Father's good luck and he didn't. "Thank you – but you're sure he's well? And Mother?"

Sato nodded. "Yes. Your father is very well protected and your mother is safe," she said. "As I told you before, I'm still with her."

"How is that—?"

She stopped me. "No way to explain it in English, I'm afraid. Best if you just accept that I can be in several places at once, and try not to think about it too much." She looked over my shoulder. "Oh, good. Your ride has arrived."

She turned me around to face a stocky gentleman who had kind eyes, a massive dark beard and a mantle of hair that surrounded his face like a lion's mane. Unlike the static people around us, he moved and breathed as Lady Sato, Hugo and I did. Obviously, Lady Sato's trick with time encompassed him just as it did us. Unsurprised by the vista of human statues, he approached us casually. He was in his shirtsleeves, and suspenders held up his brown trousers. I noted with some shock he stood barefooted. I shuddered to think what he'd walked through, knowing what sorts of muck ended up in the streets.

"Lady Ariana," he said in a thick Russian accent, "it is pleasure meet you. I am Gregor Datsik at your service." He bowed and clicked his bare heels together though they didn't make a sound. "I will take you from here to airship. Do you know horse riding?"

I looked at Lady Sato, who nodded in encouragement at me, then turned my attention back to Mr. Datsik. "I beg your pardon?" I asked.

Mr. Datsik smiled, and I saw his eyes were a deep, warm brown color. "Can you ride horse?" he asked again.

I looked around in confusion. At that moment, there were no carts, carriages or horses in front of the hotel. "Yes, but... I don't see a horse, Mr. Datsik."

"Ah," Mr. Datsik said. "Please, calling me Gregor. I provide horse for you. I ask only you not pull mane too much." He indicated the side of the hotel. "I will go there, and horse will come back. It will be dark, like me," he indicated his beard, "but the left ear will be white. If you wish speaking, reach up and grasp white ear, and we speak."

That sounded completely bizarre. "Is the horse's ear a telephone? Or detachable? Is it some sort of clockwork animal?"

Gregor barked a laugh. "No," he said. "I am real horse. You climb back, and we go to airship."

He turned and ran around the side of the building. I turned back to Lady Sato, who wore the gold gown and her hair up once again, with Hugo pacing at her feet.

"What the bloody hell is going on?" I hissed at Lady Sato. "Where did that Russian come from? He's talking like *he's* the horse, and your dress has changed."

Lady Sato smiled. "I'd forgotten how direct you were," she said, "but I dare say your mother would disapprove of your choice of words. Bloody Hell? Hardly the discourse of a lady."

I expressed myself in several more choice epithets, which only made Lady Sato smile more broadly. "The Russian?" I spluttered, having reached the end of my colorful vocabulary. "Who is he?"

"Ah. Yes. Gregor? Let's call him an associate. He's a recent addition to our group. His English does improve, but we're in early days yet."

I couldn't make sense of that comment. "What?" I asked.

Hugo croaked and waved his beak in the direction of the side of the hotel to which the bearded Slav had retreated. I spun around to see a dark brown horse with a white left ear approach, devoid of saddle or bridle, but clutching a white shirt and a brown pair of trousers with suspenders still attached in his teeth.

"Why is the horse carrying Mr. Datsik's garments?" I asked Lady Sato, then twigged to what must have transpired. "Oh God," I whispered. "He's a Facti. He *is* the horse." The horse whinnied and nodded, the clothes bobbing up and down as he did so.

I brought my hand to my head and felt my body start to shake. "That's it," I muttered. "I've finally gone starkers. Equine transformations? Temporal stagnation? Odin the Norse god? Someone's going to lock me in a madhouse and throw away the key."

Hugo squawked and in a couple wing flaps had perched himself on the horse's head.

"Ah, yes," Lady Sato said, her tone business-like, "taking the clothes along is a capital plan. Well done, Gregor. " She reached out and took the clothing from the horse, wadded it up into a ball and handed it to me. "Up you go," she said, indicating the horse's back.

"There?" I said, appalled. "There's no saddle or bridle. How will I get up there, and what will I hold on to once I do?"

Lady Sato cupped her hands and bent over, providing a stirrup of sorts. I hesitantly put my booted foot in her grasp and before I knew it, I was on the horse's back.

"Put his clothes in front of you," she suggested, "lean forward and wrap your arms around his neck. Move your skirts so your legs can grasp his back and sides without obstruction. That should keep you secure enough. I've created a time field around the two of you as an extra precaution. Don't worry. Gregor knows the way. Don't let the airship leave without your mother and me, or Gregor, once he's changed back into his human form."

"All right," I said uncertainly. "Which airship—"

"Gregor, time to go," Lady Sato said, interrupting me.

Gregor lurched forward in response. I barely managed to wrap my arms far enough around his neck while I braced my legs and feet to keep myself on his back though his clothes were secure underneath my chest. Hugo took off from the Russian's head and kept pace with us as Gregor careened through the streets of York at the fastest speed he could manage. It was more a game of dodging inanimate objects than anything else. True to Lady Sato's word, we moved between moments, while everyone around us remained ignorant of our passing.

Where is the airship depot? I wondered. *How did Gregor become this horse? How does he know Lady Sato?*

I scooted myself forward so that I could get a firmer grip on Gregor's heaving neck with my right hand and arm while I tentatively reached my left hand up to grip the white left ear. I concentrated on timing my movements with those of the horse so that I could remain more securely on the bare back under me. Buildings flew past, as did other horses, carriages, lampposts and people on the street, and the only sounds were the rapid cracks of Gregor's hooves on the brick pavement. I managed to touch his white left ear and hold on to it, but barely.

Yes, Miss Trevelyan? came a voice in my mind. It was masculine, polite, and distinctly Russian.

"My God," I said, amazed. "I can hear you."

Yes, came the phlegmatic response. *It is as I saying, yes?*

I smiled at the interesting turn of phrase. "How did you know to come to the Royal York Hotel?"

Sato tell me. I come. You must be safe.

"Are you only able to become a horse?"

Nyet. I become all animal. Big, small... all animal. He grunted. *We turn sharp. Hold hard.*

I looked ahead, noted the corner approaching, let go of Gregor's ear and held on tight as he bolted around the tight turn. I heard Hugo squawk in alarm behind us. Once past the turn, I reached up to clasp the ear again.

Ha! Hugo not liking the streets, I think, Gregor said, and I could feel the smile in his thoughts though he could not express it on his equine face.

"How are you able to become these animals?" I asked.

I am of Thetis. She change, so I change.

"Thetis?"

Goddess of Greek, yes? I am inheritor of her. It is much honor, and unexpected for you, I am thinking. I am horse with secret, like at Troy.

He whinnied at his own joke.

So Gregor's abilities meant he could shapeshift, as Lady Sato manipulated time and Hypatia manipulated the rain. The tale of the Trojan Horse was one of the few I knew, and I couldn't help but think Gregor wasn't the only person I'd met recently with hidden secrets, though for my sake I hoped they were happier ones than the Trojans had experienced.

We arrive depot soon. You will like, I think. Is nice ship. Hold hard. I go faster. Is better we speaking later.

"Thank you, Gregor," I said and slid back so I could get a better grip with arms and legs. Once Gregor sensed I was ready, he increased his speed. I closed my eyes and concentrated on holding on, feeling only the movement of Gregor's equine body underneath me, letting the shock and sadness of the day's events and revelations wash over me as I did so. Luckily, between Gregor's speed and Lady Sato's time tricks, no one saw the struggle to accept what I'd done on my face.

Chapter Thirty-Five

When Gregor finally slowed and stopped, my hair was free of half of its pins and hanging about my shoulders in a tangled mess of up and down curls. Gregor's flanks, flecked with foam, heaved underneath me. I opened my eyes, wiped my cheeks, sat up and discovered we stood in some sort of large staging area with three walls made of wooden slats nailed to large wooden beams which in turn held up a tin roof. Hugo flew up to perch on one of the rafters above us. The place smelled of new wood. Blazing torches in metal holders provided a flickering, but surprisingly bright light, and the floor beneath us was brick. Clearly, the depot was very new and intended for cargo rather than passengers. I couldn't see the airship that was meant to be our transport to Scotland. Presumably it was out in the dark, tethered, fueled and ready to leave. I couldn't see anyone in the building. *Perhaps the crew is on board the ship?*

"This the place?" I asked Gregor and sniffled. I tried to wipe my nose discreetly but had limited success. I doubted Gregor had a kerchief I could borrow. He whinnied and nodded his big head up and down.

I heard steps on the brick floor heading toward us, and the protective presence of Odin sparked in my mind, anticipating trouble. I was a target on Gregor's back, he indicated. I needed to get on the ground and get a weapon ready. I tried to get off Gregor in a way that would allow me to defend myself, but the day's exertions and the pell-mell trip through York had taken their toll on my body. My muscles quivered from holding on so tightly, and I slid from Gregor's back in a limp-noodle sort of flop, dragging the shirt and trousers with me as I landed in a heap on the brick pavement.

Gregor looked over at me and neighed in what I took to be an expression of concern. I tried to stand up but found my legs trembled so much I couldn't. My vision swam and I couldn't seem to focus on anything. The steps I'd heard drew closer, and I tried to toggle my bracelet to use as a weapon, but failed. Before I could make another move, huge hands grabbed my upper arms, lifted me up off the bricks and enveloped me in a big bear hug, pressing my face into the shoulder of a well-worn leather jacket. Gregor's clothes dropped to the ground.

"Ari!" Max cried, squeezing the air from my lungs in his enthusiasm to greet me properly. "You made it! Thank the stars and my dear Aunt Fanny!"

"Urgh," I gasped in response.

"Don't you worry—we'll get you safe to Scotland with no trouble at all," he continued, spinning me around in his embrace like I was a child's doll.

"Max," I croaked, head spinning, "please – "

He pulled me out of the embrace and placed my feet on the bricks, holding me at arms length to look me up and down. I was grateful for that, since I was quite sure if he let go I'd drop to the ground again.

"Are you all right, my girl?" Max asked. "You look dirty, bloody, windblown, exhausted and," he wrinkled his nose, "you smell of horse."

"It's been a very long day," I said. Seeing Max in front of me in his aeronaut clothes was a balm to my mind and soul. I knew that where Max was, the *Bosch* had to be. I felt my eyes well with tears as I stammered out, "I can't tell you how glad I am to see you. People have tried to—" I gasped, "— and I had to use the knives and —"

Max saw the emotion on my face and resorted to patting my head and shoulder with one hand in an awkward attempt to sooth me while he held me up with the other. "There, there, Ari," he cooed. "Deep breath, now," he urged. "You're safe with us, and you'll be safer once we're aloft. We're waiting on Lady Sato and her guest, and – "

"The guest is my mother," I said, wiping my eyes and nose with my hands and right sleeve. What was done was done. I had to get my emotions under control. "Have you received word on where they are? Are they all right?"

"I'm sure your mother is very safe if she's with Lady Sato. I promise we won't leave without them." He cupped a hand to his mouth and shouted into the darkness: "Griff! Can you come help Mr. Datsik? We need to get him airship ready toot-sweet!"

I clenched my fists and focused on calming down. I found if I didn't try to move, I could stay standing with relative success and Max's help, though my legs trembled and I still felt the movement of the horse in my body, like the roll of the deck one feels on land after a long time on a boat.

"Coming!" came Griff's return shout.

I looked around the hangar again. "What is this place? Are we safe here? There aren't any Enhanced fellows nearby or hiding somewhere?"

Max shook his head. "This is the private airfield we rented specifically to pick you up. Only been in use a couple months. For security's sake, we did a complete search of the area. No evildoers about. Needle, Lizzie, and Andrew await us on the ship on standby – once we're all present and accounted for, we'll be off."

I looked up at Hugo in the rafters. "Hugo?" I called.

Hugo flew down and landed on my shoulder, then snuggled up so his beak was near my ear. He nibbled a little of the hair close to my earlobe in a gentle tug and I felt some of the tension leave my body. He leaned against my head and cooed a little in an attempt to comfort me.

Max eyed the raven on my shoulder. "Millie told me about your beastie," he said, nodding toward Hugo, "but I must say, he's even more impressive than I've heard." He looked over my head. "I wish Griff would hurry up. If Gregor joins us as he is now, it'll be hard to explain to your mother."

Gregor neighed. I turned to look at Gregor in his equine aspect and then looked back at Max. "Wait. You know he's a man? How do you know he's a man?"

Max let go of me and watched to verify that I could stand on my own. I wobbled a little but stabilized. He nodded in approval.

"We've been briefed on the Facti and the Obscurati." He rubbed an earlobe thoughtfully. "Made for the strangest business meeting I've ever attended. We only knew we had the contract with something called the Pessarine Consortium until that meeting I told you about, which was moved up to this afternoon unexpectedly. Then Lady Sato, Andrew and Gregor showed up, told us some tall tales about these evil Obscurati blokes, wafted about terms like 'artifacts' and 'magic' and expected we'd just take their word for it."

I frowned. "I know what that's like," I said.

Max shrugged. "We demanded proof, of course – we didn't fall off the turnip cart yesterday, after all. To prove to us they spoke the truth about their unique abilities, we watched as Lady Sato stopped time, Mr. Datsik turned into various animals and Andrew showed us how he reads thoughts and heals wounds."

He cleared his throat. "That was plenty of proof for our piece of mind, but then they showed us how much the Pessarines intended to pay—a considerable sum—and we accepted the contract. Then Sato stuck us 'between seconds,' she said, to make the final changes to the *Bosch* in next to no time, which was handy, since Griff had one of the engines half in pieces."

"I can see how Lady Sato's magic would help with that."

"Then came the call for us to meet you here, and here we are." He shrugged. "We've yet to meet the chap with the gift with plants. Once we get to Brentwood Close, I should imagine we'll meet up with your Great Aunt and the 'flora' fellow."

"The chap with a gift for plants?" I parroted. Apparently the *Bosch* crew knew more about what was going on than I did. That didn't seem fair.

"We can't tell anyone what we know, of course—that was part of the agreement—but otherwise we can't complain about the contract terms." Max beamed. "The Pessarines have been very generous. If it hadn't been for the time crunch to get us here in time to pick you and the others up, we'd have made even more changes to the *Bosch*… expand the frame for the hydrogen ballonets, maybe add another engine…"

I couldn't keep the alarm from my voice. "Max—it's a generous contract because it has to be dangerous work. I'm still not sure what all this is about or even how I'm involved. I don't want you or the others to get hurt."

He chuffed my chin. "We know. Andrew explained what happened on the road and how the Obscurati are after you. We don't want you to get hurt, either."

I opened my mouth to ask a question, but Max put a hand up to stop me. "Yes, before you ask, he restored Lizzie's memories of the attack and apologized for having to mess about with her memories in the first place. What you did with the cobblestones made quite an impression on her once she remembered everything again. I always knew there was something magical about you." He smiled, enjoying his little joke. "I'm dying to know how you did it, if I'm honest."

So am I, I thought. "But—"

"Ari, the way we see it, working for the Pessarines is a way to go professional and keep you safe at the same time. We're the first of the Icarus Squadron to manage the transition. The existence of this new airship station is proof that moving people and cargo by airship is the wave of the future in England." He smiled broadly. "We're getting in on the ground floor, and if things go as I think they will, we're going to be very successful. As to the danger, well… it makes life all the sweeter, don't you think?"

Griff ran in, kitted out in a tan pair of canvas coveralls with smears of grease, paint and oil on them. His moustache was impeccably waxed to curve up at the ends and his eyes twinkled when he saw me. He swept me a courtly bow.

"Your Ladyship," he intoned, "a pleasure to see you. Can I get you to look over Needle's navigational equations quick-like before we leave? I'm sure they're fine, but another pair of eyes checking them over would be most appreciated."

"Of course, Griff," I said, my spirits lifted by the request. At least checking navigational equations was something normal and familiar.

He reached down to snag Gregor's clothes before he straightened. "You'll find the course papers at your station on the bridge."

"Thank you. I'll look them over right away."

"My thanks." He turned to face Gregor. "Come on, you Cossack," he said as he walked over to stand in front of the horse. He indicated they needed to head to the right and out of sight. "We can't have you fluttering the dovecote with your naked nether regions." Gregor snorted but followed Griff out into the night, taking his nether regions with him.

"How much of the refit did you get done?" I asked Max. "You said something about being ready for the end of the week, but we're not there yet."

"True enough. We did the best we could, but there's a great deal more to be done. We re-arranged the storage areas and put a couple walls up in the cleared space with some rudimentary furnishings and plumbing to make places for passengers to sleep. Bridge and crew quarters are unchanged, except I'm sharing my room with Andrew until we can get the refit completely finished." He motioned at the dark expanse outside the shelter. "Come on. Let's head to the bridge. We'll be able to see your mother and Lady Sato arrive from there."

We made our way out into the darkness, Max's hand on my left arm guiding me toward the *Bosch's* gangplank. I felt the effects of my bareback ride through York, so I walked stiffly, but we made it up the gangplank and onto the ship without incident. We went to the bridge, lit by its usual hanging phosphorite globes. Lizzie greeted me with a hug and tried not to look alarmed by my appearance. I hugged her back quickly.

"Where are Needle and Mr. Michaelson?" I asked, looking around.

"Engines," Lizzie told me. "Griff is handling the boarding—" she looked out the front windows, "and he's helping Mr. Datsik up the gangplank now," she said, lifting her chin at the two human figures moving below us. "The Russian will be in one of the guest rooms while Lady Sato and your mother will occupy the other one." She indicated the navigational instruments at my usual bridge station. "Your bit's exactly as you left it."

"Thanks," I said.

I moved to my station to grab the papers with the course calculations to check the headings. I looked over the instruments and familiarized myself with the current conditions of the weather and the ship while Max and Lizzie went over the standard pre-flight protocols. Hugo remained perched on my shoulder and scanned the instruments in front of us silently. I worked and snuck glances out the window, waiting for Mother and worrying that it seemed to be taking too long for her and Lady Sato to arrive. *How can someone who controls time be late for anything?* I wondered.

Then I saw a carriage roll up in front of the building where Gregor had dropped me off. It was a relief to see Lady Sato and Mother step out of the cab. Mother, with hat and hair somewhat askew, paid the driver while Lady Sato watched, wearing her gold gown and looking cool as a cucumber. Before the cab driver could turn the carriage around, Griff bowed to the women and led them toward the gangplank. Mother moved quickly, speaking to Griff urgently. He responded as he looked up at the bridge windows and motioned that we should prepare to leave. Then he helped the women onto the gangplank and out of sight.

Max pulled up the speaking tube from the console in front of him that connected the bridge to the engine room. "All right, lads," he said, "Griff's releasing us from the mooring buoy. Be ready to start the engines on my mark."

Muffled affirmative noises surfaced on the bridge end of the speaking tube, and Max grinned. "This'll be our first professional job, ladies. How about that?"

Lizzie beamed and I smiled too, but more because Mother appeared to be well despite the rapid hotel departure and the precarious state of her fascinator and coiffure. I wondered if she'd like traveling by airship.

We felt the ship lurch as Griff released the mooring bolt so the *Bosch* floated free and started a slow rise into the night sky. I watched Griff run from the bow back to the gangplank, now a couple feet off the ground, and leap up to land on it with a solid thump that jostled us. Then he disappeared from view, running up the gangplank and working the winch to pull it up into a folded position under the ship. He closed the hatch with a thud, followed by a crunch as he slid the latch on it home.

That was the cue for Needle and Andrew to start the engines. Max moved the chadburn dial to 'ahead slow' and suddenly our silent hovering had a mechanical thrum and vibration to it. Lizzie and Max worked the throttle and propellers to aim the *Bosch* up into the air so we'd gain altitude while I monitored the pressure of the eight rubber hydrogen ballonets within the silk-covered rigid aluminum frame. The higher we went, the more the pressure changed, and I spent time regulating the ballonets accordingly. My instruments showed the wind blowing south-southeast and I made notes to the side of Needle's calculations accordingly. No doubt we'd have to make some minor course corrections when we reached our cruising altitude and then again once the sun came up, since its rays would warm the air, making the ballonets expand. I figured we were five or so hours from sunrise. I hoped I'd have a chance to catch a little sleep before morning, but I'd wait to be relieved before I left the bridge.

The *Bosch* continued to rise. York spread out below us, lights twinkling in the streets and windows. Max moved the chadburn dial to 'ahead half full' and steered while Lizzie monitored the engines and propellers. I felt the increase in our forward acceleration but continued to watch the instruments in front of me for signs of trouble.

Needle stepped onto the bridge. "Captain," he said, "Griff is at his station in the engine room. Permission to take my station?"

"Aye, Needle, and thank you," Max said.

Needle stepped over to me. "I suggested Lady Sato and your mother take the air on the deck. The Duchess looked concerned, but well when she boarded." He indicated the sheets in front of me. "How was my math?"

"I made some notes," I said and indicated where I'd written. "I think you did well. Once the sun rises – "

He nodded. "I'll watch for changes. Now—away with you, Ari," he said, hiking a thumb over his shoulder to indicate the hallway. "You look knackered. See if you can get some rest."

I nodded. "Max, do you mind if I—?"

"Go. We'll make do. I'm sure you want to make sure your mother is all right."

Chapter Thirty-Six

Hugo and I headed up to the storage area above the bridge that now functioned as the guest rooms which Gregor, my mother and Lady Sato occupied. I crested the top step only to see Lady Sato clutching Mother's upper right arm as she hustled her into the room on the right. Mother had her left hand clasped over her mouth while her complexion wavered between ash grey and nauseous green. Her throat moved convulsively though she tried to control it. She noticed me and nodded briefly to indicate she'd seen me, but another nauseous convulsion took her, and she dashed into her room, leaving Lady Sato to sketch me a small wave and follow her, shutting the door behind them. I heard wretching sounds from behind the door and decided right then was not the best time to visit Mother. Obviously, she wasn't well suited to air travel.

Though I worried about Mother's being ill, it was a relief to know any conversation with her about what I'd done in the hotel room clearly had to wait. I took a moment to thank my lucky stars that I had no tendencies for nausea while on airships.

I turned to head downstairs to my own cabin and nearly walked into Andrew, who was behind me on the stairs. Like Griff, he wore tan coveralls with the collar of a white shirt poking out near his neck. I hadn't heard him come up the stairs behind me, but since I knew he was now a member of the crew, it wasn't really a surprise to see him again.

Hugo squawked briefly at Andrew in reaction to his sudden appearance and flapped his wings a little to help him resettle on my shoulder.

I gave the blonde American a cursory inspection. Andrew smelled of the engines and there was a small smear of grease on one of his cheeks. He wiped his hands on a rag, then tucked it into a side pocket of the coveralls. He looked as delighted to be on the *Bosch* in flight as I would have been, if I hadn't been so tired and sore. His blue eyes twinkled with delight to see me, until he looked me over. The twinkle faded.

I exhaled slowly, resigned to the disaster I knew I appeared to be. I was dirty, partially blood spattered, very much mud and street-grime spattered and wrinkled beyond hope of recovery, and that was just my clothes. I'd not ridden a horse in a couple years, and never astride or bareback. As a result, I had muscle aches in places both mentioned and not mentioned in polite society. It was all I could do to keep myself upright. Being on the *Bosch*, my home away from home, helped, but I found I wished to be left to myself to sort through my emotions and figure out what I needed to do next. Seeing Andrew was both a relief and a source of consternation. I felt awkward standing there in silence and rubbed Father's watch chain on my wrist absently. He'd know what to say in this situation. I didn't.

Andrew recovered from the shocking nature of my appearance and spoke first. "Miss Trevelyan," he said, concerned, "are you all right?" Then he noticed the blood on my skirt. "My God—have you been hurt?"

"No. The blood isn't mine."

He furrowed his brow. "Whose is it, then?"

"Molly Silver's," I said, shooting the cuffs of my shirt and trying to seem nonchalant though I was anything but. "She paid me a visit in York. It didn't end well."

Andrew looked from my face to the raven on my shoulder. His eyes widened, and it was obvious Hugo was communicating the days' events to Andrew. His face showed amazement, concern, anger, pride, and concern again in quick succession. Though I was glad Hugo told him the story so I wouldn't have to, I did wonder how it was Andrew could mentally hear Hugo when I couldn't.

Andrew returned his attention to me. "I'm sorry—"

I put up a hand to stop him. "You promised me an explanation. I'd like it now."

He paused, trying to interpret my flat tone. "We need privacy," he said, indicating I should precede him down the stairs to where the crew quarters and bridge were.

I moved past him. "We'll use my room," I said, heading down the stairs.

"Is it appropriate for the two of us to be alone in your cabin?" he asked, following me down the stairs. "It can't be good for your reputation. Maybe we should—"

I stopped on the stair and Andrew halted behind me abruptly so he didn't knock me down. "I killed a woman in my hotel room two hours ago," I said, not bothering to look over my shoulder as I spoke, grimly determined to keep my voice from breaking. "I hardly think being alone in my cabin with you could do more harm to my reputation than that."

"No," he said, his voice sad. "No, I don't suppose it would."

I made my way down the rest of the stairs without comment and turned left to go into the small cabin I shared with Lizzie. Andrew entered as I reached up to touch the globe and light it. That done, I put down the lower bunk and sat. Hugo hopped off my shoulder to perch on the tiny sink as Andrew shut the cabin door. He sat down with me on the bed.

Andrew ran a hand over his face, obviously trying to decide what to say. "Miss Trevelyan... I'm sorry... are you all right? You seem very much out of sorts. Hugo filled me in on what happened to you at the doctor's office and in York. I must say you look awful. You're sure you aren't hurt?"

"Yes," I said, looking at my hands. "Today's exertions haven't treated my outfit well, but other than being sore from the ride on Gregor, I am physically unharmed."

"You must understand," he said earnestly, "had we known the attacks would escalate like this, we'd have gotten you out of Cambridge much more quickly."

His apology seemed a bit late, but I inclined my head in acceptance of it. After all, I'd refused to leave Cambridge when he suggested I do so. I stood up from the bunk and walked the three paces that brought me to the left-hand wall of the cabin, covered with a poster advertising a production of *Pirates of Penzance*. I ran a finger over the words on the poster. I'd never seen the show, but Lizzie had. She thought the poster a romantic reflection of what we did on the *Bosch*.

"You arranged to employ Max and the *Bosch* specifically to get me out of Cambridge?" I asked.

"Not precisely, but it seemed a wise thing to do, particularly when you refused to leave. I thought a vehicle primed for a getaway was a good investment of the Consortium's funds, with the handy side effect of getting you to safety with great rapidity."

I turned back to face Andrew. "Who is Odin? Other than being a Norse god, I mean."

He could see I had no patience for anything but the absolute truth, so he obliged my curiosity. "He's the Norse god of wisdom, war, the hunt, magic, poetry, and the dead. His chosen daughters are the Valkyrie, who decide which warriors get to spend their afterlife in Valhalla."

"Valhalla?"

"The Norse heaven."

"Ah." *That explains my deadly accuracy with darts and knives,* I thought. *The god of war and death needs those skills in abundance, and I've clearly inherited them.* I felt a shiver run down my spine. "The other members of the Consortium, and their god counterparts, if you please?"

"Ari—"

"Please," I insisted.

"You have yet to meet Harith Otieno, a tall, dark fellow who hails from Masailand in West Africa. He's the heir of Inari Okami, a Japanese god of agriculture, and he's bringing your father to Brentwood Close. He's a good man with an excellent sense of humor. As to the other member, you've met your Great Aunt Miranda, of course."

"Of whom is Aunt Miranda an heir?"

"Odin," Andrew replied.

I froze. "Can there be two heirs of Odin?"

He looked decidedly uncomfortable. "Yes and no."

"Yes and no? What sort of an answer is that?"

Andrew unbuttoned his coveralls to reveal the white shirt he wore underneath. He then unbuttoned his shirt and pulled it aside to reveal the gold swirls embedded in his skin and the gold pendant he wore hanging from a heavy gold box chain. I could see the pendant was a figure of a kneeling man with a hawk head, complete with hooked beak. The gold was old, and the face and details of the kneeling figure were nearly worn away.

"Every heir has artifacts from the god they agree to work for. Usually, it's a pendant and another piece of jewelry that's bound into our flesh. It's these artifacts, passed down from one heir to the next, which gives us the connection to the ancient god, and by extension, the super-human abilities we possess. For the Facti, the swirls are gold. The Obscurati wear silver."

"Aunt Miranda never gave me anything like that," I pointed out.

"Right. You're a consecrated heir. You didn't receive artifacts. Odin sort of... adopted you on your own merits."

I put my hands on my hips. "I'm the adopted child of a death god? Bloody hell. What sorts of merits made me attractive to a god of *that* sort? I couldn't be adopted by a god of something *benign*? How did this happen?"

Hugo snorted and flapped his wings, a movement that seemed to indicate amusement. "Oh, yes," I said, throwing up my hands. "Let's have the bloody raven laughing at me on top of everything else. Damn and blast!"

Hugo snorted again. I resisted the urge to utter significantly inappropriate oaths, but not by much.

Andrew pulled his shirt together and began buttoning it back up, looking down at his hands as he did so. My questions and overall alarm didn't seem to affect him at all. "Language, your ladyship," he admonished. An inappropriate oath slipped past my lips.

Andrew ignored my colorful comment. "In fact, Odin is known to history and legend more for his attributes of magic, wisdom, and poetry, but I suppose, yes," Andrew said, his tone dry and matter of fact, "if you wish to be pessimistic, you could say a death god adopted you." He finished buttoning his shirt and looked up at me.

"I am not being pessimistic," I said. "I killed a woman today, clearly following in my adoptive father's footsteps."

"In self-defense," he countered. "You didn't have a choice."

"Molly Silver didn't start out as the... thing... she was in my hotel room tonight. Obscurati *made* her that... and I ended her life in the blink of an eye." I let out a brief, bitter laugh. "There was no 'magic' or 'poetry' in it... only the calculus of a knife's throw and the spray of blood on my skirts. I've never used my ability to harm another living creature until today. The fact that I did it in self-defense doesn't make the act less unpleasant, and it doesn't make her less dead."

"You can't focus on what the woman was like before tonight, Ariana," he said, trying to comfort me. He stood up and stood in front of me, facing the *Pirates* poster. "Dark magic killed who she was long ago. That isn't your fault, and you've the right to defend yourself. Surely you know if Molly Silver had succeeded, they'd have done bad things to you?"

I held up my left hand and pointed at my wrist. "There's something in there," I said, teeth gritted in revulsion. "I felt it twitch before Molly Silver found me." I dropped my hand. "Bad things have already been done to me. What I want to know is why? Laufeson and the Obscurati or whoever the Hell these people are, don't want me because they have a fondness for sonnets, Mr. Michaelson. I dare say they want me because of my association with Odin's other, more deadly aspects. Isn't that so?"

"Yes," Andrew said reluctantly. "We think so."

"Of whom is Laufeson an heir?"

"Loki, the Norse trickster god. He was a consummate liar and betrayed people at every opportunity. He engineered the death of one of Odin's sons just to show he could. Odin punished him with an eternity in the underworld chained below a snake dripping acid venom on him."

I stilled. "That's what Mellie said," I muttered, surprised. "She told me 'Laufeson' meant 'Son of Loki.'"

Andrew shrugged. "Sometimes the enemy sits in plain sight. The heir of Loki has many aliases, of course, but he decided to be more overt in his initial attack. That alarmed Miranda, so she sent me to keep an eye on you."

"My aunt orders you around?"

Andrew smiled warmly. "Your Aunt Miranda is the seneschal, or commander, of the Pessarine Consortium. She orders all of us around. From what I've seen, she orders everyone around."

I snorted. "That's true enough."

"I'm her second in command."

I took that in. "So are you really a graduate student with Dr. Maitland, or was that a lie to allow you to get close to me?"

"I am, but we'll see how long it lasts." He shrugged and looked down at me with sparkling blue eyes. "Have to see you safe first."

I looked at the floor. Part of me liked Andrew being so close to me and looking down at me like that, but part of me was uncertain what to make of his regard. "So," I said, moving around him to stand by Hugo at the sink, "Laufeson holds a grudge? That's why he kidnapped me all those years ago, put this thing in my wrist, and is now trying to get me back? Some glorified attempt at revenge against Odin for what he did to punish Loki?"

Andrew turned, looked at his hands, thinking, and then turned his gaze up to meet mine again. "While Laufeson held you over those three days, he put many devices inside your body. Some of them were... diabolical and nasty. Then he put you in Odin's path by hanging you on the World Tree so you'd end up as you are now," Andrew continued.

The memory of the dream I'd had with the huge pig bloomed in my thoughts. "The goddess Freya," I said. "She came to me in a dream with her boar and showed me the World Tree. She wanted me to know it as it knew me."

"You bled on it. Blood is a very powerful magical substance, particularly when it's shed in sacrifice. That's how the tree knew you."

That made me stop and stare at Andrew for a moment. "Sacrifice?" I said. The images the World Tree had placed in my mind loomed up in my thoughts. I saw the girl bound, in pain and dripping blood hanging in the branches of the tree. "Oh God. That girl I saw... was me?"

"Indeed," Andrew said grimly. "The Pessarines saved you from dying on the World Tree and carefully removed all Laufeson's devices. That took days, since some of the devices," he paused, frowning, "moved around like living things. You nearly died. Between the efforts of my grandfather Jeremiah, the prior Heir of

Khonshu, and the rest of the Pessarines they managed to catch all the devices except the one in your wrist, and they did what they could to disable that one."

I rubbed my upper arms, feeling my skin crawl as I thought about the thing in my wrist. "Why did he put all those things in me and then hang me in a tree?"

Andrew cleared his throat. "The Norse sacrificed people to Odin that way. Odin hung himself in the World Tree for nine days in sacrifice. Putting you there, bleeding, made you a sacrifice—"

"—to Odin," I finished, "or like Odin? Or both?"

Andrew nodded. "We think Laufeson wanted Odin to adopt you with his devices inside you. Once you came of age and started connecting to Odin's claim on you, he sought you out, intent on using the connection to Odin by controlling you."

I shook my head. "But I didn't even know who Odin was until today, and I don't remember being kidnapped or sacrificed. How could I connect with Odin?"

Andrew's shoulders slumped. "You started throwing darts."

"Sorry?" I said, not certain I'd heard him correctly.

"Your parents did what they could to keep you from anything associated with Odin's powers, on Miranda's advice. That's why they encouraged you to study mathematics and limited your exposure to literature. They turned you away from any games that involved throwing anything accurately. Then—"

Realization dawned. "I came to Cambridge, met Max, joined the *Bosch* crew—"

"—and won every dart game you played," Andrew finished. "In the legends, when Odin throws his spear, he never misses." His smile was wry. "Neither do you. When you throw darts, and in Penzance when you told those stories, it wasn't you doing those things. It was Odin. He used his connection with you to sort of... well, hijack your body, I guess you'd say. The more you threw darts, the stronger the connection became—"

"...and the more he put on my body like shrugging into a suitcoat," I said, annoyed, "wandering about as he pleased, bold as brass. Lovely."

"True," Andrew said, "but his intervention has saved you more than once, and made you nearly enough money to start your aeronaut business. He is protective of you... very much so."

I couldn't keep the annoyance from my voice. "I think you'll agree, Mr. Michaelson, if I'm under constant attack, it'll be singularly difficult to maintain a storefront, much less live my life as I wish. As it is, my taking the Tripos in June looks increasingly unlikely, if I'm even able to return to Cambridge and Towson House. I've no idea what I'll tell my parents about all of this," I indicated the ship around us, "much less explain my pagan adoption, my ability to throw darts, my use of magic, and my killing someone. Yet you speak of this odd circumstance as if it's some sort of interesting, but helpful, twist of fate. At this point, I don't know whether to weep or knock you sideways."

Hugo trilled and flapped his wings though I wasn't sure how to interpret his actions.

Andrew looked sharply at the raven. "What?" he said, alarmed, and then the *Bosch* lurched suddenly to starboard, knocking all three of us to the floor. I landed with an *ooompf* on top of Andrew.

"Ah," he said, breathless, "looks like 'knock me sideways' has won the day." He moved my elbow out of his chest. "And please," he wheezed, "call me Andrew."

The Odin Inheritance   Victoria L.   Scott

Chapter Thirty-Seven

Andrew and I struggled to our feet while Hugo flapped his wings and squawked in alarm. "Hugo," Andrew gasped, still trying to catch his breath, "go to Miranda now—tell her we're under attack!" Hugo squawked agreement and promptly disappeared into thin air.

We opened the door to my cabin just as the *Bosch* tilted alarmingly to port. We held onto the door and managed to keep our feet until the ship righted itself again.

"This isn't normal weather phenomena," I said, gasping as we stepped into the hallway. I put my hands out to brace myself against another rapid roll to one side or another. Andrew did the same.

"Bridge!" he declared, and we made our way to the command center of the ship, hands out on the walls to hold us steady as we moved.

The phosphorite globes on the bridge swung wildly on their ceiling hooks, casting odd shadows across the consoles and stations manned by my friends. Needle and Max struggled visibly to hold the wheel steady, while Lizzie frantically monitored the propellers and engines. Griff, I knew, was down with the engines, no doubt swearing a blue streak at the sudden rapid movements of the ship. The engines groaned under the strain. Oddly, the vista outside the front glass windows was placid—no sign of clouds or any atmospheric disturbance. The night sky was clear and full of stars, with the moon high in the sky. Andrew ran to the window to peer out into the darkness, pulling his gold pendant from his shirt.

I dashed to the navigation console and stared in amazement as the gauges and dials spun wildly. None of my usually very reliable instruments functioned properly. I had no clue as to the source of the rough buffeting we'd experienced—The *Bosch* flew upward, pushed by a sudden gust of wind and I hit the deck, the air knocked out of me again. —*are experiencing*, I thought with a groan.

"Ari! Report!" Max shouted.

I grabbed the edge of the console and pulled myself up to a kneeling position, staring in dismay at the wild, impossible readings. "Navigation is completely knackered," I told him. "All gauges and meters unreadable. I've no idea what the Hell is going on."

Max swore under his breath. "Understood. Andrew—what do you see?"

Andrew turned to look at Max, his face drawn as he gripped his pendant tightly. "Persian wind demons," he said. "Servants of Pazuzu and thugs of the Obscurati."

"What in blazes are they?" Lizzie demanded, "and what can be done to stop them swatting us about like a shuttlecock?"

Andrew's gaze grew distant as he concentrated on something far away. "What are they? Nasty," he said grimly. "They're trying to encourage us to land without killing us just yet."

They want me alive, I thought, my anger blazing up.

"Are these mortal creatures?" Max asked, his face set. "Can they be killed?"

Andrew's attention returned to the bridge. "They used to be people until they allowed the demons to possess them. Now they look nothing like humans, but the core of the..." he grimaced, "...creatures is eminently killable."

"How many?" Max asked.

"Four," Andrew replied. He brought a hand to his temple, closed his eyes and concentrated. "I'm telling Gregor and Ahisa mind-to-mind now," he said. "We'll see what we can do magically to stop the attack."

The ship lurched downward and I braced so I didn't fall down again.

Max looked at me. "Ariana," he said. "In the closet of my cabin you'll find a harpoon gun and a gas canister backpack. There are twelve small harpoons in a belt next to the gun. Grab the gear, suit up and head to the deck. I want you to shoot the monsters out of the sky."

There wasn't any other choice, of course, but the idea I'd be killing more attackers wasn't a pleasant one, though I knew if I didn't there was the distinct possibility we'd all be killed. What Max asked of me wasn't easy. With the demons knocking the ship about, even with my ability to hit anything I wanted I could inadvertently puncture the *Bosch's* envelope, which might also kill us all.

Andrew, done communicating with Gregor and Lady Sato, met my eyes. He didn't need to read my mind to know what I thought. He knew the danger as well as I did – as well as we all did.

"On my way," I said and headed out, arms outstretched and ready for the next wild movement of the ship around me.

"Shall I call battle stations, Captain?" Andrew asked as I crossed the bridge.

"Aye, Andrew, and get a parachute to the Duchess just in case," Max ordered, then grunted as the ship lurched again. He and Needle reset their feet and readjusted their grip, straining at the wheel.

I hit the hallway and moved as quickly as I could to Max's cabin, entered it, opened the closet and the harpoon gun fell out, the business end, thankfully unloaded, aimed at me. It was a very long, very big rifle. The barrel was bronze with a wooden stock. It was front loading, and a nozzle at the end of the stock showed where the gas canisters that propelled the harpoons attached to the gun. The leather backpack with the steel gas canisters leaned against the back of the closet, next to the canvas belt with the harpoons attached. A flexible metal pipe in overlapping segments that reminded me of a centipede lay on the floor next to the belt.

The handles to open the pressure valves were on the sides of the canisters rather than the tops, along with nozzles for the flexible metal tube, so the operator could open and close the valves easily as well as switch canisters when one ran out of pressurized air.

The ship shuddered as another blast of wind hit it and I staggered, holding on to the closet door for support. As the ship righted itself, I grabbed for the equipment. The backpack was heavy, and I struggled to get the buckles tightened around my torso. My corset helped me stand straight despite the weight of the pack. Once I'd managed that, I screwed in the tube to the right side gas canister, picked up the ammunition belt and tied it around my waist, and finally grabbed the gun, screwing on the other end of the flexible tube into the bottom of the gun's stock. The ship lurched again and I fell back into the closet, the weight of the canisters on my back affecting my balance. The closet door shut with a slam, and I was lucky not to get my fingers smashed by the damnable thing. I got myself out of the closet with a grunt and made for the hallway and stairs that would take me to the deck and the open air, grabbing a rope on my way.

The deck was windy and cold. The moon illuminated the wooden planks beneath my feet that were not obscured from the light by the cigar-shaped envelope above me. My hair billowed out, sending the remaining pins flying, and my red curls writhed in the gale like a living thing. My skirts mimicked my hair and I struggled to stay upright. Andrew, Gregor, and Lady Sato stood on the starboard side of the deck holding hands and concentrating, presumably working some sort of magic to assist in our eluding the wind demons. Focused as they were, they didn't see me.

A quick look around told me we'd lost altitude. I cursed silently. Bending over to lessen the effect of the wind on my movements I moved to the port side of the ship and tied myself to the rail so I wouldn't get knocked off the deck. I looked up and around, seeking our assailants, grateful the width of the envelope was so narrow. From the side of the ship, I'd have a greater open space within which to aim at the demon-creatures attacking us. Since the envelope curved above me at a steeper angle on the side of the ship than at the front or rear, I figured my chances of popping a hole in a ballonet by accident and blowing us into the afterlife were somewhat reduced.

I pulled a harpoon out of my belt and holding the gun between my skirted legs, I shoved the rear of the bolt into the barrel of the gun until I heard something catch on the inside. Taking care to hold the sharp pointy end away from myself and the envelope above me, I turned the gun so the pointy bit faced outward. Then I opened the valve on my right hand side and felt the flexible tube stiffen with the pressurized air from the tank accompanied by a sort of pop inside the gun itself. I brought the gun up so I could sight down the barrel and scanned the sky. Despite the light of the moon, I couldn't see much. I felt a gust of wind and was grateful for the rope I'd used to secure myself to the ship, feeling the poor old girl shudder violently and dip downward, losing even more altitude.

Andrew popped up beside me and grabbed the nearby rail with a white-knuckled grip. "There's a demon at each of the cardinal points," he shouted in my ear, pointing up and to the left. "Can you see them?"

I squinted and willed my eyes to bring the creatures into focus, but only saw grey smudges. I shook my head.

Andrew held up his right hand. "I can show you where they are," he said, "but it means mucking about in your brain a bit. Since the moon is out I can see the demons far better than you can."

I ground my teeth and nodded to indicate he had permission to 'muck about', realizing the necessity of the intrusion but still not liking it much.

Andrew reached up and put the palm of his hand up under my waving hair so he touched the back of my head.

Vision functions are in the back of the brain, he explained telepathically. This won't hurt, but you may find it somewhat disorienting. Brace yourself... three, two, one— And suddenly the night sky became more focused and detailed, as if it were daytime and I had on the most amazing spectacles ever invented. I gasped, took a second to get my bearings and saw the demons.

My initial impression was one of abomination and deformity so profound that I felt my gorge rise as I looked at the awful monsters. I swallowed convulsively and looked away. *Shoot first, then vomit,* Andrew suggested pragmatically.

I sought the demon in the sky again and held back my nausea as I looked at the creature. Andrew had said they'd been human once, but I wasn't sure what to call what I saw now. The demon hovered off the port side flapping two sets of wings: one set resembled those of a bat while the other wings resembled those of a vulture. It had elongated, ugly taloned feet like a huge bird of prey, but rather than having a bird head, this demon had the head of a dog with red eyes that burned like coals in a fire. There were no arms to speak of, just writhing tentacles dripping ooze. Scales covered its torso and a whip-like tail cut the air back and forth as the dog head opened its mouth. A gust of wind hit the *Bosch*, knocking the ship to starboard. Andrew and I held on until the ship stabilized again and I took aim with the harpoon gun.

Just then, Gregor ran up to the rail to Andrew's left, completely divested of his clothing. Before I could do or say anything, he leapt over the side of the ship and into the open air, dropping like a stone into the relative darkness. I let out a cry and put out my arm in a futile attempt to catch the Russian, but Andrew's thoughts rang in my mind.

Ari – he's fine! Watch!

He just—! He'll die! I thought back.

Then I heard a terrifying cry somewhere between the sound of a lion, an eagle and a steam engine and the largest, strangest bird – if I could call it that – flew up from under the *Bosch*. It had a huge head like a crocodile with an odd crest-like ridge along the back of the skull, with what had to be a forty foot wingspan lifting a huge body proportional to the wings. It had rear legs and a long tail though its skin was brown and leathery like a lizard. It had no feathers, and though biology was not my primary course of study, I knew there was no way that animal existed on the Earth as I knew it.

What in bloody blue blazes is that?! I asked, completely astonished.

Lady Sato suggested it, Andrew told me. *She's using most of her magic to help Gregor maintain the form, since it's so much bigger than he is. Apparently that lizard bird lived on Earth millions of years ago.*

Lizard bird? My God. Were they carnivorous? I asked.

With a tooth-filled maw like that? I hope so. He'll get the ones on the other side of the ship while you go after the ones on this side. Just don't shoot Gregor by mistake.

I blanched. *He's going to—* I thought, then stopped myself. Better to focus on my job than think about what Gregor would be eating.

I aimed the harpoon gun again, feeling the calm descend on my thoughts as it always did when I focused on hitting something. The demon seemed to sense I targeted it, and it began to fly erratically to avoid being hit. I felt a grim determination occupy the presence in my thoughts as my awareness of the world faded further. Odin manifested himself more fully and used my throat to speak an incantation. I felt vitality leave my body as glowing blue symbols crawled across the surface of the gun to cover the harpoon. I felt my finger pull the trigger. The harpoon left the gun like a bullet but without the explosion and smell of gunpowder. The recoil knocked me backwards and if it hadn't been for Andrew's hand on the back of my head, I would have landed on my rear end.

The harpoon sped toward the demon. Odin followed its progress mentally as he made my hands reach for another harpoon and load the gun for the next shot. As my body moved under Odin's command, my awareness of the trajectory of the harpoon was less precise than the god's. I felt it from afar as a glowing blue streak. It moved in time with the demon's movements, since

Odin's magic locked on to the creature no matter how it moved. When the harpoon struck the monster in the middle of its chest, the non-human elements of the being slid off like a film of oiled snake-skin and flew away, leaving its unclothed human host to clutch at the spike in his chest as he fell to the earth like a stone.

My hands slid the harpoon home and I felt the click of the firing mechanism grab the projectile.

One down, Andrew noted. I could feel him concentrating, seeking out the other demon. He projected a picture to Odin and me of the *Bosch* from above. Gregor flew on the starboard side, one of the demons in his huge prehistoric maw, flopping about as Gregor shook the demon savagely. The neck of the human host broke, and the demon slid away, leaving the naked man limp as a rag doll in Gregor's jaws. Gregor dropped the corpse and flew far enough away to make a turn and head back to attack the next demon. The two remaining demons hovered at the front and back of the ship.

Two down. Our next target is—

Andrew's thought was cut off as a roar thundered through the sky, loud and powerful enough to shake the whole ship. Through my mental connection with Andrew, I had an impression of an impossibly huge snake-like winged dragon pop into existence directly above the *Bosch*. Someone in a black coverall sort of suit seemed to be riding on the neck of the beast. Another roar cut the air.

Amazed as I was by the appearance and size of the dragon, fascination mixed with fear as I waited for its next move. Would it dive on the ship? Rip us to shreds? Set us afire?

Son of Osiris, Andrew swore, and I felt his dismay at the sight of the great creature. *How are we to stop that thing?*

Odin turned the harpoon gun up in an attempt to aim at the dragon, but the *Bosch's* frame was in the way. There was no way the dragon could be hit by the harpoon that would not also puncture the *Bosch*. Odin retreated from my thoughts a bit, trying to puzzle out our next move. I felt the thing in my left wrist twitch as it had before Molly Silver entered my room. A desire to put down the gun and go out to meet the dragon oozed its way into my thoughts. Alarm spiked in me as I forced the impulse down. I knew who rode that dragon.

Andrew felt that my concern was beyond that of seeing a huge dragon. *What?* he asked.

The dragon opened its mouth and instead of a roar a different sound emerged, one that was maliciously melodic. Music that wasn't quite music cut through everything in my mind, knocking Odin aside and leaving my consciousness to take the full brunt of the dragon's attack. Exhaustion flowed over me like a wave. I lowered the harpoon gun and dropped to my knees as Andrew dropped his hand from the back of my head and brought it up to his own head, trying and failing to fight the influence of the dragon. He dropped to his knees beside me, his hands limp at his sides. Lady Sato knelt on the other side of the deck, overcome by the mental attack as we were.

The dragon, black wings and scales shimmering in the moonlight, flew down and wrapped its long sinuous body around the *Bosch*. The head of the dragon snaked its way onto the deck, its jeweled segmented eyes glinting with malevolence as Laufeson gracefully slid off its neck and onto the planking.

He looked older than he had in the library, I noticed. A streak of white at each temple and wrinkles on his face indicated his age, which I guessed to be around fifty or so. His overall physique was unchanged from what I'd seen at the Faraday – long, angular and thin. The goatee on his chin emphasized his stark look. His black outfit seemed to be made of silk, since it flowed over his limbs gracefully. If I'd not known him to be one of the 'bad guys', as Andrew would have said, his poise and air of command would have been impressive. Knowing what I did, I found him repulsive in the extreme.

Perversely, the thing in my left wrist twitched and made my arm ache, reacting to Laufeson's presence near me. I worked very hard not to panic as part of me strained to get close to the villain. Notions of how easy it would be to give in and obey the German fiend flitted in and out of my mind. Gritting my teeth I fought the dragon's hold on my body and Laufeson's influence on my thoughts, trying desperately to raise the barrel of the gun to hit either the dragon or Laufeson, but the gun remained unused in my unmoving hand.

The German smiled in satisfaction as he took in the scene on the deck and waved a hand at the dragon in a 'get on with it' sort of gesture.

I felt the dragon order Griff to turn off the engines and in seconds, the thrum under our feet ceased. The dragon ordered my crewmates and Mother to join us on the deck, then pulled its head out from under the *Bosch's* envelope to steer the ship itself. It flapped its wings and the ship started to rise in an up and down sort of motion, the buoyancy of the hydrogen not quite in sync with the efforts of the dragon.

Laufeson walked up to me, his expression delighted as he ran a hand first through my hair and then along the side of my face the way one would caress a lover. I shuddered in revulsion for the most part, but the black tendrils of magic I'd felt the first time I'd encountered the man returned. I could do nothing to stop him touching me and, though I hated to admit it, part of me enjoyed it

Andrew seethed beside me, furious at his inability to move.

The lout sensed my conflicted feelings and smiled. "I'm

sorry I took so long, my dear," he cooed, his German accent present, but much less prominent than it had been in the library. "Pazuzu and his heir are very helpful friends, but they do require a great deal of persuasion and human sacrifice in exchange for their favors. Thankfully, Hades was a great help in securing Pazuzu's assistance."

Andrew stiffened at the mention of Hades, and his eyes burned with hatred at Laufeson.

I wracked my brain. Hades was a name I'd heard before... was he an Ancient Greek god? Cora had mentioned him in unflattering terMs. If he was helping Laufeson and assisted in human sacrifice, he had to be a bad god... and if Laufeson had the help of a god like that, we were at a distinct disadvantage. *Damn and blast*!

"I lost track after the twentieth victim, but all the screaming and mess were worth it," he continued. "The deaths sated Pazuzu's need for blood and Hades' craving for human souls. As a result, I have you, an airship and two Pessarine Facti in my power."

That made me pause and a sliver of hope grew within the alarm and fear I felt. Gregor had escaped the dragon's mental control. I'd no idea where the Russian had gone but prayed it was off to get help. Hugo was also free, thankfully, and would let Aunt Miranda know what had happened to us.

The door that led to the interior of the ship opened and Max, Needle, Lizzie, Mother and Griff walked onto the deck, their movements stiff and unnatural, like automata. Mother wore a half buckled parachute, the free ends of the straps flapping in the breeze. Her hat was gone while her face was pale and drawn with fear.

Laufeson turned his attention to the new arrivals. "Usumgallu," he said, "increase your control and make them kneel, please."

I felt the dragon's command like a lead blanket on my mind. My crewmates and mother knelt as ordered, arms at their sides, their faces blank, their eyes dull.

The remaining two demons swooped down to land on the deck, tentacles undulating briefly before the demonic attributes sank into the skin of the hosts, leaving two naked, dark-haired Persian men standing to either side of Laufeson. They smiled wickedly.

Laufeson turned slightly to acknowledge their arrival. "You will divest the red-haired woman of the harpoon gun," he ordered, pointing at me, "and carry her through the air to our agreed upon destination." Then he stopped and looked between Lady Sato and Andrew, thinking. "Which to take, I wonder," he said. "You've both overtaxed yourselves, or else Usumgallu wouldn't have overcome your minds as he did." The German shrugged. "Take the blonde," he said, waving dismissively at Andrew. "I have a use for him."

The two Persian men moved forward quickly. I closed my eyes to avoid looking at the naked man removing the gas canister harness, harpoon belt and the rope that had tied me to the rail. He plucked the gun from my hand and threw the whole apparatus overboard. I heard the other Persian pull Andrew to his feet. I was pulled to my feet shortly thereafter, and the Persian demon host half-maneuvered-half carried me over to stand next to Laufeson. I glared at the man.

"You do know my attempts on your life up to now have been tests, I hope," he said, smiling and oozing charm.

I hadn't known that, of course, and the information did nothing to endear him to me, no matter how pleasantly he smiled. Anger helped keep his magic from overwhelming me, so I focused on that. Being so close to him made my skin crawl.

"I had to see what skills you possessed and what sort of connection you'd forged with Odin," he continued. "It cost me several operatives, which was unexpected but very encouraging. Now that you're suitably prepared, the time for tests is over. I will have you, and you will do my bidding."

I felt the Persian man step behind me and wrap his arms around my abdomen. I flinched and watched in horror as the arms became the oozing tentacles again, wrapping themselves around me two and three times. I felt and smelled the horrid breath of the demon on my neck and gagged.

"Don't worry," Laufeson soothed, "you'll remember nothing of the trip." A tentacle reached up and touched my right temple, coating it with cold, stinking ooze. The world went black.

Chapter Thirty-Eight

I awoke to find myself tied to a heavy wooden chair in a chilly, cylindrical stone room. A weak light that I thought to be sunrise shone through the shuttered rectangular window to my right, illuminating my surroundings with a dim glow. The roof above me was wooden and pointed, like the top of a tower, and the floor under me was made of stout wooden planks, worn with age and oddly stained. A trapdoor in the floor that led, I presumed, to stairs descending down into the tower was to my far left. The fireplace in the room was empty. There was no other furniture in the room save the chair to which I'd been bound.

My clothes and face smelled of the ooze the demon's tentacles had left behind and I stifled a gag at the rotting stench. My red curls, completely free but tangled and matted, flowed like ribbons over my shoulders and down my back, some of the curls trapped by the ropes that held me to the chair. I still had my bracelet on my left wrist, its concealed blades a sort of comfort. I also still had the clockwork brooch pinned to the front of my shirt at my neck. Remarkably, Father's watch chain and fob remained solidly on my right wrist, a warm reminder of paternal concern. I didn't know why I still possessed the bracelets, but I was glad I still had them, particularly once I saw that my skirt and shirt were even more dirt-covered and torn. It made me wonder what the trip I 'didn't remember', thanks to the tentacle to my head, had been like.

It also made me ponder, with some alarm, what had happened to the *Bosch*, my friends, and my mother. Fear and worry for them overcame me. Father had been on his way to Brentwood Close when I'd been captured, I realized. *What if Laufeson grabbed him, too? What if he did something awful to him?* I thought. My exhaustion from all I had experienced up to that point allowed my imagination to run wild, presenting horrible scenarios of pain and destruction to my frantic mind. A couple tears ran own my cheeks, I hoped fervently they'd been left alone. *Please God,* I prayed, *please let them all be safe and out of Obscurati clutches.* I also prayed Hugo and Gregor had escaped and gotten help, somehow. With Andrew and me as the only ones taken by the demons, our only source of rescue would be the Facti, I was sure, unless together he and I could make an escape.

Unfortunately, I had no idea where Andrew was, or even if we were in the same place. I sent up a prayer on his behalf and more unpleasant possibilities began to bubble up from my overactive imagination. I shook my head to dispel the images. With my hands tied, I couldn't wipe the tears from my face and if I cried much more my nose would start to run. So, I took a deep breath to compose myself, pushing my concern for my friends and family aside. I had to think.

The air in the room was cold and smelled of damp overlaid with the metallic tinge of blood. It made my nose and brain itch. I could swear it was familiar, which tugged at my mind and unsettled me a little. Deep inside me a small voice whispered in pain and fear, but I ignored it. I couldn't afford to wallow in panic and worry. This was no time to be frightened. I had to find a way to escape. *Right,* I thought.

I tried to wriggle within the ropes and found I couldn't move enough to make much of a difference. I endeavored to move the chair by trying to hop up and down initially, and then by using my feet to slide the chair across the floor. I found the chair to be too heavy for me to budge, and I was so tired my muscles trembled after a while of fruitless effort. Then I tried to toggle the blades in my bracelet so I could cut my bonds, but though I could move my wrists, I couldn't do so in a way that let me make use of the blades.

Finally, not knowing what else to do, I closed my eyes and tried to center my thoughts, seeking the presence of Odin in my mind. I called to the god, explaining my difficulty and expressing my concerns about what Laufeson intended to do. I pointed out that the Obscurati obviously had some kind of big plan to use the abilities he'd given me to harm other people. I begged him to use magic to release me from the ropes.

Odin chose not to respond.

I then spent several seconds expressing my frustration in language so inventive and completely unladylike it would've scandalized my mother into disowning me.

Frustration somewhat allayed by inappropriate utterances, I forced myself to calm down. Eventually, someone would come to get me. I just had to wait until then and hope that my being moved from one place to another would give me a chance to get away long enough to find Andrew and get us both out. Knowing where I was would've been a great help to the success of that plan, I was certain, but I'd no way to determine my current location.

I was so tired. Most of my body ached and I felt my muscles stiffening up. I sighed. *Whatever the ooze on the tentacle had been*, I thought sluggishly, *it did nothing to make me feel better*. I leaned my head back against the back of the wooden chair and stared at the roof above me. It, like the smell of the room, also seemed familiar, though I wasn't sure why or what that meant.

Weariness overtook me and I drifted into a restless sleep.

****

"Recognize the room?" said a German accented voice.

My head snapped up from the back of the chair and I opened my eyes to see Laufeson sitting on a wooden stool opposite me. He wore an impeccably tailored tan suit that emphasized his angular features, with a navy blue cravat around his neck held in place with a ruby pin that looked like a drop of blood. He'd shaved off the little goatee, but his hair was perfectly coifed and his eyes regarded me with a flat grey gaze.

I looked around the room. We were alone. The trap door was open and light streamed up into the room from the lit stairwell below it. A quick glance out the window showed me it was dusk. I'd fallen asleep and obviously been out for hours.

"I'm glad you shaved the goatee off," I said, fighting to get my mind functioning properly. I knew I had to act much braver than I felt. "It did nothing for you."

Laufeson smiled in delight. "You are nothing if not surprising, my dear," he said.

"I'm not your 'dear,'" I said. "What have you done with Andrew?"

Laufeson's smile wilted a little, a look of calculation in his eyes. "He's here, awaiting his fate, just as you are." He indicated the room around us. "My apologies for the sparse accommodations. Sometimes I'm too greatly influenced by nostalgia. You see, when I kidnapped you as a little girl all those years ago, this was your room." He indicated the floor. "We scrubbed the pentagram and blood away years ago, of course."

I just looked at him. Now I knew why the room looked familiar, if he told the truth.

"Even then, as a four year old, you were very stubborn. If I hadn't tied you to the bed, I've no doubt you'd have tried to escape through the window." He pointed at the chair. "That's how I knew to truss you up like this."

"Why am I here?" I asked, working hard to sound unconcerned and only partially succeeding.

Laufeson leaned back and regarded me for a moment. "Because you belong to me and I have a use for you."

I grimaced. That answer told me nothing new. "I don't belong to you," I said.

My captor noticed my reaction. "I see. Your Aunt Miranda and her Pessarines did such a thorough job of erasing your memory, you don't recall your time with me and, therefore, don't know what your future holds." He sighed. "I will enlighten you." I said nothing.

"You know your mother nearly miscarried you, I assume?" I nodded, not sure where this was going.

"Your Aunt Miranda asked a Facti named Jeremiah Michaelson – Andrew's grandfather – to heal you and your mother so she carried you to term. Obviously, they succeeded since here you are... but Facti healing magic leaves a trace behind. It marks you as special. In particular, it gives your blood a certain magical essence that, if properly employed, can be very useful."

"You kidnapped me for my blood?" I asked. Andrew had said blood was a powerful substance, but I hadn't realized he'd mean it literally.

"Indeed. It was here we drained your blood, healed you, and drained you again repeatedly over the course of three days.

That blood has been the source of great power for me since then."
He stuck a hand in a jacket pocket and pulled out a glass vial half full
of some sort of brown powder. He shook the vial thoughtfully. "I
still have some left."

I closed my eyes for a moment, slightly ill at the thought this
man carried what he claimed was my blood around in his pocket.

"Once I retrieved all the blood I could, I installed several
devices in your body designed to mold you to my purpose and hung
you on the World Tree to attract Odin's attention."

I remembered what the World Tree had shown me and saw
my childhood-self dangling and bleeding in its branches. Andrew
had also told me about the devices. "Why?" I asked.

A head on a very thick neck popped up in the light of the
trap door. The man had long dark hair pulled back in a queue, a
face flattened from frequent punches and silver-orbed eyes.

"Beggin' yer pardon, Boss, but we're ready for you
downstairs," he said in a rough voice. "I've told them technicians
they'll need to start the things up in the great hall, as you ordered."

Laufeson nodded and stood up. "Quite right. It would
seem duty calls. There are few minor matters to be dealt with
before we begin in earnest. Thank you, Mr. Toby," he said and
pointed at me. "Please untie our guest and escort her to my
office." He tilted his head to point at Mr. Toby. "Mr. Toby used to
be a boxer," he explained as he moved to the trap door and stairs
below them. "You'll find he is the perfect gentleman, unless you
don't do what he, or I, want. I suggest you follow his instructions."

Mr. Toby stepped up into the tower room and moved
toward me as Laufeson made his way down the stairs and
disappeared from view. The thug's clothing was impeccably
tailored but oddly gaudy, as if he was new to affluence. The cut of
his jacket was the height of fashion. The fabrics were expensive

but too brightly colored, paisleys and stripes fighting for dominance of the ensemble, but it felt like the siege between the two had been a long and inconclusive one. His hands were huge, with thick, calloused fingers. He must have been a bare knuckle fighter, I decided.

"Now, yer worship," Mr. Toby said, looking down at me, "we can do this easy-like, or we can do this hard."

I regarded the man. "I like options," I said, working very hard to keep my voice even.

He quirked a smile. "My my. Aren't you cool as a cucumber. Easy way is I'm going to untie you, and we're going to walk down to the great hall, no fuss, no muss."

I looked down at the ropes that held me to the chair. "And the hard way?"

"I knock you into next week and carry you unconscious downstairs." He brought his hands up and cracked his knuckles, evaluating me. "Should only take one punch, but I do like to be thorough."

"You'd hit an unarmed girl?" I asked, feigning shock. He'd probably done much worse.

Toby chuckled. "I hit who the Boss tells me to hit."

"Hmmmm..." I said, thinking. "Good to know."

I certainly didn't need my brains addled any more than they already were. To escape, I had to get out of the chair, and it seemed foolish to provoke an attack when playing along would get me closer to my goal of finding Andrew and getting away.

I sighed. "Let's do this the easy way," I said and waited as he freed me from the chair.

The Odin Inheritance   Victoria L. Scott

Chapter Thirty-Nine

Heading downstairs to Laufeson's office was not quite as easy as Mr. Toby had thought it would be. My legs were stiff and sore from being cold and tied to the chair, making the walk down the stairs of the tower an awkward operation. Mr. Toby gently, but firmly, gripped me by the upper arm and helped me make my way. I took in my surroundings as we moved, keen to keep track of where we went. We were in a castle, obviously. The stairwell, cut from grey granite, curved down twenty worn steps to a landing, which led into a grey stone corridor. I used a hand along the wall to help me move down the stairs, my feet clumsy as we descended despite Toby's help.

"Down the corridor, to the left and down another corridor is the great hall," Mr. Toby told me, pointing. "Off that room is the Boss's office."

"What's in the great hall?" I asked, starting to feel the muscles in my legs loosen up a bit.

"Diabolicals, yer worship," Mr. Toby said.

That didn't sound promising. "Diabolicals?"

"Fancy machinery and magic all mixed up. They turn blokes Enhanced. Sometimes they come out dashing and dapper, like myself. Sometimes the poor sods come out thick as two planks..." he paused, "...or mangled and horrible... brains in the armpits, or missin' spines and hands and such. Don't know why that is, but it don't seem to bother the Boss none."

I gaped at him. "That's horrible! Why would anyone willingly submit to something like that?" I asked, rubbing my wrists and taking care not to toggle my bladed bracelet.

Toby laughed. "The Boss don't tell chaps that beforehand, o' course," he said, shaking his head ruefully. "Otherwise he don't get any volunteers."

That really didn't sound promising. "That doesn't bother you?" I asked. "These people don't even know about the possible unpleasant outcomes?"

Toby shrugged philosophically. "'You pays your money, you takes your chances,' my Ma used to say. Most of the chaps who go for the transformin' ain't got nothin' to lose anymore. That was the case with me, and no mistake. As it is, workin' for the Boss you get fed regular and a decent wage besides without bravin' the Diabolicals. Those who do and come out the other side improved and useful –like myself and those fellows riotin' in London and Birmingham - get loads more." He waved a hand over his eclectic wardrobe. "Fancy togs, fancy meals, money in our pockets and birds, if we want 'em. It's a fair cop, so long as you does what the Boss wants."

"And that's enough incentive to risk body and mind?"

"I ain't a philosophical type, but seems to me that kind of choice is just the consequences of livin', your worship," Toby said. "You took yer chances tryin' to keep outta the Boss's hands, and what I hear is you done a pretty good job of it until the Boss called out the dragon on you. Can't say as I like yer odds of getting' outta here intact, but you made yer choice. For you, it just didn't work out so well, is all. The Boss had his eye on you for years without you knowin'. It was only a matter of time before you came into his possession."

I nodded, acknowledging his point. "So you say," I responded, sounding braver and calmer than I felt. "I'm counting on a different outcome."

Mr. Toby gave me a pitying look. "Ain't we all, yer worship," he said, "ain't we all."

Chapter Forty

The great hall was the size of a small church, lit with phosphorite glass bulbs attached to two banks of rectangular machinery. The walls were the grey stone I'd seen everywhere else though large, but worn and faded, tapestries covered the walls and the floor was made of wood rather than stone. A fireplace sat at the far end of the room from where I'd entered with Mr. Toby. Above it there was a massive wooden mantle and a family crest of some sort carved into the stone of the chimney. The space felt old and fatigued, like a second rate residence for a very minor and unsavory noble family.

The machines, cobbled together from a variety of other devices, were steel silver and golden bronze mishmashes as big as hansom cabs. Their more modern – if haphazard – look was a direct and startling contrast to the Old World nature of the great hall they sat in. Next to the huge machines stood two man-sized rectangular chambers with windowed doors. The chambers connected to the machines with coiled wires, long quartz crystals and copper pipes. One of the machines glowed with green magical energy, obscuring the occupant of its accompanying chamber. Two Enhanced men with silver eyes observed the process, watching the gauges and dials of the green-lit machine carefully. The charge in the air from the odd energy made the hair on my neck stand up and my wrist blossomed with a steady ache that ran up my arm. What I sensed rang all sorts of alarm bells in my brain, though from the outside I couldn't actually see that the man was in distress. Every fiber of my being screamed that this was not somewhere I wanted to be.

I looked left and right, eager for an escape. Mr. Toby still held my arm in a firm grip. There were two other exits from the room I could see beyond the machines by the fireplace, but I had no idea where they led. I also didn't know how many other guards or Obscurati cronies there were in the castle.

"I see you thinkin', yer worship," Mr. Toby said. "I don't recommend your tryin' anythin'."

From the entrance to the left side of the fireplace, another Enhanced thug brought Andrew into the great hall.

"Ah. I see Mr. Silas is escortin' the other guest," Toby said.

Mr. Silas, hearing his name, found us in the hall and dragged Andrew over toward us. I gasped. Andrew looked exhausted. His coveralls were torn and stained and as he approached, I saw dark circles under his eyes and the haunted expression on his face. He looked at me and I could see the fear and anger in his eyes: fear of what Laufeson would do to me and anger that he'd failed to keep me safe. He made an effort to break away from his captor and come toward me, but his struggles only amused Mr. Silas.

"I think Moon Boy here has a thing for the guest of honor," Mr. Silas said, giving Andrew a good shake.

Like Mr. Toby, Silas had the silver eyes of someone Laufeson had altered, but his body type was much different. His short black hair was peppered with grey and his complexion was swarthy, like he'd worked on boats most of his life. He was not a big man, but he seemed heavy in an oddly physical sense. From the way he held Andrew it was evident he was extremely strong, but that strength didn't come from human muscle if his size was any indication. I blanched when I saw sinuous things undulate under Mr. Silas's well-made but garish clothing. He'd obviously taken fashion advice from Mr. Toby. The fabric of the sleeves of his mint green and yellow striped coat moved in short jerky movements, as if he had toads trapped in the coat and they were trying to escape.

"Andrew – are you all right?" I asked. I tried to move toward him, but Mr. Toby held me fast.

"None o' that now, yer worship," he warned.

Mr. Silas snorted. "Touchin', ain't it?" he sneered. "Like somethin' out o' one o' those romance whatsits."

Andrew looked up at Toby. "If you hurt her, I swear I'll – "

"You'll do nothin'," Silas sneered.

Andrew tried to pull away again. "Ari, are you –" he said, looking me over. "Have they—?"

Mr. Toby tutted and shook his head. "None of that now, Mr. Michaelson," he said. He lifted his chin at Silas. "Mr. Silas, can you make our guest here more cooperative?"

Mr. Silas smiled wickedly. A silver worm slithered out of the sleeve of his coat and touched the back of Andrew's neck. Andrew stiffened, his eyes going wide with fear.

I struggled, kicking whatever limbs or other parts I could reach on Mr. Toby in an effort to get away so I could stop whatever Silas was doing, but to no avail. I tried to reach my left wrist and the bracelet there, but Toby took full custody of me, holding me by both my upper arms so I couldn't move and squeezing so hard I had trouble breathing.

Andrew stood in Silas's clutches, standing ramrod straight as the worm appendage slithered around his neck like a collar. Once the collar settled in place Andrew's muscles relaxed to a parade rest sort of stance, his mouth moving without sound, while his eyes burned with equal parts defiance and fear.

Silas chortled. "Never thought I'd be walkin' a Facti like a bleedin' dog, and no mistake," he said, grinning. "Do you think the Boss'll let me keep him? Always wanted a dog."

"What're you doing to him?" I said, wriggling in Toby's grasp and trying to kick him in the legs.

Toby leaned down, unaffected by my attempts to injure him. "Mr. Silas is currently in control of Mr. Michaelson's motor functions," he explained in my ear. "Now, if you come along nicely, Mr. Silas will allow him to breathe and move without hurtin' him. If you make a fuss, Mr. Silas will do bad things to your young gentleman friend, like," he thought for a moment, "...stop his breathin' or force him to put out his eyes with his own thumbs." Mr. Silas smiled. Andrew's eyes took on a frantic cast.

I stilled immediately, fearing for us both, but mostly for Andrew. "Please. I'll do whatever you ask. Just don't hurt him."

"Much better," Toby said. "Now, your worship, let's take you to the Boss." He let go of my right arm and guided me by my left. Silas moved Andrew's body. Together we turned left and moved away from the Diabolicals.

Andrew's gait at the end of the leash was stiff and awkward. Whatever control Silas had it clearly wasn't precise, and it looked uncomfortable for Andrew. I mentally cursed my inability to help him.

Behind us, I heard the hiss of steam and the sound of a door opening. What followed was a blood-curdling scream of anguish and agony that sounded vaguely human but mostly something else, cut off by the report of a gunshot that echoed around the great hall. Cold horror climbed up my spine and rang panicked warnings in my head.

"Poor sod," Toby muttered, shaking his head. "Best thing to do is kill 'em straight off." I looked up in alarm at Mr. Toby.

"The Boss don't play around, yer worship," he said. "He wants to remake the world and he'll do whatever it takes t' get the job done. Best you keep that in mind."

I nodded, stunned. I'd thought the stakes were high, but now I saw that notion was an epically bad miscalculation. The stakes were... everything. The people I cared about, millions of innocent people...

My heart sank. I was a seventeen-year-old math student and aeronaut, not a diplomat or general. Cora was the strategist, not me. I had no experience with these sorts of situations and no idea what to do. Andrew had told me I'd been thrust into a conflict between two supernatural forces. He'd been right. With next to no familiarity dealing with magic, little to no active memory of stories and myths that might help me and no way of knowing what was to come, I was at a grave disadvantage. If I made a wrong move or said the wrong thing, I could easily get Andrew or myself killed – or worse – get us put into one of the Diabolical machines and made into participants in Laufeson's world domination scheme.

The only person I could think of who would know what to do in such an impossible situation was Great Aunt Miranda. I smiled wryly for a moment despite my fear and worry, thinking of what she'd tell me if she were with me right now: "Buck up, pay attention, trust your instincts and do your best. This is no time to fall apart, my girl." I took in a slow, even breath, let it out and prayed I'd at least be able to get Andrew to safety.

The Odin Inheritance Victoria L. Scott

Chapter Forty-One

"Here's the Boss's office," Toby announced, indicating a heavy oak door to the right, inset in the right hand wall of the great hall. He knocked and I heard a muffled 'Come' from behind the door. Toby turned the knob and pushed the door inward, then pulled me in behind him as Andrew and Silas brought up the rear. Silas shut the door behind us.

We stood in a rectangular room that had a vaulted ceiling made of old, slightly charred wood, with grey stone walls and a flagstone floor. Candles in massive candelabras illuminated the room. Bookcases sat along the walls stuffed with ancient looking tomes. Laufeson sat behind a white Louis XIV desk on a light blue oriental rug in an opulent desk chair of the same period. He seemed to be reviewing paperwork on the desk, an oddly merchantile sort of activity in the midst of opulence and malice.

Directly behind the desk was a heavy oak table that served as some sort of altar, with an oblong stone that had the carved image of a horned and bound god upon it, kneeling in agony. A silver bowl sat in front of the stone, its interior and edges brown with dried blood. A bone-handled silver knife, also brown with blood, lay next to the bowl. A grey silk cushion sat on the floor in the center of the steps in front of the altar. Hypatia had told me the Obscurati had power because they worshipped the pagan gods they served. Apparently the Son of Loki took his worship very seriously.

Laufeson looked up from his papers, stood and walked around the desk, looking us over. Toby pushed me down to my knees. Silas moved Andrew so he knelt awkwardly to my right.

Laufeson smirked down at me. "Welcome to my sanctum, Lady Ariana," he said. Then he spoke a word I didn't understand and I felt the black tendrils of his magic seep into my mind. I grit my teeth, clenched my fists and fought the impulse to prostrate myself before him.

"Still so stubborn?" he mused. He reached into his pocket and pulled out the bottle of brown powder. Pulling out the stopper he licked the top of his index finger before tilting the bottle and inserting it into the bottle. The brown powder sifted over the digit, and when he pulled his finger out, a small patch of brown sat on the end of it. He stuck the end of the finger in his mouth and ate the powder. I grimaced, revulsion filling me.

The German spoke again in the language I didn't know, and the black tendrils I'd been keeping at bay overwhelmed my mind. Any idea I had about resisting his influence shattered under the onslaught. I looked up at the man adoringly and showed my obeisance by lowering my forehead to the carpet in abject submission.

"Better," Laufeson said. "I told you your blood had power," he said, "and the one it has the most power over is you. You may rise." I sat up and basked in my proximity to Laufeson, eager to follow any command he chose to make.

He turned his attention to Andrew, waving a hand to indicate Silas should release him. The silver slithered off his neck and Andrew collapsed to the carpet. "Using the ancient dark tongue, Laufeson? I don't know where you learned it, but God help you when the reckoning comes."

Laufeson smirked. "Ah, yes. The foolish belief that use of dark magic rebounds on the user. You know nothing about the true nature of power. You'll suffer because of your ignorance."

"What happened to the others," Andrew croaked, ignoring the threat. "On the *Bosch*? What did you do to them?"

Andrew's words floated in slow motion as my mind tried to comprehend what he'd said. Understanding came in a rush, breaking Laufeson's hold for a few seconds. *Mother? Max and the others? What had he done to them?*

Laufeson laughed, a harsh sound in the stone room. "I had no use for them. Once my friends got us off the ship," he gave a shrug, "I blew it up."

I felt like I'd been punched in the stomach. I gasped and tears sprung to my eyes but didn't fall as the spell Laufeson had cast reasserted its hold on my mind. The anguish floated away to a distant place.

Andrew clutched the carpet and cried "No!"

Our captor sniffed, unmoved and unconcerned. "*Ja*, Son of Khonshu. I cannot believe you thought traveling with bags full of hydrogen as your primary method of buoyancy was safe," he admonished. "The explosion was very impressive – it lit up the sky like the sun for a moment, leaving only small pieces falling to the ground after. All in all it was very tidy – nothing remained to merit any kind of burial."

"You'll pay for this, Laufeson.   The other Facti will come after you with a vengeance and end your life," Andrew said angrily, his cheeks tear-stained.

The German looked unimpressed.   "You're among the last of the Pessarines.   Soon you'll serve my interests, just like Ariana."

My mind suffused with pleasure at being so close to my master and hearing him say my name.   I struggled to understand why Andrew was so upset and why my eyes were full of tears.   Serving Laufeson was our destiny.

Andrew reached over quickly.   He grabbed my hand and the deceptive bubble of complacency and adoration popped.   His grief poured into me, washing out the spell.   My mother, dead – my *Bosch* crewmates, dead – Lady Sato dead… and we sat in the heart of their killer's stronghold, fodder for his infernal devices and unable to stop him.   I sobbed, letting the first tears run down my cheeks.

You are Randgriðr, beloved of Fjölnir, he thrust into my mind. *Consecrated heir, call on Odin!   Claim your inheritance or everything is lost!   Ariana-please!*

Annoyed, Laufeson motioned and Silas pulled Andrew away from me.   "None o' that foolishness, Moon Boy," Silas said, throwing him to the floor and stepping between the two of us.

'*Randgriðr, beloved of Fjölnir*' reverberated in my thoughts like an echo doubling and redoubling on itself.   It blazed like a warm light in my consciousness, banishing the hold Laufeson's spell had on me.   I recognized the name, oddly, but it was a memory that came from the deepest recesses of my mind.   It was a secret, magical name, not to be used lightly.   Father's watch chain on my right wrist warmed and tightened.   I recognized the feel of the power as Odin's and welcomed it though I'd no idea why the watch chain seemed to be its source.   Andrew had said Odin was very protective of me. He was the only card I had to play to get us out of this mess though the consequences of my asking for his help were completely unknown.

Please, I thought at the watch chain, *All-Father, help me. Randgríðr, beloved of Fjölnir calls for your aid. Please!*

I felt a stirring in my mind and the presence of something ancient and wise made itself known to me with far more force than I'd experienced before. It – he—asked a question in a Germanic-sounding language I didn't understand.

Yes! I'll do whatever you wish, I thought frantically. *Just help me. Help me save Andrew and stop the Son of Loki!*

I had the sense of agreement from Odin, but I had no idea what form his assistance would take. The watch chain on my right wrist pulsed and warmed reassuringly as if in reaction to my agreement, then melted into me, disappearing from view.

I looked up at the son of Loki and now saw the decay and darkness behind his tailored façade. He rotted from the inside, tainted with death. That was the 'reckoning' Andrew had spoken of, though I hoped there would be worse to come for the fiend. Unfortunately, Laufeson noticed I was no longer enthralled.

"You've broken my spell, Andrew," he said with a sigh, "though it will avail you nothing. She's still mine. Making her obey will just require more forceful methods." He looked at me pityingly. "The deaths of your mother and friends will seem a mercy."

I wiped my tear-streaked cheeks and pushed myself to a standing position. "You're a monster," I spat, "and I'll do nothing to help you hurt anyone else."

The villain sighed. "*Verkur,*" he whispered, and my bones exploded with anguish, dropping me in a heap at his feet. I panted, trying to draw air around the pain, stars flashing in my vision. A sob escaped my throat.

"Will you serve me, Ariana?" Laufeson asked.

"Never," I ground out.

"*Aukning*," he said, and the pain doubled on itself. I writhed at his feet, lost to torment.

Andrew lunged forward, swearing, but Silas caught him easily. "Leave her be, you bastard," he ground out, struggling in Silas' grip.

"*Nægilega*," Laufeson whispered, and the pain ceased abruptly. I pulled in a shuddering breath and pushed myself to a kneeling position, panting on hands and knees. Andrew continued to struggle in Silas' iron grasp.

"So stubborn," he said with a shrug. "I don't have the luxury of patience. Mr. Toby," he said, turning his attention to his servant, "I need one of my special gears. Can you procure one for me?"

Toby bowed slightly. "Right away, Boss," he said, and left the office.

"Mr. Silas," he said, "Mr. Michaelson's movements and commentary are tiresome. Make them stop." Silas grinned. The silver snake undulated out of the sleeve again. Andrew increased his struggles.

"No!" he said, and then the silver collar settled back into place. His body stiffened and settled into the disconcerting parade rest stance. Silas' hands dropped to his sides, the silver snake in his sleeve lengthening to accommodate the movement.

"How's that, Boss?" he asked, pleased.

Laufeson nodded. "That will do, Mr. Silas," he said, then looked down at me. "This would be much easier if you just agreed to work for me, you know." He ran his eyes up and down my body with a significant, loaded look. "We're more alike than you think. There are many benefits to cooperation."

I didn't hate many people. In fact, I couldn't think of anyone I'd ever hated in my life before that moment. This decaying, dark man standing over me had killed my mother and my friends as an afterthought, and now his servant gloated as he held Andrew in thrall. Loathing for him filled me: sharp and acrid like bile in my throat. I hated him with everything I had and swore I would make him pay, even if it killed me. I sat back on my haunches and glared at him.

"No," I said through gritted teeth. "You killed my friends. I'll not serve someone who worships an evil pagan god and wants to hurt people. We're nothing alike. Get stuffed."

Laufeson tsked at me reprovingly. "Such language... and you, the daughter of a duke. As to our being nothing alike, I beg to differ. You make mechanical devices, as I do. In fact, your fascination with mechanicals probably came from me." He tapped his left wrist, then pointed at me.

"I refuse to believe that," I said, feeling a little sick.

"You've killed people, as have I," he pointed out, as if killing people were a commonplace activity.

I closed my eyes for a moment, cursing him. I didn't want to think about that, and it wasn't commonplace for me. The more involved I became in the conflict between the Facti and the Obscurati, the more killing in self-defense was becoming a necessity. That didn't make me like the Son of Loki. I killed to protect myself and my friends. Laufeson killed for fun and personal gain.

"You have a connection to an ancient Norse god who provides you with power, as do I." Laufeson pulled up the right leg of his trousers, revealing his bare ankle and calf above a stylish black leather shoe. A thick silver band wound around the ankle, and silver swirls and curls that reminded me, oddly, of some sort of decorative chain snaked up from the band on his ankle.

"My connection is an ankle cuff—an appropriate symbol for a god bound and sentenced to eternal torment, don't you think?"

I shook my head. "Odin gave me no artifacts."

Laufeson gave me a pitying look. "Odin accepted you as a sacrifice and adopted you as a daughter. He tasted your blood, granted you his favor and protection, and consecrated you to his service and power. Part of him lives in your mind. Artifacts would strengthen that connection immensely, of course, but without them the connection is still very strong. Luckily it isn't strong enough to prevent me from using it to my advantage."

"I'll never work for you," I swore.

"Never is a long time," he responded, unconcerned.

"Why did you blow up the *Bosch*?" I asked, venom in the question.

"For someone so closely associated with Odin, you don't have a very strategic mind. I couldn't turn down a chance to kill a Facti of the Pessarines, not to mention capturing their second in command. These actions weaken your ancient Great Aunt Miranda, which means I can push forward in my plans without her interference, at least."

"What plans?"

Laufeson smiled, which served only to make him look menacing rather than friendly. "I intend to make everyone on this planet Enhanced with my…" he paused, "…unique method of mechanical alteration. Everyone will be mechanically and magically linked to me, and we'll work together to make Earth a paradise devoid of famine and war. Poverty and want will be things of the past, as will political upheaval and free will." He made a gesture that took in the room we stood in.

"Even now, my magically Enhanced servants generate chaos in the cities of England. Haven't you wondered why the remaining Pessarines haven't come to your aid? Surely someone as powerful as your Great Aunt would find and rescue you, hmmmm?"

I said nothing, in part because I wasn't sure if that was true.

"I have no doubt Mr. Michaelson has been trying to contact his Seneschal for hours, to no avail." He shot a pitying look at Andrew. "Isn't that so?" The look in Andrew's eyes confirmed the truth of Laufeson's words.

Damn and blast! I thought, now very worried. *We'll have to get out of this on our own.*

"Don't take it personally," our captor advised. "She's too busy dealing with the riots and destruction across England caused by my followers. Rest assured, those attacks will increase in frequency and intensity until your role in my plan begins in earnest. Then everyone will do my bidding."

I was far from being an expert on societal change, but nothing about that plan sounded good to me. "I don't see how you can end poverty and want by eliminating free will and encouraging your minions to hurt innocent people and destroy property," I said. "You intend to use your black magic to enslave the world, with you as its tyrannical leader. It's barbaric."

The German tilted his head in acknowledgement. "Who better than I to run the world?" he asked rhetorically. "In some instances there will be barbarism. Not everyone will transition successfully and some will survive the process with only minimal intellect."

I thought about the anguished cry of the man from the Diabolical and the gunshot that had echoed through the great hall to end his torment. I shuddered.

"In others, the Enhanced will be much more useful, like Mr. Silas and Mr. Toby. They will be absolutely loyal to me, and in some cases, as with Mr. Silas' unique skills, super-human. That's the beauty of my plan. I'll Enhance everyone – even those without artificial limbs – to whatever level of ability and complexity they can survive. It will be efficient in the extreme."

I narrowed my eyes at him. The audacity and ambition of his plan astonished and repulsed me. "You're mad. I'm willing to bet that..." I pulled a number from the air, hoping I was close, "...a billion people inhabit this planet," I pointed out, "and even if you Enhanced one a second, it would require..." I did a quick calculation, "...nearly four hundred years for you to take over everyone, and that's without taking variables like birth and death rates into account." I shook my head.

"I don't know a lot about magic, but that seems an impossible task on its face. On top of that, you may have weakened the Pessarines, but there are other Facti who'll work against you, slowing down or even stopping your plan entirely."

Laufeson nodded. "You see the problem immediately, *liebchen*," he said, moving back around his desk. He sat down and tented his fingers thoughtfully as I pushed myself to a standing position.

"Such a precise and mathematically engaging argument," he said, watching me with interest. "Thank the gods for a university education. You're right, of course. It would take far too long. That's why you're here. That's why I spent thirteen years waiting for this moment."

"Oh?" I said, crossing my arms over my chest.

"You know how to make small mechanical devices. Your dragonflies, navigational instruments, those Ladies' Helpers... even that spider-like device you used in Dr. Sanburne's office... very effective, complex and impressive." He indicated my left wrist and I felt the thing within it twitch. "I did it first, of course, but compared to your efforts, mine are crude and unwieldy."

I covered my left wrist with my right hand as if I could hide the joint from Laufeson. "So?" I asked, trying not to think about the device in my body.

"My Diabolicals are effective, but far too cumbersome for the conversion of the Earth's population, as you have so succinctly pointed out. But, miniature Diabolicals would speed up the process considerably. For instance, a swarm of your little Diabolical dragonflies could be released into a crowded area and convert those they latched onto before the people knew what was happening." He smiled, obviously imagining what he described. "Every person in Victoria Station would become my Enhanced follower in the course of an afternoon. From there, if the small devices made it on to the trains, they could spread out and convert more people in other places. They could be easily carried and hidden," he pointed out, "and with thousands under my control doing just that, the number of my followers would increase exponentially."

I shuddered, revolted by the idea that something I'd designed would be used as a blueprint for such an unholy purpose. "It would still take decades to accomplish," I said. "You'll be dead before it's half finished, assuming the Facti don't stop you first."

Laufeson beamed. "Oh, I've made arrangements to ensure I'll live long enough to see my goal achieved," my captor continued.

"Hades has been most accommodating. As for the Facti? They can barely stop the chaos now. Against countless thousands of my followers, they'll have no chance. Eventually, they'll become my most powerful slaves – Enhanced beings with supernatural abilities in addition to the magical devices I'll implant in them? They'll do my bidding like puppets on strings. Your devices working to my purpose will make that possible."

I shook my head. "I don't have the power to create magical mechanicals like that – no matter my connection to Odin. Besides, I have no intention of helping you." Laufeson's expression darkened.

Toby entered the office holding a silver gear device about the diameter of a teacup saucer that was about an inch and a half thick. He stood near the door waiting for his next order from Laufeson.

"That thing won't change my mind," I said defiantly though I had no idea what it was.

Laufeson indicated Toby should move over to Silas and Andrew. "It isn't for you," he said. "Toby, rip open the Facti's worksuit and shirt and stick the device on his stomach," he ordered.

Chapter Forty-Two

"You've got it, Boss," Toby said agreeably. He moved to obey as Andrew stood, unable to move or defend himself. I tried to intervene, but Laufeson spoke a word and I found I couldn't move my arms and legs.

"Your mind may resist my influence, but your body is under my command," he said dryly. He waggled his index finger at me, reminding me of where my powdered blood had been. "Your blood is still part of me." Then he turned his attention to Andrew, his demeanor with me becoming one of a teacher instructing a student.

"You see, that device is extremely crude," Laufeson said, watching with an academic interest as Toby exposed Andrew's abdomen and then applied the gear to it. He toggled a button on the side and a set of snakes like Molly Silver's popped out, then buried themselves in Andrew's flesh. Silas retracted his silver snake from Andrew's neck, giving him control of his own body again. He cried out in pain and frantically tore at the gear as I continued to struggle to reach him.

"It'll take days to convert him completely with the gear placed there," Laufeson said, unmoved by Andrew's attempts to remove the device. "I've experimented extensively with its placement. Near the neck is usually the fastest and least painful, in a relative sense. With the device on his abdomen, my probes will have to find his spine by going through all the organs between them and it." He shook his head at Andrew's struggles. "You can trust me on this. He may become one of my pets by the time the probes reach their goal, or he may die of sepsis. It's all a matter of trajectory and luck."

"Take that thing off him," I bit out, horrified. "It's me you want – not Andrew."

Laufeson considered my words. "That's true enough," he agreed, "but I have you already, even if you continue to refuse to serve me. I have him as a sort of... bonus, shall we say? You're not in a position to demand anything of me. So far as I'm concerned, Andrew is expendable in the extreme."

The gears on the device turned again and a new set of probes plunged into Andrew's flesh. He grunted and I flinched, angry that I wasn't doing enough to make the torture stop. I could see the probes moving around under the skin of Andrew's abdomen and though he tried to hide it, it was clear he was in agony.

"I think," Laufeson said philosophically, "I'd prefer it if he died. I don't think he'd make a very good pet."

"Stop this," I cried, "please!"

Laufeson stopped and looked at me for a long moment. "Ah. You wish to negotiate in earnest, then?"

"Yes, dammit," I said, stifling a more blistering curse. "Get that thing off him!"

"I see. Well, here are my terMs. I promise by Yggdrasil that I will not harm Andrew. In fact, I promise not to Enhance him. I'll even give him up. In return, you allow me Enhance you. You'll undergo the procedure without complaint, do my bidding without question and assist me in converting the population of Earth. What do you think?"

"Yes!" I cried. "Just stop hurting him!"

"*Gut*. We have a deal." He clapped his hands and waved them in Andrew's direction. "Remove the device but hold him without causing him physical harm."

Toby and Silas moved to do as they were ordered. I watched as they removed the geared device, pulling the probes out with sickening bloody pops and then caught Andrew as he fell forward. He hung in their arms, blood dripping from his torso.

"Healer, heal thyself," Laufeson ordered.

Andrew, panting from the pain, reached up to grasp his pendant with one hand and mouthed words as his free hand pressed onto the wounds made by the device. He let go of the pendant and dropped his hand. The wounds had scabbed over. He fumbled at the shirt with shaking hands to re-button it, pale as a sheet.

Laufeson waved a hand and my body became my own again. "You see?" he asked, standing up and coming back around the desk, "I've made a gesture to show my good faith, and now you'll meet your destiny. Come," he said, "and Silas, bring the American. Toby, attend to our guest of honor."

I followed Laufeson out into the great hall, flanked by Toby. We moved to the Diabolical machines. Silas brought Andrew behind us. "Ariana, don't do this," Andrew said, walking stiffly in Silas's grasp.

"When you get away," I said, "you have to stop – "

Laufeson snapped his fingers, and my jaw clamped shut, cutting off my words. He grinned, enjoying his victory. "It's too late, Andrew," he said over his shoulder. "She's made the agreement."

We reached the Diabolicals. The two Enhanced men who had been monitoring the machine from before were still there, and stepped back in deference to their leader. I noticed the gun in a holster on the hip of one of the men.

"Leave us," he ordered them, and they beat a hasty retreat. Laufeson turned to look at me. "Kneel," he ordered.

I did so, fatalistic and ironically hopeful the Enhancement process wouldn't work on me... or that if it did, I'd end up like one of the 'poor sods' Mr. Toby had mentioned. Unpleasant as such an outcome would be, if I had to be 'put down' like a dog or an injured horse, that'd put an end to Laufeson's plans. It was a price I found I was willing to pay.

But if the process worked, what then? *When will Odin decide to make his move and stop this?* I wondered, my fear increasing. *What if he doesn't do anything?*

Laufeson took my left hand. The blade-filled bracelet I wore there toggled partially open and cut a gash across two of Laufeson's fingers. A drop of his blood fell on my skin and I felt a rush of Odin's power flow through me to consume the blood.

Laufeson pulled his hand away, surprised, rubbing the small cut to wipe away the blood on his fingers and checking that none of it had landed on me. He saw no trace of his blood.

"It seems you have teeth well as talons," he said and removed the bracelet, putting it in my hand. I wished I could toggle it open and cut his throat, but if I made a mistake and failed to kill him, it'd only make things worse.

"Perhaps the conversion process will find a way to incorporate your sharp little bracelet device," he said. "Now, swear you'll serve me."

"Ari, you can't trust him," Andrew cried. "I beg you—don't do this!"

I nodded in an affirmative response, since Laufeson's magic still held my jaw firmly shut.

Laufeson pulled the jar of my blood out of his pocket, removed the stopper and turned to the machine behind him. He pushed a couple buttons so a small flap opened. He emptied my dried blood into the machine, picked two small silver spheres off a console and turned back to me.

"We'll start your service with a kiss," he said, motioning for me to stand up. I did so, reluctantly. God knew I had absolutely no desire to kiss Laufeson. Toby stepped up to stand behind me while Silas kept his hands on Andrew, who struggled in his grasp.

Laufeson stepped forward and kissed me. His lips were soft and warm. He tasted of rosemary and cloves, which turned my stomach as the odor made distant shadowy memories of pain and horror curl and coil in my thoughts. I sensed the decay and death in him from his dabbling with black magic and connection with Hades. It was all I could do not to recoil from his embrace.

Then I felt the cool metallic spheres touch my temples. Laufeson broke the kiss and whispered: "Að byrja."

My world abruptly turned steel grey as the metallic spheres melted into my skin, sending tiny magical tendrils into my flesh and mind. The world spun and I sagged into Toby's arms. Andrew cried out. I was beyond being able to respond.

"Put her in the Diabolical," Laufeson ordered, "so she may fulfill her role in the new world order."

Chapter Forty-Three

Toby moved me forward and placed me in the rectangular chamber. I wasn't sure which way was up, and couldn't seem to coordinate my movements. Toby leaned me against a back corner of the chamber and I slid to the floor in a heap as he shut the door. I tried to get my bearings, but the walls of the chamber spun like a top.

Outside the chamber, Laufeson spoke a few more words I didn't understand and the Diabolical sprang to life. The air filled with the sounds of turning wheels, steam, and gears as I felt the tingle of magic along my skin. My body floated up to hang suspended in the chamber within a nimbus of green energy. It felt very much as if someone had grabbed the back of my shirt and pulled me up so my toes dangled a couple inches above the floor. I struggled, trying to get out of the grasp of the magical energy as it swirled about me.

I heard the thunk of a lever slotting into place and the machinery began to hum and grate as it began its work in earnest. Magic moved around my body in a whirlwind, erasing the enchantment on my jaw. The device in my left wrist broke through the skin, a blood-covered two-inch long silver centipede-thing waving in the green magic. I yelped from the pain as it pulled itself out of my body and melted onto the surface of my left arm. The beginnings of arcane silver tracery formed on and in my skin from the place where the silver centipede had been. My clothes disappeared as the green magic, now mixed with silver, ate them away. I distantly felt something weaving in and around my body to create new garments, but I didn't know what they would be.

Odin moved to the forefront of my mind, bringing blue-gold light into the steel-grey that gripped my consciousness. I felt him subtly modify Laufeson's magic. Images of all the devices I'd made for myself, or for sale or even for the *Bosch,* filled my thoughts while schematics and algorithms danced in the air. Odin created a barrier between my mind and Laufeson's magic in sort of a protective embrace, lessening my fear. Then all traces of him completely disappeared.

Laufeson's magic overtook me then. My body changed at a faster and faster rate, so much so I couldn't keep track of what the magic did to me. The machine groaned and rattled around me and then something... just... broke.

The grinding sound of the gears and machinery slammed to a halt and something hissed angrily. The magic that held me suspended in the chamber cycled down and my feet touched the floor. I wobbled on my feet and put a hand out to steady myself, looking down at my body. I gasped at what I saw.

Silver tendrils covered my exposed skin, but instead of the gentle curves I'd seen on Molly Silver, mine were angular and resembled the sorts of gears and circuits I put in my mechanical devices. A blue wool sleeveless dress that dropped to the floor covered my body. A corset-like silver breastplate chased with angular designs and clockwork that resembled my brooch covered my torso on top of the blue dress. The back of the metal corset was heavier than it should be, but I couldn't tell why that was.

Silver bracers matching the breastplate covered my wrists, with hints of the mechanism from my bracelet in their design. I wore black boots on my feet, chased with silver gear designs.

I brought a hand to my head and looked at my reflection in the glass of the chamber door. I saw pupil-less steel-grey eyes staring back at me. My red curls intertwined with silver metal strips that formed a clockwork-winged helmet on my head. I felt my face. Silver emanated from my temples where Laufeson had pressed the metal spheres. The silver in the skin on my face and neck emanated from those two points, the outlines of gears prominent in the tracery.

The chamber door opened. "Step out and let me look at you," Laufeson ordered.

My hand dropped away from the wall of the chamber and though I tried to fight it, my body responded as ordered. I stepped out of the chamber stiffly and stood while Laufeson circled me, inspecting his new creation. My heart pounded in my ears. *What if he orders me to do something horrible?* I wondered. *Could I stop myself?*

"*Mien Gott*," Laufeson breathed, "you are *fabelhaft*." Toby and Silas nodded in agreement. Andrew looked equal parts fascinated and dismayed.

My skin crawled at the way Laufeson looked at me, the memory of his kiss still very vivid. I'd have blushed if my flesh were still capable of showing my embarrassment, but I didn't think it was. I looked at Andrew, hoping to communicate something with my glance, but my steel orbs conveyed nothing to him. He simply stared back at me in horrified astonishment. The bleak look on his face showed he believed me lost to Obscurati magic. My heart sank. I had no way to indicate that wasn't true... or at least I didn't think it was.

"Ari? Are you in there?" Andrew asked. I tried to say something, but nothing came out.

"Don't waste your time, Heir of Khonshu," Laufeson said, amused by Andrew's reaction. "She'll speak when I require it. My machine scrubbed her uncooperative personality away. Now her thoughts are only of how she can serve me and my goals. Nothing else remains." He turned to consider the machine I'd emerged from.

"Ariana – no," Andrew whispered. "Show me you're in there – fight him!"

I tried, screaming in my mind to give him any sign I could that Odin had protected me. Nothing worked. I stood, silent and still, and waited for my next order.

"You damaged my Diabolical," Laufeson said to me. He waved a hand at it. "Let's see what you can do with it. Take the elements of the two machines here, make sure you understand how they work, and make me," he paused, his eyes narrowed in calculation, "...five hundred miniature, functional insectoid Diabolicals."

My body turned to face the machine I'd just stepped out of. The gears and circuits in my skin moved, much to my surprise, and information on the malfunctions in Laufeson's device filled part of my mind beyond the protective barrier Odin had erected. I read the information there the way I did a mechanical diagram. In a heartbeat I understood the hateful device completely, knowing how it worked, why it turned some people into crippled, mangled monsters while others came out 'improved', and how Laufeson had rigged the device to enslave those who braved its workings. Fury burned in me. I wanted to destroy the horrible machine and its twin.

Instead, compelled by Laufeson's command, I had to make five hundred of the damnable things as a test of his hateful, horrible plan. I didn't want to do it, but I had to obey. My mind spun as I tried to find a way around the order, but the best I could do was make sure the changes made by the Diabolicals I created could be reversed. Using that as my secret template for the work, I gave into the compulsion to do Laufeson's bidding. The gears in my skin moved as my magic evaluated the Diabolicals and plotted the necessary circuits, structures and magical requirements necessary for small versions of the ponderous, unpleasant machines.

At my command, the big machine gutted itself of its important parts. I shrank them down, replicated them by the hundreds, and configured them to fit within the bodies of small mechanical scorpions, wasps, and cockroaches.

He hadn't specified what sorts of insects he wanted. I'd be damned if I made him any dragonflies and I'd also be damned if I made them attractive like ladybugs or butterflies. They had an ugly purpose, so I chose ugly, unpleasant insects.

The infernal insects cut their way out of the carcasses of their parent machines in a sick parody of birth. Glowing green with Laufeson's magic, the crawling insects poured out and down the sides like lava flowing over the edges of a malevolent active volcano, their metal legs, geared wings and clockwork claws clicking and clacking as they rolled down to the floor in a wave. The wasps flew out of the top of the mass of machines, buzzing around the great hall in a swarm above their crawling brethren. When the scorpions and cockroaches hit the floor, they crawled and buzzed over top of each other, roiling like foam in an agitated mechanical sea.

When they all had exited, I commanded them to stop. The wasps landed themselves along the edges of the gutted Diabolicals, while the crawling insects slowed their rolling and stopped, poised statue-like waiting for their next order. Laufeson's eyes glittered with triumph as he reached down and picked a scorpion up off the floor, inspecting it carefully.

The body of the scorpion, a mixture of tiny bronze and steel parts, was the length of an index finger, with its tail curled up over the top of its body. The legs were coiled wires attached to gears and levers in the body of the scorpion. The claws were hinges, and the tail consisted of circuits and wires woven within washers and other flat circular parts. The algorithms and circuits that made the scorpion move were deep within the body of the mechanism, and the magical power source of the device was in its belly. It glowed a sickly green, illuminating Laufeson's palm.

I started to sway, suddenly fatigued. Toby quickly stepped up and grabbed me before I fell and held me steady. Even though the magic that Laufeson forced upon me had powered the vast majority of the insects' creation, some of Odin's magic and my life force had gone into the spells as well, it seemed. Therefore, creating five hundred brand new mini-Diabolicals had drained me. I felt my vitality return slowly, but I felt very much like I needed a lie down.

"Do you see, Andrew?" Laufeson gloated, holding out the small mechanical scorpion. "I've crafted her mathematical and mechanical skills to serve my interests. I'm using Odin's magic in new ways, and neither he nor the Facti, can prevent it. My creation," he indicated me, "straddles the space between mechanics and magic and she's adept at both."

"Making those devices knocked the wind out of your creation," Andrew noted grimly. "I don't see how she'll have the stamina to create millions or billions of mini-Diabolicals to fulfill your insane needs."

"Ah. With the appropriate amount of magical power, Ariana will craft all the devices I require to change the world. I just have to access it."

"You can't access more magical power," Andrew retorted. "You'll need an infinite source. Even if you make another ritual sacrifice and worship Loki at that disgusting altar in your office forever, the amount of magical power any human can possess is finite."

"Listen to the clever American," Laufeson taunted, "so wise in the ways of Obscurati power. I'll gain the power I require."

"We'll stop you," Andrew said, fury in his voice. "By Osiris, I swear we'll stop you."

"No," Laufeson said simply, confidence oozing from him like a bad smell, "you won't."

He tucked the scorpion in his pocket, snagged a clockwork cockroach and snapped his fingers. One of the silver –eyed technicians ran in. "Yes, Sire?"

"Bring me Sylvester," he ordered.

The technician nodded and ran out, then returned with a thin man who looked to be about thirty years old. He had dark eyes and hair and a crude claw replaced his left hand, obviously the handiwork of an English back alley mechanist. His clothes were clean, serviceable garments. A dishtowel hung off his right shoulder, green fingerprints and food stains on the cloth, showing that he worked in the kitchen. There was nothing out of the ordinary about him except the crude and difficult to hide Enhancement he possessed. I winced mentally. With such an obvious artificial limb, his fellow citizens of the Empire would've treated him badly.

"Welcome, Sylvester," Laufeson said.

"Sire," the man said, his delight at the specific attention of his master evident in his tone.

"Would you like to join the ranks of my elite?" Laufeson indicated Toby and Silas. "You may find it worth your while."

Sylvester shifted from foot to foot in his excitement at the prospect. "Yes, Sire. I'd like that very much."

"Don't do this," Andrew said, low and urgent. "Sylvester – get away while you can." My thoughts mirrored Andrew's, but I couldn't express them.

Andrew's comments obviously troubled Sylvester. His excitement dimmed somewhat, and he looked at each of us in turn in an attempt to figure out what was going on and what the truth was.

"Don't listen to him, Sylvester," Laufeson said, holding out the cockroach. "Take this, and you'll end up like Mr. Toby and Mr. Silas."

Sylvester took the insect tentatively and turned it over, looking at the mechanism with interest. "What does this do?" Sylvester asked, curious.

Laufeson waved a hand and the cockroach started to glow with a brighter shade of green. "It changes your life," he said.

The beetle's legs moved with lightning speed to grab Sylvester's hand, making him jump in surprise. Green magic suffused his body and he stiffened as the device began its work. His left claw became a silver hand. From there, silver cords ran up the arm to attach to Sylvester's neck. Armored plates bloomed from the cords, covering the left side of Sylvester's left arm, side, neck and head in flexible silver armor. Then the magic went to work on Sylvester's body. His eyes turned completely silver. He grew half a foot and his shoulders and muscles expanded in proportion to his new height. He became a behemoth, and the expression on his face changed from one of an eager desire to serve to one that indicated an eager desire to do violence. The shift chilled my soul. The fact that I'd created the vile device chilled my soul even further.

I realized Laufeson's boast about the success of his mad plan wasn't as far-fetched as it seemed. I imagined Victoria Station filled with unsuspecting people bathed in green magic and turning into silver-eyed monsters with a penchant for violence. I had to find a way to stop Laufeson before that happened, but I'd no idea how.

The insect let go of Sylvester's human hand and dropped to the floor. Its job completed, the legs of the device curled up underneath its body and it ceased moving as the green glow of magic faded from it.

Sylvester staggered as the magic stopped coursing over him. He had to adjust to his new height and girth. He ran his steel gaze over his new hand first, opening and closing it to test it. Then he moved his armored arm and head, experimenting with the new addition to his body. "Thank you, Sire," he said in a gruff, thick voice, awed and pleased with his transformation.

"I think," Laufeson remarked, nodding in approval, "you'll no longer be needed in the kitchens." He motioned at the technician. "Take him. See what he can do and report back to me when we return. While I'm gone, prepare for distribution."

The technician nodded and indicated the hallway he and Sylvester had come from. They left, Sylvester lumbering back and forth as he grappled with moving his new body.

Laufeson turned to Andrew. "You see? How is that not an improvement over what he was before?"

"You've made him even more a victim of your evil," Andrew said tersely. "There's nothing 'improved' about that." He stuck his hands in the pockets of his ripped coveralls, the white shirt open and bloodstained. He tilted his head in thought. "You'll never convince me that you're acting in the best interests of anyone but yourself. I'm more interested in where we're going."

"You'll see soon enough, Facti," Laufeson said. He turned to his left and spoke an incantation in a language that sounded like Ancient Greek as he drew a circle in the air with his left hand. A circular door made of swirling black smoke appeared where he'd drawn the circle. He turned to look at me. Toby let go of me and I found my energy mostly restored.

"Ariana, bring Andrew and follow me," he ordered. "Mr. Toby, Mr. Silas: attend us."

Silas handed Andrew off to me and I took custody of him as ordered. I propelled him forward to join Laufeson in front of the dark arcane door while Toby and Silas took up a position behind us, like guards.

Andrew glared at me, then put a hand to my cheek in an attempt to touch my thoughts, which failed. Then he tried to use his healing abilities to reverse what the Diabolical had done to me, which also didn't work. I didn't stop him, since I hadn't been ordered to keep him from using his abilities as Khonshu's Heir. It was then that I began to see Odin's plan.

Laufeson's magic didn't allow for initiative or independent thought. The Son of Loki believed so completely in his ability to control everything he didn't trust anyone else to think for themselves, even if they were magically compelled to serve his monstrous interests. Clearly, I was a weapon of great power but limited scope, and Laufeson saw that as an advantage. I wasn't sure how it would happen, but I knew that belief would bring about his downfall. I'd already changed the insectoid Diabolicals so their magic could be reversed, and my captor was none the wiser. He assumed I did what he wanted and didn't think much beyond that.

Odin had altered the nature of the magic used on my body, but it was what he'd done to preserve my mind that was the key to getting myself, Andrew, and the world out of this mess. I was a Trojan Horse. I just had to figure out how to make use of the advantage he'd provided. I remembered Odysseus had been a crafty, clever warrior who made good use of his skills to survive. I wished he'd been with me as an advisor since I felt very much alone and worried.

Andrew closed his eyes and focused hard, trying again to touch my mind, but the barrier Odin put up to keep my mind insulated from Laufeson kept Andrew out as well. My throat tightened to see his sadness at what he obviously thought of as some sort of death of me. I tried to push through Odin's barrier from my side to touch Andrew's mind and tell him I wasn't lost, but the barrier held firm against my efforts.

The smoky door opened. "Come," Laufeson ordered, and the five of us stepped through the door into abject darkness.

Chapter Forty-Four

The trip through swirling smoke was disorienting. We dropped at breakneck speed, the curls of smoke around us sometimes incorporeal, sometimes not. I heard screams of agony – felt the pain they came from as a visceral ache – and generally bounced around like a doll in a butterchurn. My grip on Andrew's arm didn't falter despite the confusion, and when we landed I still had him firmly by my side, though smoke enclosed us and I couldn't see much beyond Andrew's head. Toby and Silas behind me wavered a bit on their feet, expressions of dismay spoken in low tones pitched so Laufeson wouldn't hear them. I heard Laufeson speak more words in Ancient Greek and a cold wind blew the smoke off of us. I smelled sulfur mixed with heated stone and felt the heat radiate from the walls around us. Decay and offal completed the olfactory landscape. The miles and miles of stone and earth above our heads bore down on us, increasing the unpleasant and oppressive feel of the place.

"Laufeson," Andrew said, looking around, "where are we?"

"That depends on the pantheon you ascribe to," Laufeson said simply. "Near the roots of Yggdrasil for the Norse is one way to think about it. The Romans called it 'Dis', but the 'Realm of the Dead' is probably the best explanation."

"Hell," Andrew swore.

"That description is also accurate," Laufeson continued smoothly, "though this area only bears a resemblance to that Christian concept. This is the afterlife as conceived by the Ancient Greeks, not the fools who worship the Christian god," he sneered. "Come along. We have an appointment." He motioned us forward, and we started walking into the blackest darkness I'd ever known, Laufeson confidently leading the way.

Toby and Silas continued their susurrus conversation behind me and Andrew. He noticed and looked back at them. I kept my eyes forward, not having been given permission to look behind me.

"You still think Laufeson is someone you want to serve?" he hissed at them. "He's brought you to Hell – the domain of Hades. He's a god who does not forgive trespasses lightly. The number of people who have entered and exited Hades' realm alive and well over the course of history is infinitesimal, and he's striding in bold as brass!"

I hadn't known our odds of escaping alive were so small, yet my feet took me inexorably further into what was clearly an extremely dangerous place for living beings. *Why,* I wondered, *would Laufeson place himself at the mercy of Hades like this?*

"I trust the Boss," Toby said defiantly. "This is all part of his big plan, and Hades is on our side."

"Really? That's what he's told you," Andrew hissed back, "but who knows? Has the Boss filled you in on this part of his grand scheme? Was a trip to Hell on your schedule for the week?"

A greenish light popped into existence in Laufeson's hand, illuminating the corridor ahead of us with a sickly glow. Blue-white multi-legged creatures scrabbled away from the light, their blind eyestalks waving in alarm as they sought the shadows. I tried not to wonder what other creatures lurked in the darkness.

"Andrew," Laufeson called over his shoulder, "be quiet or I'll have Silas use his snake on you."

Glowering, Andrew turned back to face front and stopped talking. He tried again to touch my mind as we walked, but Odin's barrier held firm.

Laufeson stopped. The green glow of his hand revealed a door made of obsidian with silver hinges and handle. He said a few words and waved his hand.

The door swung open toward us, blasting us with a wall of brimstone-scented heat and smoke. Toby and Silas gasped and coughed while Andrew waved his free hand in front of his face to keep the smoke away. Once the smoke rolled over and beyond us, we saw a jagged black and grey peak in the midst of a huge cavern. Red and orange magma lit the cavern, the lava flowing around the peak like a moat. Gouts of flame roared to the top of the cavern at regular intervals, sending waves of heat blasting outward.

A classical temple in black stone with columns and a pediment that reminded me of the pictures I'd seen of the Parthenon sat on the top of the peak. The figures on the pediment writhed in agony, tormented by monsters as they begged for mercy with hands and arms outstretched. A stone pathway to the palace curved up from where we stood, crossing the lava by way of a stone bridge. The whole vista filled me with dismay. *How will Odin's plan get Andrew and me out of a place like this?* I worried. *How can the remaining Facti, assuming they intend to rescue us, find us here?*

"Blimey," Toby whispered behind us. "I'd heard Hell was hot, but I never really thought – "

"My Ma was right," Silas breathed. "Eternal torment in flames. God help us."

"Bit late for that," Andrew murmured.

"Boss?" Toby said, loud enough for Laufeson to hear, "we ain't gonna burn up before we get the job done, are we?"

"Of course not," he snapped. "Follow me."

We crossed the threshold into blazing heat, surrounded by the glutinous sound of liquid stone flowing around in its riverbed, the chunkier bits on the top crashing and rubbing against each other and the sides of the riverbank. Flames roared around us. *This must be what standing in a volcano is like,* I thought.

Laufeson spoke more words I couldn't quite make out, then turned to face us. "Three steps will take us into Hades' presence," he said, then looked to me, holding out his hand. "You will take my hand, and the others will clasp hands so we stay together as one group. You will not let go until I command you to do so."

As commanded, I changed my grip from Andrew's upper arm to his hand with one hand while I grasped Laufeson's outstretched hand with the other. Andrew reached back to clasp hands with Toby. Toby took Silas's hand and we were ready.

"On the count of three, we step together. One, two... three!"

We stepped forward as a group. There was a blur of red magma and a swirl of brimstone heat around us for a moment. When we'd finished, we stood on the other side of the stone bridge and the Greek temple-like palace loomed above us. Its columns and walls were made of obsidian. The walls glowed red as they reflected the lava flowing around them. The writhing figures on the pediment flowed back and forth in agony, lit from below with the red glow. The tormenting monsters bared their teeth and growled at their victims.

Laufeson indicated a second step forward. After a three count and another moment of disorientation, we stopped inside the covered porch of the palace, surrounded by obsidian columns, their fluting beautiful and as sharp as broken glass. The wall we faced was a solid sheet of black volcanic glass with a double door of silver in its center.

Laufeson nodded at the door. "Our last step will take us into Hades' audience chamber," he said. "One, two…"

Chapter Forty-Five

The interior of the obsidian temple was a huge cavern lit with magma torches and stone braziers of molten rock. Heat came off the torches and braziers in waves. Sweat ran down the faces of the men around me, but although I felt the heat, it didn't bother me. The floor of black stone under our feet was polished to a mirror shine, reflecting the red and yellow glowing light of the torches. Obsidian with veins of silver stone that travelled up and down made up the cavern walls. The silver doors remained closed behind us while a wall of grey-black smoke obscured the end of the cavern opposite the doors.

"You may let go," Laufeson said, letting go my hand. The rest of us followed suit. He pointed at the wall of smoke. "We're heading there. Don't speak unless I tell you to," he ordered, shooting a look at Andrew. Andrew narrowed his eyes suspiciously but said nothing. "Follow me," Laufeson ordered.

We did so in silence. As we got closer to the wall of grey-black smoke, it retreated from us like a curtain, revealing the god who ruled the Greek Realm of the Dead.

Hades was a huge creature of smoke. He had the form of something human, but his edges blurred and swirled as puffs of smoke traveled in curls around the space he seemed to occupy. Red coals served as his eyes, and an ugly slash in the head-like shape worked as a mouth, its interior darker than any cave I'd ever seen. His foggy body sat on an equally huge throne made of thousands of writhing people floating on a sea of bleached human bones.

"You see the spirits of the dead, and the bones those of the bodies they once inhabited in that throne," Laufeson explained. "I suppose the Christians would call that the 'wages of sin.' Hades enjoys punishing impure mortals very much."

Faces and body parts flowed like water across and within the throne, distorted by the corners and sides of the massive chair. Occasionally, Hades pulled one of the spirits off an armrest and consumed it, a faint horrific scream accompanying the grey fog of the dread god's chewing. Once swallowed, the swirls of smoke in Hades' torso became the face of the tortured soul he'd masticated, its mouth open in a silent image of profound agony.

"Welcome, Son of Loki," came the coal-laced voice of the ancient god of the Underworld. The walls reverberated with the power of his words. "You come to fulfill the last part of our bargain?"

Laufeson smiled and bowed. "I do, my Lord. I trust you will hold up your end of the deal."

"Of course," he said. He looked our group over, noting Andrew's presence. "You bring a Facti into my presence," the dread god grumbled. "Why is this?"

"He's my prisoner," Laufeson said.

"An interesting turn of events," Hades said. He pointed a smoky finger at the Facti. "He is far from the protection of his god.

Your Egyptian father cannot help you here, Facti," he ground out. "This is a place of death, not healing."

Andrew's eyes took on a look of defiance as he met Hades' gaze, unafraid and unmoved by the god's comments. Behind me, Toby and Silas shifted nervously but said nothing.

Hades tilted his smoky head in thought. "The Facti healer is unafraid of death. How unexpected." I felt the red gaze of Hades fall on me, its heat on my skin. "This is the female you sought?"

"She is a Daughter of Odin and a chooser of the slain, stolen from the knife of the Fates themselves."

"Why should she help you, Son of Loki?" Hades asked, tugging a soul from his chair, putting it in his mouth and chewing absently. I watched, fascinated and sickened, as the smoky face of an old woman strained in a misshapen rictus of torment across Hades' chest.

"I have made her my creature," Laufeson said. He picked up my left arm and showed it to Hades as proof of my bondage. "See? Her form is bound with silver. She serves me and no one else."

Hades stretched his smoke head out on a smoky neck to inspect the angular silver traces in my skin. The smell of brimstone and oily decay filled my nostrils as he looked me up and down. I stood silently as ordered. What Hades saw on me seemed to pass muster, and his head flowed back to sit on his swirling body.

"Has she the power you require?" Hades asked. "Your magic is strong, but Odin is not easily conquered or outwitted."

Laufeson nearly glowed with triumph. "Yet I have done it — with your help, of course," he said, inclining his head in gratitude. "She carries Odin's attributes, but no longer merits his favor. Of her own free will, she gave herself, body and soul, to me."

"I sense only your mark upon her," Hades ground out. "She has great power. I congratulate you on your success. Only two more steps are required for our bargain to be complete."

Laufeson inclined his head in thanks. "Indeed, my Lord," he said.

Hades reached down a smoky hand to surround us, warm and sulfurous. "I will take you to Loki," he said and closed his massive foggy fist, enveloping us in a dark mist of tortured faces that obscured everything.

Chapter Forty-Six

When the fumes of Hades' hand dissipated, we stood at the entrance to a rocky, steamy cavern lit with low burning torches. The stone under our feet was slick with dirty wet moss and the air smelled of animal fear, mold and old urine. It reminded me of the cloying smell of the cages at the London Zoo.

Andrew, Toby, and Silas coughed and choked, working to rid Hades' brimstone from their throats and lungs. The fumes didn't bother me though I didn't know why. I stood unmoving behind Laufeson, who wiped his eyes and mouth before he turned back to look at the rest of us.

Suddenly, an olive-skinned, dark-haired man with a lean body and a hooked nose appeared next to Laufeson. He wore a black robe and his eyes burned red like coals.

"Hades," Laufeson said to the newcomer as he turned back to face forward, "so nice of you to join us – and in mortal form."

"Yes. It's easier to move about in this part of my realm this way. Since you're clever, Son of Loki, I'll stay close to ensure you keep your bargain," Hades said, his accent exotic and smooth. "I know your father's reputation well, as I do yours. I will have what you promised me."

I didn't like the sound of that. *What could Laufeson have promised the god of the Underworld?* Toby and Silas shifted and looked at each other, clearly wondering the same thing I was.

Andrew crossed his arms and glared at Laufeson and Hades. "I knew this trip would get us all killed," he said coldly. "Bargains made with the son of a Trickster god? You've been too long underground, my Lord Hades."

Hades' eyes blazed like fire, and a hot wind, tinged with brimstone, blew over us, making his black robe undulate across his body. "The Facti speaks," he ground out. He waved a hand and Andrew doubled over, gasping in pain. "Speak again, mortal, and I will take your Moon god's artifacts and end your pitiful existence in the most painful way possible."

Andrew said nothing and looked up to meet Hades' fiery gaze without fear.

Hades snapped his fingers and Andrew gasped again, then slowly stood up straight, the pain apparently gone. The God of the Dead turned, strode to the front of our group and indicated the mouth of the cavern. "Come. Loki gets few visitors, especially since he's here in my domain and not in Helheim. The Norse rarely come here. We mustn't keep him waiting."

He entered the cavern, holding up his hand and generating a red light in it to illuminate the way. Laufeson followed, beckoning the rest of us to follow him.

As we walked further down the tunnel, the zoo smell increased in intensity, as did the heat. Toby and Silas pulled out handkerchiefs to cover their noses and mouths, gagging on the smell. Andrew put his hand over his mouth and nose.

We rounded a corner and Hades stopped, waving his right hand to send pulses of red light to the sconces on the walls of what was a cave. A huge tree root, gnarled with age, crawled down the wall to our left, smaller and smaller roots spreading out from it to crisscross the wet floor under our feet like a carpet. Three pointed monolithic stones rose ten feet from the floor. Loki lay pinioned across the three points, his hands and feet bound with reddish-blue ropes that glistened with blood and moisture and shook as the man writhed in agony. His eyes were screwed shut as he moved his head back and forth in an attempt to avoid something dropping down on him from above, with little success.

Loki's skin was filthy, as was the loincloth that covered his lower torso and hips. The animal smell of urine and the stench of a long unwashed human body emanated from the Trickster god, as did the smell of offal from the entrails binding him to the stones. On our side of Loki, a worn set of stone stairs led up to the top of the monoliths near his head, but at the moment they stood empty. Behind him, the cavern extended in a narrow tunnel.

Hades sent more red spheres of light to hover higher in the air, revealing a stalactite plunging down from the top of the cavern. Coiled around the stalactite was a huge black snake, its mouth open showing huge dripping fangs and a forked tongue flicking back and forth. Venom dropped onto Loki's face. With each drop, he let out a hoarse cry and twisted more frantically in his bonds.

"Where are you, cow?!!" Loki screamed. "Why do you delay?!!!"

A wraith-like woman in filthy brown rags came from around the back of the monolith out of the narrow tunnel at the man's feet. She moved up the steps wearily. A coarsely woven scarf covered her face below her eyes and much of her head, while stringy blonde hair caked with grime tumbled out over the top of the scarf. She put a basin with gnarled dirty hands above Loki's face that caught the drops of venom, and the spasms in his limbs eased. His complaints did not.

"Sigyn, my wife," Loki ground out, distaste in his voice, "you move too slowly! One would think you live to watch me suffer, you bovine wretch!" Sigyn held the bowl and said nothing in response to her husband's insults.

I shuddered to think what the god had done to earn the eternal torment we witnessed. The red light of Hades' magic cast everything in a flickering bloody haze. Shadows flitted in and out as Loki writhed and Sigyn strained to hold the bowl in place.

Loki turned his head, green eyes open now that the drops of venom hit the bowl above his head. His face was burned and eaten away by the venom, but as we watched, the muscles and flesh rebuilt themselves on the exposed bones though the repairs were red, scarred and puckered. Old blood palattered his neck and torso, removed wth new droplets. Loki noticed our presence in the cavern and his scarred lips sneered at us.

"Hades, you son of an ugly whore of Ishtar, why do you invade my cavern? My cries are not loud enough to be heard in your throne room?" The ends of Loki's fingers glowed with flickering green fire and he flexed his fingers, sending balls of green flame from each careening around the cavern so we had to duck and dodge to avoid them.

"Now Loki," Hades admonished, unmoved by Loki's attack, "is that any way to treat guests... or your gracious host?"

"Release me, Hades!" Loki roared. "Have I not suffered enough? Release me!"

"You know I cannot," Hades replied, his tone matter of fact. "Odin and the other members of your pantheon condemned you to this existence here with me. They couldn't leave you under the control of your daughter Hel in Helheim for fear she'd release you. By their command, I haven't the power to alter your confinement.

Perhaps if you had not engineered the death of Baldur, your punishment would have been less..." he paused, face wrinkling in distaste, "...gooey." He waved a hand in dismissal. "But that hardly matters now. Every time I come, you and I have the same pointless conversation. You know as well as I do that I can't release you." The god indicated us. "I've brought you visitors. That should lighten your torment a little, surely."

Loki growled bitterly. "I am not some exhibit in a museum," he spat. "Begone, mine host," he sneered, "and leave me to my fate."

"Great Loki," Laufeson said reverently, kneeling on the filthy carpet of roots and grime before his god, "it is I, your Heir. I have come as promised and seek your favor."

Loki's eyes narrowed in calculation. "Ah... my Heir, in possession of my artifact," he said, his tone oily with suspicion. "I've done all I could to answer your prayers for power and dominion. What power I could be spared I sent to you. Bound as I am, I can do nothing more. I meant you to use that power in the world above. Your trip here has been in vain. Leave me and hope Hades does not take your life instead of granting you safe passage home."

"Father," Laufeson persisted, "I seek to assist you. I beg you, examine my companions. What do you sense about them?"

Loki looked at Hades. "What trickery is this, Hades?"

"No trickery, Deceiver," Hades responded. "Do as he asks. You may be surprised."

Loki looked us over carefully, his inspection obviously more than visual. "You have brought me a Facti of some minor Egyptian healing god, and two servants who stink of your mechanical sorcery... but the female..." he paused, thinking, "...she is almost Valkyrie and carries the favor of Odin, but she too has the marks of your arcane mysteries upon her.   How can she be your creature and Odin's, and how does this help me?"

"The Valkyrie can break Odin's bonds upon you, Father.   I worked for years to craft her into the tool you see here.   Under my instruction, she'll end your suffering and bring about your release."

Loki shook his head.   "If Hades can't release me, neither can this hybrid female you created.   Odin will not allow it."

Laufeson lowered his head and hands so he lay prostrate in supplication.   "Father, may I try to release you? If I fail, you've lost nothing, but if I succeed you'll have gained everything.   What say you?"

"He's immortal," Andrew said, scoffing at the thought Loki could be released.   "His torment isn't supposed to end.   Loki is destined to stay here, bound by the entrails of his son and suffering forever."

"Haven't I suffered enough, mortal?!" Loki roared.   "I engineered the death of Baldur, yet he didn't suffer as I do!   His pain was brief, while mine is unending!   He has hope of rebirth while I languish in this stinking prison; my only companion this feeble, hated harridan!   Her attempts to ease my torment are frail and laughable!   You know nothing of the pain I endure!"

"Will you allow me to try, Father? May I attempt to free you?" Laufeson asked again, sitting up.

Loki laughed manically.   "Try, son," he giggled, "but face my wrath if you fail!"

The Son of Loki stood.   "Watch carefully," he said to Andrew, "while I prove you wrong." He turned to Hades.   "I am ready, my Lord," he intoned.

Hades tilted his head and narrowed his coal red eyes. "But the price has not been paid," he said gravely.

Laufeson indicated Toby, Silas, and Andrew. "There are three men here," he said. "Take any of them you wish as payment. I give them to you."

Andrew tensed, ready to defend himself or run. The other two men looked at each other in confusion, understanding slowly that Laufeson had just given them to the Lord of the Underworld to do with as he saw fit.

"Choices, Son of Loki? How very generous," Hades said, looking over the men.

My mind raced. *But... Laufeson had given his word*—I thought—and then, I understood. I cursed my own foolish stupidity. I struggled against Odin's mental barrier, pushing against it with all the cognitive force I could muster, some of my effort driven by panic. *Come on... come on...* I willed, gritting mental teeth as I pushed. It didn't work, of course. I tried to move my limbs and interpose myself between Hades and Andrew, but that didn't work either. *Damn and blast!* I swore, wishing I had control of my mouth so I could do more than think my curses. *I'm a fool!*

Laufeson had promised not to hurt Andrew and said he'd 'give him up'—which he'd just done, by giving him to Hades. Hades had made no promise to leave Andrew unharmed, and he'd already threatened to kill Andrew once. Trapped as I was in my own body by Odin's impenetrable magic and Laufeson's damnable sorcery, I could do nothing to prevent Hades hurting Andrew. He'd die deep in Hell, and all I could do was watch.

The Odin Inheritance Victoria L. Scott

Chapter Forty-Seven

"So what's the bargain you struck?" Andrew asked, his gaze flickering from Laufeson to Hades and back.

The woman in rags removed the bowl from above Loki's head and made her way down the stairs to empty it. Loki's animal howls of pain and maniacal giggles slashed through the cavern as the venom began to dissolve his face again.

Laufeson winced at the sound while Hades just looked bored. The others put their hands over their ears in an attempt to drown out the ululations. I stood unmoving, my continued attempts to do something—anything—unsuccessful.

"Ariana's calculations of how long it will take to spread my magic across the world were sadly accurate," Laufeson said, stepping forward and speaking louder to be heard over Loki's cries. "Even after she constructs more of the smaller Diabolicals and they begin to disperse across the world, it'll be decades or longer before the job is complete. No matter how much I worship Loki, he can't extend my life as far as required to see the plan to its end."

"But Hades can, I take it?" Andrew bit out, moving slowly toward the cavern's entrance.

"All I need is one life in service to me in exchange for another," Hades explained, "and a Facti of a healing god will do very nicely, however minor."

The Son of Loki clasped his hands behind his back and smiled in satisfaction. "I give you to Hades, he gives me hundreds of years of life without fear of disease or growing old," Laufeson explained, as if trading in lives was as mundane as buying a horse. "Add in one or two other men as a bonus, it's an equitable trade, I think."

"Now wait a minute, Boss—" Toby stammered as he started to back away, grabbing Silas as he went. He jostled into me, knocking me toward the gnarled root along the wall of the cavern. Andrew attempted to make a break for the exit in the confusion, running around and behind Laufeson's two Enhanced thugs and pushing them more in my direction as he did so. I put out my left hand to catch myself against the root and my palm made contact with the bark.

I stiffened in surprise as a wave of power and awareness flowed though me. The tableau of horror in front of me slowed to a crawl as Yggdrasil's silent recognition and assurance wound its way up my arm and around the perimeter of my thoughts. Without warning, it moved through Odin's barrier and into the protected part of my mind to make contact between us easier.

My initial wonder at Yggdrasil's ability to pass through Odin's barrier gave way to relief at finally being able to communicate with someone, even if she was a supernatural tree. Any questions I might have had devolved into a desperate attempt to tell the World Tree everything I'd experienced and thought all at once. My panicked fears about Andrew and what Laufeson wanted me to do to the world flitted about like frightened moths at the top of my mind, fueled by the deaths of my friends, the destruction of the *Bosch* and my metamorphosis into a human/mechanical/magical hybrid at the mercy of a madman.

The World Tree dealt with change on a glacial scale, only truly understanding large spans of time. To Yggdrasil, a season like autumn passed by in the blink of an eye. Therefore, short term events presented in a flurry of frenetic mental activity were harder for the tree to grasp. Yggdrasil made me understand she knew I was distressed, was aware my essential essence had been altered and that beings had died, though she had difficulty with the concept of the massively infinitesimal span of time within which these things had happened. She offered sympathy for my concerns and magical energy if I required it, but she was clearly at a loss as to what else she could do.

Can you prevent Hades from hurting Andrew?

No, she said, her response sad.

Can you help me do something to save Andrew?

Perhaps, but her response made it clear she didn't know what she could do, and the time frame in which it had to be done confused her.

I wondered if energy from the tree would enable me to reverse the changes Laufeson's Diabolical had made to me. That, at least, would put a stop to Laufeson's plan to convert the inhabitants of Earth into his puppets. If that worked, I'd only have to destroy the mini Diabolicals back in the great hall.

No, she whispered in my mind. Despair filled me and I tried to pull my hand from the root but found I couldn't.

Wait, it urged, sibilant and unhurried. *Be still and wait. Let me see you, and then through you.*

The power in the voice enforced its desire and I stilled, standing as Yggdrasil examined every cell in my body, every swirl of silver on my skin, and every bit of magic that was now part of me.

You have complete control over your exterior, the World Tree noted. *Remove the covering on your feet so your bare flesh touches the floor.*

I concentrated and found that I did have control over my attire, which was essentially a magical construct woven from both Odin's and Loki's magic. I willed the boots to disappear and the soles of my feet touched the grimy mat of roots along the floor of Loki's cavern. Yggdrasil's awareness seeped into me from there, like sap moved up from the roots of a tree. She filled my mind, calculating and glacial in her patience, and I became the eyes and ears of the World Tree.

Chapter Forty-Eight

The tableau of chaos wound back up to its normal speed. Toby, Andrew, and Silas scrambled to get away from Hades, but he snapped his fingers and closed off the end of the cavern, cutting off the only escape route. Then he curled his right index finger and the wall he'd erected began to move inward, forcing the three men back into the cavern. The men faced the Lord of the Underworld, their backs against the wall and arms outstretched, trying to keep the wall from moving forward by planting their feet.

It didn't work. The wall stopped moving and the three stood against it like men facing a firing squad.

Loki's howls, less loud but more hoarse, reverberated against the cavern walls. "Sigyn, you stinking harpy!" he screamed, "why do you delay?!!! I curse your miserable hide, worthless nag!"

"I'm not goin' without a fight," Silas said, looking at Toby and Andrew, his eyes wild with fear. He went on the attack. He ran forward a few steps and sent his silver snakes from his outstretched arms to strike Hades in the head.

"Silas, no!" Toby cried, but too late. Hades waved his hand and the silver snakes turned to dust. Silas howled in agony and dropped to his knees, his hands twisted in a rictus of pain, his face a study in torment. The silver appendages had been a living part of him, and their sudden disappearance was like having a limb amputated without warning or anesthesia. His screams were horrible and unending and rivaled Loki's in intensity.

"Ashes to ashes, dust to dust," Hades said dryly, and with a second wave of his hand Silas's body disintegrated into nothingness.

"NO!" Toby cried. He dropped to his knees and desperately tried to scoop up the powder that had once been Silas. His hands turned grey from the man's remains, and Toby stared at them, stunned.

If Hades turned Silas to dust with a wave of his hand, I wondered in a panic, *what will he do to Andrew?* I squirmed in Yggdrasil's grip, fighting against the pull of her patience. It was like trying to stop the sea with a broom.

Laufeson tsked at the tableau of Toby in the dust. "Oh, Toby," he said, "how weak you are."

"He served you faithfully!" Toby shouted, leaping to his feet. "He became yer creature, and you threw him away!" Angry, Toby took a step toward his master, murder in his eyes and grey hands outstretched for Laufeson's neck. "It ain't right!"

Laufeson laughed, unconcerned. "What's one man in the army of millions I will command, you fool? Dust under my feet is a fitting end for him!" He pointed, and green energy pulsed in his hand. He threw it at Toby and covered the man in green magic. Toby stiffened and shook, fighting Laufeson's influence, but it was a battle he lost. He stopped shaking and lowered his arms like a man in a daze. "Hades," Laufeson asked dryly, "do you want this worm?"

"I think not," he responded. "The Facti will do quite well."

"Stand next to Ariana to await my will, or I'll bring you to a worse end than Silas," Laufeson ordered, spitting the words out.

Toby nodded dully, dusted off his hands and moved to stand at my right, whatever spark of personality he'd possessed now dulled or gone.

Andrew grabbed the pendant around his neck and started to whisper an incantation in an attempt to save himself from Hades, and a grey-white glow surrounded his body.

Hades looked pointedly at Andrew. "A feeble attempt, Facti," he said. He waved his right hand and a thick band of red power encircled Andrew's torso, lifting him off the floor. The red nimbus quickly overcame and absorbed Andrew's grey-white protective magic.

Andrew grunted and struggled within the red nimbus. "Why do I have the feeling Silas wasn't the 'payment' you wanted?" he asked, his tone pained but sardonic. Hades smiled, his grey, pointed teeth a ghastly sight.

"Enough talk," he said, pointing his right hand at him. A black ribbon of power leapt from the hand and spun itself into the red ring of power surrounding the Facti. "I bind you as a slave to my will," Hades said in a flat tone, "your soul trapped in an unliving body to serve at my pleasure until I allow death to take you."

Andrew writhed and kicked, fighting the black magic that seeped into his body. As I watched, screaming in my mind, Andrew's hair turned white, his skin became grey parchment, his blue eyes turned black, and his face lost all expression. Black bands circled his wrists. The red nimbus dissipated and Andrew's feet touched the floor, arms at his sides and still as death. Though his face was pallid and unmoving, I saw torment and anguish in his black eyes. No matter what the condition of his body, part of Andrew was aware of what had been done to him.

No! I cried, furious and helpless, trapped in my own body, just as Andrew's soul was trapped in his. *Yggdrasil, do something!* I thought to the World Tree. *Please!*

Wait, the tree responded.   I swore mentally, despairing and frightened.

Hades then motioned at the wall where the stupefied Toby stood. "Step to the wall, slave," Hades ordered.

Andrew's animated corpse, moving slowly with a shuffling gait, did as commanded. Hades spoke an incantation and Andrew's mouth dropped open in a silent scream. Clear red crystal formed around him, so he stood like an insect trapped in amber.

Hades then turned to Laufeson, rotating his hands to create a sphere of grey-white energy about the size of a cricket ball. He juggled it from hand to hand, considering it. Then he threw it at the Son of Loki.

Laufeson laughed as the energy ball hit him square in the chest and the grey-white light enveloped his body, only to be absorbed. "Now," he said triumphantly, "to Loki."

Chapter Forty-Nine

Loki's howls and curses on Sigyn had faded to weeping cries, the acid of the venom having eaten away much of the center of his face. It seemed Sigyn had taken longer to return this time, and the damage was, therefore, more extensive than it had been when we first arrived.

"Ariana," Laufeson ordered, incandescent with triumph and pointedly ignoring the pathetic mewling of the god bound behind him, "attend me."

The command took hold. I let go of the big root and walked to Laufeson as he'd ordered, still in contact with the World Tree and feeling its infinite patience like a lead blanket on my mind through the soles of my feet, forcibly dampening my incandescent rage at what I'd been forced to witness.

Think, Yggdrasil urged, her power and presence emanating into me from the floor of the cavern. *Odin kept your mind unencumbered. Use it.* With that, the tree's personality faded into the background, its power ready to be used, but its presence out of the way. I was alone with my thoughts once again.

It was good advice. With a supreme act of will I shoved aside my fear, fury and despair, and decided I'd find a way out of the mess I was in by out-thinking my opponents. My mind was the only weapon I had.

The woman in coarse rags returned with the bowl and made her way up the stairs quickly. Her head was covered as before, giving no hint of the face under the rags. She put the bowl underneath the dripping mouth of the snake to catch the venom, and Loki's face began to rebuild itself as his cries lessened. He swore viciously at the woman, but she remained unmoved by his curses. Her hands were different, I noticed: clean and not gnarled, and even a little tanned.

Whoever held the bowl, it wasn't the woman I'd seen doing it before. I didn't know if that was good or bad, but neither Loki or Hades seemed to notice. I had no reason to inform them, so I didn't. Laufeson grinned at me as I reached his side and turned to stand at his right, facing Hades.

Hades laughed. "She's a pretty girl, but can she really do what you require?" he asked. He moved to stand beside me, looking me up and down. He brought a hand up to finger a strand of my curling hair. "A shame you mechanized her," he cooed. "I can think of other tasks for her to perform... tasks that require flesh, not metal gears."

Laufeson pulled me away from Hades. "I'll ascend the stairs to stand beside Loki and Sigyn," he told me, "and then you will follow my instructions exactly."

I nodded, as compelled by his magic. He led me to the bottom of the steps, then left me behind as he climbed up to the top. The woman in rags didn't react to his presence but continued to hold the bowl.

"You must succeed, son," Loki rasped. "Your power will be without limit if you free me. I swear it."

Laufeson looked down at the wrecked face of the god he worshipped. Certain of his success, he sneered down at the captive beside him. "I will have power without limit without your help, Father... but worry not. Your pain will end as I promised. In death, you'll know peace."

"No!" Loki screamed, his hands glowing with green fire, the fingers flexing and straining in fury. "I'll not allow you to kill me!" Green fire flashed from his fingers, hitting Laufeson but having no effect.

"You've shared too much power with me for your fire to hurt me now," he pointed out.

"Treacherous dog!" Loki howled. "I'll withdraw my artifact from you! I'll curse you to the nine realms!" He looked to the woman holding the bowl. "Sigyn! Knock the slave off the steps! Do something useful, you beef-witted shrew!"

The person pretending to be Sigyn said nothing and did nothing to Laufeson. She held the bowl and remained still as a statue.

Laufeson looked me in the eye and I felt the magical power of the command wash over me even before he spoke. He dipped his hand down to wipe up blood from Loki's skin, then flicked it at me, a droplet striking my cheek. "I require Loki's power, Ariana. I command you to make me exactly like Loki."

"No! Hades! Stop her! Stop this!" Loki cried.

Hades shrugged. "This is a family matter, Loki," he said smoothly. "It's not my place to interfere."

Loki swore blistering oaths, condemning Hades, Laufeson, Odin and every member of the Norse pantheon as Laufeson watched and waited for me to do his will.

My senses narrowed to take in Loki's body. Everything else around me faded as the magic I required grew within me. The blue magic I had from of Odin diagrammed the green power that Loki possessed, showing me how it was bound to his tissues, and how the entrails that bound him counteracted Loki's magic.

Loki's power was much greater than Laufeson's by an exponential degree. If I took the power from Loki and gave it to his son, he'd be able to do everything he'd planned. I fought against following the order I'd been given, not wanting the power of a god in the hands of a madman. The gears and circuits in my skin moved as calculations blazed in my mind, diagrams of how Loki's power could be diverted considered and discarded one by one.

Laufeson's command pushed at me with great force. Part of me worked on how to draw the power from Loki in a way that was like what I had done to create the Diabolical scorpion. Compelled by the command, I began crafting the spell, and then stopped by sheer force of my will. The compulsion to complete the spell burned through me painfully, but I refused to give in. The words of the command echoed in my ears like a chant: 'Make me exactly like Loki,' as the ache of my disobedience increased.

I looked at Loki again, then at the madman who'd issued the order. I had to make Laufeson like him in every detail. He wanted to have Loki's power, I knew... but that wasn't what he'd ordered. I had to do exactly what he'd ordered. The spot where Loki's blood had landed on my skin burned as I examined it, forging a connection on a flesh and blood level between Laufeson and Loki. Blood was power. I intended to use it.

"What are you waiting for?" Laufeson demanded.

My bare feet still touched Yggdrasil's roots. I asked her to give me the power I needed.

Power surged up into me from the floor, merging with the magic I already possessed and making it mine to command. I re-plotted the calculations and the gears and lines in my skin glowed with power as I completed my spell and cast it at the Son of Loki.

Green waves of magic flowed over and into him. He laughed as he felt his magic swell to a god-like level. "Yes! Yes!" he cried, triumphant. Loki felt the draw on his magic and screamed his outrage.

Then the rest of the spell began its work. Laufeson's triumph faded as the pain started. He clutched at his body as it morphed and changed.

"What's happening?!" Laufeson cried. "What are you doing?!"

Loki's curses stopped as he noticed not all was going as planned for his would-be murderer. He laughed wickedly to see the tables had been turned. "Overconfident fool!" he shouted. "Kill me? Look to yourself and hope your punishment is brief or your death is swift!"

Hades looked on, clearly intrigued by the turn of events but not inclined to offer any assistance to either Loki or Laufeson.

The Diabolical scorpion crawled out of Laufeson's jacket pocket and scuttled to his chest. Its green energy merged with mine and it grew, its eight legs grasping his twisting body in an embrace and holding it upright.

Laufeson screamed in horror. His head remained unchanged, but everything below his neck became boneless and malleable. Clothes disappeared. The scorpion stood on the lower two sets of legs while it used the upper ones to gather up the shrinking limbs and torso of the Son of Loki. It used its claws to hold the head carefully until what little remained of his body was nothing more than a ball of raw flesh attached to the base of his neck.

Laufeson's screams ceased since his lungs and ribcage were gone, but he was still alive and aware. His eyes rolled in his head, taking in the hideous changes his command had wrought. Then the scorpion took Laufeson's head in both claws and scuttled over to Loki's side.

"What devilry is this?!" Loki cried, trying and failing to squirm away from the mechanical arachnid. "Be gone, beast!" he ordered. His attempts to stop the scorpion with his green fire failed, since it was as immured to Loki's own magic as Laufeson had been.

The scorpion climbed halfway up Loki's chest and deftly applied the raw flesh end of Laufeson's neck to the left side of Loki's neck, midway between the neck and shoulder. Loki cried out in revulsion as the raw flesh merged with Loki's and the head stuck, the join between the two becoming seamless and unbreakable. The flesh join smoothed out so it looked as if Loki had always possessed two heads.

Laufeson's gaze roved wildly as he took in his new surroundings and position. The magic continued its work, connecting the head with Loki's circulatory, nervous and pulmonary systeMs. Laufeson's head drew breath to howl in terror and outrage, the volume and number of the curses he expressed in direct competition with Loki's. The two heads quickly began to argue bitterly, their voices indistinguishable.

I'd fulfilled my command. Laufeson was now exactly like Loki: bound with entrails while being burned with acidic snake venom for eternity. With the completion of the spell, the scorpion shrank back to its prior small size and dropped to the stone landing, still and dead.

The magic that had held me in thrall dissipated. Odin's magic flowed through me, wiping away the evil of Laufeson's arcane sorcery. I felt the Obscurati silver on my body turn to Facti gold. The metal breastplate, bracers, and winged helmet converted from silver to gold, and my eyes went back to their usual green color, the orbs no longer cold steel. I took full possession of my body and stretched, grateful to be able to move freely but fully aware I had more work to do. I concentrated, crafting the magic in my grasp to do my bidding. I took the scorpion apart and magically applied its parts to the entrails that held Loki and Laufeson, thereby strengthening their bonds with a second layer of Odin's magic. I made doubly sure they'd never escape their eternal prison of torment.

Laufeson had killed my friends and my mother, blown up my airship, handed Andrew over to the Lord of the Underworld, and richly deserved his fate. He'd trouble me no longer.

I turned away from the bound god to face Hades. My job in Hell wasn't done yet.

Chapter Fifty

Hades waved a hand, blocking the sound of the two heads yelling at each other, then snuffed out the red magical lights he'd hung above Loki, plunging the two-headed wretch into semi-darkness. The red lights in the sconces on the cavern walls continued to glow, illuminating Andrew covered in red crystal; Toby in a magically induced stupor next to the root of Yggdrasil; me in the armor of a Valkyrie and full of Odin's power, and Hades in his black robe.

He broke the silence he'd created with his applause, grinning at the turning of the tables on his erstwhile ally and my transformation into Odin's heir.

"Well done, young woman," he said, delighted. "I've not seen anything that nefarious happen in eons. Taking his command literally—brilliant! A two-headed mad god trapped for eternity... I never could have predicted that. Thank you for providing me with such rich entertainment!" He leered at me. "I do enjoy surprises."

Before I could react, he'd surrounded me in a red nimbus of his magic as he had Andrew. Pain shot through me as he tried to drain Odin's magic from my body. "Such a clever, treacherous young woman... I hope I can convince you to stay," Hades mused, watching me struggle.

Just then someone in armor very much like my own leapt between me and Hades, slashing with a gleaming sword to cut the red magic away from my body. I dropped to my knees and put out my hands to grasp the root-covered ground, gasping at my sudden release.

Hades yelped as the magic he'd expended backfired on him. He looked with loathing on the armored woman between us, her blonde hair in a braid down the middle of her back, her sword at the ready to defend both of us.

"Freya," he spat, "you half-wit child of Aesir! What right have you to interfere in my business?"

"That mortal body has slowed you down, Eater of Souls," she taunted, then sobered. "Ariana offered you no offense and made no move against you. Despite that, you attacked her without provocation. Odin does not take kindly to such treachery perpetrated on his daughters. Know you, Dread Lord: she is Valkyrie and a chooser of the slain in her own right. You will not have her."

Mortal body? I thought, scrambling to gather my wits. *If he's in a mortal body, he can't be invincible.* He'd certainly be easier to contain as he was than as a huge being of smoke. That gave me an idea.

"Take her to Valhalla then, and damn your eyes!" Hades retorted. "Be gone, the both of you!"

"No," I said, shaking my head. I didn't know where Valhalla was, but I didn't want to go there. "I'm not leaving without Andrew."

Freya, sword still at the ready, backed up a couple steps and looked down at me, dividing her attention between me and Hades. "Cousin," she hissed, "we cannot save the Facti healer. Hades' power in Hell is absolute. There's nothing you can do to release him. Let us go while we can – the young man is lost!"

I ignored her. "Hades," I shouted, my voice low and dangerous, "let Andrew go. Let him go now."

Hades tilted his head slightly, as if my demand was unexpected and somewhat curious. "Let him go? But he's such a valuable prize!"

"He leaves this place with me," I maintained. "I warn you – release him or there will be consequences."

Hades laughed. "Oh? Clearly you're new to this Facti business. You can't order me around, child. I am Death, and as inevitable as the tide and the turn of the planet. I have ruled here for thousands of years, master of all I survey. If I decide a soul will lodge with me, there's nothing you can do to alter that decree."

I narrowed my eyes at the god, a plan in my mind. "Nothing *I* can do," I said softly, "but *you* can do something, Hades."

"You should take the Aesir's advice. The Facti is beyond your grasp. Leave him and return to the world while you still can."

I called to Yggdrasil, her roots under my hands and feet. She responded, and at my mental request the roots that covered the floor rose up around Hades, encasing him in a sheath of slender, grime-covered shoots and roots. Crossbeams jutted out from the upright branches and roots, pinning Hades in place like a bug on a specimen plate without piercing his flesh. Then fine white roots crawled up Hades' feet and ankles, entwining themselves with his flesh as he grunted in pain and writhed in a futile attempt to squirm out of Yggdrasil's grip. When it was done, Hades stood in a woven tube of the World Tree's own substance, his face and one hand up to the wrist visible, but the rest of his body hidden behind layers of wood and foliage.

Freya, seeing the immediate threat from Hades was gone, sheathed her sword and regarded him critically. She looked at me and smiled. "Wily as the All-Father, young Ariana," she praised. She slapped me companionably on the shoulder, then helped me stand up. "If only Hildisvini were here to see this! You do the Valkyries proud. The God of the Underworld trapped like a bug in a cocoon. Wait until I tell the other gods."

I nodded and brushed some of the dirt off my skirt, my mind converting to the calculation of my next step now that I'd imprisoned Hades. "I hope someone will fill me in more completely on what a Valkyrie is and how I happen to be one," I told her in a low voice. "I'm playing this by ear, and I've no idea of the rules."

"So far, that hasn't been a problem," Freya noted pragmatically. "I'd say keep going. I'll back you up."

Hades, the shock of his sudden confinement fading, laughed though it was bombastic and forced. "What is this? You seek to hold me in a wooden prison?" he asked derisively.

"Release Andrew," I told him, unmoved.

Hades scoffed. He generated a globe of red burning energy in the hand that wasn't trapped, then applied it to the wood he could reach. The wood started to smolder and burn. Hades grinned, thinking he'd found a way out until the pain the tree felt became his pain. Sweat broke out on his brow as he tried to endure the discomfort, but the more he burned, the more it hurt. Panting, he gave up and swore several lengthy oaths in Ancient Greek.

Freya looked on, intrigued. "A shame I don't know Ancient Greek," she mused. "New oaths are so hard to come by."

"I learned most of mine from the stableboys at home," I told her, adopting the same attitude. "Very colorful."

"What have you done, Norse witch?!" Hades growled. "No one can command Yggdrasil – yet you confine me in her roots!"

"You're right," I confirmed. "I didn't command her. I just asked. The Son of Loki forged a connection between us and she did me a favor. She made you a part of her. So long as her roots are in your flesh, she will nourish you and keep you alive. Any attempt to hurt her will, as you've discovered for yourself, hurt you. Your mortal form is now an immortal one. So long as Yggdrasil lives, so will you."

"I am the Lord of the Underworld and the God of Death! You condemn me to eternal life?!"

"The irony of the situation is part of what made it so appealing," I told him, and Freya laughed. "Your power in this realm is absolute, Hades, as you said," I explained. "Yggdrasil's power isn't absolute – it's primordial. She holds the Norse planes in place. She is an embodiment of life, and her power runs deeper and stronger than any you will ever possess." I crossed my arms over my golden breastplate. "Therefore, she was the only one capable of containing you."

"How dare you confine me in my own realm!" Hades screamed. "I am no mere mortal! I am the god Hades, the bringer of death!" Pulling a great deal of his power together, his face screwed up with the effort and concentration required for great magic, he created a huge red ball of flame that floated in his free hand to throw at me. I could feel the heat of it across the cavern as it grew in size and strength.

Chapter Fifty-One

"Kill me and you'll be trapped forever," I pointed out. "Yggdrasil won't release you until I give the word for her to do so."

"I will end you, witch!" he spat, his face contorted in rage as the ball of flame continued to grow.

By God, I thought, my anger rising, *there's been enough blood and death. Too much has happened to me for Hades to kill me now. Too much has yet to be done for my journey to end here. End me now? Not bloody likely!*

I let go of some the anger I'd been holding in check. Fueled by that and at all that had been done to me, my friends and my loved ones, Odin's blue magic surged through me like a wildfire, illuminating the chamber in blue light. In response to my call for power, geared metal wings sprang from the back of my breastplate to unfurl on either side of my body with the swish of oiled metal and the crackling of magical energy. Out of the corner of my eye, I saw that the 'feathers' of my mechanical wings resembled the scalpel blades from my bracelet. The ones attached to the frames of my ten-foot wingspan were far bigger, but they were just as sharp.

At my mental command the wings moved, swirling air up and around Hades in his cage in a mini-whirlwind, its blue magic extinguishing his ball of flame like someone putting out a candle. Hades shut his eyes against the onslaught of wind and clenched his fist in frustration, screaming curses down upon me at the top of his voice as the wind died down.

"I will call hellhounds and demons down upon you," he shouted. "They'll tear you limb from limb!"

I felt Yggdrasil's presence react and Hades' eyes widened in surprise. "You're welcome to try," I said.

Mouth set in a stubborn line, he began to chant an incantation but struggled with the words as the glacial presence of the World Tree started to blanket his thoughts. His chant slowed and sputtered to nothing. "You'll never leave my realm alive," he said as Yggdrasil's influence retreated. "You'll die before I let you leave."

I felt a belt form around my hips, the left side of it weighted down with a sword, which I drew. Its hilt was gold, with the grip wrapped in black leather and a steel surgically-sharp blade that was three feet long if it was an inch. It was far lighter than I expected, and I found that, like my wings, I could use it intuitively. I made a few practice passes with the weapon, then pointed it at Hades as I walked toward him. Freya took up a position to my right, winged and armed, but she wasn't surrounded with magical energy and driven by wrath. I certainly was.

Odin flooded my mind with possible ways to kill or hurt Hades, feeding me trajectories for sword thrusts and information on what sort of power I truly had over mortals, if I chose to employ it. He then told me what to say.

"I am Randgríðr, Beloved of Fjölnir, Shield-Destroyer of the Wise-One and First of the Daughters of Odin!" I said. I placed the point of my sword under Hades' chin and forced his head so he had to look in my eyes, blazing blue green in anger. The sword point sat right at his jugular vein.

"You will not take my soul, dread lord," I told him, my voice taking on the gravitas and weight of the god. "I am a chooser of the slain. Should I choose *you* here and now in your weak mortal form, I will take you to Helheim personally. There you'll serve as Hel's personal slave. I have no doubt," I sneered, "that Hel will revel in the chance to torment the god who's overseen the punishment of her father, Loki, for the past few millennia, not to mention being the god instrumental in a plan to kill him."

My sword bit into the flesh of Hades' neck. Blood welled in the wound and ran down the blade in a slow trickle.

"As I am sure you know from personal experience, gods can be remarkably inventive when it comes to the persecution of those they dislike. You have Sisyphus and Ixion as examples. Be warned: Hel is especially adept at the art."

Hades' eyes burned red with his own anger, but the prospect of eternity as the wretched plaything of Loki's daughter seemed to give him considerable pause. "I hear you, Odin," he ground out. "Call off your daughter and name your price for my freedom."

Chapter Fifty-Two

I gently removed my sword point from Hades' neck and took a step back, flanked by a very alert and cautious Freya. Odin faded into the background of my mind and most of the blue magic dimmed.

"Let me guess: I have to release the Facti," Hades sneered.

"You'll need to do more than release him, Hades," I said. "I want him back in a healed, healthy state. Return what you took from him. Make sure he's unharmed and shows no residual effects of what you've done to him."

Hades looked singularly unimpressed. "If I do that, I've nothing for myself. Surely you don't expect me to give up what little I managed to gain from this fiasco? Besides, we both know you can't really take me to Helheim." He sighed. "Even if I wanted to let the young man go, I can't release him confined like this. Let me out and then I'll consider giving his life back. Perhaps we could discuss an even trade."

If I released Hades, he'd do everything he could to kill us. I didn't have time to negotiate. I wanted Andrew free and I'd have him safe, even if it meant there'd be Hell to pay.

Odin's fury blazed up within me at Hades' prevarication. The manifestation of the god's power before had been an impressive show of strength, but Odin in his godlike wrath put the previous display to shame. Blue magical energy blazed from every part of me, the gold gears and circuits in my skin moving and burning with the release of energy. Angry blue sparks jumped and ran along the metal feathers of my wings, discharging into the walls like mini-lightning strikes.

The cavern shook and dirt and other debris rained down from the ceiling as I pummeled the Greek god of the Underworld with Odin's power. Hades' spell to deaden the sound of Loki and Laufeson's cries and imprecations shattered under the onslaught. The rumbling of the cavern combined with their wails and oaths in a cacophony of sound that was nearly deafening.

The sword I held came back up to sit with its point at Hades' jugular. I began the spell for a Valkyrie to choose the slain, with Odin burning the words into my memory as surely as the gears were enmeshed in my skin. I felt the power of the spell begin to take hold, and so did Hades. His red eyes widened in surprise and I felt something shift in the energy in the cavern.

The red crystal surrounding Andrew's corpse-like form melted away. Freya ran over to him quickly, looking him over and turning back to me. "He still looks dead!" she shouted in order to be heard over the roar Odin's magic generated.

More of the incantation spilled from my lips, the elements of the spell seeming very much like parts of complex mathematical equations to me. I looked Hades in the eye as I drove the spell forward, my intent to give him to Loki's daughter Hel foremost in my mind. I felt things—important, needful things – beginning to fracture inside me. The magic drew mostly on Odin and my connection with him, but some of me made up the spell, too, and my life energy had a finite limit.

"Ari!" Freya yelled, "he's turning to dust!"

Hades had released Andrew, which was good, but he hadn't re-animated him. Whatever was left of Andrew inside the shambling wreck of a body didn't have enough life force to hold his tissues together. That wasn't good enough. I wanted Andrew back and fully alive.

I began the last part of the incantation, feeling Hades' intellect and what constituted the soul of the god in the mortal body start to flow into the blade of my sword. Pain suffused my body as the force needed to draw him out consumed more and more of me. Fear and disbelief gripped Hades as he realized that I really could 'choose' him. Panicked, I felt him pull energy out of himself and in an act of desperation hurl it at Andrew.

Out of the corner of my eye, I saw a grey-white aura envelop the alcove where Andrew was, but I continued with my spell, not trusting that Hades had restored him fully.

"Ariana!" came Andrew's hoarse shout, "I'm back! Stop!"

It would have been so easy to finish—I was two phrases away—and Hades had helped Laufeson kill my mother and my friends... but I stopped the incantation and allowed Hades' soul and mind to return to his mortal form, feeling my eyes fill with tears. Andrew was alive. That would do for now.

Odin's fury cycled down and I lowered my sword, suddenly weary of gods and magic. My whole body ached and I found it hard to breathe. Struggling to draw air into my lungs, I folded my wings up so they hung behind my shoulders, the trailing edges of the wings almost brushing the floor, the bent joints above and to either side of my head.

Loki and Laufeson argued and swore at each other as a distant murmur of background noise. In the absence of Odin's roaring magic, the cavern felt as quiet as a tomb even with the two-headed god's cries. Hades looked very much the worse for wear and slumped inside his wooden prison though I didn't know if that was due to relief or exhaustion. He still looked angry, but it was the anger of one who'd been beaten and taken the loss with bad grace. I didn't care.

"I'm so glad we were able to come to an understanding," I said grimly, then turned away from Hades and went to Andrew, wiping the tears from my cheeks.

Chapter Fifty-Three

Freya had sheathed her sword and made her wings disappear so she stood with Andrew's right arm draped over her shoulder, helping to hold him up. She shot me a proud but worried glance and tilted her head at Andrew.

His skin was back to the hue of the living, but only barely. His blue eyes sparked with life and intelligence, but they had a deeply haunted look to them now. The grey hollows under his eyes added to the tormented look. Drenched with sweat that could be seen through his coveralls, he shook visibly though he mostly stood on his own two feet. He smiled weakly at me.

"I'm relieved to see you working for our side," Andrew said. "There was a bit there when I wasn't sure if you'd end up with us."

"You need to get out of here, cousin," Freya said. She pointed at Hades with her free hand. "Hades is not one to forgive easily... or ever, come to that. The sooner you get gone, the better."

"We can't forget Toby," Andrew said, "though he clearly isn't himself."

I looked over my shoulder at the Enhanced thug, unmoving against the wall. I closed my eyes and sent out my magical senses to analyze Laufeson's last spell, cast to prevent Toby from resisting commands. It hurt to do it, certain evidence that I'd overtaxed myself fighting Hades.

A green aura surrounded Toby, conforming to the contours of his body like treacle. Ribbons of green swirled up and entered his forehead. I also saw the green pulse of energy deep in his brain. Toby's magical mechanical parts centered around the middle of his backbone, tied into the green magic deep in his brain. Some of the vertebrae there were crushed and I winced, seeing the extent of the injury. Silver wires curled around Toby's damaged spinal cord and circumvented the injury so he could move like a normal man. I already had some familiarity with the nature of Laufeson's magic, but it was instantly clear that if I altered it too much in that area, Toby would lose the ability to walk.

I thought of Sophie's little box – the one I'd changed out for her what seemed like ages ago. Surely that was some sort of control circuit. I pulled up what I remembered of it, taking it apart and reassembling it in my thoughts as I examined it. I decided it would do the job, if I infused the design with my magic to replace Laufeson's.

I plotted what I needed to do and began. It took a great deal of careful, delicate work to make the changes necessary to free Toby from Laufeson's evil magic and leave him able to walk. I succeeded but staggered from the effort.

Freya put out her free hand to stabilize me. I quickly hid any external expression of pain, though it had gone from a minor ache to a constant full body throb. I'd used too much magic, but I couldn't let Hades see that.

Toby shook himself and blinked, looking around the cave with brown eyes that were no longer chased with silver swirls. He took in a trapped Hades and the three of us. He clenched his fists, his anger returning. "Where's the Boss?" he asked, moving toward us. He cocked an ear and listened to the arguing of Laufeson and Loki. He looked up and started at the sight of Loki with two heads... one of which he recognized.

"Trapped for eternity," I said wearily.

"Did you do that to him?" Toby asked, hiking a thumb at the bound god.

"I did. I got my different outcome. Come to think of it, so did your boss."

Toby tilted his head and let go of his anger. "Good. Bastard deserved it."

"I've freed you from his control," I told Toby. I wiped a hand down my face in exhaustion and wished the ache in my body would stop. "No more steel eyes or swirls in your skin. You're your own man now."

Toby shrugged. "Thank you, yer worship," he said. "With the Boss otherwise engaged, I dunno what I'll do with meself, but I suppose I'll worry about that later." He looked me up and down. "You look different. Like the wings." He nodded at Andrew. "Mr. Michaelson. You look like death all warmed up."

"That's not far from the truth," Andrew admitted, leaning against Freya.

Toby knuckled his forehead at Freya. "Ma'am," he said respectfully.

"Mortal," Freya nodded back in greeting.

"What a touching reunion," Hades mocked, moving within his prison.

I ignored him. "We're leaving," I told Toby. "Do you want to join us, or would you rather stay here?"

"Leave the thug," Hades cooed. "Laufeson owes me a life."

"I'm all for leavin', yer worship," Toby agreed, his expression grim. "I'd rather not pay the Boss's debt."

"Not to mention Hades looks madder than a wet hen at a chicken broil," Andrew added.

I turned to Hades and asked Yggdrasil to release him. The branches flowed away from his body and wove themselves back into the floor. He lurched forward, fists clenched and face contorted with hatred.

"You've made an enemy, Valkyrie," he said. "I'll make you pay for your work this day."

"You conspired with Laufeson to kill my friends and family and do untold damage to the population of the world. Rest assured, I'll not forget that."

Hades raised a hand as if to cast a spell on us. I spread my wings, covering Toby, Freya and Andrew behind them. I held up my sword, pointed it at him and prepared to begin the choosing spell again. "I almost 'chose' you, God of the Underworld. Let us leave your realm without incident or else. I hear Hel gets lonely."

"Be gone, you Norse harpy," he growled. He waved an arm and the wall he'd created to close the cavern disappeared. "I trust you can find your own way out," he snapped.

The body Hades occupied turned to dust that dropped in a cascade to the floor. A creature of grey smoke remained but quickly dissipated as Hades disappeared. Freya shook her head. "I predict future difficulties with that one," she muttered.

"Can't be helped," I said, lowering my wings.

Suddenly the cavern shook with the loudest barks I'd ever heard, the sound coming from down the hallway, accompanied by the scrabbling of nails on stone. The four of us flinched at the noise, which seemed to be getting closer.

"What in the bleedin' 'eck is that?" Toby asked, eyes wide. "Makes a Great Dane sound like a lap dog."

"Hades' pet dog," Andrew said, frowning. "Three heads, very big, usually hungry, and not friendly."

"Then it's time to skeedaddle, I think," Toby said. "I don't fancy a trip through a dog's gullet. Can you work yer 'Moon magic' and get us outta here?"

Andrew shook his head. "Need moonlight – none of that here. Valkyries have the power to travel between the realm of the dead and the realm of the living. Freya only has the power to move herself and the spirits of the dead from one realm to another, since she's an Aesir of Asgard, yes?"

"You speak truly, Son of Khonshu," she confirmed. "I haven't the power to transport corporeal beings. For me to save you, you'd need to die first."

"No thanks," Toby said.

Andrew looked at me. "Think you can manage it?"

The barking began to alternate with howls and yelps. Dust and small stones started to rain down on us from the cavern's ceiling as the stalactites hanging from it shook. The scrape of the beast's nails on the floor of the corridor reminded me of someone running their fingernails down a chalkboard. Both the beast's yowls and footfalls grew closer to us at an alarming rate, and I detected the distinct smell of a lot of unwashed canine in the air.

I wasn't sure I had enough magical or even life energy to get the three of us out of that cavern by magical means, but that was the least of my worries. I slid my sword into its scabbard and returned Andrew's gaze.

"I'm certainly willing to try—" I said, speaking loudly to be heard over the din in the corridor. A stalactite fell with a crash against the wall to my right, "—but I don't know the spell to get us out of here!"

Chapter Fifty-Four

Suddenly, a black paw the size of a writing desk shoved its way into the cavern through the corridor opening, its nails big and sharp as the appendage moved back and forth, trying to scoop us up. We quickly moved to the rear of the cavern, which put us only a few feet out of the beast's reach and at the end of Yggdrasil's roots. I sagged as the tree's energy within me diminished to a trickle.

The dog howled its frustration in triplicate, shaking the room and filling the air with a stench of carrion. My eyes watered and I put my hands over my ears, as did the others. Toby, clearly realizing the overall size of the monster in relation to the paw, paled visibly.

"Good God!" he shouted, pressing himself against the wall as best he could, "that thing's as big as a house! How's it fit in that corridor?!"

"I'm more concerned about what it'll do once it gets in here," Andrew shouted back. He no longer stood with Freya's assistance but leaned against the wall, looking for an escape route.

"Any ideas on a way out of here that bypasses the hungry dog?"

Toby looked around and up. "Maybe behind Loki? No way out above us and those pointy hanging things're movin' too much... we might get crushed before we get eaten!"

The paw withdrew, taking part of the opening with it, and two dark eyes sitting in two different heads peered through the ragged enlarged doorway to look at us. Huge tongues ran along the edges of huge jaws as the dog huffed, sniffing at the air of the cavern. He whined and barked.

More stalactites crashed to the floor to either side of us. I covered my ears more tightly and wracked my brain, searching desperately for a way I could get us out of there, but the pain and noise made it very hard to concentrate. I couldn't sense Odin within me at all. I felt oddly disconnected even though our lives were in danger and the cavern was falling apart around us.

Freya grabbed one of my hands. I felt her mind touch mine and she shoved a spell into my thoughts, burning the words there as Odin had done with the 'choosing the slain' spell, but with less finesse. I felt more of my own energy leech away as the information took up permanent residence.

"I have given you the means of escape, cousin," Freya shouted, letting go of my hand, and then she disappeared.

"Oy!" Toby shouted, "where'd she go?"

The black paw came into the room again. It tore away more of the cavern opening in a crash of boulders and dust. Toby saw a stalactite shake loose of the roof and pulled Andrew and me out of the way so it crashed beside instead of on top of us. Stone bits of various sizes flew in all directions, forcing us to shield our faces from the debris and taking the cuts and blows on our backs, wings, shoulders and arms.

"We may be done for!" Andrew shouted.

I shook my head to clear it as best I could.   Forcing my brain to examine the spell Freya had left me, I struggled to calculate the amount of energy it would take to get the three of us to Great Aunt Miranda's house on Earth, or 'Midgard' as Freya thought of it.   The math involved was the easy part until I realized I barely had enough magical energy to work the spell.   I asked Yadrasil to give me one last jolt of energy, but trapped as I was at the endo f her carpet of roots, what I was able to absorb was a fraction of what she'd supplied.   It would have to do.

'Barely enough' is still 'enough,' I thought.

"Take my hands!" I ordered, holding mine out to Andrew and Toby.

They did as I directed.   I pulled every bit of energy I had into the spell, feeling incredible pain as I did so.   More connections within me broke, but I held on and completed the equations in tandem with the incantation.   There was a flash of blue light.   The cavern disappeared as the last of my magic sent us back to Earth.

Chapter Fifty-Five

The blue light dissipated and I found I stood in a place I was quite sure wasn't Brentwood Close.

"Hello, Little One," came a male voice. The *basso profundo* syllables echoed in the huge chamber around me as well as reverberated back and forth in my thoughts. I staggered and winced. I felt a wave of unending, indescribable fatigue and nausea flow over me. I'd used far too much magic. The needful and important things that had loosed their moorings while I'd battled Hades for Andrew's life and then cast the spell to get us out of his realm made themselves known. The general pulsing ache roared to a crescendo and became a solid wall of physical and mental anguish. The wide planked wooden floor beneath my bare feet obligingly rose to meet the rest of my body, the impact a minor note in the symphony of agony I experienced. My metallic wings spread out to either side of my body, limp. When I'd had power, they'd been light as air. Now their weight effectively pinned me to the floor.

I just lay there after, breathing and hurting, not responding to the greeting of the huge man who towered above me.

"Welcome to Glaðsheimr," the voice thundered. "It's been a long time since we spoke face to face."

My face remained pressed to the floor. I couldn't see his. I breathed some more and tears ran down my cheeks. I couldn't pull together enough energy or thought to speak. There were only pained and broken things inside me.

I heard the shuffle of feet approaching, then the swish of fabric and someone knelt beside me. I saw a hem of a pale green dress trimmed with gold swirls. Gentle, cool fingers touched my temples. A female voice spoke words I couldn't understand and some of the pain receded from my mind. I knew instinctively that didn't mean the pain was gone for good. I'd been given a reprieve from enough of it that my mind could function though I couldn't move to push myself up off the floor. Her hands left my head and she backed up and away from me.

"Little One," the voice boomed, "rise. I command it."

The words flowed through me, urging obedience. "'I'm sorry. I can't," I said, my voice strained. "Not I won't... I can't."

The woman responded angrily to the man, again using language whose intent I could glean from the tone and vehemence of the words even if I couldn't understand what specifically was said. She thought asking me to stand in my condition was unreasonable. I needed time to recuperate. I felt the floor move beneath me as the man approached, speaking calmly to the woman on the other side of me. The words made no sense. I closed my eyes and ached.

Randgriðr, the man whispered deep in my mind, *rise*.

The use of my secret name – the one given to me by Odin - shuddered through my exhausted body. I found I could move my limbs. Bolstered by whatever power the name 'Randgríðr' had over me, I slowly pulled my wings in with a metallic glide, pushed my hands under my torso and managed to rise to a wobbily standing posture. The pain still rang through me like a low note from a bass viol. I resolved to keep it from showing on my face and set it to a different part of mind with obstinancy born of pride and contrariness. Looking down at myself I saw a thin layer of blue light enveloping my body. That was the outward sign of magic allowing me to stand in Odin's presence.

The Head of the Norse pantheon stood towering above me, seven feet tall if he was an inch and looking me over with a one-eyed calculating, cold stare. He wore silver armor chased with golden runes and had silver greaves tied over black leather boots. A blue woolen cloak hung from his shoulders down to his knees, held to his shoulders with golden pins attached to the armor. White hair braided from the crown of his head hung down his neck and back. A black leather eyepatch covered his left eye, the leather strap that held it in place a thin black line across his face and around the back of his head. His right eye was a blue somewhere between midnight blue and a dark grey-blue, the hue changing subtly with what I could only guess was his mood, but I had no way of knowing for sure. He was ancient and ageless at the same time, at one moment vibrant with the power of a youthful warrior, the next moment crafty and wise with age and experience.

He stood in front of a raised wooden platform made of the same wide dark planks as the floor I'd been laying on just moments before. On the platform against the wall behind Odin sat a silver throne. It was large, regal, ornately crafted and very obviously Odin's. Twelve smaller wooden thrones sat to either side of the silver throne, six per side. In those seats were the shadows of men dressed in armor, shimmering and only partially corporeal, like ghosts who hadn't quite decided whether to appear to mortal eyes or not. I sensed they were retainers to Odin... or maybe lesser gods in the Norse pantheon. I was far from being an expert on such things and I didn't think I had a lot of time to puzzle it out. I had no idea how long the magic surrounding me would last.

Above the thirteen seats and covering the wooden walls of the hall as far as I could see were huge, vibrantly colored tapestries. I saw a few figures I recognized, like a very large blonde man in a wedding dress – Thor in the story Odin had told through me at the pub in Penzance. I also recognized Loki grinning with malicious glee as a blonde woman wept over the body of a handsome young man pierced through the heart with a wooden arrow. The wooden ceiling above the tapestries was carved with ornate dragons and other creatures I didn't recognize, some of their more monstrous features highlighted in swirls of color that matched the vibrancy of the tapestries.

To my right was the woman I'd heard arguing with Odin in the language I hadn't understood. She had eyes the color of spring grass and a gentle, caring face, her expression as she looked at me one of great concern. Blonde hair framed her face in curling wisps and two long braids draped over her shoulders and down the front of the gown. Gold trimmed her pale green woolen dress on the ends of the long sleeves as well as the hem. Golden buttons held it together at the shoulders and along the tops of her arms, the white flesh of her arms visible in small ovals between the buttons. She had a golden belt tied around her waist and thin golden bracelets on her wrists.

Odin, fists on hips, regarded me. "You stand in my hall, Little One. I rule here. Behind me sit the judges who determine who enters Valhalla. I interrupted your journey to Brentwood Close so I could speak with you. The Son of Khonshu and the minion of the Son of Loki arrived there unharmed."

Relieved that Andrew was safe in a place where he could get help and hopeful that Toby would behave himself, I carefully maneuvered myself into a rickety curtsey, lowering my eyes respectfully as I did so. At least some of Mother's advice about how to behave in the presence of a monarch seemed to have stayed with me. Hopefully, I could apply the training, combined with my manners and deportment, to dealing with pagan gods.

"I greet you, All-Father," I said. I rose from the curtsey ungracefully and focused on the wooden floor. One did not look a monarch in the face. It seemed a wise precaution to take with Odin.

"Do you know why you're here, Little One?" Odin asked.

"No, my lord," I said.

"You are close to death. Your soul remains attached to your body only through the efforts of Eir and myself. Her healing powers and my magic hold you here, on the precipice between life and afterlife."

I swallowed. I knew I wasn't well. I hadn't realized just how 'not well' I apparently was.

"These judges are here to decide if you are worthy of Valhalla if I allow you to slip over the precipice... unless..." I looked up at the god, his one blue eye cold as he regarded me. "...I choose to let you live. What is your life worth, Little One?"

That stiffened my spine and I felt anger rise in me. *Going to Valhalla?* I thought, shocked. I wasn't a pagan, for a start, and if God had heard only half of my imprecations and blaspheming when I'd been tied to the chair in Laufeson's tower, the only place I was headed *post mortem* was Hell. *No matter where I spend eternity*, I resolved, *I'd be damned if I beg for my life, no matter who this god thinks he is.*

"I know my worth, my lord," I said coldly, enunciating so that I could be heard throughout the hall, "but I dare say it's your opinion of my value that matters. What do *you* think my life is worth?"

The twelve spectral judges in the seats behind Odin moved in their thrones, looking at each other in surprise at my words. Mother would have fainted to hear me address a social superior –

much less a god in his own hall—in such a way, but she wasn't with me.

She was dead. So were my friends. I'd avenged them and nearly killed myself in the process, but at least Andrew was safe. Therefore, hurting as I was, I hardly cared what happened to me anymore. I'd done my best. If death and Hell awaited, so be it. *At least I know what the Ancient Greek Hell is like*, I mused sardonically. *I wonder if the Christian Hell will be better or worse?*

Odin tilted his head and skewered me with the gaze from his one eye. I didn't look away. "You made an agreement with me, Little One," he rumbled. "Do you not remember it?"

I did remember it. Having made it under duress and not understanding the language in which he'd proposed it, I wasn't sure, precisely, what I'd said I'd do on Odin's behalf. That could be a bad thing.

"I do, but I'm a bit unclear as to the terMs. Perhaps if you explained them to me in English?" I suggested.

Again the judges behind Odin looked shocked and whispered among themselves. Odin's eye narrowed in calculation.

"I gave you power to defeat the Son of Loki," he said, his voice echoing through the hall in a proclamation-like timbre. "I protected you from the most invasive and insidious of his magics so that you could turn his evil plan against him. In return, you agreed to serve... and... worship... me."

It was my turn to be surprised. *Worship... him?* I thought, the implications of that running through me like cold steel. My brain ramped up to lightning speed, the pain I'd been holding at bay forgotten amid my blazing and panicked cogitation. My minds' eye showed me the altar in Laufeson's office with the bowl on it stained brown with sacrificial blood, which was the only personal example I had of what constituted pagan worship. Andrew had told me those who worshipped Odin hung their sacrifices in trees... as Laufeson had done to me as a child. It was a far cry from sitting in a church pew, singing hymns and listening to a sermon, praying to the Almighty of a Sunday morning.

Since I hadn't known the terms, I'd made the agreement without an opportunity to think things through or perhaps find another way to stop Laufeson that wasn't so personally compromising. I'd had no choice at the time and Odin had known it.

My panic faded, turning to determination and cold fury as I then understood two things. First, I'd been tricked by a god who'd 'adopted' me and wanted to protect me from harm because he loved me—or so I'd been told—but who now required worship in exchange for my doing his sneaky dirty work; and second, no matter what I'd agreed to and whether I'd understood it at the time or not, there was no way in Hell or any other miserable afterlife I would worship the one-eyed fiend in front of me.

"What say you, Little One?" Odin asked, watching me closely. "Shall I teach you the proper ways to venerate me?"

"No," I said, icy wrath in my tone.

The judges, who by that point should've been unsurprised by my lack of polite reverence for their boss, again whispered among themselves in shock and dismay.

"You already know the methods then?" Odin asked, turning away from me and walking a couple steps to my left.

"No," I said again, watching him like a hawk and fuming at the trap Odin had snapped around me.

He stared at the wall in front of him, his back to me. "You agreed to worship me. Do you not understand what that means?"

"I only have your word on what I agreed to. I do understand what worshipping you means." I shrugged. "I simply refuse to do it."

Odin turned to face me and the room and his face darkened with rage. The men in the chairs behind him became still as statues. "I gave you power beyond that of mortals," he rumbled. "With it you saved humanity from the Son of Loki's malevolence. You even faced down Hades and succeeded in freeing the Son of Khonshu. I've fulfilled my end of the bargain, but you refuse to do the same. Why?"

"I worship another," I said simply and the statement, though true, surprised me. I didn't really consider myself to be the best of Christians, I supposed, but I did believe in God. I'd met a few pagan gods in the past couple days and witnessed their great abilities. They had power that was clearly manifest, but somehow it didn't impress me. My conviction in my belief in God glowed within me as a steady, forthright light. The foundation of my refusal to worship Odin rested solidly on that, though how I'd come to realize it was a mystery to me.

"The puny Christian god?!" Odin cried and laughed derisively. A spear appeared beside him out of thin air and Odin grabbed it, thumping the flat end of it against the floor and making the room shake. "You prayed to him and he didn't come to your aid. When you asked, I came and gave you such power that you fought a death god to a standstill, Little One!"

"I disagree," I said, unmoved by Odin's theatrics. "God did answer my prayers. Isn't it possible he set you in my path to give me the power I needed to stop Laufeson's evil?"

"I was not an instrument of Jehovah," Odin rumbled.

"Why not? I was *your* instrument," I pointed out. "Perhaps I was God's instrument through you?"

"He didn't craft the plan to stop my enemy. He didn't wait for years to spring it. Had I not acted, the Son of Loki would have succeeded." Odin laughed derisively. "Jehovah is weak and useless in comparison to me."

"God is stronger," I said.

Odin laughed again and leaned on the spear. "How so, fool?!"

"He's given me the strength to stand up to you," I said, my voice even. "I will not be moved though you do your worst."

At that, Odin stood very, very still, the spear gripped in his hand and his eye narrowed in calculation. I was suddenly very weary. The pain roared back into my thoughts and I just didn't care anymore.

"Pick up the spear and kill me," I said with a sigh. "I won't change my mind, we both know you won't miss, and I'm ready for the afterlife though I'm not sure if the afterlife is ready for me." I put my arms out so he had a clear shot at my chest. "Have at it, All-Father," I said, meeting his gaze. "I'll not flinch from the blow. I am worthless to you. Push me over that 'precipice' you mentioned and be done with it."

Much to my surprise a tear welled up in Odin's eye and slid silently down his cheek. He turned to the judges behind him. "Is she not magnificent?" he asked, his voice husky with emotion. "Her courage and conviction do us great honor. What say you, warriors? Will she not serve the world well as the First of the Valkyries? Does she pass the test?"

I put down my arms, confused, then watched in dumb astonishment as the judges looked at each other, then at Odin. As one, they nodded their assent and disappeared.

Odin turned back to me and with a gesture the spear disappeared. Unfortunately so did the blue magic holding me up. The room started to brown out and I felt my knees buckle as the song of agony within me crescendoed again, my ability to block it out having left me. Odin rushed forward and caught me, lifting me gently as if I were a small child. He spoke a word and I felt my wings and armor disappear, leaving me in the blue wool dress, my hair tumbled over my face and shoulders, my feet bare.

"I don't understand," I whispered.

"It was a test, Ariana Grace Trevelyan," he murmured and moved the hair out of my face so he could see it clearly. The use of my full given name sent a chill down my spine. "It was the final and greatest test. You passed it and showed your worth. If you choose to work for me, you'll do me great service."

That statement made me tear up, *though it's probably from the pain*, I thought. I suddenly missed my father very, very much. "The agreement?" I croaked.

"There was none," he said. "That, too was part of the test." He looked up from me. "Eir," he said, "quickly – she needs healing. Let us go to Frigg without delay."

"I don't—" I whispered.

Odin covered my eyes with his hand. "Sleep, my daughter," he said. "When you've recovered, I'll explain all to you."

Dark oblivion rose from the depths and swallowed me whole. The world went dark.

Chapter Fifty-Six

After the darkness and quiet, a room coalesced around me in a blue haze. I had no true sense of just how much time had passed. It felt like Odin had cradled me in his arms only a half second before, but the dark after had been silent as the grave and just as timeless. The abrupt transition from that to a standing position rattled me for a moment and I felt my heart rate increase.

I saw books. Books on a shelf in a wall full of shelved books. I stood in a library and I felt... normal... not disconnected or weary or in pain... and I nearly sagged in relief. My heart slowed. I didn't hear anything or anyone, nor did I have the sense that there was something to be feared from my surroundings. I took a moment to close my eyes and thank my lucky stars I hadn't been dropped from the dark into immediate danger.

Opening my eyes again, I looked down at my body to see if the golden gears and circuits still ran along my flesh. My arms were bare and looked just as they had before Laufeson's machine and Odin's magic had changed me. I still wore the blue wool dress, though the breastplate was gone and a quick hand to my head verified I no longer wore a golden helmet. My hair was neatly plaited, however.

I spun on my bare feet to take in the room full of books, on my guard against an attack. None came.

It was a narrow rectangle of a room that hearkened back to the early days of the century. It ran along the side of what seemed to be a great house, illuminated with the light from four tall French windows in alcoves along the exterior wall, framed by wooden shutters and saffron draperies. Outside, a garden, still grey from winter, spread outward in a rectangle from the French doors.

Built-in bookcases ran the length of the other three walls, framing a marble-mantled fireplace decorated with Greco-Roman items meant to evoke the decor of the houses of Pompeii, which I recognized from Cora's books on the place. To my right was a large wooden door, closed to what must have been a hallway on the other side.

The parts of the walls that didn't contain bookcases were painted a terra-cotta color, with thin black-brown lines framing them, again in imitation of Pompeiian decor. A long narrow reddish-brown rug ran the length of the room, upon which sat a long cherrywood table, several cherrywood armchairs with saffron velvet cushions, and two richly red damask couches near the fireplace with small end tables beside them. A low table sat in front of one of the couches. Brass candelabras with unlit tapers abounded, and the room smelled of beeswax and book leather. I stood in the middle of the room, now facing the fireplace with the wall of my books at my back and the long table in front of me.

It was the room a Roman aristocrat would've owned, as imagined by someone who had never been to Pompeii. I found I quite liked the room, despite the obvious dissonance between the inspiration and result. The warm colors made it cozy, and the windows let in a great deal of light.

The Odin Inheritance   Victoria L. Scott

Problem was, I was alone there and I had no idea whose library it was. Something about the place tickled the back of my mind with familiarity, but every time I tried to grasp the memory it darted away from me. Even though I didn't know whose library I stood in, I felt safe. No one would hurt me here. I was alone and secure for the first time in what felt like forever though I knew it had only been a few days.

I moved over to one of the couches and sat down, a little stunned. So much had happened in such a short period of time. So much had changed. I'd gained and lost so much. *What am I to do now?* I wondered. Fear, uncertainty, grief, disappointment and anger fought for control of my thoughts. I'd no idea if any of the choices I'd made had been the right ones or what the consequences of those choices would be. *How long will I be safe here?* I wondered.   I longed for home and familiar things. I longed to see my father, to know he was safe and well out of the mess I was in. I wondered about what had happened to Gregor and Hugo after the dragon attacked. My eyes burned and my vision wavered. I wished I'd had a chance to say goodbye to—

The tears began to flow before I was aware of it, but once I felt them on my cheeks, the floodgates opened. I wept openly and messily, placing my hand over my mouth to suppress the sound of my sobbing. My nose began to run and I felt my cheeks heat up from my crying and distress. I didn't have a handkerchief to wipe my face. I grabbed a fistful of the blue dress and used that for lack of something better. It left the fabric wet and crumpled, but I didn't care.

Eventually, the sobbing subsided and it took another handful of dress to wipe my face dry a second time. I leaned back on the couch, tired but feeling a little bit better, as I knew my friends did after a 'gutter-washing lacrimonious interlude,' as Cora called them. I was not prone to 'gutter-washers' as a general rule though many of the girls at Towson were. I hated exhibiting such a 'weakness of spirit,' but I supposed I'd been though enough that the 'lacrimonious interlude' was understandable, if messy. At least I'd been alone when it happened.

I still had no idea of what to do next, however. *Should I leave? Will I be allowed to leave? Where will I go? Where am I?*

"Interesting room, don't you think?"

I jumped off the couch and whirled with my fists up to see Odin standing in front of the room's closed door. He wasn't as large in the library as he'd been in his great hall, standing now at what I estimated to be a little shorter than six feet. He wore tweed and looked for all the world like a country gentleman about to embark on an afternoon of bird hunting. The patch over his missing eye was brown to match the tweed and it added an odd, almost piratical air to his appearance. His white hair was cut short and combed down on his head, his beard neatly trimmed as one would expect of a rich, older gentleman of leisure. But, despite his mundane appearance, he exuded an aura of power and wisdom slightly tinged with menace. I knew better than to assume a different appearance meant a different being. He was still a pagan god who could kill me outright if he chose... if I wasn't dead already.

I paused, uncertain what else to do. I realized I must look a mess, with my face blotchy from weeping and the evidence of my distress on wrinkled, moistened parts of my dress. I kept my fists up and hoped my willingness to get pugilistic would distract from my disheveled appearance.

Odin put up his hands in an 'I mean you no harm' sort of gesture. "Little One," he intoned gravely, "Be at ease. I will not harm you. I had hoped we'd sit down," he indicated the chairs and couches, "and I could answer your questions."

I lowered my fists and narrowed my eyes as I looked at the Norse god. *Now he was playing nice?*

"Why?" I asked, my tone wary.

"I honor my promises," he said simply. "I promised you an explanation."

Hmmm, I thought. *Is this another test?*

"Where are we?" I asked, not moving.

"This is a version of the library at Brentwood Close. I thought it'd help you feel less out of place. You like libraries. When you were younger, you spent a great deal of time in here." He pointed behind him at the closed door. "If you don't wish to speak to me, simply leave and you'll return to Midgard unharmed and," he paused, "...uninformed."

I wanted answers. I wasn't going anywhere until I got them. "I'm still in Asgard, then?"

Odin nodded. "Essentially. Such workings," he indicated the room, "are within my power here."

What sort of knowledge did he have of the world beyond here? I wondered. "You said you sent Andrew and Toby on to Brentwood Close. What about my father, aunt, Mr. Datsik and Hugo? Are they safe?"

"They are," he said. "They're worried about you, of course, but they're unharmed."

I took that in, relieved. "Am I in this construct of Aunt Miranda's library because you healed me completely, or did I die and this is the chat I get before I head off to... well, wherever God chooses to send me? Or is something else going on?"

Odin stepped further into the room. His movement forward was slow and deliberate, indicating he didn't want to alarm me. I tensed but kept my fists lowered.

"Frigg, Eir and Yggdrasil work to stitch your soul back to your flesh, while my magic keeps your body alive. While they work, I have chosen to meet you here, in this realm of the mind," he said. He smiled at me. "It's a good thing you're so stubborn. A more fragile young woman would have been lost, but you hold onto life with a grip of iron now, just as you did on the World Tree thirteen years ago."

I frowned. "I used too much magic," I said. "I knew when I cast the spell to get Andrew, Toby and me out of Hell, I'd have very little life energy left over."

"True, but that isn't what slipped the moorings of your soul. Part of that's my fault. I allowed you to follow through on your threat to Hades but didn't tell you the rules."

"There are rules?"

Odin chuckled. "There are always rules, Little One. The Universe operates within certain principles and parameters. Otherwise, there would be chaos. Surely through your study of mathematics and the sciences you can recognize that?"

"Yes," I said uncertainly, "but fact and experimentation made those rules known to humanity. Newton based his laws on what he observed in the world. You're saying magic has rules like that? If so, how did my breaking a rule untie my soul from my body?"

"You didn't break a rule *per se*," Odin explained, "but you had no idea of the consequences of the spell you cast to 'choose' Hades and take him to Helheim." He indicated the couch I'd occupied before he'd arrived. "Please, sit. I'll sit on the couch opposite," he pointed at it, "and answer all your questions."

Chapter Fifty-Seven

I thought about it a moment and sat back down on the couch. I wanted answers and Odin seemed inclined to provide them. *Best for me to find out what I can*, I thought. "All right," I said tentatively.

Odin walked over and sat opposite me. He leaned back and regarded me with a mixture of pride and exasperation. It reminded me very much of the expression I'd seen on my own father's face more than once.

"So..." I began, feeling my way into the conversation, "...what rule did I bend that nearly killed me?"

"As a Valkyrie—even a temporary one—" he explained, "you have the power to choose which recently dead mortals will spend their afterlife in Valhalla. I burned the spell for choosing the slain into your memory as you used it on Hades, yes?" I nodded.

"Though Hades was in a mortal body at the time," Odin continued, "that mortal body contained the immortal soul of a god, like me."

"The god of the dead wasn't recently dead," I said, putting it together.

"Exactly so. Your decision to choose Hades for Helheim and make him Hel's plaything was inspired, to be sure, but not truly within the realm of your abilities as one of my Valkyrie."

I furrowed my brow. "But I felt his soul start to leave his body as the spell did its work," I said.

Odin nodded gravely. "It did, but the effort of casting that spell untied the links between your soul and your flesh. Had you completed it, you'd have taken Hades to Helheim as you intended... but your soul would have escorted him there personally. You would've trapped yourself for eternity right beside Hades, suffering the same torments as he did. And, I'm sorry to say, Hel likes new toys."

My eyes widened in realization. "Oh," I said. "That sounds... unpleasant."

Odin smirked, his eye twinkling. "Your determination to save the Healer and ignorance as to the rules gave you the strength to pull Hades halfway to an afterlife he couldn't escape."

"I am stubborn," I said, looking at my hands.

"You are indeed," Odin agreed. "Between that and encasing Hades within Yggdrasil, you made quite an impression."

"I also made an enemy," I muttered.

Odin's expression sobered. "True. Hades will not forget the insult and eventually there'll be a reckoning... but not for a bit, I think."

I didn't like the sound of that, but I couldn't do anything about it now. "So now what? You put me back together and...

then...?"

Odin put out his hands in a gesture that indicated anything was possible. "I give you a choice," he said.

I scoffed. "That's a change," I said cynically. "Very little that's happened to me over the past few days has felt like I had any choice in the matter." I crossed my arms over my chest. "No matter how you ask me, I'll still not worship you."

Odin chuckled. "Yes, Little One, you made that quite clear. I don't need a worshipper. Jehovah and I, while not exactly friends, do have certain goals in common. Your allegiance to him is without question. The choice has to do with something else."

"What about *your* choice, Odin?" I asked.

"My choice?"

"Why me? Why have all these things happened to me? Why didn't you just leave me on the World Tree to die? If you had, I dare say more people would be alive now." I stopped for a moment, my heart squeezing painfully in my chest. It was hard to keep my voice even as I continued speaking. "I was an insignificant little girl. Had you done nothing to save me, my death would have stopped Laufeson's plan cold. That was the logical, cold-blooded thing to do, well suited to a god of war and death. Why didn't you do it?"

Odin blew out a breath slowly. "I found you hanging in the World Tree in sacrifice," he began, his voice sad. "The shedding of your blood in that place made your life mine to do with as I wished. I could have claimed you for death, and that thought did cross my mind. The Norns, who see the future and advise me occasionally, told me to leave you to die. They showed me what the Son of Loki hoped to do with you if I didn't destroy you." A look of fierce pride and wistful memory crossed his face. "You were brave. You had spirit. By Yggdrasil, child, had you been born a thousand years ago, what a warrior you would have made! How could I end a life that burned with such determination and strength at so young an age?" I said nothing.

Odin continued, "It's true I'm a god of war and death, but I am also a god of magic, poetry and above all, *wisdom*. Therefore, I decided to let you live under my protection until you fulfilled your destiny," he said, "and the possibility of failure be damned. I believed your destiny was to thwart the Son of Loki's plans... which you did, with my help."

He's been playing a long game with my life and me none the wiser, I realized. "And now, having done that, what do you intend to do with me?"

"As to what happens next... that depends." Odin clasped his hands in his lap, watching me, saying nothing.

I rolled my eyes. "That depends? You set me up from the beginning to trap Laufeson. You set up everything in my life to do what I did in Hell. You've made it so I have no choice as to what I do from here."

"Call for your wings," he said, unmoved. "Call on your magical power. Right here, right now. See what happens."

Confused by the non-sequitur but curious as to what would happen, I did so. I felt nothing. I looked down at my arms, which still showed no sign of the golden gears and circuits from before. I wore no magic breastplate and felt no wings on my back, which upon reflection was a good thing, since I wasn't sure what the razor-sharp feathers would've done to the couch I sat on.

Odin reached in the pocket of his vest, pulled something out, let it dangle in his hand for a moment and allowed it coil, serpent-like, into a pile on the table between us. It was my father's gold watch chain – the one I'd wrapped around my wrist that had altered Laufeson's magic. The fob at the end, a worn golden saint's medal Father had called 'Old Tom,' sat on the top of the coiled golden chain.

"As you are right now, Ariana Grace Trevelyan," Odin intoned, "you possess no magic. I am no longer part of your mind. You are not Valkyrie. You are what you would've been had the Son of Loki never touched you." He indicated the chain. "I removed the artifact from your body and severed my magical ties to you."

"That's Father's watch chain, not an artifact," I said, staring at it.

"Your Aunt Miranda gave it to your father years ago upon my order. She and her father found it on the body of Aithyrr, the last woman to bear the artifacts of my Heir. You saw the tomb?"

I remembered Aunt Miranda's story. "Yes. She was buried with a man, and she had red hair, like mine."

"Her husband died at the hands of a misguided Christian and she chose to join her husband in death. She now serves in Valhalla."

He put his hand over the golden coil on the table for a moment and when he removed it a worn golden pendant that resembled a raven had taken the place of the old saint's medal.

"When you called on me as Randgríðr, I made this artifact part of you. It is no longer, just as you are no longer Randgríðr." He snapped his fingers and a dart appeared on the table beside the golden chain and its raven fob.

"Pick up the dart," he said and waved a hand to indicate the bookcases. "Pick a target. See how you do."

I grasped the dart, the feel of it in my hand familiar from more dart games than I could count. Looking up, I picked a book spine out of one of the shelves, aimed and threw the dart as I'd done thousands of times before.

The dart missed the book and bounced off the glass of one of the French doors with a bang. It dropped to the ground with a plop. I stared at my hand and then the door in disbelief. It had been an easy shot and I never missed... until now. It shouldn't have bothered me, but my mouth went dry and fear fluttered in my belly.

"If you want to get good at darts again, it'll take a great deal of practice," Odin said. "You'll have to acquire the skill just like everyone else does. I'm afraid that means you'll not be able to rely on pub winnings to help fund your aeronaut endeavors."

"That ability – that was all you?"

"It was," he agreed. "You do have some natural ability, but I stepped into the forefront of your mind and threw the darts with your hands. You had very little to do with it."

"But," I said, thinking furiously, "there's more to this – more to all of this – than my throwing darts," I said. "The choice isn't about that – it can't be."

"True enough," Odin agreed. "It's about the future."

"I don't understand," I said. "How can my choice make any difference in the future of anyone but me?"

Odin leaned back on the couch and looked at me for a long moment. "The era I came from was one of ignorance and hardship. Life was short for most and the world didn't change very much for hundreds of years. Many were born, lived and died in the same place and didn't travel beyond their own village. That's no longer the case. Humans create new devices, make new discoveries, develop new theories about the world at a rate that's astonishing and breathtaking to someone from the Iron Age. When I was the primary god of my people, long distance travel in a short period of time required considerable magical power and mortals couldn't even imagine such rapid movement across land or through the air. That was then. Now, common mortals traverse vast distances in short spans of time without giving it much thought. They ride in great metal beasts driven by steam that roar with mechanical voices and it's no magic trick. Humanity has harnessed ingenuity and it's spread like wildfire across the world."

He rubbed his chin. "I thought the changes that happened when the Christian god came to my lands were rapid. What's happening now..." He shook his head. "...I can barely keep up."

"But you're a god," I said. "A god of wisdom, of all things. How can you *not* keep up?"

He chuckled. "I'm an old god – and an old man. I have limits. Those limits were harder to see twelve hundred years ago, but the world was a vastly different place then. Now I see the world from my silver throne and I can track most of the changes as they happen. But, just because I know what's happening in the world doesn't mean I *understand* all of it, Little One. Believe me: in the Iron Age, being 'all knowing' was considerably easier. Nowadays my abilities as a god still function relatively effectively, but I'm wise enough to know when I need help."

I could see how the pace of the modern world would seem incredibly fast to someone who'd lived during the time of the Vikings. "Do all the pagan gods who help the Facti on Earth have this difficulty?" I asked.

"To differing degrees, I should imagine, but they'd hardly admit it, now, would they?" he said with a rueful grin. "It isn't the Facti gods that I'm worried about. The Obscurati tend to be far more... inventive, shall we say, with changes in mortal knowledge. Loki, Hades, Ahrimanes, Set and other gods like them have deep ties to the mortal world. Their desire to cause harm serves them well, and new inventions are easily turned to evil purposes."

Realization struck me like a physical blow. "My God," I said, "Laufeson mixed magic and technology in an effort to take over the world. He understood enough about mechanics and Enhancements to do that much..." I thought about the mini Diabolicals he'd forced me to make, "...and he came very close to succeeding."

"Indeed, though he needed your blood to do it. You took him out of the world permanently, but the Son of Loki had many followers. They may try to continue his work, assuming other Obscurati heirs don't beat them to the punch. I'm not convinced his plans are completely frustrated just yet." He looked at me, his one blue eye dark and serious. "We seem to have lost track of the mini machines Laufeson ordered you to make. Will they still function magically without Laufeson to direct them?"

Oh, God, I thought, horrified. I didn't know if the devices could work independently of Laufeson or me. "I... I don't – I'm not sure—" I stammered. "I made them so the changes they wrought on their victims could be reversed. It didn't occur to me to make them cease functioning if Laufeson wasn't around." I squeezed a handful of my dress in frustration, silently cursing my oversight. The damage those devices could do was horrible to contemplate. "I should have thought of that."

"The fact that you put the reversal spell into the mechanisms right under the Laufeson's nose is impressive."

"But—"

Odin put up a hand to stop my spluttering. "We'll find out soon enough if the devices became inert or if they'll have to be dealt with."

"Dealt with? What do you mean 'dealt with'? How will you deal with them?" I asked.

"If the Facti can reverse the spell on the devices, then they'll do that. If they can't—"

My heart sank. "You'll have to kill them?"

"That's a possible outcome," Odin admitted.

I felt sick. "You're saying I may have condemned hundreds of people to death."

"That remains to be seen."

"I can't say that makes me feel better," I murmured.

"These are difficult times, Little One. Laufeson will not be the first Obscurati to merge mechanics and magic, but the threats to come from others won't need your blood as a catalyst," Odin told me. "I've seen that. So have the Norns and your Lady Sato. The Obscurati are seeking out new Heirs just as I am, and theirs are not so keen to do the world a good turn as you are."

"You're saying you need me," I said as a frisson of apprehension made the hairs on the back of my neck rise. "You need me because I used the magic you gave me to straddle your Iron Age world and my industrial one. You linked that magic with my knowledge of science and math and the principles behind mechanical devices. That's why I see spells as equations and had the gears in my skin. I'm a... hybrid. Laufeson started the process when he kidnapped me and you exploited it to destroy him. I'm the new blood you need to stop the Obscurati recruits."

Odin beamed. "Yes."

"But..." I looked at where the dart had fallen, "...you removed the magic. Now I'm just a normal young woman. Laufeson's followers or other Obscurati may use the devices I created against my will... and you've left me helpless to stop them or help their victims." Odin nodded. "Why? If you need me—if you need how I use magic—why did you take it away?"

"That's the choice," Odin said. "You were the Son of Loki's victim when he left you on the World Tree. I turned you into a weapon out of necessity, without consulting you. If you wish to go back to Midgard as you currently are, free of magic, you have that right."

Alarm spiked within me. "But Hades—"

"If you choose a normal life, I'll deal with Hades," Odin assured me.

"But what about—"

"There are other Facti who can fight those arrayed against us," he explained calmly. "It doesn't have to be you. If you decide to be done with magic, you'll no longer be involved in the conflict between the Facti and the Obscurati. You can take the Tripos and finish at Cambridge, establish your business, or marry, or do whatever you wish unencumbered by magical entanglements. Your mind will be your own, but the outcome of your dart games will be far less predictable." He smiled. "I'd suggest you give up wagering until you've had some time to practice."

I took that in. I could have a life like Cora and Mellie had. I'd not have to worry about random attacks or abduction attempts. There was something very appealing about that possibility, but I knew it wasn't a choice I truly had open to me. Victim of Laufeson or not, I felt responsible for those who might be hurt by the mini Diabolicals... and Odin knew it. I'd already lost most of what I'd known as my life, but I was curious how my normal life would be if I chose it.

"I assume," I said, my tone thoughtful, "if I decided to walk away from using magic and all of this," I waved my hand to encompass the room, the coiled gold chain and Odin, "you'd conveniently erase any knowledge of Facti and Obscurati? I'd go back to ignorance about magic and the rest of it?"

"That's usually how things are handled, yes," Odin said. "Fewer difficulties that way."

"What would I remember about the death of my mother and my friends on the *Bosch*?" I asked, my tone sad and bitter. "Laufeson blew the ship up with them on it. How do you propose to wipe that memory away? Or would you bring them all back from the dead?"

Odin smiled. "Very easily," he said with a wink.

Chapter Fifty-Eight

Suddenly, I was on the darkened deck of the *Bosch*, the ship swinging widely back and forth as a result of the dragon... or whatever it had been... uncoiling from the balloon and body of the ship. Its massive wings flapped and a gust of wind rattled the airship. I put my arms out to steady myself against the movement only to find my arms were ghostly, filmy appendages. A quick look down verified that my whole body was nothing more than a spectre, making me immoveable in relation to the ship, though the swinging of the deck below me was disconcerting. I could see the wind billow the pegamoid silk of the balloon above me, but I couldn't feel the moving air or the night's cold.

Apparently, I was an observer of past events within the 'realm of the mind' Odin commanded. I'd have a front row seat for the explosive destruction of the airship and the horrific death of my friends and my mother. "Please—no!" I cried out. "Please! I don't want to see this! I don't want to see them die!"

Odin didn't respond. I clenched my fists in frustration, trying to will myself back to the library, but nothing happened. For the second time in as many days, I had to watch, helpless, as bad things happened to those I cared for.

As the *Bosch* struggled, rudder loose, engines silent and the bridge devoid of the direction its crew provided, my friends and Mother remained rigid on their knees on the deck, their eyes vacant and faces expressionless as they started to slide toward the starboard rail. They made no move to stop their potential drop over the side into the open air.

"No!" I shouted, more frightened for my friends and mother than I'd ever been in my life. I waved my spectral arms at them, knowing it was futile but not able to help myself. "Wake up! Stop yourselves!" I screamed. "Please!"

Lady Sato blinked, shook her head and stood up in a flash, throwing her arms out wide, her face intent with concentration.

"BATILTU!!!" she screamed, and everything on the ship… just… stopped.

My mother and the crew of the *Bosch* collapsed to the deck, panting and shaking. Mother gripped the deck with such force I thought for sure she'd make finger holes in the wooden planks. I nearly fell over from relief. They'd not slid off the deck into darkness. *They might have a chance*, I thought, hope filling me.

"Bloody Hell!" Max said, sitting up and slamming his fist into the deck with a loud, angry thump. "By God, Sato, I'm not a damnable puppet on a string! What on God's great green gob *was* that horrific thing, and what's that German bloke with his dragon and demons going to do to Ari and Andrew?"

Mother's head popped up, her eyes wild, but the set of her mouth was determined. "We need to follow them," she insisted. "I don't care what it is – who he is—we can't let that fiend harm my daughter!" She shoved her free arm through the loose half of the parachute only partially attached to her body. Pushing herself to a standing position almost as quickly as Sato had, she reached over to grab Griff by the arm and pull him up. He stumbled a bit but managed to keep his feet. Lizzie, Needle, and Max followed suit.

"Get down to those engines, young man, and start the infernal things up!" Mother ordered Griff. "We need speed! We have to save Ariana!"

"No," Lady Sato intoned. Her eyes blazed with white fire while waves of energy flowed outward from her body, holding the ship perfectly still. It felt very much like what Lady Sato had done when I'd made my escape on Gregor's back, the two of us and Hugo moving at speed within the infinite space between two seconds. Then it had been Lady Sato in control of the magic. Clearly, she wasn't in control this time.

"Bloody Hell," Needle whispered, frightened. "She'll set the balloon alight, she keeps that flaming eyes bit up."

"LEAVE THE SHIP, LEST YE DIE," the being within Sato said, its voice insistent and commanding, "I, MAMMETUN, GODDESS OF FATE, HAVE SEEN IT."

Max looked at the others and rubbed the back of his head in a quick, decisive movement. "That's good enough for me," he said. "Grab chutes and let's be off, toot-sweet! Abandon ship!"

Needle, Griff, and Lizzie scrambled for the stairs that led down into the body of the ship, their movements silent and efficient.

"We have to—" Mother started, but Max cut her off.

"I want Ari to be safe as much as you do," he hissed, reaching down to tighten the parachute straps around her body, "and God knows I don't want to lose the *Bosch*, but we can't catch that dragon and I'm willing to bet Sato's risking a lot to allow this Mammetun lass take her over like that. She says we go, we go."

"But—" Mother spluttered.

"YOU MAY NOT PURSUE THE GIRL," Mammetun intoned, her voice striking the air with the sound of a church bell.

Mother tore herself away from Max and stormed over to Sato, fury on her face. I watched, amazed. Clearly I'd come by my 'defiance in the face of pagan gods' honestly. I'd never seen my mother so emotional before – I wanted to tell her I was all right, that she should get off the ship... but I was a spectre watching a memory. She wouldn't hear me.

"I don't know what the Hell you think you are," Mother bit out, "but my daughter's in danger and I'll not stand by and do nothing, no matter what you say! I'll fly this bloody ship all by myself if I have to, by God!"

"NAY," Mammetun said, implacable. "YOU LEAVE OR DIE."

"I don't care!" Mother snarled.

Max put up a hand. "I do care, Your Grace," he said, his voice calm but firm. "I'll not be the one to tell Ari of your death when she gets back. I'm the captain of this ship." He pointed in the direction Laufeson had taken Andrew and me. "We're not going after that devil and his minions. Even if we caught them, that damned creature would overcome our thoughts again and we'd be helpless. Duchess or not, I'm ordering you to come with us. If you don't, I dare say I'll grab you bodily and throw you over the side myself!"

I was in complete agreement with Max. Chasing Laufeson was a suicide mission. I flowed over to stand by my mother. "Listen to him," I urged though I knew she couldn't hear me. "He's right. Get off the *Bosch*!"

"Not acceptable," Mother said, her face taut with fear. "We can't just let her be taken like this." Mother angrily pointed a finger

The Odin Inheritance   Victoria L. Scott

at Sato's face. "I've no idea who you are, what you've done with Sato or what the Hell is going on, but I swear I'll not see my daughter harmed. If I can't go after her and you've got magic powers, you use them to help Ariana, damn you!"

Sato's face took on a mournful cast and she tilted her head slightly to one side. "Nay," Mammetun said, "From this, as before, you cannot save her. Forces are in play beyond your mortal scope." The god's voice softened. "You I may save. She must save herself."

Mother stepped back like she'd been struck, dropping the finger she'd been pointing. "You're saying this is related to the kidnapping," she growled, "when that bastard nearly killed Ariana."

So Aunt Miranda hadn't altered Mother's memory of my being taken as a child. *Had she known the magical nature of what had been done to me?* I wondered.

Max looked from Sato to Mother and back. "Kidnapping? It's happened before?"

Mammetun, relentless as a granite wall, nodded. "Aye. That was the opening gambit. This is the endgame."

"We need to get to Lady Brentwood," Max said, "and with due speed. She'll know what to do."

Mother just stared at Sato a long moment, swallowed with an effort and hugged herself, looking away. "As flies to wanton boys are we to the gods," Mother whispered. "They kill us for their sport."

"They also serve who only stand and wait," the god said, unmoved. "That time, for all of us, is now."

Needle, Griff, and Lizzie arrived back on deck, parachutes fastened to their backs, carrying two extras: one for Max and one for Sato.

Max reached over and took a parachute for himself. "Lizzie," he ordered as he pulled the chute on and started to buckle himself up, "strap Lady… er… Mammetun… into a parachute, if you would."

"On it," Lizzie said, moving quickly to apply a parachute to Sato's statue-like form. Mammetun allowed it but kept her arms up holding time at bay, leaving Lizzie to tighten the straps and place the loop of the pull cord in Sato's hand.

Max completed putting on his own parachute and went over to my mother. He looked over the parachute she wore one more time and leaned down to finish tightening straps. He looked up at Mother's tear-streaked face.

"Ari's a resourceful woman, Your Grace," he said gently as he put the loop for the pull cord in Mother's right hand. "You'll see her again – we all will."

Needle stepped up behind Mother. "Too right we will. Stubborn as Ari is, that Laufeson bloke's no idea what he's in for, taking her with him. She'll out-think the blighter and be back with us before you know it."

Mother nodded somberly.

"Sato? You ready to go?" Max asked as Griff and Lizzie joined him, Needle and my mother at the port side rail.

"Aye, Mortal," Mammetun rumbled, walking toward the group. Time returned to its normal speed. "We depart."

The ship started its barrel roll again, the wind picking up. As a spectre I didn't feel the effects myself but witnessed them, along with the flinches of my friends and mother when the cold wind hit them hard.

Mother finally seemed to realize what she was about to do. She put up a hand to shield her face from the cold gusts flowing along the deck. "I don't know how this works," she said over the wind, squinting first at the parachute, then at the pull cord in her hand and then at my friends.

"Gravity does most of the work," Max shouted back with a wink. "Count to three and pull the cord. Scream if you like and try to avoid trees!"

With that, the group clambered over the port rail and dropped into darkness. Seconds passed. I heard a hissing sound above me and looked up in time to see three burning red flares strike the *Bosch's* outer balloon, piercing it and plowing right into the hydrogen-filled ballonettes. They exploded with a deafening boom and a blinding blaze of light, sending metal, wood and fabric shrapnel flying in all directions, including through my ghostly form. I covered my head and ears, crouching instinctively to protect my softer bits against the blast.

Chapter Fifty-Nine

I found myself back in the library with Odin. He sat on the couch, while I huddled in a fetal position on the floor opposite him, near the couch I'd been sitting on, covering my head and ears with my arMs.

"They dropped into the countryside with no injuries, Little One," Odin said as I unfolded myself. "They're safe, well and waiting for you at Brentwood Close." He rubbed a finger under his nose. "The *Bosch* is lost, I'm afraid, but your friends are drawing up plans for their next airship. I'm sure you could get in on their newest enterprise if you expressed an interest."

I closed my eyes and felt tears start again. I put my hand over my mouth to muffle my sob of relief as I lowered my head onto my knees. I couldn't get all lacrimonious in front of Odin. *Thank God for Lady Sato, Mammetun and Max*, I thought, and used that as a starting place to steady my nerves. Everyone was alive and well. Laufeson had destroyed the *Bosch*, but not the people I cared about.

Odin moved to sit on the couch beside me, handing me down a handkerchief. "Better than the dress, I think," he murmured.

I nodded and wiped my face with it, strenuously pulling my feelings back into line. I had to think clearly and not let my emotions cloud my judgment.

"Right," I said, clutching the handkerchief. I cleared my throat, stood up, smoothed my very wrinkled dress and put myself back on the couch beside Odin. *Best if I change the subject*, I thought. "If I become a Facti, what does that mean?"

"You become First of the Valkyries, replace your aunt as the Seneschal of the Pessarines and serve as my heir on Earth."

"Does my aunt need to be replaced?" I asked, wary. "She seems in fine fettle to me."

"Miranda continues to be a force of nature, as you know first-hand. That being said, she, like me, possesses knowledge of the world that's far less up to date than yours. For the future, the Pessarines and the Facti need a more modern take on the world. She's been my... employee, I suppose you'd say, for decades. She'd like to retire from active duty and act in an advisory capacity to her replacement."

I furrowed my brow. "I see. What difference does it make if I'm the 'first' Valkyrie?"

Odin settled back on the couch. "That varies from person to person. Much of what will determine your role as my First Daughter will come from on the job training, you might say."

I frowned. I knew an evasion when I heard one. "You don't want to tell me, do you?"

Odin grinned. "You are a new sort of being, Ariana," he said. "No other Valkyrie has been offered in sacrifice as you were. I adopted you – which is itself a sign of great favor and power. If you choose to take the position as First Valkyrie, you'll inherit my artifacts directly from a female blood relative, which also confers power. What shape those magical abilities will take other than your connection to and manipulation of machinery and technology are unknown at this point. It isn't that I don't want to tell you. You'll just have to figure things out for yourself."

"You can't put the spells and how to use the magic into my mind like you did the 'choosing' spell?"

"No," he said, putting out his hands in a sort of shrugging 'I can't help it' gesture. "I'll no longer inhabit part of your mind as I did as you grew up. Some of the abilities you had that came from me will remain, like the accuracy with darts and knives you grew up with, but everything else you'll have to learn how to do."

"Such as?"

"Control and use of your magical abilities, obviously, but you'll also need to learn to fight with a sword and an axe. Some instruction on strategy and diplomacy will be required, as will learning what's required to lead the Pessarines."

I frowned. "Is that all?"

"To facilitate ease of communication with those here in Asgard and enable you to use the old spells properly, you'll also need to learn Old Norse."

Old Norse? "Damn and blast," I said, "How in the world will I do that? I'm horrible at languages – always have been."

"Ah," Odin said, enjoying some joke I'd not understood. "Who, precisely, is the benefactress of Towson House?"

"Lady Sato," I said automatically. "I find it hard to believe she'll be able to teach me all of those skills."

"Indeed. Who are your friends at Towson House?"

I couldn't believe I'd not seen it before. Excitement and surprise rose within me. "Mellie, who's studying Norse mythology and languages," I said, "and Cora, who's studied battle tactics and strategy of all different cultures as part of her studies." I thought for a moment. "Gertrude is a biologist, but I'm sure I could learn something from her as well."

Odin nodded. "Lady Sato anticipated your needs if you chose to become a Facti and tailored the residents she admitted to Towson House accordingly. Your friends already possess many of the skills you need."

My mind boggled. "You're saying she set up Towson House specifically for me? Good Lord."

Odin inclined his head. "There are advantages to seeing the possible futures. It's one of the reasons she's very valuable as a Pessarine."

"I should say so," I agreed.

"For diplomacy," Odin continued, "and the day-to-day operations of the Pessarines, your Aunt Miranda can advise you. There are several people on Earth and in Asgard who can teach you to fight with swords, axes and any other weapons you wish. Who you choose as your instructors for those lessons is up to you." The All-Father indicated the coiled chain and raven pendant on the table. "Pick up the artifact and you'll become Valkyrie. Leave it behind and you'll have a normal life, free of magic."

He stood up. "I'll leave you to think," he said and disappeared.

Chapter Sixty

I stared at the coil of gold for a long time. I pondered the past few days, amazed at how my life had changed. If I left the artifact behind, I'd return to the world I knew: the one where magic didn't exist. I'd be able to finish at Cambridge without fear of being attacked and start my aeronaut business. I could live the life I wanted – the one I'd chosen for myself – and not have to worry about the fate of the world.

But... there were four hundred ninety eight mini-Diabolical mechanisms I'd been forced to create that'd gone missing, according to Odin. It was possible they'd become inert when I'd confined Laufeson to Hell for eternity. If that was the case, then the devices were harmless. If that wasn't the case, someone could use the devices to turn people into mechanized monsters. Great Aunt Miranda had her hands full dealing with the Enhanced the Son of Loki had already created and released on England. How would she and the other Facti deal with *more*? What if they had to kill the newly Enhanced? Could I live with that, knowing my unwilling but definitive part in their deaths?

I reached over and grabbed the golden coil off the table in my fist, my hand shaking a little as I did so. I looked up at the ceiling of the replica of the library I sat in and addressed Odin.

"All right, All-Father," I said, determination in my voice, "I choose to become your First Valkyrie."

Victoria L. Scott

      Victoria L. Scott teaches Social Studies, Latin, Steampunk Studies and Quilting to middle schoolers at a private school in Southeastern Michigan. She has studied Shakespeare in England and at the Folger Shakespeare Library; communicated extensively in spoken Latin at Latin Language immersion camps in Kentucky, Michigan and Massachusetts; and studied Roman History and Archaeology in Rome and environs as a student of the American Academy in Rome. She is an avid quilter and Steampunker who enjoys Doctor Who, walking her dog Red 'the Wonder Husky', and writing.

Coming Soon...

More from *The Pessarine Chronicles...*

Book Two:

The Odin Apprentice

Ariana begins to learn the ropes of her new life, looking forward to her duties as a Valkyrie and setting up her aeronaut supply business. The threat of the Diabolically Enhanced seems to be waning, until something sinister starts happening in London. To Ariana's mother's great delight, Ariana has to enter high society and play the role of the 'proper duke's daughter' to find the source of the evil that plagues the social scene. Can Ariana stop the menace before it spreads to the highest echelons of the Empire?

Coming Soon...

More from *The Pessarine Chronicles...*

Book Three:

The Odin Expedition

Ariana receives a troubling message from her friend Cora Allerton, now working at the ancient city of Carthage on an archaeological dig. The archaeologists dug up a tomb Ariana urgently needs to investigate involving someone named 'Ba'al'. Ariana rushes to the dig site only to find Cora gone under mysterious circumstances. While she tries to track down her friend, small children start dying in Tunis. Ariana has to find Cora and solve the mystery of Ba'al before another child dies and an ancient evil rises again.

www.ingramcontent.com/pod-product-compliance
Lightning Source LLC
Chambersburg PA
CBHW060751030726
47503CB00002B/236